THE BASTARD KHAN

Wastelands of Drachenia

Kimberly Evette Ortuno

Kimberly Evette Ortuno

DEDICATION

First and foremost, this book is dedicated to the one and only
Almighty God. He has given me the strength and perseverance to
push through the hardest of times. I would continue to be lost if I
did not have Him as my guiding light. This book is also dedicated
to my wonderful children; they selflessly sacrificed their time so I
could work diligently completing this book.

CHAPTER 1

A faint creaking sound rumbled like thunder in the calm of the early morning, and it coaxed Everly out of her peaceful sleep. Without opening her eyes, her brows furrowed together as she focused on the abrupt silence that followed. The deep, steady breaths of her slumbering husband mingled with the occasional squeals and screeches of the night creatures as they flittered through the open window. After a few tense moments, she heard the door handle click, alerting her that it could now be pushed open. With a deep breath, Everly forced the tension from her body and waited motionlessly, patiently waiting as she gauged the apprehensive steps of the intruder. Suddenly, a small puff of hot air wafted over her face as the unexpected visitor knelt beside the bed where she lay.

"Grandami?" came a hushed voice, breaking the uneasy silence.

"Hmmm?" murmured Everly, arching her brow inquisitively, while barely opening one eye to peer at her grandson. Kneeling, his chin resting on the edge of the bed as he gazed at her. The scant lavender flecks that peppered his otherwise onyx-black eyes sparkled in the faint amount of light peaking in through the open window.

"Are you awake?" asked Wesdin, even in his whispered tone, his excitement was evident.

"Wesdin," grumbled Everly as she closed her eye, "what time is it?"

"Umm... still a... umm... little early," he stammered slowly.

"And why does one come to disturb me at such an hour?" mumbled Everly with annoyance.

"So that we may go train," came his eager reply. "Oh! And maybe hunt this time!" he added enthusiastically. "Please, Grandami?" he begged softly, reaching out to gently shake Everly by the shoulder.

The corner of Everly's mouth twitched slightly as she fought back the urge to smirk in amusement.

"Pleeeeeeease?" repeated Wesdin, his tone still hushed so as not to wake his grandfather. Contorting his face in mild frustration, Wesdin tugged at Everly's arm while raising on his haunches to peer at Manijor nervously.

After a few moments passed, Everly lifted her head off the bed and opened her eyes. With a grin, she finally said, "Very well," to which Wesdin shot upright zealously.

"Yes!" he hissed eagerly before immediately wincing apologetically when Everly swiftly hushed him. "Sorry, Grandami," he whispered before slowly inching his way back toward the door. Leaving the door slightly ajar, Wesdin waited patiently for his grandmother in the hall.

Shaking her head from side to side, Everly rolled her eyes and smiled to herself in delight. *"His skills improve every day,"* she silently thought to herself as she quickly changed, donning a linen tunic, a pair of leather breaches and her training boots. Turning to gaze at her still sleeping husband, Everly raised her hand, pressed a kiss to her fingers and smiled as she blew a kiss toward him. Without further delay, she grabbed the sheaths housing her twin throwing blades and fastened them to her hips before joining Wesdin.

Once the door to the chamber was closed, Everly turned to her grandson and pulled him into her embrace. "Good morn, my darling," she said softly before kissing his cheek.

Wesdin returned his grandmother's hug and pressed a kiss to her cheek in return. "Good morn, Grandami. We need meal mush," he stated while impatiently withdrawing from her embrace.

"Indeed," replied Everly with a nod of her head as she guided the way to the kitchen.

"Grandami," said Wesdin pensively and paused, eyeing the food vessels his grandmother was filling with greenish-yellow colored, pudding like, food, "why must it always be meal mush?" he finally asked in disgust.

Everly peered at her grandson briefly as she arched her brow before responding. "Because my darling, it is quick to prepare and consist of all the basic necessities to sustain us as we train," she reminded him gently.

"But it does not taste so good," admitted Wesdin as he made a face of abhorrence causing Everly to chuckle.

"You sound just like your Grandapi," chided Everly with a feigned sternness to her voice. "Here you are," she said as she placed the vessel in front of Wesdin. "The faster it goes down…" she said and waited for Wesdin to finish her sentence.

5

"The less I have to taste," grumbled Wesdin as he picked up his serving of meal mush and eyed it once more with distaste.

"Come now, it is not so bad," added Everly as she set her empty vessel down. Using her tongue, she cleared the gritty textured remnants of the bland-flavored contents from her mouth and teeth. "Be hasty child," she chided with exasperation as Wesdin continued to stall, "or I shall return myself back to bed."

The threat spurred Wesdin to motion; holding the container to his lips, he then tossed his head back and swiftly gulped down the contents. "Gah!" he exclaimed once he finished the meal mush and shuddered with repulsion.

Nodding her head curtly in approval, Everly then spun on her heels and navigated her way toward the training grounds with Wesdin following close behind her.

* * *

"You mustn't doubt yourself," said Everly as she held out a throwing blade for Wesdin to take. "In the middle of a hunt or battle, the slightest hesitation could…" she intentionally paused and quizzically peered at her grandson as he grasped the hilt of the blade.

"Could cost me my life," he finally replied with a frown on his face.

"Or that of another," added Everly critically.

"But Grandami," he began and was instantly interrupted.

"I will not hear any excuses," she stated firmly. "You must practice in order to advance your skills. And also," she halted mid-sentence to let loose a throwing blade, "to maintain your skills." The *thwack* of the blade finding its mark on the practice target resounded in the early morning. "Now… let loose again!" she stated firmly but softened the command with an encouraging smile.

Wesdin held the blade lightly in his hand and heaved a sigh; with his fingers wrapped loosely around the handle, he shook his hand up and down to test the weight of the weapon. The action made the blade appear to wobble. Closing his eyes, he fought to control his breathing and calm his racing heart. After a few moments of silence passed, he opened his eyes once more. Without hesitation, he took a step forward while simultaneously drawing his arm upward and back beside his ear; in less than a moment, he flung his hand forward, letting the blade loose. The faint whistling of the blade as it flew towards its target was quickly halted with a *thwack* as it found its mark.

"Wonderfully done!" exclaimed Everly as she excitedly clapped her hands together.

6

Furrowing his brows together, Wesdin continued to stare at the throwing blade, lodged in the practice target beside the one his grandmother had previously thrown. Disbelief slowly gave way to pride as he realized he had finally nailed his target.

"Grandami!" he exhaled breathlessly. "I did it!" he said, his voice dripping with excitement. "I did it!" he repeated while jumping up and down joyfully.

The sun, barely cresting over the horizon, reminded Everly it was near time the others would be rising for the day. *Such resemblance to your father and grandfather,* she thought silently while reaching out to ruffle Wesdin's hair; the metallic grey locks with silver highlights clung to his steel-blue flesh from the sweat pouring down his face. *And yet so different,* she mused about the darker skin of her husband and lighter skin of their own son. Wiping a bead of sweat from Wesdin's face before it could fall in his eye, she then cleared her throat. "Come. It is near time the others will be rising," she reminded him with a gentle nudge toward the palace.

* * *

Sitting in her preferred chair in the Dining Hall, Everly casually leaned back with a glass of freshly brewed *lavendia* tea. "You slept well?" she asked while smiling as she glanced toward the open door as her husband entered.

"Indeed," said Manijor with a slight nod of his head as he approached his wife. Leaning down, he briefly brushed his lips across hers in greeting, drawing a broader smile from Everly. "What is it that you have there?" he then asked curiously as he straightened to his full height once more.

With the glass held up to her lips, Everly replied, "*lavendia* tea," before taking a cautious sip of the hot contents. "Shall I prepare one for you?" she graciously offered.

"Not this morn," he responded with a smile while slightly shaking his head from side to side briefly. "I am more in the mood for *berria*," he admitted; his mouth immediately watered at the thought of the fruit juice medley ordinarily served with morning meal.

"I shall fetch the fresh batch for you, Grand Brute," immediately offered a nearby palace keeper, aware a flagon had not been set out.

Turning toward the palace keeper, Manijor offered a fleeting smile and brief nod of his head in thanks. Without waiting, he then picked up a nearby plate and began making his selections from the array of morning meal items laid out before him on the banquet table. "Excellent," he said aloud softly to himself as his eyes settled on the vessel of *kayzia,* a pale, green, spread made from Vertalia mountain goat milk. After lathering a generous portion of *kayzia* atop the loaf of bread

7

on his plate, Manijor returned to sit across from his wife. The palace keeper returned with a mug of *berria* just as Manijor finished settling himself and placed it on the table beside Manijor. "You have my thanks!" exclaimed Manijor, his mouth once more watering in anticipation.

Lifting the bread loaf from his plate, Manijor tore a section off and shoveled it in his mouth hungrily. "Mmmm," he sighed and closed his eyes while slumping back slightly in his chair with delight. "*Kayzia* is my absolute favorite," he admitted sheepishly.

"I have noticed," retorted Everly with a chuckle. "It is indeed delicious," she added in agreeance to which Manijor nodded.

After glancing around the Dining Hall, Manijor finally asked under his breath, "How goes the training?"

Everly pursed her lips briefly before shaking her head from side to side. "He still doubts himself," she finally replied. "I sense it is because he has not experienced his *transformation,*" she continued softly.

Manijor drew his brows together slightly. "Do you think he will?" he asked after taking a swallow of *berria*.

"I am not certain," responded Everly with a shrug of her shoulders. "The other children have already experienced their *transformations,*" she recalled of the children with at least one Weretigal parent. "I have not seen any go past their fifth cycle without experiencing their *transformation,*" she admitted slowly. *Except for those who lacked the ability to transform.* The unsaid thought lingered in the air between the two.

"Well," began Manijor before clearing his throat, "it is of no real concern if he cannot. We will still foster his abilities, whatever they may be," he reassured Everly.

"Of course," agreed Everly after raising her glass to take another sip of tea.

Just then, Wesdin charged into the Dining Hall. "Good morn!" he said happily as he raced toward his grandparents.

"Good morn, my darling," greeted Everly with a smile, reaching upward to embrace Wesdin as he leaned over to hug her.

"Good morn, runt," replied Manijor with a teasing grin.

"Hmph!" grunted Wesdin in response to Manijor in displeasure before replying. "I am no runt," he finally said as he gave his grandfather a brief hug.

"Nay, not any longer," agreed Manijor with a chuckle. "You have since overtaken the others your age. You appear nearer to ten cycles," he said, arching his brows and shaking his head in amazement.

"It is still difficult to believe you are only but five cycles," added Everly as she stood to prepare a plate for her grandson.

"Was Api as big as me?" asked Wesdin, curious to know if he was of similar stature to his father.

"Oh, my darling!" exclaimed Everly as she set the plate of Wesdin's favorite fruits and meats down in front of him along with a mug of *berria*, "you are twice the size of your father!" she finished, drawing a broad smile from Wesdin. "I expect you will grow to be much larger," she added with a laugh.

Wesdin's smile slowly faded and was replaced with a pensive frown. "Will Ami and Api be home soon?" he suddenly asked.

"Indeed," responded Manijor assuredly. "The Khan and Khantessa are due to arrive later this eve with the others."

"Why do Ami and Api go on so many expeditions?" Wesdin asked with a pout. Without waiting for an answer, he proceeded with multiple question. "And when will I get to go on the expeditions? And when can I start training with the troops? And why can't I..."

"That's enough for now, runt*,"* Manijor interrupted Wesdin sternly. "You already know it is the desire of the Khantessa that you do not begin training with weapons until you have mastered your healing abilities."

"But Grandapi..." began Wesdin, his voice pleading.

"None of that, now," interjected Everly, her voice just as stern as her husband's. "Your parents set boundaries that we must obey. They must make sure the kingdom, as vast as it is, is always safe. And as Khanzito, you are required to learn of your abilities, history of VerTexItas, the politics and all else necessary to rule a kingdom so you are prepared to take over in your father's place when that time comes," she finished in a tone that welcomed no rebuttal.

Wesdin contorted his face in disgruntlement.

"You must also learn to control your emotions," added Manijor in a softer tone while winking mischievously at his grandson. "You cannot always allow others to know what you are truly feeling. Keep your face expressionless," he finished in a whisper. Clearing his throat after catching Everly openly glare at him, Manijor added, "now eat your morning meal before Grandami skins us both."

"Lest you are late for Erudition," added Everly with a steely gaze.

Wesdin tried to stifle a giggle as he and Manijor both shoved a piece of bread in their mouths.

CHAPTER 2

The pounding of zebril hooves on the hard-packed dirt road drowned out the muted thuds of paws as the variety of mounts stirred up a cloud of dust behind the expedition party; staying on the primary road, the group continued their trek between the main cities of Restway and Capitalia. Capitalia, having replaced Feralia as the capital city nearly seven cycles prior, served as the leading defense post between the *Forbidden Wilds* and the remainder of Savenius.

"Whoa!" called out Avenor as he rose his right arm up with his hand open. *"Whoa, Drayd. Whoa, boy,"* he said silently to his mount.

The massive cat chuffed in response, acknowledging Avenor's silent command. Panting, Drayd slowed to a slight canter before coming to a complete stop.

"Whoa, boy," called out Galhix and gently tugged on Pylo's reigns to bring him to a halt in response to Avenor's signal. Pylo came to a halt abreast his brother, Drayd. The pair of white, *colossal jaguars* stood regally beside one another. Their white fur, speckled with minuscule aquamarine-colored spots, appeared to shimmer in the daylight as they protracted and retracted their claws while stretching.

"We'll break here. Water your mounts and eat swiftly," stated Avenor as he dismounted. Reaching up, he gently scratched the massive cat under his chin.

"Aye, Khan Avenor," came a chorus of replies in response to their leader's command.

Galhix gracefully dismounted from Pylo's back; her motions were fluid and effortless as she swung her leg over and landed silently on her feet.

"Khantessa," greeted Azelly, dipping her head respectfully, as she approached Galhix and Avenor.

"General Azelly," replied Galhix with a slight dip of her head in return.

"Sister," said Avenor as he raised his right forearm in welcome.

"Your Grace," answered Azelly as she knocked her right forearm against her adoptive brother's arm in greeting. "We must ride hard if we are to make it back to Capitalia before dark. That last skirmish with the Goons has delayed us," she informed him, obviously perturbed.

"Indeed," he grunted with a curt nod of his head.

"The skirmishes are becoming more frequent," added Galhix tentatively.

"Aye," agreed Azelly with her brows knitted together. "I believe it is because the Goons are increasing in numbers. Their youth are maturing and joining the fighting forces," she said speaking of the outcasts once known as *Trolls* before the ancient curse had been lifted.

"As well as other exiles joining them," grunted Avenor. "We will discuss the issue when we are home. For now, eat and water your mounts," he instructed the pair.

"As you desire, Your Grace," Azelly responded while bringing her right forearm up over her chest and dipping her head respectfully in salute before turning to head back toward her mount.

"Come, my Khantessa," said Avenor, his tone gentle and loving. "We, too, must address our mounts and eat before we ride once more." Avenor reached out to take Galhix's hand and interlocked her fingers with his. Without thinking, he brought her hand to his mouth, brushing his lips against her knuckles.

Galhix smiled, adoring the practice Avenor had sustained. It was a habit he had developed two cycles after their allegiance had been established between VerTexItas and the Weretigals of Savenius. It was when their courtship had begun. "Yes, my Khan," replied Galhix softly, her voice still laced with love and devotion for her husband even after six cycles of wedlock.

* * *

Early as usual when visiting Capitalia, Laynee sat quietly in her favorite seat with her head downcast. "Ugh!" she huffed irritably while shoving her silver locks back from falling in her sapphire blue eyes. She clamped her teeth down on her bottom lip while scrunching her nose; with extreme focus, she clenched a plume between her fingers and practiced writing the series of letters and numbers assigned by the Erudite, the Master of Education.

Ding-Dong! Ding-Dong!

Laynee grimaced and at once covered her ears upon hearing the first clanging of the bell atop the newly constructed Erudition building. Laynee lowered her hands after the most obnoxious tones of the bell had faded, becoming a faint echo in the distance. Aware that the bell called all the pupils that would be attending morning lessons, she turned her attention back to her task. Pressing down heavily, Laynee dragged the plume over her parchment sheet.

Erudite Kaminah flinched slightly as she heard the plume of her best pupil scrape over the parchment sheet.

"Not again!" wailed out Laynee suddenly as her plume ripped through her parchment sheet. She tossed her plume on the desktop, sat back forcefully in her chair, and crossed her arms over her chest.

"What have I told you before?" gently asked Erudite Kaminah as she looked across the room at Laynee, noting how the girl pulled back her lips, almost as if snarling with irritation.

"To scribe as if I was using a feather when painting by making gentle strokes," grumbled Laynee in resignation, knowing she would have to begin her task anew on yet a different parchment sheet.

"Indeed," replied Kaminah as the corner of her mouth twitched slightly in amusement. "Begin again," she calmly instructed Laynee while managing to force the entertainment from her voice.

"Aye, Erudite," groused Laynee under her breath without making eye contact.

The chorus of voices echoing throughout every corridor was accompanied by the light pitter-pattering of slipper clad feet mingled with louder boot thuds as students raced through the halls of the Erudition Building toward their assigned chambers. Without warning, the door to the first Youth Chamber flung open as two children scampered in.

"Take that!" shouted Wesdin as he chased after Geodani. Grunting, Wesdin brought down his wooden sword.

Geodani swiftly raised his own practice sword to greet Wesdin's above his head.

Clack!

"Blocked!" mumbled Geodani. Grunting, he then used both hands as he shoved his sword against Wesdin's, struggling under the force and strength of his sparing mate.

"Block this!" retorted Wesdin, bringing his foot up and kicking his cousin in the stomach.

"Ooof!" grunted Geodani as he stumbled backward and collided with his twin sister's side.

"Ey!" cried out Laynee as Geodani bumped her, causing her to smudge the undried letters on her parchment.

Leandra hastily pursued her companions; her pale green gown swirled around her legs as her feet moved silently on the marbled floor. Pausing just as she passed through the doorway, she closed her eyes and raised her arms out beside her. With her lips moving rapidly, she quietly began an incantation. "Nieve pelloticas!" she finished as she arched her arms, bringing them to the center of her chest. In her hands, she held small balls made of snow. Without waiting, she unleashed a rainfall of snowballs on Wesdin and Geodani.

"Oy!" shouted Wesdin grudgingly, "We said no incants!"

"Pupils!" roared Erudite Kaminah as she slammed her hands down on her desk. "Why must every day begin in such a manner whenever we have visitors?" she exasperatedly asked.

"Well, Erudite…" began Geodani sheepishly.

"Oy, Geodani…" interrupted Kaminah as she rubbed her temples, "my question did not require an answer."

Wesdin immediately approached Kaminah. As if on cue, Kaminah lowered her hands which were replaced with Wesdin's; without hesitation, Wesdin began softly incanting to ease his Erudite's pain.

"You have my thanks, Khanzito," she said softly. "Now, please, take your seats," she announced to her pupils. Just before the second bell rang, indicating the start of learning, the remaining pupils trickled in. "Good morn, Erudite Kaminah," they greeted in unison before finding their seats.

* * *

The alternating repetition of *clat, tap, clat, tap, clat, tap* resounded through the corridors as the visiting Weretigal leaders, Chief Gelriz and Chieftess Baylay, casually strolled through the palace; with each step, the heel of Baylay's hardened leather boots struck with a *clat* followed by the softer *tap* of Gelriz's pliable leather slippers. Baylay's chestnut brown hair was braided tightly and hung over her shoulder; braided in a similar fashion, Gelriz's silver hair hung down his back. Sitting atop of their heads rested matching *damiund* bands adorned with alternating red and gold gems.

"Good morn," said Chief Gelriz in greeting while passing the nearby palace keepers as Baylay smiled and partly dipped her head.

"Good morn, Your Graces," replied the palace keepers in unison, recognizing the visiting Tigalia leaders from their identical crowns.

"Oy!" exclaimed Odeera once the Chief and Chieftess had turned a corner and were gone from her vision. "Did you notice how large their gems were?" she turned and openly gaped at Taylin.

"Indeed!" Taylin managed to squawk out, her eyes still bulging in amazement. "I 'ave never seen *Fire Spark* or *Star Strike* gems o' that size buh'for worn like that," she admitted as she recalled those embellishing the Grand Brute's, General Manijor's, battle-hammer. "I ca'not even fath'm the added strength a *Fire Spark* gem that size could pruh'vide," she finished in awe of the red gems.

13

"Nor can I imagine the increase in one's attack speed from the *Star Strike* gems," added Odeera of the precious gold stones, her voice dripping with admiration. "Perhaps one day we will have our own," she sighed longingly.

"Yea, pur'haps," agreed Taylin with a hopeful smile before returning to her daily assigned tasks.

The grin tugging at the corner of Baylay's mouth did not go unnoticed by Gelriz as he cast a sideways glance at his wife. "What amuses you so?" he asked with a slight arch of an eyebrow.

"The chattering of the youth when they believed we were out of hearing range," admitted Baylay, flashing a smile at Gelriz as they continued walking toward the training grounds.

"Mmm," hummed Gelriz in reply. Gelriz extended his arm out, and he waited until Baylay tucked her hand in the crook of his arm. He then gently pat Baylay's hand as they continued walking. "They are still young yet. With time, they will learn that just because it appears no one is around, it does not necessarily mean no one else is listening."

"Aye, it is true," replied Baylay with a brief snort as she thought of her children.

"Let me guess," stated Gelriz with a grin as he gazed at Baylay's face before asking, "you think of Layn and Geo?"

Baylay giggled briefly before a full chortle brought her to a stop mid-step. "Aye! Those two…. have yet to learn this," she finally managed to say between bouts of merriment.

Gelriz rolled his eyes upward briefly as the countless times Baylay and he had foiled their twins' practice of ambushes entered his mind; he then shook his head slightly as laughter began to bubble up from inside of him. Without warning, he threw his head back before doubling over in amusement, tears streamed down his cheeks, as the startled and contorted faces of his children flashed in his mind causing him to laugh harder. "Oy!" he gasped, clenching his side, as his entertainment slowly subsided. "Let us… go spar… as we had… planned…" he finally managed to suggest between chuckles as he reached up and wiped the remaining tears of mirth from the corner of his eyes to which Baylay nodded in response.

CHAPTER 3

The faint chittering of insects and scurrying of small prey in Overlook Cave were drowned out by the gurgling from the natural spring as it bubbled fresh water from underground; the water splashed its way out of the cave as a waterfall and created the pool below that sustained life at the Veiled Oasis.

Sunlight filled the main cavern where Gunter stood across from his mate. Reeyah watched Gunter's jaw muscles bulge as he clenched and unclenched his teeth. After a fleeting moment, Gunter crossed his powerful arms over his bare muscled chest. Reeyah observed the numerous scars marring Gunter's chest from the battles he had fought defending his position as Overlord, and she noted how they intensified his menacing appearance.

"The Boy goes," growled out Gunter after what seemed to be an endless time. Aware she had not responded, Gunter's eyes narrowed in anger as he glared at his mate.

Reeyah stood unmoving across from Gunter. There had once been a time when she would have flinched under his steely gaze; it had been six cycles since the last time she had cowered from his intimidation. "He is not yet of age," Reeyah countered bitterly. Snapping her mouth closed, Reeyah braced herself as she watched Gunter's anger flare to rage in his eyes.

Lowering his arms to his side, Gunter took an ominous step closer to Reeyah. Distorting his already disfigured face, he repeated in a threatening tone, "He goes."

Reeyah rolled her shoulders and straightened herself to stand as tall as possible; with her back stiff, she defiantly responded, "He will not."

SLAP!

Reeyah's head abruptly snapped to the side from the force of Gunter's expected open hand blow. Controlling her breathing, Reeyah fought to remain conscious and push the stinging pain from her mind.

Slowly, she turned her head back toward Gunter. An oozing sensation caused her to crinkle her nose briefly, knowing if she moved to wipe the blood away, he would strike her again.

"Being Lordess does not give you the right to challenge me," Gunter reminded Reeyah in a snarl.

"Overlord...," began Reeyah, her speech void of emotion.

"Silence!" roared Gunter, his voice reverberating through the cave. "The Boy goes. That is final!" Gunter grinned to himself as he watched Reeyah's temples appear to pulsate as she struggled to maintain control of her emotions.

Reeyah refused to tear her gaze away from Gunter's. "As you demand," she finally growled out between her clenched teeth. Without waiting for another response, Reeyah swiftly spun on her heels to leave the cave. "Agh!" she cried as a hand closed tightly on her upper arm and yanked her backward.

"Oh, no...," snickered Gunter as he tangled his other hand in Reeyah's hair. "Not so soon," he finished before jerking her head back and leaning down to force his tongue into her mouth.

"Ugh!" groaned Reeyah in disgust, feeling the evidence of Gunter's sudden arousal as she wrestled against him.

"Why struggle?" sneered Gunter as he gripped her hips firmly. "You are mine," he reminded her as he licked the blood staining her upper lip up to her nose. Effortlessly, he hoisted Reeyah off the ground and carried her across the cave to their personal grotto; Gunter tossed her on the bed before falling on top of her. Without hesitation, he ripped the fasteners securing her tunic. He harshly grabbed her ample bosom, squeezing and biting until Reeyah wailed out in anguish.

"Get off!" cried Reeyah while fiercely thrashing against Gunter and beating his shoulders in vain. Gunter quickly shucked his trousers, pulled Reeyah's breeches down, and violently had his way with her.

* * *

"Get up, Boy!" shouted Sordun. "The longer it takes to get back up," he grumbled as he struck the unsightly growth on his trainee's shoulder, "the more likely you will become a meal."

"Ugh!" grunted Dondree under the power of Sordun's attack. While uncomfortable, the blow did nothing more than fuel Dondree's desire to land his own strike. Rolling to his side, Dondree pushed himself up onto his stronger leg, and he hobbled in place as he eyed his trainer who was unable to stand straight up but still managed to move speedily.

Dondree waited patiently. *"Wait for your opponent to make a mistake,"* he remembered from his previous training. *"Do not be so hasty in your attacks." "Do not strike the growth,"* he suddenly remembered just as

16

Sordun charged toward him. Side-stepping at the last minute, Dondree spun around behind Sordun. He swung his staff down without delay; remembering to avoid the misshapen mass on Sordun's back, he changed the angle of his attack.

Thwack!

Sordun grunted in pain as he felt his knee give way from Dondree's assault and crashed to the ground.

With ragged breaths, Dondree hurried over to Sordun with his staff raised above his head. He then brought down his weapon rapidly.

Sordun turned his head to the side and flinched just as Dondree halted his attack. "Well done, Boy," gasped Sordun as he eyed the staff just mere inches from his head. "If possible," murmured Sordun as he struggled back to his feet, "never strike the growth."

"I remembered at the last moment," grumbled Dondree with a frown of disappointment plastered on his face. "The growth is like armor," he recited.

"Do not fret over it," said Sordun as he pat Dondree on the back. "You still remembered."

"Why do we have these growths?" pondered Dondree aloud. He already knew, but he enjoyed Sordun's explanation.

"No one is certain," admitted Sordun with a shrug of his broad shoulders. "But it is said that once long ago, there was a *Great Falling*. With it, beasts were born and banished far away. Those who were left eventually succumbed to the *Filth* and became tainted.*"

"Where is the *Filth* found?" asked Dondree curiously as he always did.

"It is all around," replied Sordun in a troubled whisper. "Over the cycles, it has seeped into the ground, the water, the food. It has left all the animals disfigured and deformed just as we are."

"Is that why we are known as *Deflings*?" probed Dondree as he scratched the side of his head where a new growth was emerging.

"You know this already," murmured Sordun irritably and nodded his head curtly. "Enough questions, Boy! Go and get washed up," he instructed his trainee. "It is almost time to feast." Sordun watched as Dondree navigated his way through the Veiled Oasis toward Overlook Cave before making his way to his own hut.

* * *

"Ssssssss," exhaled Reeyah painfully as her head lolled to the side. Rapidly blinking, she tried to focus her eyes within the dimness of the cave, aware that the sun had already begun its downward decent in the sky. "Ugg!" she grunted as she shifted to her side and attempted to push herself to a sitting position. "Aah!" she shrieked, immediately regretting her decision, as searing pain pulsed through her body and caused her to collapse onto her back.

Squeak... purr-eee-eee... squeak, squeak. The calling of a nearby elusive *capybarat* as it scurried along the ground drew Reeyah's gaze, blurry from blood that had trickled into her eyes. A crease appeared between her brows as she squinted, forcing herself to try and focus on the easily camouflaged large, nocturnal, cave rodent.

"There," murmured Reeyah thankfully as she finally managed to distinguish the animal from its surroundings. Outstretching an unsteady hand toward the creature, Reeyah began incanting quietly.

"Tuyom lif...exia...," she whispered raggedly before taking a shaky breath and continuing. "Et soulexia... sar... *meyah*," she finished harshly. Suddenly, a scarlet specter emerged from her palm and raced straight toward the rodent. The *capybarat's* agonizing screeches and shrills echoed through the cavern as its lifeforce was drained by the undead figure and transferred to Reeyah.

Reeyah inhaled slowly as she absorbed the strength and energy of the animal, grateful as she felt her wounds healing and pain subsiding. After a few moments, the shadowy phantom dissipated. Reeyah stood and tipped her head to one side. *Crack.* Grunting, she then tilted her head in the other direction. *Crack.* "Mmm," she moaned slightly before interlacing her fingers together and raising her arms high above her head. *Crack... prap... crraack... prraaap... prap... crack!* "Uhh...ghhh," groaned Reeyah as she stretched and felt her spine realign. Lowering her arms, she shook out her hands and quickly surveyed the grotto she was forced to share with Gunter. Her eyes locked on the lifeless husk of the *capybarat;* she approached it tentatively and reached out her foot. She then lightly kicked the corpse and watched it crumble to a pile of dirt.

"Oy," she muttered in fascination before hastily stripping her torn attire from her body. She swiftly snagged a suitable replacement and donned it; without pause, Reeyah snatched up the bloodied blankets and garments. She then tossed the items in before slamming the lid closed. She glanced around once more and heaved a sigh of relief, satisfied nothing looked amiss. Not waiting any longer, Reeyah departed from Overlook Cave.

* * *

Sordun patted his chest and arms before knocking the remaining sand and dirt from his breeches; satisfied he had removed much of the debris, he then pushed aside the drape that covered the entryway to the hut he shared with his mate.

"Da training goed good?" asked Kifta, her gaze shifting sideways as light filtered through the doorway.

"Aye, *the* training *went* good," grunted Sordun, his voice tinged with slight displeasure, as he stressed the correction to Kifta's words.

"Dat... *that*... makes... me happy," replied Kifta with forced concentration at choosing the correct words to form her sentence.

"There are not as many days when you speak incorrectly," said Sordun, nodding his head in approval which drew a smile from Kifta.

"Thank you," she responded happily before turning her attention back to stitching together a blanket made from the hide of a *fire hound*.

"Do you think she will have your ability?" asked Sordun as he crossed the hut and peered down at the basket beside Kifta where their infant lay sleeping peacefully. Her black hair, thick and wiry, stood straight up on her tiny head, unable to be tamed. Turning to gaze at Kifta, Sordun chuckled to himself softly.

"What make yous laugh?" asked Kifta with a frown.

"The way her hair stays upright," admitted Sordun as he reached out and grabbed a stray lock of Kifta's hair, giving it a gentle tug. "I am certain it will eventually fall as yours," he continued, as he released Kifta's hair and watched it settle back against her shoulder. "It is too short for now."

"Hmm," mused Kifta softly. Even after nine cycles, she had not become accustomed to her physical change.

"What troubles you?" asked Sordun as he observed the variety of emotions transforming Kifta's face.

"Nothing," she replied while shaking her head from side to side and shrugging a shoulder.

Sordun crossed his arms over his chest and tried to stand as straight as possible. Arching a brow, he stood quietly and motionless as he gazed at his mate. Her black hair was secured at the nape of her neck with a leather strap. A few locks managed to free themselves and hung loosely around her once unblemished face.

Reaching up absentmindedly, Kifta pushed back a stray lock that had fallen over her face and into her eye. Her hand brushed against the newly forming lump on her brow. "It is the recent most one," she said quietly, more to herself than to Sordun.

"I see," grunted Sordun as he heaved a sigh. She and the others had been without deformities when they arrived. Over time, just as everyone, they began to develop lumps and disfigurements.

"You thinks she will have them?" asked Kifta suddenly as she gazed down at her sleeping infant, her flesh flawless and without malformations. Kifta did not bother to look at Sordun when he failed to respond; truthfully, she did not seek an answer. It was common knowledge that if children were not born disfigured, they would eventually develop a deformity.

"I will carry the infant," said Sordun as he bent down and scooped the tiny bundle up in his massive arms. "It is time to feast," he continued as he held out a hand to assist Kifta to stand. Closing his large hand around her smaller one, Sordun easily pulled her to her feet.

"Eep!" squealed Kifta in surprise as Sordun hoisted her upright. He was just as strong as any *Troll* she had ever known. *"They are all big and strongs,"* she silently thought to herself as she was reminded of the immense size of the *Deflings* while standing beside Sordun.

* * *

Gunter raised his arm and nodded his head once, the signal that feasting could begin. Situated along side of the clear waters of the lake, the gathered *Deflings* erupted in chatter amongst themselves as *lowlings* began serving the nourishments. Without waiting a moment longer, a nearby *lowling* hobbled forward and set a thin, stone slab stacked with nourishments down before Gunter.

"Overlord," greeted the *lowling* before placing a similar rock platter down in front of Reeyah. "Lordess," continued the *lowling*. Reeyah nodded her head in acknowledgement of the *Defling* unable to hunt but still capable of performing tasks around the village.

"Boy," said another *lowling* as she skulked forward.

"Lowling," replied Dondree tentatively as he watched the girl dragging her right leg as she walked. Absentmindedly, he began softly beating the heel of his left foot repetitively on the ground. Reeyah reached under the table, placed her hand on Dondree's knee, and pressed down firmly to halt the anxious behavior. Dondree placed his hand over his mother's without making eye contact; Reeyah immediately turned her hand over to gently squeeze her son's hand before letting go.

Suddenly, Gunter stood and held his arms out wide, quieting the gathering. As silence gradually spread throughout the encampment, Gunter lowered his arms to his side. "The season is upon us!" he began, his voice booming throughout the village. "The Boy is to go on his *Hunt!"* he boldly announced to the gathering, drawing astonished gasps.

Reeyah clamped her teeth together tightly in response to Dondree's sharp intake of breath, and she forced herself to remain motionless as she peered out at the crowd. The renewed tapping of Dondree's foot had an increased fervor; trying to calm her son, Reeyah slightly pressed her leg against his. Sensing the pressure of his mother's leg against the side of his own, Dondree slowed the tapping of his foot and eventually stopped.

"In order to become *Lord*," continued Gunter, oblivious to the silent communication between his mate and offspring, "the Boy must return with his first kill."

Murmurs instantaneously erupted and spread throughout the gathering. Whispers of concern, doubt, and hesitancy spread like wildfire.

"It is a death sentence," ground out Reeyah between her clenched teeth. "You know he is not adequately prepared," she continued under her breath so that only Gunter and Dondree could hear.

Gunter dropped back down in his seat and leaned forward, his face no more than a breath away from Reeyah's. Turning her steely gaze, Reeyah met his menacing glare.

"Then so be it," he hissed in return as he shifted his gaze past Reeyah to glower at Dondree in disgust. "To be *Lord*, he must be able to provide and hunt. I will not have a *lowling* as my offspring," he spat vehemently.

Dondree fought back the tears that unexpectedly stung his eyes, leaving his vision hazy. He had always sensed the loathing from his father, but he had never heard his father express it aloud. He had never thought his father would send him out from the Veiled Oasis to his death. Dondree immediately stood, grabbing the table to steady himself, and he forced a smile to his face as he raised a hand. "I will return victorious!" he called out passionately. After drawing a cheer from the gathering, he excused himself and retreated to Overlook Cave.

CHAPTER 4

Wesdin, already tucked in bed for the evening by Everly and Manijor, curled his hands slightly and rubbed his bleary eyes as he fought the urge to drift to sleep. *"Ami and Api will be home soon,"* he reminded himself wordlessly as he opened his mouth wide to allow a yawn to escape. He then turned onto his side, and he drew the blanket up over his shoulders as he nuzzled into the warmth that cocooned him. Batting his eyelids sluggishly, he resisted the comforting heaviness that settled around him. Within moments, his deep, peaceful breathing was the only sound resonating through his chamber.

"I wager he will be awake," whispered Galhix as she stood outside of Wesdin's chamber with her hand resting on the door handle.

"And I wager he will *not*," retorted Avenor with a slight chuckle. "The hour is late," he continued with a doubtful arch of an eyebrow.

"He has surely missed us," countered Galhix hopefully.

"I am certain of it," agreed Avenor with dip of his head before turning his head to the side as a yawn interrupted him. "Aarrgh," he grunted aloud at the end of his yawn, and he shook his head vigorously to ward off the sleep threatening him. "However, it is well past evening meal."

"Perhaps you are right," murmured Galhix timidly. "Perhaps we…"

"Say that once more," interrupted Avenor with a grin tugging at the corner of his mouth. Galhix turned and scowled at him in response to which Avenor snorted as he suppressed his laugh. "I do not hear it enough," taunted Avenor lightheartedly as he reached out to softly jab Galhix in her side.

"Hmph!" exclaimed Galhix before turning back to the door, "and you will not be hearing it again any time soon," she finished in a huff. Not waiting for her husband's reply, she turned the handle and pushed the door open. Galhix peered in the darkness to the bed where it was stationed centrally along the right wall from the entrance, and she made out the form of her son sleeping quietly.

"He is a beautiful child," murmured Avenor as he stood behind Galhix, placing a hand on her shoulder.

"I am glad he has your ability to see in the darkness as well as you," replied Galhix, reminded that Avenor and Wesdin were able to see as if the sun shone at every hour of the day. "At times I am envious," admitted Galhix under her breath.

Avenor leaned down, and he lightly kissed Galhix's shoulder before whispering in her ear, "You are capable of seeing in the night as well. Why be envious?" he questioned.

"Indeed," she replied quietly with a slight shrug of her shoulders, "but not as well as you both. To be able to see every detail at every moment would be glorious," she admitted with a sigh.

"Mmm, I suppose" replied Avenor, uncertain of how to respond. "In truth, I had never considered how beneficial an ability it is until just now," he finished with a frown, realizing he had always taken his ability for granted.

Galhix turned to kiss Avenor's hand before flashing a smile at him over her shoulder. "It is easy to forget how fortunate one is to have certain abilities."

"Indeed," he said as he squeezed Galhix's shoulder lightly while nodding in response. After a few moments, Avenor lowered his hand to Galhix's waist. "Come," he said calmly, "we must rest as well."

"Mmmhmm," murmured Galhix before immediately raising her hand to her lips to cover the yawn that followed. Galhix gently pulled the door closed, and she then turned to place her hand in Avenor's. The delicate pitter-patter of steps resounded throughout the corridors as they proceeded through the palace to their personal chambers.

* * *

Azelly handed Pylo and Drayd both an evening treat in the form of a kodiak shank before closing the stall door. Leander reached through the stall door and handed his and Azelly's mounts both a bushel of carrots before rubbing the length of their snouts.

"Good eve," called out Azelly as she raised a hand in farewell. The remainder of the expedition party members responded in turn as they continued bedding down their mounts.

"Ready?" asked Azelly as Leander joined her.

"Aye, my sweet," replied Leander as he reached out to tuck a wild lock of hair behind Azelly's ear. Azelly turned her head and kissed her husband's hand briefly as he cupped her cheek, enjoying the continued affection and adoration he continued to bestow upon her even after seven cycles of wedlock. After a fleeting instant, the pair turned and began the trek toward their home. The steady *clanging and tapping* of their metal and leather boots striking the cobble-stone street in unison sounded louder than usual in the still of the night as the two marched in silence; as they approached their home, Azelly could see the torchlight flickering and dancing in the night breeze as it illuminated the entryway. Stopping at the entrance with Azelly by his side, Leander raised his hand and rapped on the wooden door lightly. Within moments, the pair heard the locking bolt being slid to the side before the door was pulled open.

"Good eve," Trittni greeted brightly as she stepped back to allow Leander and Azelly to enter.

"Good eve," replied Leander and Azelly in harmony as they stepped passed their home keeper who also served as Leandra's *watcher*.

"Is she already in bed?" asked Azelly with a skeptical grin, drawing forth a quick bark of laughter from Trittni.

"If only it were that easy," replied Trittni with a chuckle as a *thud* sounded from above them, drawing their gazes upward.

Leander guffawed as he shook his head from side to side. "Has she learned to control the *transformation?*" he asked while arching a brow as he turned his gaze back toward Trittni.

"Nay, not as of yet," responded Trittni with a slow shake of her head. "And it sounds as though she be in her form," she finished as a louder *thud* followed by a *crash* echoed through the home.

"Very well," replied Azelly as she began removing her iridescent gauntlets and wrist guards. "It is late. You are free to stay or go as you please," she stated warmly.

"My gratitude is yours," responded Trittni with a slight dip of her head, "but I have made a promise to my brother that I shall meet him in the morn."

"Then swift travels," replied Leander as he stood with Azelly, placing a protective arm around her shoulders as she wrapped an arm around his waist.

"Goat's piss! I nearly forgot!" exclaimed Trittni before she transformed. "The Erudite was not pleased again while you both were away."

"This does not surprise me," groaned Azelly as she tossed her head back and stared at the ceiling with exasperation.

Leander pursed his lips while casting a side-ways glance at his wife, and he immediately flinched when he saw her eyes narrow to a glower. "What?" he suddenly asked sheepishly. "It is not as if I had something to do with it..." he finished, allowing his voice to trail off implicitly.

"Just because Wizard abilities course through her veins, does not mean it is directly related to me," she muttered blandly under her breath, but knew the statement was an untrue statement.

"Pfft," scoffed Leander with an arched brow. "Khan Avenor has already made the declaration that *HybraRunners* can possess abilities that are dormant in one's bloodline." Suddenly, he snapped his fingers before asking, "Oy, riddle me this... How can the ability come from me? There are no tigal Wizards..." he added while raising both brows and shoulders simultaneously in what appeared to be a confused look.

"Bah!" grunted Azelly as she crossed her arms over her chest defiantly, unaware of who the Wizard in her lineage could have been.

Trittni stifled a giggle as she watched Azelly. The sudden *poof* followed by a cloud of white smoke drew Azelly's attention back to Trittni. The *transformation* process failed to startle Azelly as it once had. In place of Trittni's human form stood a tan tigal. Trittni tossed her head from side to side then shook her entire body as she adjusted to her tigal form. Huffing quietly in farewell, she then turned and darted off into the night.

Leander closed the door without waiting; he then reached up, and he slid the bolt in place to make sure the door was locked for the evening. Another *thud* drew their attention and caused Leander to grimace as if he experienced a physical blow.

"Ready?" asked Azelly, her face a mask of uncertainty.

"Aye," replied Leander hesitantly as he followed his wife toward the stairs.

The couple paused outside of their daughter's personal quarter to listen to the myriad of chuffs, hisses and growls coming from within. After a moment, Azelly turned the handle and shoved the door wide open.

Leander and Azelly peered into the room and examined the wreckage. Linens spilled over the side of the bed while both pillows rested on the floor. The table lay overturned with books and shredded parchment sheets scattered nearby.

A feline head suddenly popped up from the opposite side of the bed; her light brown eyes twinkled with mischief. Her eyes widened in delight as her gaze settled on Leander and Azelly. Without hesitation, Leandra sprang up on to her disheveled bed, and she launched herself across the quarter into her mother's waiting arms.

"Ooof!" grunted Azelly as she caught Leandra, the weight of her daughter causing her to take a staggering step backward. "You've grown!" she then exclaimed as she hoisted Leandra up to adjust her hold.

Leandra began purring deeply as she nuzzled her mother's neck before turning to lick her father's face in greeting.

"Child…," began Leander in a stern tone. "Why are you not in bed?" he asked to which Leandra lowered her eyes in embarrassment.

"And what is this we hear that you have displeased the Erudite?" questioned Azelly, thankful for the strength her Aggressor Knight ability granted her, as she held Leandra out in front of her. Leandra flattened her ears in response to her parent's scolding and kicked her hind legs, her paws nearly touching the ground, as she shifted uneasily in her mother's grasp. "We will discuss it in the morn," finished Azelly as she handed Leandra to her father.

"Aye," agreed Leander as he scooped Leandra from her mother's arms. He then hugged her against his chest. "For now, it is time to sleep," he finished as he settled Leandra on the bed.

Azelly picked up the discarded pillows and placed them on the bed under Leandra's head. "Rest well," murmured Azelly as she bent down to place a loving kiss on the tip of Leandra's nose.

Leander grabbed the blanket, and he placed it over his cub. Smiling, he watched as Leandra's light brown eyes, the exact shade as her mother's, fluttered closed as sleep claimed her.

Satisfied Leandra had succumbed to slumber, Leander and Azelly silently eased their way from her personal quarter. Wordlessly, they then proceeded down the hall to their own personal quarters before preparing for bed themselves.

CHAPTER 5

Avenor rolled onto his back and stifled the urge to grunt as a yawn escaped his mouth. The sun had not yet crested over the horizon, but he could already feel the warmth of the day creeping through the open window. Turning his head, he peered at his wife sleeping peacefully beside him with one hand tucked under her cheek resting against the pillow. Her deep, even breaths assured him it would still be a while before she would rise. Reaching out, Avenor tenderly pushed back Galhix's silver hair that danced across her brow from the breeze wafting through the window. It still bewildered him how her hair appeared to pulse with life; the *humming* sound faint as energy coursed through every strand.

After a few moments, Avenor turned his attention toward the shady area closest to the open window. A slight crease formed between his eyes as the shadows began swirling together and conjoined as a single entity. Avenor watched the light streaming into the chamber fade as the shutters gradually closed from his nonverbal command of the shadows.

Silently, he then blended with the shadows to slip unfelt from the bed so as not to disturb Galhix. In his shadow form, Avenor proceeded to the changing area of their chambers before resuming his normal self. Soundlessly dressing, Avenor donned comfortable linen attire before making his way toward Wesdin's chambers.

Avenor delicately pushed open Wesdin's chamber door, and he tip-toed across the distance to Wesdin's bed without making a sound. Peering down, Avenor noted the likeness of himself in Wesdin's features. *"The only true difference is the shape of his nose… it is like his mother's,"* mussed Avenor distractedly to himself. *"His complexion is a tad darker… and his hair,"* he continued to think as his eyes were drawn to the pulsating silver streaks that highlighted Wesdin's metallic grey hair. Shaking his head vigorously, Avenor freed himself from becoming completely enthralled in a trancelike state.

"Oy!" he exclaimed mutely. *"I mustn't forget his ability,"* Avenor reminded himself of the natural protection Wesdin's silver tresses

generated, evident from the barely audible thrumming of energy as he slumbered.

Avenor skillfully situated himself at the end of Wesdin's bed and grinned impishly; he then lowered himself to a squatting position. Inhaling deeply, Avenor then vigorously propelled himself up and forward, vaulting himself high into the air.   "Rise!" roared Avenor at the exact moment he landed on the bed beside his son.

"Aagh!" shrieked Wesdin in surprise as he immediately leapt out of bed. Instinctively, he assumed a battle stance and quickly spun around to survey his chamber. As his heartbeat slowed and his eyes adjusted, he stood staring at his father still standing on his bed.

"Api!" he exclaimed as Avenor hopped down from the bed. Without hesitation, Wesdin rushed into his father's open arms, and he rested his head against Avenor's rock hard chest.

"Good morn, my son," greeted Avenor as he embraced Wesdin fiercely. Dipping his head, Avenor brushed an adoring kiss over Wesdin's forehead. "You rested well?" asked Avenor before he tousled Wesdin's hair.

"Aye, Api," grunted Wesdin happily as he squeezed his father with all his might. "Is Ami still sleeping?" he finally asked as he turned to gaze up at his father.

"Indeed," groaned Avenor with a slight chuckle. "You have grown stronger. Shall we go train before she wakes?" he asked while waggling his brows in mischievous suggestion.

"Aye!" Wesdin nearly bellowed with his enthusiasm before disengaging himself from his father's hold. He then promptly changed into suitable training attire and joined Avenor in the hall.

* * *

Valcaly swiftly dipped under Jonetal's arm as he swung his sword out in attack; she then side-stepped instinctively. Immediately, Valcaly lifted her dominant leg and landed a kick to Jonetal's midsection.

"Ooof!" grunted Jonetal as he staggered backward from his wife's powerful kick. Jonetal gasped for air, struggling to regain the breath that had been knocked out of him.

Valcaly seized the opportunity to dart away from Jonetal, and she placed twenty feet distance between them. Turning, she flicked her wrists to let loose the wooden throwing daggers she used in sparring.

A loud *knock* and *thump* were instantly followed by, *"Puq!"* as Jonetal cursed in surprise as Valcaly's dull daggers nailed him in the forehead and the center of his chest.

"Ah ha!" exclaimed Valcaly victoriously just as a series of claps and cheers erupted from the edge of the sparring enclosure, eliciting Valcaly's attention.

"Hmph!" groaned Jonetal, scowling at Valcaly as he rubbed his forehead. Turning sideways, he openly glared at the onlookers before smirking awkwardly.

"Khan Avenor! Khanzito!" called Valcaly, her voice warm and welcoming as she joined the pair outside of the sparring enclosure. "How long have you been observing?" she asked while wiping sweat from her brow on the sleeve of her tunic.

"Only the entire time *Onia* Valcaly!" replied Wesdin, addressing Valcaly as a respected older female, with a giggle as he waved happily at Jonetal.

"Indeed, High Trapper" agreed Avenor with a slight dip of his head in response to his mother's closest friend and the Overseer of Savenius. "Good morn, Major Jonetal," greeted Avenor as Jonetal joined them.

"Your Grace," murmured Jonetal as he knocked his right forearm against Avenor's. "How goes it?" he asked casually.

"Well enough," responded Avenor. "Wesdin," he began and placed his hands firmly on his son's shoulders, "is in need of training. I figure you could use an opponent... closer to your skill level," jested Avenor with a sly grin directed at his former trainer.

"Bah!" grunted Jonetal as he rolled his eyes upward. Valcaly threw her head back and erupted with laughter, causing Jonetal to cross his arms over his chest and glower at his wife.

"It seems as though High Trapper Valcaly has bested her teacher!" taunted Avenor as he chuckled softly.

"You will require this," said Valcaly after she managed to calm the mirth and handed a training sword to Wesdin.

Without waiting for instruction, Wesdin grasped the sword and held it out to his side, testing the balance and weight of the dulled weapon.

"Excellent," murmured Jonetal in approval. "It is important that you know if the weapon is balanced."

"Aye," agreed Valcaly as she nodded her head in agreeance. "If not, you may be easily thrown off balance during battle."

"I remember," replied Wesdin as he eagerly turned to Jonetal. "Ready, *Onio* Jonetal?" he then asked while raising and lowering his brows repeatedly which drew a chorus of laughter from those around him.

"Aye, Khanzito Wesdin," mumbled Jonetal in feigned exasperation. "I shall follow you," he said, bending at the waist in a slight bow and extending his arm out, signaling for Wesdin to proceed past him into the sparring enclosure.

"Train him well," murmured Valcaly as she stood on the tips of her toes to lightly kiss her husband's nose.

"I shall not harm him," replied Jonetal with a smile and an amused shake of his head. "But he will be trained," he finished and winked reassuringly at Avenor.

Avenor nodded his head and grinned in response, remembering his training as a youth with Jonetal. *"He is the best close-combat trainer aside from Api,"* Avenor recalled silently to himself as he stood and watched his son in the enclosure with Jonetal.

"Block!" hollered Valcaly as she watched Wesdin and Jonetal sparring. "Parry!" she then called out, her excitement causing her to lean over the fence of the sparring enclosure.

"Do not help the boy!" huffed Jonetal in slight displeasure as Wesdin blocked his attack before parrying. "He must learn to assess his opponent independently!"

"Hmph!" responded Valcaly, crossing her arms across her chest, but continuing to watch the dual.

"Khan Avenor," came a somber voice from behind Avenor, drawing his attention.

Avenor turned his head sideways and looked at the soldier that had addressed him. The soldier, with his right forearm clasped over his chest in salute, stood holding a sealed scroll. "What is it?" asked Avenor as a frown slowly transformed his face.

"A message, Your Grace," replied the soldier as he held out the scroll, "from Texicar."

"Oy," murmured Avenor softly as he tried to force the apprehension from his voice. "You have my thanks. Return to your post," he said as he dismissed the soldier.

"As you command, Your Grace," replied the soldier, drawing up his right forearm to his chest before retreating to his assigned location.

"Valcaly," called Avenor, his voice loud enough for only her to hear him.

"Hmm? Your Grace?" she responded in question as she looked over her shoulder. The concern etched in Avenor's features compelled her to approach him. "Are you well?" she asked, worry evident in her voice.

"I must address a message," he replied instead of directly answering her inquiry. "Watch over Wesdin and return him to the palace once he has completed training," he instructed Valcaly gravely.

"As you desire, Your Grace," she said as she brought her right forearm up to her chest, saluting Avenor and wordlessly promising to guard the Khanzito.

"You have my thanks," responded Avenor as he raised his right forearm to his own chest, returning the salute before making his way toward the Grand Hall of the palace.

* * *

Scrolls lay placed in neat rows on the desk of the Grand Hall as Avenor sat holding the most recent in his hand. Sighing to himself uneasily, he eyed the wax closure marked with the seal of High Trapper Kenzelo Ozulben, the Grand Council member assigned as Overseer of Texicar.

"He rarely sends messages," said Avenor aloud yet hardly perceptible in the empty chamber of the palace. After a few moments of hesitation, Avenor finally broke the wax and unfurled the scroll.

"Khan Avenor Crusendir: With your forthcoming expedition, I am pressed to inform you of the increase in civil unrest. The Battalion Majors report all is well, however, I have noticed otherwise. Citizens show fear of the soldiers. I have heard whispers that blame the Khan. I suspect there is abuse of power within the ranks. Use caution when you arrive. – Faithful Servant, High Trapper Kenzelo Ozulben"

Lost in his own thinking, Avenor failed to hear the door open or the soft *pitter patter* of approaching footsteps.

"What troubles you?" asked a familiar voice, startling Avenor out of his thoughts.

Lowering the message, Avenor met the black eyes and steady stare of his grandmother. "Grandami Iriva," greeted Avenor affectionately as he held the piece of parchment out to her.

Walking around to the other side of the desk, Iriva placed an arm around her grandson's shoulders and squeezed him gently before taking the parchment sheet he extended to her. Reading the contents swiftly, she then placed the scroll down next to the others.

"Overseer Mulbin of Itagrio has also sent word that the *Raiders* have increased their attempts to recruit others," mumbled Avenor, the frustration evident in his voice.

"High Wizard Juldeyah Mulbin has done well to keep you informed," returned Iriva as she pat Avenor on the back in reassurance. "You must gather the Generals and prepare to extinguish the threats before they are no longer manageable," she suggested grimly.

"Indeed," grumbled Avenor just as Azelly shoved open the door to the Grand Hall.

"How did you know I would be here?" asked Avenor with a slight arch of his brow as Azelly approached him and Iriva.

"General Iriva," greeted Azelly as she turned to salute Grand Soother Iriva Jander.

"General Azelly," returned Iriva as she, too, brought her right forearm to rest against her chest.

"Leander and I planned to take Leandra to the training fields," Azelly then said as she addressed Avenor's question with a frown. "As we passed the sparring enclosure, I saw Khanzito Wesdin training with Major Teyio and Overseer Valcaly. You and Khantessa Galhix rarely allow him to be about unless he is accompanied by a personal protector. I assumed you would be here," she finished nonchalantly with a slight shrug of her broad shoulders.

"There is truth to that," interjected Iriva drawing a nod from Avenor.

"What information has arrived?" inquired Azelly as she glanced at the desk with one brow arched, her curiosity peaked.

"There is a possibility we may deploy the Grand Military to Texicar and Itagrio," replied Avenor with a heavy sigh as he picked up the letter from Kenzelo and handed it to Azelly.

"We cannot leave Savenius unprotected," Azelly reminded Avenor as she tossed the scroll back on the desk in front of Avenor. "The attacks on the smaller towns have become more frequent. Not every citizen is capable of defending themselves against the Goons."

Standing, Avenor ran a hand through his metallic grey hair before shrugging his shoulders back and tilting his head from side to side. "I'll call together the Generals for afternoon meal. We will discuss the situation then," he informed his grandmother and sister.

* * *

Avenor stood beside the *strategy slate* staring down at his proposed plan of action; raising the remainder of his candied bread laden with braised bear meat, he placed it in his mouth and chewed thoughtfully. After a few minutes, he took a deep breath and held it briefly before exhaling forcefully; he then gazed around the armory before raising his right hand and making a series of brief sweeping motions toward the nearby palace keepers. The pink gem nestled in the center of the *damiund* band adorning his middle finger reflected the light from the sun filtering in through the open windows. The glinting from Avenor's band, the one all members of the Grand Council wore, drew the nearest palace keeper's attention. Swiftly dipping his head in acknowledgement, the palace keeper signaled for the others to close the shutters and disperse.

The armory doors, cast wide open, allowed sunlight to fill the entire building as Avenor waited for the Generals to arrive. A faint rustling of fallen leaves just outside of the entrance drew Avenor's attention. *"There is no wind to cause such a disturbance,"* he silently thought to himself and immediately began searching the shadows.

"Had I known you would be hosting an elaborate gathering, I would have brought formal attire," jested a familiar voice, echoing through Avenor's mind. Avenor grinned just as his eyes clashed with a mischievous pair of sapphire blue orbs.

"When did you arrive? I would have extended an invitation," Avenor silently responded in a cheerful tone as he cracked a grin.

"The Apex escorted Chief Gelriz, Chieftess Baylay, and the twins. We arrived last eve," replied the newcomer as he allowed his shadow blending ability to fade.

"Oy!" exclaimed Avenor as a frown creased his brows. "You all have been here that long?" he gaped incredulously as the fair skinned visitor nodded his head, dislodging his thick, black locks which settled lightly around his face.

"Aye," responded Novex as he approached Avenor. Without hesitation, he raised his right forearm to his longtime friend.

"Damn pretty felines," grumbled Avenor under his breath regarding Novex's flawless, silky locks as he knocked his forearm against the tigal's. Novex chortled briefly in response and reached up to tuck the loose tresses behind his ears. "Oy!" Avenor exclaimed abruptly as a thought suddenly entered his mind. "Summon the Chief and Chieftess. This is a gathering of the Generals. But since my allies are here, I require their attendance," Avenor finished tersely.

"As you desire, Your Grace," responded Novex briskly before blending once more with the shadows and departing just as hastily.

Galhix walked wordlessly beside her second-parents as they navigated their way toward the armory.

"Odd," murmured Everly as she rounded the corner and walked through the open doors of the weapons vault to find her son standing alone.

"Hmm? What is?" inquired Manijor with a slight turn of his head toward his wife, briefly catching his second-daughter's gaze on the opposite side of his wife. Galhix's expression mirrored the same confusion he knew was plastered on his own face.

After a few hesitant moments, Everly finally replied, "I am nearly certain I heard him speaking to someone." She immediately cast a swift survey of the area which revealed nothing amiss; her eyes narrowed as they settled on the prepared *strategy slate*. Without thought, her stride changed from a casual stroll to a purposeful march as she joined Avenor in the center of the armory. "Your Grace," she said firmly as she raised her right forearm in greeting, her voice tight as she reigned in her questions.

"General Everly," responded Avenor as he turned to his mother, raising his right forearm, and knocking it against hers.

"Your Grace," greeted Galhix warmly as she slipped into her husband's open arms and wrapped her own arms around his waist.

"Khantessa," replied Avenor before dipping his head without hesitation and capturing his wife's lips in a swift kiss. Turning back to his father, he continued, "General Manijor," while extending his right forearm once more.

"Khan Avenor," replied Manijor as he knocked his forearm against his son's arm in salute. "I assume we must wait for the others?" asked Manijor as he turned and surveyed the *strategy slate*.

"Indeed," replied Avenor with a curt nod of his head before saying, "we have much to discuss."

"Aye," agreed Iriva as she joined the others in the center of the armory; without hesitation, she raised her right forearm to her chest. The others silently responded in similar fashion, saluting Iriva in return. "It appears we may be here for a time," she said as she eyed the nearby table, set with an assortment of foods and drinks.

"Prepare yourselves a plate while we wait for the others," instructed Avenor just as Betaro walked through the open doors. The clanking of metal boots on the stone floor drew Avenor's attention. "General Azelly," called out Avenor swiftly, "wait just a few moments longer before you secure the doors."

"As you desire, Your Grace," she responded before turning to take the few steps back to the entrance. Without warning, Novex appeared before Azelly; he stood huffing and panting as he struggled to calm his ragged breathing. "Oy!" grunted Azelly in surprise while taking the slightest step back before absentmindedly clasping the intruder by the throat. "Ugh!" groaned Azelly as she strained to heft the densely muscular man off the ground single handedly.

"General!" squealed Chieftess Baylay in horror as she openly gawked at the giant of a woman as she appeared to crush Novex's throat.

"*Puq!*" cursed Azelly as recognition finally registered. "Ambassador Clawbane!" she groaned as she relinquished her hold and dropped Novex to his feet.

"You are nearly as swift as a tigal," rasped Novex with a brief smile as he extended his forearm to Azelly.

"Surprisingly faster than you," taunted Chief Gelriz with a chuckle, knowing Novex was one of the most lethal members of the *Apex*.

"Heh," scoffed Novex in response. "Indeed, she near laid me to waste without a struggle," he admitted sheepishly.

"Enough!" shouted Avenor, the frustration in his voice immediately sliced through the mirth of the recent arrivals.

The three Weretigals made their way to the center of the building while Azelly turned toward the doors. The heavy, wooden doors creaked and groaned as Azelly pulled them from the wall and swung them shut. A loud *bang* echoed through the armory as the doors slammed closed. Azelly quickly joined the others preparing a platter of afternoon meal for herself.

Avenor waited until the others had settled themselves in seats around the *strategy slate*. "I've called you all here because I received a message from Overseer Ozulben of Texicar," he began tentatively.

"What sort of message has High Trapper Kenzelo sent?" inquired General Betaro, his greying brows drawing together as he sensed the gravity in his grandson's voice.

CHAPTER 6

Gloomy clouds collecting above the oasis obscured the moonlight and cast an eerie blanket of darkness over the encampment. A faint glow, the only light visible, spilled from the mouth of Overlook Cave where a small fire burned within; the occasional crackling and spitting of the flames as they hungrily devoured the logs fought back the deafening silence. As if sensing Reeyah's frustration, a hidden cricket began its evening song of harmonious creaks and chirps; Reeyah's face knotted with annoyance as she struggled to concentrate on her task.

"Hound's piss!" grumbled Reeyah to herself as she sat beside the fire. "Damn insect," she hissed while bent over a leather hide that had been stretched as thin as possible.

"Lordess," whispered Dondree softly as he crept as soundlessly across the cave as possible.

"Dondree!" gasped Reeyah, her head snapping up in surprise. She silently stared at her son for a few moments as she watched him hobble across the cave toward her. "Why are you not resting?" she asked harshly, causing Dondree to flinch as if she had physically struck him.

"I am preparing for my travels," he replied solemnly as he settled himself down across the fire from his mother.

Reeyah nodded her head curtly before turning her attention back to the thin hide. "When will you depart?" she asked without looking up.

"Next eve," he replied as he watched his mother place just the steel tip, fastened to a wooded rod, in the flames. Canting his head to the side, he continued observing as Reeyah cautiously removed a similar rod and lightly pressed the steel tip into the leather, burning the hide. "What is that?" he asked curiously.

"It is called..." said Reeyah before pausing, sitting up and leaning back so she could observe her creation, "a map," she finished simply. With a nod of approval at her work, she shifted her gaze and motioned for Dondree to sit beside her while saying, "come."

36

Turning so that his dominant leg was under him, Dondree shoved himself upward.

"Tchuh!" growled Reeyah. "What have I told you?" she asked, her voice stern.

"To use my weaker leg so that it does not become lame," replied Dondree, his gaze downcast, as he joined his mother.

Reaching a hand outward, Reeyah vehemently struck Dondree across the face; the unexpected slap caused Dondree to jerk his head upright. "And?" demanded Reeyah.

"Never lower my gaze. Never show fear. For it is a sign of weakness," he responded tentatively.

"Remember it, Boy!" she spat angrily as she battled her own uncertainty and worry. "For your life depends on it!" she finished. Reaching up, she ran an unsteady hand through her maroon-colored hair. After taking a calming breath, Reeyah placed the map out before Dondree.

"What is a map?" asked Dondree as he inspected the thin hide.

"You have never been outside of the oasis," stated Reeyah tersely. "This will assist you in your journey," she said as she began pointing out different areas that she had burned into the hide.

"Here is the Veiled Oasis. This is our home," she said as she pointed toward the upper right corner of the hide. "The Arid Mountains," she said while pointing to the mountains that surrounded the oasis, "are the mountains that protect us from the searing winds. They form the northern border and the upper eastern border."

"How will I know which way to go?" asked Dondree, the apprehension evident in his tone.

"There are stairs where the hunters always depart. They gradually turn into a path that then leads out of the oasis. You will follow it," continued Reeyah, her voice hushed. "When it ends, do not walked straight out from the path or you will burn in the Scorched Barrens. The barrens reach the western boarder and meet the Arid Mountains to the north. Stay along the eastern border but do not venture into the Salt Flats. None have ever returned. Always," reaching out, Reeyah grabbed Dondree's leather tunic, "*always* stop at the trees."

"I hear you," replied Dondree as he locked his eyes with his mother's, noting the seriousness in her voice.

"While not pleasant to the taste, the leaves provide sustenance and water. Squeeze the leaves to replenish your water pouch. Do not discard them. They are safe to eat," she continued to instruct Dondree. "You will first be here," she paused briefly to point at the map before continuing, "at the Geyser Grounds. Do not approach the pools. As tempting as they may seem, they will erupt with scalding water. Many have perished because the flesh was melted from the bone," she warned her son.

Dondree swallowed hard, forcing down the bile that had abruptly risen in his throat as his mother mentioned the many dangers he would likely encounter.

"If you find the ground has changed from the dried, packed ground of the desert to lush grass, you are near the south eastern border of the Lost Plains," she said while pointing out the area on the map. "It extends from the south eastern border upward toward here," she said while tracing the lower central area of the map, under the Scorched Barrens. "Be cautious of the Deaf Raptors and Plain Stompers," she warned. "The raptors will devour you. While the stompers will not, they are easily angered and will not hesitate to crush you under their weight."

"And what of that area?" asked Dondree as he pointed to the lower left corner of the map dotted with multiple trees and what appeared to be small circles.

"That area is known as The Wilds. Stories tell of creatures that are part fish with a song so beautiful that it delights its prey and lures them to their death. There are stories of enormous flowers. It is claimed their scent is so sweet that it entices those to come nearer. Once within reach, the plant suddenly snatches up the individual and consumes them," uttered Reeyah as she remembered her own trek through The Wilds cycles ago.

"Do you believe I will be triumphant?" Dondree suddenly asked as he watched his mother intently. The various emotions that crossed her face answered his question even before she spoke.

"It is a cruel and desolate place outside of the oasis," rasped Reeyah quietly. "Those who venture out alone rarely return unscathed," she continued with her eyes downcast. "To be considered worthy, you must return with a kill equal to your own girth or greater."

Dondree took an unsteady breath, recognizing the unspoken meaning of his mother's words. It was unlikely he would return successful. The likelihood that he would not return at all was even greater.

Reeyah took the hide from Dondree and picked up a small flask close at hand. "At your first stop… while still within the safety of the foothills… drink the elixir," she instructed tensely while swiftly folding the map before placing the container on top of it. She then bound the two items together with a leather strap. "Remain there until the effects subside," she continued with a frown.

"What effects?" Dondree asked apprehensively as he watched his mother's frown deepen.

"I know naught," she admitted quietly. "The elixir... it is the first... a trial... a test..." she stammered, trying to find a way to explain what she had done. "Bah!" she grunted in exasperation after a few tense moments. "Just do as I say, Boy!" she nearly shouted before lowering her voice. "Do *not* lose the elixir or destroy the map," she emphasized the importance of the hide before placing it in his hands. "The map will serve as your guide home," she finished before hastily leaning forward and depositing a wisp of a kiss to his forehead. Without waiting for a response, Reeyah left Dondree and proceeded to her resting place within the deeper hollows of the cave.

* * *

A soft sneeze followed by a gentle cough stirred Kifta from her sleep. Just as she began sitting up, she felt a large hand restrain her. "I shall bring the infant," rumbled the scruff voice of her mate.

Sordun rubbed his eyes and waited for them to adjust to the dim light provided by the single candle lit in their hut. After a few moments, he was able to make out the large items within the home partially illuminated by the muted light, and he navigated through their hut toward the basket where their infant lay kicking and flailing her extremities. Reaching down, Sordun picked up the tiny bundle just as she began to fuss. "Hush, little one," he murmured gently as he pressed her against his chest.

"Gah!" gasped Sordun at the unexpected sharpness on his chest followed by suckling as the babe attempted to feed.

"What is it?" asked Kifta as she sat upright, alarm suddenly flooding through her.

"She bit me!" exclaimed Sordun as he held the child out away from himself.

"I do not...," Kifta replied slowly, confusion evident in her voice. After a brief pause, she continued, "Sordun... she has not yet growd'ed teeth," she said as she tried to stifle her giggle.

"Well," Sordun said as he tried to shake the sleep from his head. "Something was sharp," he finally said with a slight laugh as he thoroughly inspected the child.

"Perhaps she scratched you," offered Kifta as her laughter intensified.

"Hmph!" grunted Sordun before adding, "and she attempted to feed at my chest!" he finished while laughing at himself. Placing a kiss atop the child's head, he then deposited the squirming bundle in Kifta's waiting arms.

Kifta brought the babe to her bosom; without hesitation, the infant turned and rooted against her mother's breast. The whimpers and grunts drew another chuckle from Sordun as he watched his offspring.

"It is here," said Kifta as she guided the eager babe to the place she impatiently sought. Kifta took a sharp breath in and winced briefly as the infant latched on to the rosy peak.

"Does the pain subside?" asked Sordun curiously as he watched Kifta slowly relax and settle down on the sleeping mat with their child.

"Aye," replied Kifta slowly. "The pain is not as strong as before," she admitted as she peered down at her nursing infant.

Sordun yawned before laying behind Kifta; tucking a protective arm around her waist, Sordun drew her possessively against him. Turning his hand, he placed it protectively against his daughter's back. "What shall we call her?" he asked, his warm breath tickling Kifta's ear.

"What you think of Eetzee?" replied Kifta as she turned her head slightly to peer over her shoulder.

"Why Eetzee - eearghs?" asked Sordun with another yawn.

"Because she always wants to eats," replied Kifta with a giggle.

Sordun grinned and chuckled in response. "Eetzee it is," he agreed before settling back down. Within moments, Sordun began drifting back to sleep.

"You think he will be successful?" Kifta abruptly asked, arching her head to look over her shoulder at her mate.

"Hmm?" mumbled Sordun in his near sleep state.

"The Boy," grumbled Kifta as she scowled over her shoulder.

"What boy?" grumbled Sordun as he nuzzled his face in Kifta's hair.

"Bah!" grunted Kifta as she turned back to peering down at her daughter, her innocent eyes batting drowsily as sleep began to claim her once more.

"The Boy is being sent to his death," said Kifta quietly to herself, a frown slowly spreading across her face. "Reeyah," she said before becoming lost in her own thoughts. *"You haves gone through so much. How wills you handle the loss of Dondree? Do you stills hate us?"* Kifta was drawn from her own thoughts as Eetzee kicked in her sleep, trying to find a comfortable position. After a few moments, Eetzee quieted back down. "You are right," Kifta agreed sleepily to her daughter with a smile. "Time to sleep," she murmured while snuggling back against her mate and drawing her daughter closer before allowing sleep to engulf her as well.

* * *

Erudite Kaminah sat at the front of her class, observing every student as they focused on their own parchment sheets. A crease gradually developed between Kaminah's brows; she watched wordlessly as the eldest in her tutelage - a lass from one of the surrounding colonies – sat at the rear of the chamber fidgeting nervously with her plume. After a brief time, the girl attempted to peek over her neighbor's shoulder.

"Tsk! Tsk! Eyes on your own parchments…" Kaminah scolded, her voice laced with disapproval, pausing momentarily prior to adding ominously, "lest you remain for remedial erudition."

Lana frowned and tried to sink further into her seat as a red glow instantly stained her cheeks, drawing forth stifled giggles from those sitting closest to her.

Kaminah slowly shook her head from side to side, displeasure evident in her expression. *"Oy! They learn nor recall naught!"* she thought sourly to herself of the colonial children. *"She should be well past basic erudition…"* Kaminah mussed silently as she studied the unkempt youth. After a time, sympathy softened her expression as she realized the girl would probably never receive advanced erudition or find a *Master* to accept her as an apprentice. Exhaling sorrowfully, the Erudite continued her survey of downturned heads. "Time is up!" she curtly declared following the first clanging of the main bell that signaled the end of Erudition for the day. "Place your pages with answers faced down," she instructed from her position by the door.

Hushed chatter burst forth from pupils who had already turned in their answers to the surprise assessment, eagerly discussing the activities planned for the next two days they were not required to attend formal learning. Muted "Oy!" and "Pardon me…" blended with intermittent "Ugh!" and "Boundaries!" as the throng of students impatiently fought to submit their answers. Lana dropped her plume without a second thought and proceeded toward the front of the class. She hastily set her parchment sheet down and turned toward the door.

"Woblana Peygul…" Kaminah began. Lana grimaced at the use of her formal name, and she then sighed gratefully when the unexpected volley of shouts and questions distracted the Erudite.

"Erudite Kaminah!" shouted Wesdin after he placed his assignment with the others.

"Erudite!" yelled Leandra as she raced after Wesdin toward their instructor.

"Personal space!" grumbled Wesdin as he pushed back against Leandra as she crowded behind him.

Lana ducked her head and slipped through the entryway with a group of older pupils, unnoticed by Kaminah.

"Get out of my space!" retorted Leandra hotly as she pushed Wesdin forward.

"Stop!" growled Wesdin under his breath as he refused to move.

"Children…" began Kaminah, her voice deliberately low. The bickering immediately halted. "Now what is this disagreement about?" she asked while turning to Leandra.

"I say the Great War happened before the Great Falling. But Wesdin keeps saying I am wrong. He says the… the… the Great Falling was first," she finished in a huff while crossing her arms over her chest.

"Mmm…" murmured Kaminah softly. "I see. Do you recall what brought about our abilities?" she finally asked.

"Umm… hmm… it was…" stammered Leandra as she thought about the question. "Oh!" she squealed excitedly. "It is because of the Great Falling."

"Indeed," replied Kaminah with a slight dip of her head. "And how did the Great Rift occur?"

"It was because everyone with abilities forced VerTexItas to separate!" interjected Wesdin enthusiastically, drawing a glare from Leandra.

"This is true," Kaminah admitted with another brief nod. "Now… knowing that we have abilities because of the Great Falling… and knowing that the Great Rift was caused by using abilities… it makes sense that the Great War would have occurred when?" she finished, asking her question deliberately slow. Watching the mask of confusion on Leandra's face, Kaminah added, "The Great War happened because the Mountain Runners, now known as Shadow Runners, attacked the southern regions."

"Oh," mumbled Leandra tentatively as she absorbed the information. "I see. Wesdin is right," she added after a brief pause.

"Ha! I told you so!" sneered Wesdin triumphantly. "Thank you, Erudite!" he quickly added before laughing tauntingly at his classmate and racing from the class.

"Shut your mouth!" snapped Leandra aggravatedly as she glared at Wesdin's back.

"Leandra…," Kaminah said gently, her expression of reprimand softened by her tone.

"Apologies, Erudite Kaminah," Leandra replied uncomfortably while turning her gaze to the ground.

"You are forgiven," Kaminah said with a smile. "Now, go enjoy your informal days."

"Aye, Erudite! Thank you!" exclaimed Leandra happily before darting off down the hall of the Erudition Building in search of her friends.

CHAPTER 7

"No..." barked Galhix irritably before adding sarcastically, "*enlighten me...*" as she interlocked her arms over her heaving chest.

Avenor stood wordlessly with his lips curled distastefully as he glowered at his spouse standing before from him; the rise and fall of his solid-muscled chest as he took deep, controlled breaths along with the occasional jumping of his jaw muscles flexing were the only outward signs as he resisted the urge to roar his answer back. He clearly noted how Galhix did naught to mask the unbridled wrath clearly skewing her beautifully symmetrical face. A single brow was arched, her arms irately crossed, and she stood supporting much of her weight on her left leg whilst her right foot tapped the ground impatiently.

"Well?" Galhix finally demanded after what seemed an eternity, her tone commanding a response.

"I am Khan," he began, his speech intentionally unhurried. Pausing long enough for the tension to rise, he then continued, "The matters in Texicar require my presence-," he managed to say before Galhix effectively interrupted, leaving him with his mouth ajar.

"*Puq,* Avenor! That is pure goat's piss... and you know it!" she spat vehemently and threw her arms up in the air. "As Khan, you have the right to send your **Generals***,*" she continued, making certain to stress the highest-ranking leaders at his disposal. Not waiting for a response, she pressed on while halting between names. "General Manijor. General Azelly. Blast! Even General Everly!" she finished, nearly bellowing as she began pacing the length of their personal chambers. "Why must **you** continually lead every expedition?" she fumed.

Avenor's frustration gradually dissolved as he squinted slightly, keenly observing Galhix storming from one side of their quarters to the other. *"Beautiful, yes..."* he mutely mused to himself, his own thoughts drowning out the ranting of his wife. *"Formidable..."* he finally decided as Galhix passed by him, her rose colored gown whooshing as her legs slashed through the fabric. *"Indeed. The perfect Regent to lead in my absence,"* he continued thinking as a pleased smile tugged at the corner of his lips.

Galhix, oblivious to Avenor, had become increasingly animated as she sustained her verbal spewing of rationales for Avenor not to journey to Texicar.

Absentmindedly, Avenor turned his head slightly and thoughts of smiling fled his mind; a curious expression spread over his face as he absentmindedly leaned forward, attempting to discern the location of the buzzing noise trailing after his wife.

Abruptly, Galhix halted, aware Avenor was leaning oddly towards her. "Oy!" she quietly gasped as she felt herself nearly carried forward by her own momentum. Her silver hair glided forward before being jerked back and settling in a disoriented array around her face. "Puuph," she partially exclaimed with a powerful puff, attempting to blow the loose strands out of her eyes. After peevishly reaching up to shove the hair aside, she turned toward Avenor, her eyes flashing hotly. "Why do you stare at me in such a manner?" she panted rancorously, mildly winded from her forceful pacing.

"Is..." Avenor began hesitantly and paused, cautiously taking a step closer before continuing, "are... what..." he stammered as his eyes widened with bewilderment.

"Well? Spit it out already!" retorted Galhix, her mood darkening with every moment that passed.

"It is!" Avenor finally whispered in awe, his eyes fixated on Galhix's silver tresses, vibrantly pulsing with energy. In a trance, Avenor approached his wife and reached out, snagging a lock. "How have I never noticed this before?" he murmured in wonder.

"What nonsense are you blabbering about?" replied Galhix, her fury replaced with confusion as she looked down at her own hair. "Oy..." she said in a tone barely audible.

"You have no knowledge of this?" asked Avenor incredulously as he turned his gaze to meet Galhix's.

"Nay..." she admitted uneasily, picking up a separate section that had become tangled and teased it until it became unknotted. "An occasional humming, at times appearing to pulse... faintly yet noticeably becoming brighter and fading... but... but never this!" she expressed. Her mind racing, Galhix tried to recall any previous time a similar event had occurred. "Nay, I recall no other..." she began before unexpectedly stopping, her mouth agape.

"What is it?" asked Avenor, suddenly worried as he watched various emotions transform his spouse's face.

"*The Rectifying*..." Galhix murmured pensively, recalling the day when the *Pillar of Life* had been reestablished correctly many cycles prior.

"When we defeated your brother?" questioned Avenor, his tone relaying his confusion.

"Hmm?" mumbled Galhix, her thoughts still a blur. "Oh, nay... nay," she finally added with a shake of her head. "After the *Battle of the Ancients*. After the death of that monster! It was when the *Pillar of Life* was restored to its proper position, and the curse was lifted!" she cried out softly, remembering how her energy coursed through every fiber of her being, her fur included. Her fur had thrummed with the same energy as her hair did now.

"Oy..." whispered Avenor as he took an unsteady step back, recalling how a green explosion, the light so magnificent, that it forced him to look away so as not to be blinded by the intensity. "What do you suppose this means?" he asked anxiously.

"I am uncertain," Galhix admitted furrowing her brows and turning to stare down at the ground though not seeing anything. "Perhaps..." she began hesitantly... "perhaps it is because I am experiencing emotions stronger than ever before..." she finished and allowed her voice to trail off as she turned away from Avenor, crossing her arms low across her abdomen as if cradling herself.

"How do you mean?" prodded Avenor, catching Galhix by her elbow before she could walk away from him. "My most cherished... talk to me..." he begged softly, placing his hands on her shoulders, and turning her to turn to face him. Reaching up, he placed his hand under Galhix's chin and gently forced her eyes to meet his own. "Explain your reasoning to me. What troubles you to this extent?"

"You depart in two days' time..." she muttered quietly, a single tear escaping from the corner of her eyes.

"You truly worry about my departure?" Avenor questioned in return as he tenderly caught the tear with his thumb and wiped it away.

"You are a dolt!" exploded Galhix unexpectedly as she pressed hard against Avenor's chest, shoving him away from her. "Of course, I worry about your departure! Why would I not?" she replied passionately. "This is the first... the absolute **first** excursion... in eight... **eight**... cycles... that I will not accompany you!" she nearly shrieked as she began anxiously pacing once more.

"This is not true..." denied Avenor and paused briefly before continuing, "there have been many days when I traveled throughout Savenius," he finished with a scowl.

Galhix halted abruptly and spun around to glower at her husband. "A single day, perhaps three at most for a short journey," she spat in return. "An expedition where you will travel for longer days, weeks, months, possibly a season or longer…" she allowed the unfinished statement to linger.

Avenor dipped his head in acknowledgement with a slight shrug of his broad shoulders.

"You think I relish the idea?" she demanded furiously with her shoulders pulled back as she stood her full height. "You think I enjoy the idea that you could perish, leaving me a widow to raise Wesdin without a father? If you believe that I savor the thought of you passing, then you truly are a zebril's arse!" she finished, her voice rising until she nearly shrieked her response.

"Oy!" exclaimed Avenor, taken aback by his wife's vulgar language.

"And if you believe that is acceptable, I want nothing else to do with you before you go!" she hollered before spinning on her heels and storming from the chamber, yanking the door so fiercely behind her that the sound of the bang echoed throughout the palace.

Avenor stood mutely staring at the closed door in shock. After what seemed an eternity, he finally shook his head to clear the fog that seemed to cloud his thoughts. "What in blazes was that about?" he managed to grumble, reaching up to scratch his head before heading toward the door to seek out his wife.

* * *

Betaro inhaled a deep, audible breath, expanding his chest so that his chiseled muscles strained against the cloth of his linen tunic. The sound drew the attention of the others seated at the table; while holding his breath, Betaro raised his brows and simultaneously shook his head briefly before forcefully exhaling.

"What are your thoughts, second-father?" asked Manijor, the concern conveyed in his voice equally reflected in the expressions of the others present.

"Khan Avenor gave his direction," interposed Novex before Betaro could respond.

"That he did," said Azelly slowly, her tone welcoming no argument as she shifted her gaze between the Khan's grandparents.

Betaro's eyes clashed with those of Iriva's across the table, observing the silent turmoil raging within their black depth. "We will obey the Khan's command," Betaro finally said after what seemed an eternity.

"Damn," whispered Iriva under her breath, hoping Betaro would allow the Generals to challenge their grandson's orders.

"Api!" roared Everly as she bolted to her feet and slammed her hands down on the table. "I will not allow my *son* to journey without proper escort!" she seethed, the unsaid threat lingering in the air.

Betaro met his daughter's stare, her eyes narrow and flaring passionately. After a few tense moments, he finally nodded his head in agreement. Even had he denied his daughter, he knew it would be futile. "*You have every right to travel with him,*" mussed Betaro silently to himself, understanding why Everly was rarely far from Avenor. The detestable memory of his grandson kidnapped as a child and sold into slavery caused Betaro's stomach to churn and its contents to rise in his throat. "Very well," he rasped after swallowing down the bile. "I will accompany General Iriva to Itagrio."

"Is that wise?" Azelly unexpectedly questioned tentatively. "I mean no disrespect... however... uh...," she stammered, her cheeks suddenly stained pink. "General Betaro and General Iriva... you both... are seasoned..." she continued brokenly, embarrassment causing the light pink color to darken and spread to her ears. Resisting the urge to avert her eyes, Azelly met the icy blue ones of Betaro.

Iriva, attempting to suppress her mirth, clamped down on her lower lip. Stifled giggles bubbled up from within her before she finally began cackling uncontrollably. "Oy!" she gasped while clutching at her side. "Betaro! She calls us old!"

Betaro grunted, a single brow raised as he glowered at Iriva which caused her to chortle even harder. "Hmph!" he snorted before adding, "At seventy-nine cycles, it is a fair enough statement." Abruptly he added, "But I fight as if I was still fifty cycles! You, General Iriva... if you feel your age, I am certain I can locate a suitable replacement to accompany me in your absence," taunted Betaro relentlessly.

"Hmph, yourself, aged imbecile!" squawked Iriva as she glowered at Betaro in return. "I feel as though I am still as youthful as a spring-chicken!"

"Indeed! A spring-chicken seventy-six cycles past her prime!" Betaro immediately retorted, drawing muffled snickering.

"Generals!" snapped Novex irritably, halting the unnecessary bantering. "As Ambassador of Tigalia, I speak on behalf of the Chief and Chieftess," he said before the remaining council members could oppose.

"Where did the Chief and Chieftess disappear to?" suddenly asked Iriva as she surveyed the chamber, her lips pursed with distaste.

"Chief Gelriz and Chieftess Baylay requested a private audience with Khan Avenor," Novex responded bluntly before continuing. "My leaders have decided to remain in Capitalia to entertain the Regent Khan, Khantessa Galhix. The *Apex* members that escorted Tigalia's leaders will stand guard here in the Khan's absence," he finished before curtly nodding at Betaro to continue.

"That is acceptable," responded Everly with a sigh as she hesitantly sunk back down into her seat, recalling how intimidating Aylox was and how ferociously he fought during the *Battle of the Ancients* before her father added in approval, "excellent!"

"General Everly… General Manijor… General Azelly…" said Betaro, pausing to meet each commander's eyes for acknowledgement. "You three shall accompany Khan Avenor to Texicar. I believe a stronger show of force is necessary in Texicar than Itagrio at this point."

"Aye, I agree," added Iriva reluctantly. "The occasional raiders are easier dealt with than conspirators and those with false loyalty."

"Ey!" exclaimed Novex, feigning offense as he raised a hand and touched his knuckles to his forehead. "What of this tigal? Am I not considered a warrior worthy to escort the Khan?"

Azelly scoffed before chuckling in response; she then crossed her arms over her chest, her action relaying her skepticism.

"Bah!" grunted Novex and rolled his eyes upward in exasperation. "I, too, shall accompany Khan Avenor!" he stated firmly.

"Very well, Ambassador Clawbane" sighed Betaro with a stern nod of his head. "It is decided then. Make the proper preparations. We depart in two days' time." Murmurs of acknowledgement spread throughout the gathering area prior to the group dispersing.

* * *

Gelriz and Baylay stood on the bridge connecting the palace courtyard to the interior foyer of the Grand Palace; casually, they leaned over the rail and peered over the edge, mesmerized by the fish swimming below them. The sound of splashing water cascading over the edge of the *Pillar of Light* created a melodious tune as it landed in a small pool at one end of the enclosed yard. From the sparkling pool, the water snaked across the courtyard, burbling gently as it traveled under the bridge where Baylay and Gelriz listened to the soft babbling as it meandered lazily along. Opposite the tower where the stream originated, a neatly manicured hedge of flowering bushes concealed the stream's exit - a barred passage along the far wall.

"You meet with the Khan soon," murmured Baylay, pausing momentarily before continuing. "What do you plan to say?" she then asked without moving, her voice hushed so only Gelriz could hear her.

"I still have not yet decided," admitted Gelriz apprehensively while peeking around nervously to ensure no one else was within hearing range. "But I must inform him," he whispered.

"Perhaps it will alter-," began Baylay. A sudden *bam* startled the pair, causing Baylay to jolt upright and squeal in surprise. "Ah!" she yelped as the thunderous sound echoed throughout the corridors of the palace.

"Oy!" exclaimed Gelriz in time with Baylay, instantly pulling her protectively against his chest. After the initial shock subsided, Gelriz released his hold and took a step toward the palace foyer. Turning his head, he strained to determine if there was trouble afoot. The hasty pitter-patter of slippers slapping the stone floor caused Gelriz to frown.

"What is it?" questioned Baylay as she turned to listen as well. "Someone is fleeing..." she murmured and allowed her voice to trail off as the individual approached their general location.

"Indeed," replied Gelriz while grabbing hold of his wife's hand. "Come. We shall discover who," he finished before purposefully striding toward the palace in search of who was causing the disturbance. Just as Gelriz and Baylay passed through the middle of the foyer, they fleetingly glimpsed a silver wave of tresses flying past.

"Galhix?" gasped Gelriz, the statement more of a question as he increased his pace. "Galhix!" he called, louder than his usual tone, in hopes of capturing her attention. "Bah!" he grunted and released Baylay's hand before breaking into a sprint down the hall and tightly skirted a corner after his sister.

Baylay watched as Gelriz raced after Galhix. The repetitive tap-tap-tap behind her drew her attention. "Oy!" she exclaimed, watching as Avenor galloped down the hall with a scowl plastered on his face.

"Which way has she gone?" demanded Avenor as he reduced his speed as he came abreast Baylay, his dark expression focused on his second-sister.

"She turned there," responded Baylay as she pointed in the direction where she had seen Gelriz disappear. Without hesitation, she picked up a light canter to join Avenor in search of their spouses.

"Galhix!" Gelriz finally shouted and listened to her name reverberate throughout the palace walls as the repetitive clapping of her slippers slowed before coming to a halt.

Galhix, panting harshly, dropped the fabric of her gown clenched in her hands, placed her hands on her hips, and tilted her head back to stare at the ceiling as beads of sweat formed along her hairline; with each ragged breath, her bosom strained against the hardened leather corset worn under her ruby colored robe. "Blast!" she groaned to herself as she waited for her brother to join her.

"Why... do you... run..." gasped Gelriz as he stopped beside his sister and turned to face her. Bending over at the waist, he placed his hands on his knees for support as he struggled to control his erratic wheezing.

Galhix cast a curious glance at Gelriz and scoffed. "Dearest Brother… it appears you have not been running much of late," she said while laughing intermittently between forceful huffs.

"Hah…" mumbled Gelriz as he rolled his eyes in return. "What need… do I have to run… through the palace?" he managed to rasp before straightening to his full height. "Or even through The Citadel of Tigalia?" he finished before Baylay and Avenor arrived beside them.

Mutely, Galhix turned away from Avenor, and she instantly crossed her arms over her chest.

Breathing deeply to calm her own puffing, Baylay looked from Khantessa to Khan and back. Sensing the increased tension, the Chieftess approached Galhix and tugged one of her arms free; she then tucked her arm into Galhix's before gently guiding her away from the two men. "Come," Baylay said determinedly. "Let us discuss what is troubling you."

"Brother," said Gelriz sternly as he clapped Avenor on the back, stealing his second-brother's attention. Transitioning his hand to Avenor's shoulder, he informed Avenor, "I am seizing this opportunity to hold private counsel with you… as you assured me, we would."

Avenor's glower deepened temporarily, recognizing Gelriz's unwavering gaze and tone, before exhaling grudgingly. "Very well," he replied gruffly and allowed Gelriz to lead him in the opposite direction of their wives.

* * *

Lana lifted the hood of her cloak and settled it on her head, pulling it down snugly in the front to shield her face. Nervously glancing around, she then stepped out of the shadows from behind the Erudition Building. With familiarity, she dodged her way through the crowded streets, avoiding direct communication with bystanders as she proceeded toward the palace.

"Blast…" Lana grunted softly as she heard a conversation carried by the breeze.
"At no time… and that is *no time*… shall this post be unattended," instructed one of the guards. "Unless ya wou'd enjoy Gen'ral Az'lly rippin' ya a fresh arse hole," added another soldier before snickering. "Ya shou'd feel hon'rd. Protectin' the Khan 'n his fam'ly are Gen'ral Az'lly's main conc'rn," he finished, the mirth suddenly gone from his voice. "She dun' take the saf'ty of the Khan nur his fam'ly ligh'ly."

Hastening her steps, Lana inconspicuously joined a flock of women prattling on about their errands; the boisterous group neared the main palace entrance still oblivious to the stranger following close behind them. Lana peered passed the occupied guards, swiftly scanning the courtyard beyond and committing the details to memory. *"Blast…"* Lana silently fumed to herself, suddenly aware she had been abandoned by the babbling bunch.

"Am I heard?" demanded the guardsman that Lana remembered speaking first.

"Aye, Major, you are heard," responded the replacement guards in unison as they snapped to the position of attention and saluted their superior.

"Very well," replied the Major before straightening to the same position as the soldiers. "May your patrol be uneventful," he added while crossing his right arm over his chest as he returned their salute.

Lana glanced over her shoulder just in time to watch the commander salute in return before he and his companion began the trek back to the armory. Exhaling a sigh of relief, she then turned quickly away.

The fluttering of a cloak as someone swiftly spun away in his peripheral vision drew Jonetal's full interest. "Halt!" shouted Jonetal, glowering as he watched the small stranger.

"Hmm?" replied the Major's companion as he turned his head to watch as a youth nearly stumbled to the ground.

"Captain Catorlino… should we approach?" questioned the soldier concurrently assigned to stand guard as she watched Jonetal flick the hood back from the girl's face.

"Nay," replied Ernist, still unaccustomed to his new title of Captain. "Major Teyio is capable of handling the lass… lest we be caught abandoning our post," he reminded the soldier.

"Aye, very well," she replied curtly but continued to observe the interaction.

"I am Major Jonetal Teyio, commander of *Force Champion*. What is your name, child?" demanded Jonetal as he grasped the youth by the chin and turned her face from side to side, his frown deepening to a scowl as his eyes were met with golden-amber ones. *"Oy! What distinctive eyes!"* he admired silently. *"I cannot recall ever seeing eyes such as hers… except… who was it?"* he continued to muse wordlessly. His thoughts were interrupted as the girl began to answer.

"Uh… my… uh…" stuttered Lana, her eyes widening in fear as she stood before the commander of the largest, fiercest, predominately melee force in the whole of VerTexItas.

"Well, dun keep 'im wait'in!" exclaimed Eezien Holdir as he reached out to smack the youth on the side of her head.

51

"Youch!" exclaimed Lana as she reached up to rub the sting from her temple.

"Captain Holdir!" snapped Jonetal as he released his hold of the child, turning his steely gaze toward one of his unit leaders.

"Aye, Major," grumbled Eezien as he crossed his arms, understanding the silent command to refrain from striking the lass.

"Well?" probed Jonetal after he turned his attention back to the girl.

"My name is Lana... Woblana," she replied apprehensively.

"And what of your family name?" inquired Jonetal with a single brow arched.

"Peygul... Peygulroq," she finished and swallowed hard, her mouth suddenly dry.

"Peygulroq," repeated Jonetal as he watched Lana shift her weight nervously from one foot to the other. "And Woblana Peygulroq..." he began, his voice intentionally unhurried, "should you not be attending Erudition?" he finally asked.

Lana heaved a sigh of relief before blurting, "Erudition has ended for the day!"

"I see," murmured Jonetal with a brief nod of his head. "Well then, what brings you to the palace?" he questioned, his face and voice expressionless.

"I... um... I..." stammered Lana once more, suddenly gripped by panic. Coughing softly to clear her throat, Lana finally managed to reply, "I... am lost. I am... not... from here."

"Mmm. I see," returned Jonetal as he crossed his arms over his chest. "And where is home?" he continued his interrogation.

"A... uh... a small colony... east of the city," replied Lana, darting her tongue out and moistening her dry lips between stuttered responses. Captain Holdir's scoff spurred her to continue. "It is called Camp Yorando. When the proper seasons arrive, I journey with my mother... we stay at the *Encampment*... so I am... uh... able to... uh... receive formal Erudition," she finished in a rush.

"I see," Jonetal replied after what seemed an eternity. "Should you not have committed to memory your route by this time?" he inquired suspiciously. Waiting for the child's response, Jonetal watched keenly as a myriad of expressions transformed Lana's face. "Well?" he abruptly questioned as he became impatient. The harshness of his voice jolted Lana out of her frozen terror.

"The course... it changes with each season," she admitted, suddenly aware that it was true. "Buildings are torn down and others established," she finished while pointing toward a group of citizens completing the construction of what appeared to be a future shop.

Jonetal nodded in recognition of the child's reasoning after glancing in the direction she pointed. "Very well. Captain Eezien will see to it you are safely escorted back to the *Encampment*," he then announced, his tone firm and welcoming no objection.

"Aye, Sir," grumbled Eezien as he saluted Jonetal, waiting for the commander to return the gesture. "Get ta mov'in, brat!" commanded Eezien after Jonetal lowered his arm back down to his side. Without hesitation, Eezien led Lana away from the palace; he hastily guided her toward the field of tents erected by travelers requiring lengthier lodging accommodations than afforded by the local inns and taverns.

"Peygulroq," repeated Jonetal softly to himself as he watched Lana disappear from his sight. "Why does that name sound remarkably familiar?" he asked himself before shaking his head, dismissing the thought from his mind, and continuing to the armory.

CHAPTER 8

Clack! *Rrrraaaaak. Trrraaaak. Snap, clack, snap, snap. RrraaaAAAACK!*
"Feed the blasted beasts!" shouted Sordun as the two *desert scorpions,* solitary creatures by nature, began circling one another in the arena. "Damn!" he cursed aloud as the scent of blood wafted on the breeze toward him. As his nostrils flared, he recognized the scent of blood would soon send the monsters into a frenzy. Noticing one scorpion about to clench the pincher of another, Sordun hurled his spear.

"Rrrrrrraaaaaaaaah!" shrieked the colossal creature as the weapon landed directly ahead of it. Sordun watched as the unruly mount snapped his bone spear to splinters like a twig.

Demic, perched in the immense boulders that created the arena enclosure, knelt grasping two end quarters of a *fire hound,* one in each hand. Across the ring standing opposite of his brother, Dimor held the remaining two front quarters. Demic quickly gazed at his brother standing shirtless, his perfectly defined, solid chest was marred with white scars from previous skirmishes and hunting wounds. The jagged, bright, red marks of newly healed wounds on Dimor's shoulder and neck from the bite of a deaf raptor made a stark contrast against his otherwise tanned skin.

Dimor noticed his brother staring in his direction; hastily, he rotated his shoulders backward and tilted his head from side to side. *Crack.* His neck popped and released the tension built up as his freshest wounds continued to heal. He rotated his shoulders both forward and in reverse once more, and he then nodded his head slightly in his brother's direction.

Demic caught his sibling's signal; without hesitation, he turned his interest back to the hungry beasts. Inhaling deeply, he raised himself up to a half-crouching position and abruptly stopped; he watched as the scorpion struck out at the other in the enclosure. As the animal's stinger struck the ground, debris flew toward Demic; he instantly squinted and turned his head to prevent the dirt from blinding him. Without further delay, Demic breathed in fiercely before grunting, "Ugh!" as he turned all his attention to launching himself into the arena with the mounts in training.

A grin spread across Dimor's face just as Demic's feet left the ground. "Here we go!" he exclaimed excitedly before sprinting a short distance and hurling himself through the air.

"Those two," grumbled Sordun as he watched the elaborate feeding technique of the pair of fearless and reckless brawlers. Blood from the *fire hound* quarters splashed the dirt surrounding the beasts, immediately calling their attention.

"Kyah!" roared Demic as he landed closest to the female scorpion. The creature spun in response to its name and reached out with a *snap* of its pincher.

Sordun admired the balance and coordination of the brethren as Demic ran backward, luring the larger and stronger mount away.

The thunderous *clattering* of Kyah's legs striking the loose rock of the arena garnered the awareness of the smaller yet swifter male. Without delay, he began his advance toward Kyah and Demic.

Dimor unleashed an ear-splitting whistle, halting Malakai midway from reaching Kyah. "Oohoos, Malakai!" shouted Dimor while raising a hound quarter for him to see.

Ssssssrrrrrrrraaaa! Malakai hissed in response as he shifted his weight and turned to face Dimor. His scarlet eyes appeared to narrow as he focused on the blood dripping meat swinging from the *Defling's* grasp.

"Oohoos!" repeated Dimor sternly as he tentatively approached the monster.

"Still at it, 'eh?" questioned Gunter as he strode up behind Sordun and witnessed the greatest trainers feeding the youngest mounts.

"Aye, Overlord" responded Sordun while continuing to observe the dangerous spectacular.

"The most remarkable we've had," commented Gunter half to himself while replying to Sordun.

"Aye," repeated Sordun and paused briefly before adding, "and the most imbecilic."

Gunter snorted in response while casting a sideways glance at Sordun, his amusement evident by the upward turn of his mutilated lip. "Why do you say?" he questioned lightly.

Sordun tipped his head in the direction of the arena; Gunter turned his focus back to the trainers just in time to watch as Dimor effortlessly tossed a chunk of meat which was instantaneously caught in Malakai's deadly clutch. Void of any delay, he ripped the food to shreds. With the scraps firmly in his grasp, he exudated a salivary astringent from

Kimberly Evette Ortuno

his jowls, sufficiently liquefying the bits. With his eyes still locked on Dimor, he slurped the acidic muck down.

"Oy-yi," grunted Demic. Previously illiterate, his accent changed the sound of the original expression, as Kyah snapped her pinchers swiftly; abruptly, Demic threw a section of the hound to Kyah as her claws became a blurred whirlwind of razor-sharp edges. "Cease!" shouted Demic. Kyah's flurry slowed enough to snatch the second relinquished canine section. She then promptly dissolved the portion and downed the liquidized contents.

"A pair of putzes!" bleated Sordun as he continued to watch the brothers twirling, almost as if in dance, amongst the lethal behemoths. "Why not just feed the creatures in their cages?" he questioned in confusion.

Gunter fleetingly lifted one shoulder, allowed it to drop nonchalantly, and grunted in response. "Perhaps..." he mused as his brows drew together in contemplation, "perhaps it allows them to establish a better bond with the creatures."

"Bah!" retorted Sordun skeptically. "Surely they just enjoy tempting death," he groused while witnessing the scorpions devour the additional segments provided by the siblings.

"Oy-yi," exhaled Demic in relief as he eyed Kyah. "Oohoos!" he then called sternly as Kyah swayed from side to side; Kyah, hearing the command, hesitantly approached the *Defling*. Demic waited cautiously, noting Kyah's pinchers tucked against her sides, with the barbed end of her tail appearing to float languidly above her armor plated back.

"Oy-yi! There's my boy," greeted Dimor as Malakai casually pendulated to-and-fro in similar fashion to Kyah. Malakai responded with a series of brisk yet non-threatening *snaps* and *clacks*. "Easy," murmured Dimor as he placed his hand on a spike protruding just behind the end of the nearly-indestructible, bone-like carapace that protected Malakai's head. Aware of the foreign pressure just behind his head, Malakai stabbed the ground anxiously with his rear legs. "Easy," repeated Dimor, easing the mount's expected apprehension.

Demic, at a distance from his brother, mimicked Dimor's actions at the same time. Kyah stood motionless as she considered the familiar touch behind her head.

After a short-lived pause, Dimor met Demic's gaze and took a calming breath.

"Mount!" Dimor and Demic roared in unison, and they both skillfully hefted themselves onto their respective mount's backs.

Malakai shook violently but posthaste settled down as Dimor yelled, "Easy!"

"Rrrrrraaaaaaaah!" screeched Kyah as she reared up and bucked frantically.

"Easy!" Dimor shouted, forthwith, as he grasped the barb symmetrically protruding opposite the first and held on securely. "Easy!" repeated Dimor. His thunderous voice finally penetrated Malakai's unruly reaction.

Gunter grinned broadly as he nudged Sordun with his elbow. "Eh?" he said while jabbing Sordun in the side, eliciting an eyeroll and incomprehensible grumble, as intermittent barks of *"tut"* echoed throughout the arena as the scorpions were guided around the enclosure.

* * *

Lana grudgingly stalked after Captain Holdir; sunbeams highlighted her light amber eyes, and the rays made them appear to brightly sparkle even though her glowering stare was menacingly dark. Grumbling to herself and huffing erratically, she broke into a brief sprint to catch up to the blue-skinned Captain as he knowingly navigated through the bustling city. Approaching the end of a row of shops, Eezien noted the everyday happenings lessened, and he managed to bob his head to the passing citizens.

"Make haste, girl!" barked Eezien irritably over his shoulder,

"Eeep!" squealed Lana as she jumped in surprise to Eezien's harsh command.

"The cam'pin groun's be jist uh'head," Eezien informed her as they turned the corner of the last building.

"I know my way from here," Lana grumbled her reply as she quickened her steps to pass her unfriendly escort. "My thanks," she mumbled under her breath as she continued past Eezien without a backward glance.

"Lit'tle twat," spat Eezien, scowling after the frumpy child as she disappeared in the throng of tents and pavilions, temporary homes established by merchants and travelers. Not wasting another thought on the girl, Eezien spun on his heels and made his way toward the armory to return his specifically distributed sentry weapon.

Lana darted behind the first tent before tentatively poking her head out to search for the rude sentry. She watched the tall guard with metallic grey hair disappear from her view back into the main sections of the city. "Phew!" she sighed forcefully before finally relaxing. No longer concerned about being scrutinized, she followed the familiar trails between shelters until she arrived at the poorly constructed and rickety structure she shared with her mother and uncle. "Hail," said Lana as she pushed the flap of kodiak hide, serving as a door, aside.

Kimberly Evette Ortuno

"Hail, Lana," greeted her mother from the floor, lifting her head briefly from grinding grain into flour. "A favor," murmured Taygan, dipping her head toward the wooden food vessel on the table.

"Aye, Ami," replied Lana as she reluctantly walked across the dimly lit space. "Where is uncle?" she asked casually, lightly swinging the empty container between her fingers.

"Whot does yous have ta say?" Peygar demanded gruffly as he entered the tent, overhearing the brief conversation between his niece and sister.

"Oy!" exclaimed Lana in surprise as she snapped her head toward the entrance just in time to watch her uncle swing the bundle of crudely crafted weapons off his back and lower them to the ground.

"Eh, *spawn*?" he probed impatiently, extending his hands out to his sides.

Taygan clenched her teeth, and she forced herself to refrain from interrupting her brother to avoid an unnecessary skirmish.

Lana felt her nose and upper lip begin to crinkle with disgust.

"Uh hmm!" coughed Taygan forcefully, drawing Peygar's attention before he could see Lana's expression. "Hail, Peygar," she said purposefully and waited for his reply. He remained motionless, his brows raised and his stance expectant.

"Hmph!" he finally snorted before dipping his head to his sister. "Hail, Taygan," he grumbled, suddenly aware of her rigid posture. "Whot troubles yous?" he asked with a frown.

"You know..." replied Taygan slowly, keenly aware of Peygar's accent and poor choice of words. After a tense moment, she then added hesitantly, "Lana is a girl or child. You do not call her *spawn.*"

"I calls her whot I wants!" he retorted vehemently.

"Then they will all know we do not belong here!" interjected Lana forcefully before stomping across the short distance to her mother, extending the bowl out to her. "They know *spawns* were *Troll* youth," she spat out before turning to glare at her mother's brother.

"We are not **Trolls***!*" sneered Taygan under her breath as she shot Lana a warning look.

"No..." grumbled Lana as she crossed her arms over her chest defiantly. "We are *Goons*. And we are going to be discovered because of him," she finished in a huff while jutting her chin upward toward her uncle, a jester used to indicate she was referring to him.

"Wretch!" growled out Peygar, his eyes narrowing on Lana as he took a threatening step toward her.

"Leave her be..." Taygan warned, her voice low and menacing, halting her younger sibling in his tracks. Lana's amber eyes appeared to

58

sparkle in the dimly lit space as she shifted her weight expectantly. Making no attempt to disguise her contempt, Lana stood openly glowering at her uncle, and she unconsciously pulled her lips back as she growled aggressively. "Lana!" Taygan said firmly.

"Whot da hell…" mumbled Peygar, confusion evident in his voice.

Shaking her head fiercely, Lana tried to clear the sudden fog that clouded her thoughts. "Sorry, Ami…" she replied nervously.

"Have you any information?" demanded Taygan, ignoring her brother's befuddled reaction.

"Uh…" stammered Lana, trying to recall what her mother just asked. After what seemed an eternity, Lana finally exclaimed, "aye!"

"Well?" asked Peygar impatiently, immediately forgetting Lana's strange reaction. "Whot it be?"

Lana cast her uncle a look of detestation before rolling her eyes upward. "In the palace courtyard… there is a stream," she began unhurriedly. Taygan scrutinized her daughter; quietly, she watched as Lana closed her eyes slowly and canted her head slightly to the side. Gradual creases developed between Lana's brows as she concentrated on the memory of the enclosed space. "The stream… it does not end!" she added excitedly as her eyes snapped open. "It leaves through a small, section of the outer security wall."

"Guards?" inquired Peygar as a devious grin transformed his face.

"Nay," replied Lana as she shook her head from side to side. "I could not clearly see, but it appeared to have a barricade in place to prevent entry."

Peygar scoffed and crossed his chiseled arms over his burly chest. "It wills no stops a weapon maker or stoneworker!" he boldly declared before flashing a smile and winking knowingly at Taygan.

* * *

The two sentinels standing outside of the throne room snapped to attention with their arms down at their sides as they watched Avenor and Gelriz approaching. Once the leaders were within a reasonable distance, the guards rendered the appropriate salute.

The *clanking* of armor striking armor briefly drew Avenor's attention.

"Khan Avenor… Chief Gelriz," greeted the guards posted outside of the throne room as Avenor and Gelriz approached.

"Greetings," responded Avenor as he returned the salute by raising his right forearm to his chest. "Let no one in," he instructed the pair outside the doors.

"As you desire, Your Grace," they replied in unison.

"Salutations," greeted Gelriz with a curt nod of his head as he passed through the doors after Avenor. Gelriz, peering over his shoulder, caught sight of the younger guard just as she closed the double-doors. Satisfied, Gelriz turned back around to focus on his second-brother.

Avenor purposefully strode across the room, and he began navigating his way to the smaller council chamber concealed behind the throne itself.

"Why do you not wear your crown?" asked Gelriz as he stopped before the dais which elevated the intricately designed seats for the royal family. Gelriz placed one foot on the raised platform as he leaned closer, admiring the ornate *damiund* headpieces placed on Avenor's, Galhix's and Wesdin's thrones.

Avenor paused to gaze at his second-brother momentarily before shifting his eyes to study the exquisitely decorated *damiund* bands adorned with an impressive assortment of gems. "As magnificent as they are, I do not feel it necessary to wear my authority," he replied.

Gelriz made a face of confusion which did not go unnoticed by Avenor. "Wear your authority?" repeated Gelriz slowly. "You do not wear your authority..." he continued slowly before pausing. He raised his hand and turned the palm upward; rhythmically, he began opening and closing his fingers while slightly motioning outward as he tried to formulate a suitable response. "You are wearing your announcement of sorts."

"My announcement?" repeated Avenor, the same mask of confusion now plastered across his own face.

"Aye!" retorted Gelriz. "There is no herald announcing your presence for citizens to harken to. What other way have your citizens to identify you?" he then asked with a downward tilt of his head while simultaneously arching a brow.

"They know my appearance," replied Avenor with a scoff.

"Does every citizen... in every city, town, and camp?" pressed Gelriz as he crossed his arms over his chest.

Avenor grunted under his breath as he acknowledged his second-brother's skeptical expression.

"Ah hah!" exclaimed Gelriz as he uncrossed his arms. "Therefore, Brother, to avoid unnecessary conflict, disorder, or other unpleasantries, you should wear your crown to announce your presence to those not familiar with your appearance," he finished cheerfully. With an impish grin, Gelriz stepped up on the dais and picked up Avenor's crown. "Your Grace -" he said while turning toward Avenor and continuing, "if you would…" Gelriz allowed his voice to trail off as he raised the crown high enough to place on Avenor's head.

"Oy," mumbled Avenor with resignation as he allowed his brother to settle the crown upon his head. Immediately, Avenor felt his muscles pulse with power, his mind race with clarity, and he felt a surge of energy displace his fatigue.

"Oy!" exclaimed Gelriz as he took a step back, sensing the unexpected increase in Avenor's selected traits. "Perhaps I should have you smith mine own and that of Baylay," said Gelriz with a chuckle as he admired Avenor's crown and blacksmithing ability.

Avenor smiled then. As the youngest blacksmithing *mayven,* he had focused on self-teaching and learning to imbue metals with additional properties from crushed gems and precious stones.

"Is there naught you can do?" asked Gelriz in bewilderment while slightly shaking his head.

"Truthfully…" began Avenor pensively before shaking his head in return. "I have never considered it," he finally admitted. *In all honesty, I am certain I could master any skill or ability if I truly desired to,* he thought silently to himself. *I have already mastered the ability to Invoke a Bloodline.*

"Are you well?" asked Gelriz, aware that Avenor had suddenly gone mute. "Avenor?" repeated Gelriz as he approached the Khan, and he reached out to gently smack Avenor's cheek. "Brother?"

"Oy!" escaped passed Avenor's lips as he retracted unexpectedly from Gelriz's touch. "Aye… aye…" he repeated while pushing his hands through his locks, disheveled from his abrupt withdrawal. "Apologies, Brother. I became lost in my own thoughts."

"So, I observed," returned Gelriz hesitantly.

"What is it that you must tell me in private council?" asked Avenor abruptly, twirling on his feet to lead the way to the small chamber.

"Ah, yes…" replied Gelriz nervously as he joined Avenor in the council chamber. Gelriz surveyed the space, and he then tossed his head back nervously causing his braided hair to sway from side to side behind him. "Uh-hmm!" coughed Gelriz, the act forced as he delayed answering Avenor's question. "Well…" he continued apprehensively.

Avenor crossed his arms over his chest. His biceps strained against the fabric of his tunic which suddenly appeared too small as it molded his chiseled frame. Inhaling deeply, his chest expanded and threatened to burst the seams of the garment stretched like a second skin over his flesh. A crease gradually appeared between his black eyes as he stood curiously waiting for Gelriz.

Taking a deep, calming, breath, Gelriz finally met Avenor's gaze with his own. "I had... a vision, Brother..." he finally said as he exhaled.

"That is all?" asked Avenor with a sigh of relief. The tension appeared to physically dissipate from his frame as if washed away.

"Avenor..." began Gelriz, his voice somber as he waited for the seriousness to set in.

"What is it?" demanded Avenor as he saw the grave expression etched on his second-brother's face. Swiftly, he uncrossed his arms and approached Gelriz before reaching out to grasp the Chief by his shoulders. "What was the vision about?" he demanded while fiercely giving his brother a short jolt.

"Sorrow, Brother..." whispered Gelriz as he met Avenor's dark eyes. "You will come to know sorrow once more."

"What do you mean? What will happen? When? Who?" asked Avenor heatedly as he shook the Weretigal again.

"A child? A woman? Someone you know? Someone you love? I know not the time, but only that it shall come to pass." murmured Gelriz quietly with a puzzled expression. "You are aware my ability is limited, Your Grace. I only desire that I could be of better service," he finished quietly.

"That is too vague!" exploded Avenor as he stepped back and placed his hands on the sides of his head. Closing his eyes, Avenor's mind raced through all the women in his life that he cared about. *Galhix... Ami... Azelly... Grandami Iriva... Onia Valcaly...* "Surely no harm can befall any of them if they have personal protectors," he mused aloud to himself.

"Aye," Gelriz responded weakly with a brief nod and slight smile. *"No amount of planning or preparation will prevent this,"* he spoke to himself mutely as he watched Avenor hastily depart from the council chamber and practically sprint from the throne room.

CHAPTER 9

The previous evenings' dew, now a frozen blanket of glimmering crystals in the rising sun, crunched under Azelly's boots; the soldiers, enough to form a unit, snapped to attention and saluted Azelly as she approached the chosen personal protectors for the royal family. Halting at the front of the rows of guards, Azelly returned their salute before removing her helmet.

"You all have your assignments," Azelly called out in a voice loud and clear. "Should you fail…" she continued and allowed her warning to go unsaid. "Am I understood?" roared Azelly as her steely gaze pierced through every individual.

"Ha-ooh!" thundered the specialized group in unison as they simultaneously thumped their right forearms against their chests in response.

"Your charges have already been informed. Do not disrupt their daily routines. These precautions shall last until Khan Avenor decrees otherwise," she informed the group as she scanned each one, meeting their unwavering gazes with her own. After what seemed an eternity, Azelly nodded her head and shouted, "Make haste!"

Without hesitation, the soldiers resounded with another deafening shout accompanied by a fierce blow to their chests as they saluted. Needing no further instruction, the guards disassembled and located their partners.

"You must be addle-brained if you believe for a moment that I would permit you to embark on this mission without me," came a familiar voice from behind Azelly.

Pulling back her shoulders defiantly and settling her helm back on her head, Azelly took a deep breath before turning to meet the hostile glare of Leander. With his arms firmly crossed over his rock-hard chest, Leander stood dressed in his chainmail armor, an added layer of protection over his black, hardened leather garments.

"You do not have the ability to permit or limit my expeditions, Major Leander," replied Azelly coolly. Her eyes closed to mere slits as she dared Leander to say differently.

Grunting, Leander dropped his hands to his sides before approaching his wife. "Why must you be so difficult?" he demanded harshly, yet his eyes betrayed the ferocity in his voice. Reaching out, Leander grasped Azelly's chin and brushed the pad of his thumb lightly over her lower lip.

"I am not being difficult," she replied with a snort. Hastily kissing her husband's thumb, she then pulled away from his loving gesture. "I have sworn to protect the Khan," she finished sternly.

"And what of Leandra? What of me? What of us?" he asked fiercely, holding his arms out to his sides. "Do we not matter?" he continued probing. "Are we not important to you?"

"Do **not** question my honor or my love," snapped Azelly as she openly glowered at Leander. "Every soldier is sworn to protect the Khan and the royal family," she hissed softly while allowing her gaze to dart from side to side to avoid drawing an audience.

"Bah!" replied Leander as he threw his hands up in the air irritably before dropping them back down by his sides. "He does not **own** you," he added angrily.

"He could very well," replied Azelly simply. "I owe him my life. If naught for the Khan, I would still be a slave in Sicario Prison," she reminded her husband quietly.

"Even still!" exploded Leander as the thought of his wife traveling without him caused his stomach to churn. "I shall accompany you," he finally informed her.

Azelly stood unmoving as she listened to her husband. Slowly, she nodded her head in agreeance. "And what of Leandra?" she quietly asked.

"Trittni has agreed to remain with her as usual," he said swiftly. "You think I would not discover the reason a handful of elite soldiers were selected as personal protectors? Major Jonetal informed me… and you are high on that list."

"Hah!" scoffed Azelly briefly as she rolled her eyes upward in response. "I would not be the first choice to bring sorrow to my brother," she finished matter-of-factly.

"And why was I not selected to protect you?" demanded Leander suddenly. After a moment, his eyes widened with realization. "You did not want me to worry?" he managed to say as he watched Azelly clench and release her jaw through the front opening of her helmet. "You are my mate… my spouse," continued Leander as he pulled

Azelly into his embrace. The horrendous scraping sound of his chainmail coat against her iridescent breastplate made them hastily separate. "We share the burden. We share the worry. We face this enemy **together**," he informed her softly to which Azelly finally allowed a faint smile to tease the corners of her lips in response.

"Come," said Azelly as she took Leander's hand in her own and gave it a firm squeeze. "We depart soon," she said before releasing her husband's hand.

* * *

Galhix sat at the edge of the bed in the personal chambers she shared with Avenor, and she tensely watched as Avenor finished preparing his travel pack. With his crowned head resting on his mother's bosom, Wesdin sat beside Galhix with his arms wrapped around her waist.

"You will not reconsider?" asked Galhix quietly. Her question drew Avenor's attention, and her eyes immediately searched those of her mate.

"We've previously discussed the issue," sighed Avenor as he took in the sight of his wife and son. "General Azelly has selected the most elite soldiers to guard you and Wesdin in my absence."

"Pugh!" exclaimed Galhix skeptically with a puff of air. "I am more than capable to defend myself," she reminded Avenor while pulling Wesdin closer to her side.

Avenor grinned as he watched Galhix's unconscious action. "Indeed. No one ought to mess with an Ami Weretigal and her cub!" he jested.

"Api…" began Wesdin and waited for his father to look at him. "Why must we wear the crowns?" he asked, taking his crown off to inspect it. "Why does mine not have so many sparklies?" he continued, comparing his own to his mother's and father's.

"Ah…" replied Avenor quietly as he approached his wife and son. He gently removed the crown from his son's grasp before settling it back atop his head. "Your uncle, Chief Gelriz, insists that we **announce** our presence."

Wesdin made a face, clearly confused, which drew a chuckle from both his parents. "I do not understand."

"Yes," replied Avenor with a dip of his head. "I can see that." After a moment, he snapped his fingers. "Uncle Gelriz wants others to know you are the Khanzito without having to tell them. The easiest way is to wear the crown," finished Avenor as he tapped the *damiund* band on his son's head.

"Hmm… I suppose so," grumbled Wesdin with a shrug.

65

"And when you are older, with your abilities more evident, your crown will be re-crafted by your Api to enhance the traits that are most beneficial for you," added Galhix as she smiled down at Wesdin.

"Ami… Api," whispered Wesdin, his voice so soft his parents had to lean closer to hear him.

"What is it my beloved?" asked Galhix as she leaned back slightly so she could clearly see Wesdin's expression. Simultaneously, Avenor knelt before his child so they were eye level.

"I am not going to *transform,* am I?" he finally asked as his eyes watered.

"Oy!" exclaimed Galhix as she pulled Wesdin firmly into her embrace. "My beloved," she whispered softly as she felt her gown dampened by tears.

"Oy…" echoed Avenor as he sat back on his heels, unsure how to comfort his son. Reaching out, he placed his hand against Wesdin's back and caressed him lightly. "Come," said Avenor as he drew Wesdin from his mother's embrace into his own arms.

Galhix quickly stood and made her way to the nearby table with a pot of hot water. Selecting a small pouch of herbs, she placed it in a mug. Pouring the hot water over the contents, she waited for the *lavendia* tea to brew.

"Perhaps you may not experience the *transformation* as a tigal," whispered Avenor quietly against his son's ear. Wesdin immediately pulled back to gaze up at his father's face. Pulling him back against his chest, Avenor continued to speak quietly so only Wesdin could hear him. "Perhaps you'll transform as I do, merging with the shadows. You only need quiet your mind and see if they speak to you. Do not be afraid to allow your mind to wander. Do not be afraid to embrace all that comes to you. Should you choose, *you* have the ability to *Invoke a Bloodline,"* he finished just as Galhix returned with the freshly brewed *lavendia* tea.

"Come," said Galhix as she extended her hand to Wesdin. Without hesitation, she pulled him back into her embrace as he slid his hand into her own. "We'll sit and discuss the *transformation* to distract ourselves as your father prepares to depart," she said as she handed the mug to Wesdin and sat beside him on the bed.

Avenor felt himself dismissed from the conversation, and he felt his heart tighten with sadness, aware of the displeasure the excursion was causing his wife. Avenor pushed himself back to his feet and gazed down at two of the most important people in his life. Reaching out, he gently caressed Galhix's cheek with one hand while ruffling Wesdin's hair with the other. "I shall return soon," murmured Avenor. Not waiting for a response, he turned and picked up his travel pack before heading out of the chamber in search of the others.

* * *

"There you are, old goat," said Iriva as she watched Betaro set his travel pack by the door in the Dining Hall. "Did you have adequate beauty rest?" she continued taunting.

Ignoring Iriva's jeering, Betaro continued about his business. After dropping his personal belongings, Betaro picked up a plate and made his selections from the foods set out for morning meal. Satisfied, he joined Iriva at the table, and he sat across from her at an angle. Smiling, he nodded and finally said, "Indeed."

"Indeed, what?" echoed Iriva as she turned to stare at Betaro.

"I did have adequate beauty rest..." he answered while shifting to look at Iriva. Taking the time to caress the slight wrinkles at the corner of his eyes, he finally continued, "while you, my dear, do not appear to have received adequate rest to be considered beautiful," he finished just before scooping up a spoonful of egg and depositing it in his mouth.

"Bah!" exclaimed Iriva as her expression turned to one of horror which drew forth a deep belly-shaking laugh from Betaro.

"Oy..." giggled Everly as she and Manijor tried to stifle their entertainment as they walked in the Dining Hall. "Api!" chided Everly as she and Manijor joined the two Generals seated at the table.

"Ami..." said Manijor sternly as he lifted a brow skeptically. "My second-father does not typically engage in this type of banter. If I know any better," he murmured while looking between his adoptive mother and second-father before continuing, "you initiated this abuse yourself!"

"Nonsense!" puffed Iriva as she crossed her arms over her chest defiantly. "He just enjoys pointing out my flaws," she continued to huff.

Everly and Manijor chuckled to themselves as they prepared their own plates for morning meal. "Not too heavy," Manijor reminded Everly as she began piling her plate with candied breads. "We teleport today."

"Oy, you are right," she groaned and replaced most of the candied breads stacked high on her plate. "I do not desire to lose my morning meal when we travel," she confided with a slight pout. "Ah, well..." she groused and settled on a lighter array of cheese and meats.

Just then, Avenor walked through the doors and headed directly to the prepared buffet. Without saying a word, his foul mood was sensed by the others; the lighthearted mirth was instantly chased from the chamber. Avenor surveyed the contents, and he then made his way to the end of the table. He poured himself two different mugs after eyeing the various decanters – one with *meal mush* and one with *berria*. Without

67

wasting any time, he lifted the mug of gritty textured mush and swallowed it down followed quickly with the delicious fruit juice medley.

"I am departing," he finally said once he turned to face his family seated at the table. "Whenever you have finished morning meal, I will see you in Texicar," he continued briskly. Noticing his loved ones starting to stand, he held out his hands to halt their hurried activities. "Nay, finish morning meal. It is no rush. Ambassador Clawbane will not arrive for a few days as he is not fond of teleportation. Generals, I will see you soon," he assured them. A chorus of verbalized understanding followed as everyone settled themselves back down once more.

Partially dipping his head in farewell, Avenor turned and navigated his way through the palace, and he headed toward the back entrance.

"*Nahm-Aztey,* Khan Crusendir," greeted a sentry, snapping to attention and saluting, as Avenor appeared at the secondary entry to the palace.

"*Ahz-sulam oo-laikim,* Soldier," replied Avenor, returning the salute. "Lower the banner. I depart for Texicar," he instructed the guard.

"Aye, Your Grace. I am here to serve," replied the soldier with another salute.

Avenor returned the salute briskly before continuing his trek to the *Teleportation Tower* that housed the large, pink sphere that permitted teleportation.

Immediately after Avenor departed, the sentinel hiked up the stairway located on the outside of the palace. He then walked to the post that proudly displayed a black banner, with occasional blue veins as if the material had been marbled, emblazoned with a silvery crown and trim intended to resemble *damiund.* He then lowered the banner, indicating that the Khan was no longer within the city.

Azelly and Leander caught sight of Avenor as he walked along a cobblestone road leading toward the tall structure that contained one of the few blush-colored boulders in the world. "Your Grace," shouted Azelly from across the open pasture before Avenor entered the building.

Avenor halted mid-stride and turned to see his sister and second-brother rushing in his direction. Frowning, he returned the salute the pair rendered as they approached him. "What trouble have you encountered?" he asked once they were within hearing range.

"No trouble, Your Grace," panted Azelly as she forced her breathing to slow. "Major Swiftpaw… has requested… to join the… excursion," she continued between ragged gasps.

"Ah, I understand," replied Avenor as he turned his attention to his sister's husband. "And Major Teyio is aware? He accepts responsibility of *Force Tohunga* while you are away?"

Leander took a deep breath, his uneven breathing finally settling, and coughed once before responding, "Nay, Your Grace. I have yet to speak with him. If I may have your approval, I will then seek out Major Teyio," finished Leander as he took another deep breath.

Looking from one to the other, Avenor finally nodded his head. "Will you accompany Major Swiftpaw?" he asked.

"If you would permit it, aye," replied Azelly with a curt dip of her head.

"How long will this delay your arrival?" questioned Avenor, his lips pursed as he turned his attention to Azelly.

"If I may, Your Grace," interrupted Leander and waited until Avenor acknowledged him before continuing, "the usual travel time takes twenty-five days. However, aboard the *Sailfish*, we will arrive at Harbola in five days at the latest," he said regarding the name of the fastest ship in the Grand Fleet of the military

"Very well," replied Avenor before snapping his fingers and pointing toward the couple. "Oy… Ambassador Novex departs soon. Alert him so that the lot of you travel together aboard the *Sailfish*," he informed them.

"As you desire," replied Azelly. Nudging her husband in the side with her elbow, they both saluted. "You have our thanks," she finished, waiting until Avenor returned the gesture. Without further delay, the pair dropped their arms and hastily made their way in search of the Weretigal.

"Your Grace," greeted the soldiers posted outside of the *Teleportation Tower*, guarding the sphere that had been moved from the palace foyer cycles prior. They waited patiently until Avenor saluted in response and said, "Good morn," as he passed through the secure entryway.

The building, while not exceedingly tall, was high enough for the sphere to be fastened out of reach of the tallest *ShadowRunners*, *HybraRunners*, and Weretigals. Access to the large rock was limited; soldiers selected to stand guard surrounding the stone required incredible strength to navigate the intricate obstacles that lead to the platform where it was expertly secured by a blacksmith *mayven*.

"*Nahm-Aztey!*" cried out the soldiers in formal greeting as they raised their right forearms to their chests while gazing down at Avenor.

"*Ahz-sulam oo-laikim,*" shouted back Avenor as he struck his chest with his own forearm, suddenly filled with apprehension. *"Peace be upon you,"* he repeated to himself wordlessly, *"and yet, here I am, heading into conflict.* " Vigorously shaking his head from side to side, Avenor shoved the uneasiness out of his mind. Closing his eyes, Avenor focused on the pink sphere located in an identical tower on the continent of Texicar.

"Ey, ey!" came hushed calls from above Avenor as the guards realized he was beginning the teleportation process. The guards crowded around the rails as they gazed down at their Khan in bewilderment.

"I, Avenor, return to Harbola, fragmented no more," he whispered. His words were barely audible to himself; immediately, he felt his physical form become as light as a feather before dissipating and completely disappearing as he transported to the capital city of Texicar.

"Oy!" exclaimed one of the soldiers after watching the teleportation. "He vanished!" she said in awe, turning to meet the eyes of the fellows she was posted guard with. Their eyes, too, were wide with disbelief.

"Ah'right, ya nooblins. Ya dun seen the Khan tela'port. Now git back ta yer posts," laughed the senior guard on duty.

"Oy," exclaimed the female soldier incredulously once more before returning to her station.

* * *

Valcaly stood silently outside of the personal chambers belonging to the Khan and Khantessa, listening to the squeals of laughter coming from within. A smile tugged at the corners of her lips as she heard Galhix's playful jeers returned taunt for taunt by Wesdin. A chuckle from the tigal standing guard on the opposite side of the door drew her gaze.

"You and your brothers have a striking resemblance," she murmured quietly to one of the *Apex* members.

"Aye, we are oft mistaken for the other," he admitted with a mischievous grin.

Valcaly returned the impish smile. "So, tell me, tigal… which one are you? Clearly, you are not Novex. He ventures to Texicar this morn."

"Aylex Clawbane," returned the flirtatious feline, his voice nearly a purr as he said his name. "And who do I have the honor of standing guard with?" he asked with a frivolous bow.

Valcaly arched a brow skeptically and rolled her eyes upward before responding. "Overseer Valcaly Truceran," she replied while returning Aylex's exaggerated bow, drawing forth a hearty laugh from the tall man.

"The pleasure is mine," returned Aylex with a wink.

Valcaly remained silent for a moment as she recalled Galhix's furious outburst at Aylex's previous visits; she finally said, "If I recall correctly, you are the one that chases anything with a -" she paused for a moment before continuing, "a *velvet glove*," she finished with a devious grin. Aylex's grin vanished as a coughing fit overcame him to which Valcaly chuckled. "I have no desire for a *moppet*," she then informed him sternly.

"Ey!" he objected hotly. "I'm well into adulthood," he retorted, straightening to stand his full height as he stood staring down at Valcaly.

Valcaly turned slightly to observe the tigal, aware that he stood near a foot taller than she. Just then, Valcaly noticed someone approaching from behind Aylex. Leaning to the side, Valcaly peered around the pouting feline.

"*Nahm-Aztey*, Vice Commandant Aylox," said Azelly as she raised her right forearm to her chest, greeting the second in command of the entire Weretigal Troop.

"What?" gasped Aylex as he nearly jumped while spinning around to meet his father's ice blue eyes. "Father," he murmured and hastily saluted the leader of the black tigal Pride.

"*Ahz-sulam oo-laikim*, Overseer Valcaly," replied Aylox, his voice deep and gruff as he returned her salute. Without releasing his son's gaze, Aylox asked, "Any disturbances?"

"Nay," replied Valcaly with a shake of her head. After a few moments, Valcaly became aware of a somewhat smaller man standing close to Aylox. Valcaly smiled as she noticed he stood the same height as Aylex though shorter in stature than Aylox. Dipping her head, she noiselessly greeted Daylin.

Briefly looking at the woman, Daylin met Valcaly's eyes. Swallowing hard, he dipped his head slightly before quickly shifting his eyes away.

Valcaly stifled a chuckle as she watched a pink flush suddenly stain the quiet tigal's cheeks. *"Ah, yes, the lethal yet incredibly shy brother,"* she mutely said to herself.

"Do not be looking for a fresh honey pot to taste," Aylox telepathically scolded Aylex which was also heard by Daylin.

"Aye, father," replied Aylex with an audible sigh as he shifted uneasily from one foot to the other.

"If any harm befalls the Khanzito, it'll be your head I come for," warned Aylox sternly as he reached out, thumping his son firmly on the chest with his fist.

"Oof!" grunted Aylex at the force of his father's blow.

Valcaly stood quietly shifting her gaze between the three tigals; the myriad of facial expressions alerted her to their private conversation, and she waited patiently until they finished. Valcaly watched as the pink stain darkened to a crimson red and spread up to Daylin's ears.

"I'll be joining you," Aylox finally said after what seemed an eternity as he turned to face Valcaly. "From the information I was given, it seems as though Khantessa Galhix is a higher risk than Khanzito Wesdin," he said somberly while posting himself opposite the hall from Valcaly and Aylex.

"I'll be joining Aylex in protecting Khanzito Wesdin," finally spoke Daylin, his voice a deep, sensual rumble causing Valcaly's body to unwillingly respond.

"Uh... Aye," stammered Valcaly as she nodded her head and turned to look away from the young stud. *"Oy!"* gasped Valcaly silently. *"What magic does the boy-man possess that my body responds in such a manner?"* she continued silently questioning herself.

Clearing his throat, Daylin positioned himself across from his older brother. *"I see she refused your advances,"* Daylin silently teased Aylex.

"At least I've the balls to engage in conversation with a pretty woman," countered Aylex lightly. *"It does no good to leave them moist between the thighs,"* he finished with a roguish smirk.

Daylin cast his brother a look of dismay at the promiscuous remark. *"You know damn well it is not my intention. I cannot speak to a girl, much less a woman, without them trying to pull down my trousers,"* he continued while crossing his arms over his brawny chest.

"Do they always speak through a mind connection?" asked Valcaly as she glanced between the two brothers, their facial expressions continually changing.

"Apologies," the brothers responded in unison as their father snapped his gaze between them.

"Aye," replied Aylox curtly. "Most of us tigals do, especially when on a mission."

"I see," replied Valcaly quietly as she tilted her head back briefly before slowly allowing it to come forward.

Just then, the slow creaking of the door handle being turned drew the attention of all four guards.

"Onia Valcaly!" gasped Wesdin happily as he threw his arms around his Grandami's closest friend. Valcaly chuckled softly as she embraced Wesdin and lightly stroked his hair. Abruptly, Wesdin drew back from Valcaly but did not leave her embrace. "Who are they?" he whispered as he looked up at the unfamiliar men. "They look like Ambass'dor Clawbane," he murmured quietly, trying to use Novex's proper title, while pointing at the younger two.

"Aye, they do," answered Valcaly as she turned to face the tigals. "That one is Aylex. And that one is Daylin. They are the younger brothers of Novex," she finished softly.

"Though not by much, my beloved," added Galhix from the doorway of her personal chambers, drawing the attention of the small gathering in the hall.

"It is incredibly rare, but they are a *terzetto*…triplets… three children birthed by the same mother at the same time," fumbled Galhix as she tried to explain the uniqueness of the brothers.

"Oy! They're so big!" gaped Wesdin as he eyed the two men who appeared to stand just a tad taller than his father. After a short while, he turned his black eyes up to his mother and asked innocently, "Ami… how did they all fit at one time?"

The group abruptly erupted into a roar of laughter. Valcaly, still holding Wesdin, clutched him harder as she nearly doubled over with entertainment. Galhix, though initially trying to resist, could not contain the mirth bubbling up from within. Snorting once, Galhix then burst into a series of cackles and wheezes as she tried to maintain her composure. Aylox openly chortled, his adamantine demeanor suddenly broken. The two brothers snickered before joining the chorus of hilarity, grasping at their sides from the force of their merriment.

"What?" demanded Wesdin as his face contorted with a frown. "What is so funny?"

"Nothing, my beloved," Galhix finally managed to say. "As your father has instructed, Aylex and Daylin shall serve as personal protectors until he returns," she reminded Wesdin gently.

"As you desire," grumbled Wesdin as he pulled away from Valcaly. "And who are you?" asked Wesdin abruptly, leaning back as he turned to look high up at the goliath of a man now standing beside his mother.

"Vice Commandant Aylox Clawbane," replied the largest tigal as he saluted the youth. Crouching down, Aylox met Wesdin at eye level. "I, along with your *Onia* Valcaly, have been instructed to protect your mother," he informed the child. "I'm pretty good at what I do," admitted Aylox warmly. "And you know your *Onia* is good too."

At the last statement, Wesdin broke out into a huge smile. Raising his hand to his mouth, he quietly informed the second in command of the tigal forces, "Aye, she even defeated *Onio* Jonetal in a duel!"

Aylox barked a short laugh in response before shoving himself back to his feet. "Don't be too much of a rascal for them, eh?"

"As you desire, Vice Commandant Aylox," replied Wesdin with a giggle as he saluted the massive man. Facing his mother, Wesdin then asked, "Ami, may I go see if Geodani and Laynee are able to play?"

"Aye, but you best listen to Uncle Gel and Aunt Bay," she responded sternly while holding out a finger to her son.

"Oh, Ami! I promise," groused Wesdin, lolling his head back in annoyance.

"Very well. Have fun and stay out of mischief!" Galhix shouted after Wesdin as he raced down the hall, followed closely by Aylex and Daylin.

"You have my thanks," murmured Galhix as she saluted both Valcaly and Aylox simultaneously.

"I am here to serve, Khantessa," replied Valcaly without hesitation.

"You are well?" asked Aylox as he examined Galhix, taking her hands in his own.

"Aye," replied Galhix with a small smile. *"You have aged well,"* she silently spoke to the tigal deputy commander.

"And you have not aged a cycle," he admitted softly while caressing her hands with his thumbs. *"To be honest... I have missed you..."*

"You know it was never meant to be," replied Galhix mutely as she peered deep into Aylox's eyes.

Aylox scoffed then before looking away. *"Your age is not your true age!"* he retorted, finally releasing Galhix's hands.

"Aylox..." pleaded the Khantessa quietly. *"You know we could never have been mates. We knew not when the curse would be lifted!"* she continued while wrapping her arms around herself, desperately wishing she could ease the heartache she caused her former hunting companion and fancier.

"Khantessa?" Valcaly interrupted the silent communication. "Are you ill?"

"Nay, Overseer," replied Galhix shakily. "Well, perhaps a bit sick to my stomach," she admitted after a short time.

"Come," instructed Valcaly as she placed an arm around Galhix's waist, and she then guided the Khantessa back into the chamber she shared with Avenor. "Retrieve a platter of morning meal items and *berria,"* Valcaly called over her shoulder to Aylox as he waited by the door.

"Very well," said Aylox curtly before closing the door firmly.

"To bed with you," instructed Valcaly, her tone gentle yet her grip firm as she guided Galhix toward the bed. "We've all felt your apprehension the last few days," confessed Valcaly as she helped settle the Regent Khan.

"Oy," groaned Galhix as she settled herself. Swallowing hard, Galhix tried to force down the bile rising in her throat. The color quickly drained from her face, leaving her pale. Beads of sweat formed along her hairline as she tried to take deep, steady breaths.

"Oy!" exclaimed Valcaly in response as she hastily surveyed the chamber for a bowl. Spotting the water basin, Valcaly quickly plunged a nearby hand towel into the water before pouring the contents out. Grabbing the towel and bowl, she returned to Galhix's side. "Here," said Valcaly as she thrust the vessel into Galhix's hands.

"My than-," began Galhix before being interrupted forcefully by uncontrollable dry heaves with the occasional bile splashing into the basin she now clutched.

Valcaly folded the towel into a compress and pressed the cool cloth to the Khantessa's forehead, wiping away the sweat that now poured down her face.

After a time, Galhix finally ceased retching. Murmuring quietly, she whispered an incantation, warding off the nausea that plagued her. Leaning back onto the pillows, she closed her eyes. "You have my thanks," she said with her eyes still closed.

"I am here to serve, Regent Khan," Valcaly reassured Galhix. "Rest now. Aylox will bring refreshments, and we will both be on patrol right outside the chamber should you require assistance."

"You have my thanks, Valcaly," murmured Galhix once more with a weak smile before pulling the covers up to her chest and allowing sleep to claim her.

* * *

Reeyah's senses gradually returned, and she immediately became aware of the pain pulsing throughout her entire body. Recalling previous experiences, she stifled the groan that threatened to escape her lips; she knew too well what would happen if she woke the slumbering giant beside her. Risking a glance over her shoulder, Reeyah barely made out the steady rise and fall of Gunter's chest even though her vision was blurred. As quietly as possible, she exhaled a tense sigh of relief before rolling away from him.

Thump!

Reeyah inhaled sharply and automatically winced in response to the searing sensation that assaulted every fiber of her being. Holding her breath, she strained to hear, nearly certain she had woken the Overlord.

Gunter snorted once in his sleep before turning away from Reeyah; it was his only response to the muted sound of his mate falling to her hands and knees beside the bed. Reeyah remained motionless, waiting until she heard Gunter's breathing become deep and even once more.

Mustering all her strength, Reeyah shoved herself to her knees and managed to stagger to her feet. Sucking her bottom lip between her teeth, she clenched down hard to prevent from crying out in agony. Reaching up, she gingerly wiped the blood out of her eyes and inwardly grimaced, acknowledging her eyes were nearly swollen shut.

Reeyah stumbled in silence until she reached the nearest wall; using it as support, she made her way out of the hollow she shared with Gunter. Following the tunnel that led deeper into Overlook Cave, she blindly navigated to the last grotto within the main cave. Grunting quietly, Reeyah felt the ground change from smooth, cold, hard-packed dirt to the same cold, hard-packed dirt that had been ladened with rocks of varying sizes; while the rocks did not cover the entire area, there was a chance that every second step would land on a stone.

Feeling along the uneven floor with her bare feet, Reeyah cursed herself for not lighting the tunnel torches earlier when the thought had entered her mind.

"Ssss!" she hissed suddenly while jerking a foot up off the ground, and she immediately regretted it as a white light appeared to explode before her eyes from the pain, blinding her momentarily. "*Damn*," she wordlessly grumbled after the acute discomfort faded, and she could feel the blood trickling from her heel down the bottom of her foot and dripping off her toes. *"If I were not so weak, I would heal myself,"* she silently moaned to herself.

Dondree opened his eyes hesitantly; the scraping sound coming from the hall taught him that it could be many different things, especially because the torches had not been lit within Overlook Cave. His personal fire had grown small as the day wore on and he slept; the flames licked hungrily at the remainder of wooden pieces crumbling to ash, and they cast an eerie orange glow in his hollow. From his bed, a hollowed-out section in the rock wall that was high enough off the ground, he reached down and clutched around nervously until his hand closed around the staff of his spear. Taking an uneven breath, he turned on his side to face the cave entrance while bringing his staff up next to him.

Reeyah placed her hand on a smooth section of stone, supporting herself as her legs trembled, threatening to give way from under her. In the darkness and unable to see clearly, Reeyah leaned all her weight against her bloodied hand on the wall; suddenly, she felt her hand slide.

Whack!

"Ugh!" she grunted as her forehead connected with the wall, preventing her from falling completely to the ground. "Damn…" she cursed, keenly aware that the smell of metal had become stronger as her life's essence oozed out of the fresh wound above her eye and down her cheek.

"Lordess?" murmured Dondree, confusion evident in his voice. Apprehensively, he crept out of his sleeping space and hobbled to the entrance. Pressing himself firmly against the wall, he peeked around the corner. "Ami!" he exclaimed as he finally made out his mother's frame crumpled in the passageway. Without hesitation, he approached his battered mother and placed his arm around her waist. "Come," he instructed her while leading her to his personal hollow.

Reeyah groaned, her pride fighting the assistance for a mere moment before her body collapsed. *"He has grown stronger,"* she silently thought to herself as she leaned all her weight on her son, surprised that he could support her weight even though he remained hunched over.

"I'll kill him…" Dondree abruptly said, interrupting his mother's silent mussing. Lifting her legs, he helped his mother settle in the area he slept most of his life.

"You'll attempt no such thing," replied Reeyah weakly. "If he discovers you have not yet departed, **he** will surely kill **you**," she warned her son sorrowfully. "You must go!"

"And who will protect you?" demanded Dondree as he crossed his arms over his chest.

Reeyah peered at her son through her swollen eyes, barely able to make out his frame. She tried to smile, but she knew it looked more like a grimace. "I've managed this long on my own," she reminded him softly. "I'll manage until your return," she tried to assure him though her voice betrayed her message.

"Lordess…" he tried to reason with her.

"Boy!" growled Reeyah, her tone low yet firm. "Depart now or **I** will alert the Overlord," she threatened fiercely before she completely collapsed from exhaustion.

Dondree jerked his head back as if his mother had dealt a physical blow. After a few tense moments, he dipped his head once in response before turning away from Reeyah. He hastily picked up his travel pack and spear; briefly pausing at the entryway to his personal grotto, he softly whispered, "I'll return soon," before navigating his way out of Overlook Cave.

* * *

"This assignment shouldn't be too difficult," commented Aylex aloud as he and Daylin followed closely behind the Khanzito, their strides long to keep pace as the child raced through the palace. "How old do you wager he is? I cannot tell his age," admitted Aylex as he examined the blue-skinned child.

"I don't think he's that old," replied Daylin with a sideways glance at his brother. "Ey!" he then called out. "Khanzito!"

"Hmm?" replied Wesdin as he looked over his shoulder before stopping. "You called?"

"Aye, Khanzito," returned Daylin as he saluted the future ruler. "How many cycles are you?" he questioned as he halted before the boy.

"I have reached five cycles," said Wesdin, his eyes narrowing cautiously at the seemingly odd question. "Why do you ask?"

"Aylex and me were just wanting to know. You're about the size of a *paahkia*, maybe a tad smaller," he answered while examining Wesdin from head to toe.

"What is a *paah-key-uh?*" inquired Wesdin as he attempted to repeat the strange word.

"*Paahkias* are Weretigal cubs," interjected Aylex. "They are born of both tigal mother and father."

"You mean like my cousins, *Chiefuno* Geodani and *Chiefuna* Laynee?" responded Wesdin as he furrowed his brows, becoming deep in thought. *"Is that why me and Leandra are not as large as Geodani? But we're just as tall as Laynee."*

"Aye, Khanzito Wesdin," answered Aylex as he watched the youth's face transform from interest, to confusion, before registering comprehension. "Just curious. That is all. Shall we continue?" he asked. "Khanzito…" he repeated after a time, his tone louder, as he realized the boy made no response.

"Oy!" exclaimed Wesdin, momentarily startled. "What is it?"

"Shall we continue?" asked Daylin as he lightly patted Wesdin on the back.

"Uh, aye…" returned Wesdin as he shrugged Daylin's hand away, suddenly feeling awkward that he was not a *paahkia* like his cousins. Abruptly, Wesdin spun away from his two personal protectors and hurried toward the chambers his visiting family members occupied.

Skidding to a stop before the chamber door, Wesdin excitedly reached up and began knocking on the wooden panel that prevented his entrance. "Uncle Gel! Aunt Bay!" he shouted, relentlessly pounding on the door.

The jiggling of the handle went unnoticed by Wesdin as he continued fiercely banging.

"Ey!" shouted Laynee as she yanked the door open. "What is wrong?" she demanded hotly, her eyes level with her younger cousin.

"Hail, Layn. Do you and Geo wish to go explore?" Wesdin asked in a rush, his breathing still uneven from his dash through the palace.

"Aye!" squealed Laynee as she clasped her hands together, and she jumped up and down excitedly, her wrath already dissipated. "Ami!

Api!" she shouted over her shoulder from the entryway just as Geodani walked up beside her.

"Ey…" Geodani growled in annoyance as he covered his ear closest to his sister while openly glowering at her.

"Oops," responded Laynee. Grinning apologetically, she shrugged her shoulders simultaneously at her minute-older twin to which Geodani rolled his eyes.

"Move over," he grumbled while nudging his sister aside to see who had arrived. "Hail, cousin," greeted Geodani when he saw Wesdin. Without hesitation, Geodani stepped forward and knocked his right forearm against his cousin's. "Ey!" he then exclaimed as he looked past Wesdin, noticing Aylex and Daylin standing close by. "Commandant Mikela was just asking for you both," he informed the two tigal brothers.

Daylin looked skyward momentarily before casting an irate sideway glance at his brother. *What did you do this time?* he wordlessly demanded of his brother. *I am going to start asking to accompany Novex,* he continued to grouse.

"Very well, *Chiefuno* Geodani," acknowledged Aylex as he took an inconspicuous side-step closer to his brother. Waiting until Geodani turned his attention back to Wesdin, Aylex forcefully jabbed his brother in the side. *I did nothing to upset Commandant Mikela,* Aylex assured Daylin coolly.

"*Nahm-Aztey*, Khanzito Wesdin," greeted Baylay warmly after peeking around the door; gently, she guided her *paahkias* aside. "*Ma-ah-heen ah-ah-pas ba'ad mee-ay'en nep-ah'ut too-oon'ga,*" she murmured quietly while glowering momentarily at her children.

Way to go. Why is it that I always get in trouble when I'm with you? grumbled Geodani, mind-connecting with Laynee as he crossed his arms over his chest and glared at her. He dreaded when his mother used the - *I'll deal with you later* – phrase.

"*Ah-sham oh-lake him,* Aunt Baylay," replied Wesdin which garnered a broad smile in return from Baylay.

"You continue to improve with each passing cycle," replied Baylay with a smile, admiring her nephews earnest attempt to respectfully respond in the Weretigal language.

"Oh, shut up!" returned Laynee silently while her mother was occupied. Before Baylay turned around, Laynee held her hands up to her head with her palms open, and she placed her thumbs against her ears. Simultaneously, she forced herself to look at the tip of her nose, stuck out her tongue, and wiggled the remainder of her fingers.

79

Geodani pulled his lips back, and his eyes narrowed in a silent snarl. Contorting his face, he made an equally ghastly face in return to his sister.

"You are both aware that such behavior is unacceptable of the *Chiefuno* and *Chiefuna*," came a familiarly stern voice, causing the tigal twins to abruptly erase their absurd expressions. "You are both fortunate. Had it been another, you would've disgraced your parents," she continued scolding.

Geodani turned and met the bright sea-blue eyes of Commandant Mikela. He watched as her round pupils became narrow slits, indicating her displeasure. *Gulp.* Geodani forced himself to swallow, aware his mouth had unexpectedly become dry.

Baylay turned to see Laynee with her hands clasped together, apprehensively twirling her thumbs, and staring at the ground. Close by, Geodani stood motionless with his head held high as he accepted the reprimand. Looking farther back, Baylay observed Mikela standing in the middle of the sitting area – the common space in which four separate sleeping chambers shared – with her arms crossed over her chest. With a sigh, Baylay turned her attention back to Wesdin. "And what can I do for you, Wesdin?" she finally asked.

Wesdin, leaning to the side to peek at his cousins, shook his head and rightened himself in response to his aunt's question. "Uh…hmm… uh…" he stammered briefly, unnerved by the intimidating Commandant, before remembering why he had come seeking out his cousins. "Oy, I remember now." he suddenly commented. "Can Geo and Layn join me in exploring?" he asked softly.

Baylay gazed down at Wesdin, and she tried not to chuckle at his trembling bottom lip as he pitifully pouted.

"Pleeeeeeeeeeeease?" continued Wesdin with a wide, ridiculous smile which drew forth a stifled giggle from the Chieftess.

Puckering her lips pensively, Baylay intentionally waited to reply to the Khanzito's request. After a few tense moments, she finally replied, "Very well."

"*Ha-rah!*" exclaimed the three children simultaneously as they sprang upward with delight.

"*Tchah.* Not so fast," said Baylay as she tried to calm the exuberant bunch, but her interjection fell on deaf ears. "*Tchah!*" she repeated herself in a roar, immediately silencing the three cousins. Clearing her throat, Baylay finally said, "You are all going to have to wait until Commandant Mikela is finished speaking with Aylex and Daylin," she informed them while standing to the side and holding out her arm, signaling for Wesdin and his personal protectors to enter.

"Aye, Aunt Baylay," grumbled Wesdin as he walked past her. "We will keep busy," he added as he grabbed the twins, one by each arm, and hurried them to the sleeping chamber they shared.

"I'll be in my sleeping chamber," Baylay informed the remaining trio as they stood silently.

"Very well, Chieftess," came Mikela's quiet response though she remained still. Out of the corner of her eye, Mikela watched as the Chieftess strode across the sitting area to the door - slightly ajar - of the private quarter she shared with the Chief. Mikela waited until Baylay stepped inside and allowed the wooden door to swing shut with a heavy *thud*. Taking a calming breath, Mikela then turned to address her two youngest sons.

* * *

Blub, blub, blub. Oolp. Splish, splash! Blub, blub, blub. Oolp. Splish, splash! Blub, blub, blub. Oolp. Splish, splash!

Taygan, grateful for the burbling and rippling that drowned out her footsteps, cautiously navigated her way in the darkness alongside of the stream that flowed out from the palace courtyard. Twinkling high overhead like gems adorning a black cloth, the stars provided enough light to deceive the eyes; without the illumination from the moon, the fainter starlight gave rise to unsettling shadows. Taygan, increasingly aware that the activity of night creatures had ceased, lowered herself to a crouching position behind a thick bunch of shrubbery. Pausing briefly, she listened for any troublesome sounds before continuing to lower herself until she lay flat on her stomach. Taking an unsteady breath to try and calm her rattled nerves, she then began the uncomfortable slither on her belly toward the front of the bushes.

Blub, blub, blub. Oolp. Spliiiish, splash! Blub, blub, blub. Oolp. Spliiiish, splash! Blub, blub, blub. Oolp. Spliiiish, splash!

The repetitive song of the nearby creek began to lull Lana to sleep as she patiently leaned against a tree and waited. *"Just for a moment,"* she thought silently to herself, and she allowed her heavy eyelids to lower.

Crack!

Lana's eyes abruptly snapped open, and she instantaneously dropped to a crouching position beside the tree; the unnatural absence of animal chirps and cries was deafening as Lana strained to hear or see her mother in the near pitch-black that engulfed her. The unexpected hand that clasped over her mouth caused Lana to tense; the firm grip on her shoulder tightened and prevented her from jumping up or running.

The blue-skinned sentry halted abruptly and inwardly flinched as the fallen branch broke under his weight. Exhaling calmly, he then initiated his ability to see better in the darkness; he squinted his eyes and swiftly scanned the surrounding area. After a few anxious moments, he finally relaxed before turning back around in the direction he had come from. "Anything?" came a whispered voice from a short distance in front of Lana.

"I cannot see a thing!" admitted the female sentinel. As if on cue, Priestess Desmin's foot became ensnared in raised tree roots, causing her to lose her balance. "Oy!" Lawren yelped softly and extended her arms out blindly to brace for the impending fall.

"Shhhh," came the barely audible instruction against Lana's ear to which she wordlessly nodded. Cautiously, Peygar removed his hand from his niece's mouth.

"Nay," murmured Brute Pelar, reaching out to catch and steady Lawren. "But to be honest, even with my ability, I cannot see as clearly as if it were as bright as day," Eethin admitted sourly.

"My thanks," mumbled Lawren as she gingerly pat Eethin's torso, glad to have her face bounce off his brawny chest rather than the ground. "I have heard it is a skill only the Khan possesses," she replied.

"Aye, I've heard the same," returned Eethin as he took a step back from his patrol partner. "Come. They'll be expecting our report," he added as he waited for Lawren to get her footing before heading back toward the rear gate of the city.

After what seemed an eternity, Peygar finally released his hold on his niece. Lana stifled a groan as she stood; her muscles screamed in protest as she stretched, aching from remaining crouched and motionless for an unexpected and prolonged time.

Peygar grunted quietly, his joints popping and crunching, as he placed a hand on his knee and shoved himself back to a standing position. "Les go," he said gruffly while stepping around Lana, excitement for their mission to locate the sleeping chambers of the Khan. Soon, they'd be able to steal several royal items to sell before disappearing to live a more luxurious life.

Lana inhaled slowly, and she glowered at her uncles back. After a moment, she then released her breath in a forceful puff before following after Peygar. Peering over her shoulder with apprehension, Lana kept a nervous watch even though she knew her mother was also close by.

Shriish... Shraash... Shriish... Shraash... Shriish-shraash... Shriish... Shriish-shraash.

Lana listened to the uneven sound of her uncle sawing at the metal bars that prevented their entrance into the palace courtyard. After a time, Lana noticed as Peygar's shadowy frame appeared to reach up and wipe sweat from his face. "Any progress?" whispered Lana.

"No'yet," hissed back Peygar, frustration evident in his voice as he reached out and felt the bar he had tirelessly worked out. "Damn!" he cursed, feeling the bar to learn he had not even cut halfway through.

Lana inhaled and exhaled with extreme focus as her brows furrowed together in irritation and contemplation. Suddenly, Lana closed her amber eyes. *"Now is as good a time as any,"* she wordlessly said to herself. Turning all her concentration to herself, Lana unleashed the power she longed to release. "Rrgh!" she quietly cried as her body began to transform and grow.

Rrriiiiip!

Peygar automatically spun around at the startling sound of cloth shredding to see Lana doubled over in pain; his eyes widened with disbelief as he watched her bones break before fusing back together.

"Ugh!" Lana muttered while throwing her head back, unsuccessfully attempting to mute her cries of agony. Lana inhaled sharply, and she dropped to her knees in the water, blinded by the pain that coursed through her.

Splash! "Whot da…" gawked Peygar as he absentmindedly dropped the saw he held; dread slowly began to spread through him as he stood dumbstruck, observing a pair of ghastly, black, leather-like wings gradually emerge from between his niece's shoulder blades. Reaching up, Peygar rubbed his eyes, certain he was hallucinating.

Lana sank her hands into the muddy stream-bottom and grunted as the last section of her spine sliced through her lower back, sprouting a barbed, whip-like tail. Wincing, she felt her face contort, and her teeth lengthened to form fangs.

"Phew," Lana managed to sigh softly to herself once to the *transformation* was complete. Carefully pushing herself to her feet, she rotated her shoulders and settled her wings against her back. She then cautiously clenched and unclenched her hands to avoid slicing her own hands with her two-inch, razor-blade like nails. After re-familiarizing herself to her monstrous form, she opened her now blood red eyes.

Peygar took an unsteady step back, flabbergasted by what he just witnessed.

"My turn," said Lana as she stepped past her stunned uncle. Placing her hands on two separate bars, she then pulled in opposite directions.

Peygar continued to stare at Lana; wordlessly, he watched her back and shoulder muscles flex and strain against the remaining fabric of her robe. The screeching of bending metal broke through Peygar's trancelike state.

"I'll return soon," murmured Lana as she awkwardly squeezed through the two bars that she managed to pull apart wide enough to allow her passage. Without another word, Lana disappeared into the shrubs on the other side of the hidden gate.

"Whot da hell," Peygar finally managed to say. Frowning, he recalled the vision of his niece standing upright like a person yet possessing bizarre features - ones he had only heard about in stories - before vanishing to execute her quest.

CHAPTER 10

Avenor remained motionless as he hid behind a large, woven-reed, container watching the scene unfold before him. Confusion and fear gripped him as his mother struggled against his grandfather's hold. The sudden appearance of his grandmother as she flung the basket aside startled him. "A bastard and an abomination!" Lukesia seethed. "Look at it! Its soulless eyes!"

"Agh!" cried out Avenor as he bolted upright, the nightmare abruptly waking him. "Oy," he crooned quietly in the dark chamber as he laid back down. "Only a few days more…," he reminded himself as Lukesia's words continued to ring in his mind. Without moving, Avenor silently commanded the shadows; as if the shadows had a mind of their own, they began to swirl and converge together. Avenor listened as the lock clicked before the shutters creaked open; as the night air wafted through the open window, Avenor relinquished his hold of the shadows. Inhaling deeply, Avenor felt the cold air enter his lungs and clear the fog from his mind. "I might as well get up," he grumbled while turning to glance out of the open window, noticing the faint glow that indicated the sun would be rising soon.

Kicking the covers away, Avenor climbed out of bed before picking up his travel pack and set it in the place he just vacated. "I'll have them washed today," said Avenor with a frown as he sifted through his travel pack, noting he was nearly out of clean clothes. Quickly choosing a pair of black, softened, leather leggings and matching boots, Avenor donned them before selecting a simple, red-colored, linen shirt to wear. After slipping the shirt on, Avenor rolled the sleeves up to his elbows and lightly tucked the hem into his breeches. Making his way to the vanity table, he wasted no time in dipping his hands into the bowl of cold water waiting for him and splashing it on his face. Hastily, he washed the sleep from his face before using the hand-towel to dry the remaining water dripping from his chin; grabbing the smallest of brushes in his assortment of toiletries, he quickly scrubbed his teeth clean. Speedily, he pulled a fish-bone comb through his long hair before picking up his nearby crown and setting it on his head. Glancing in the mirror once, Avenor grunted in approval before heading for the door. Without stopping, Avenor grabbed his battle staff and continued out of his sleeping chamber.

* * *

Kenzelo, with one hand at the corner of his mouth, sat quietly twirling a section of his mustache, and he pensively examined the map set out before him. After a moment, he dipped his plume in the container of black ink, and he carefully marked out the smaller towns that the expedition had already visited. Satisfied, he set the plume down before picking up his mug of *koffie*; the scent from his preferred morning beverage lingered in the air. Inhaling deeply, Kenzelo allowed the aroma to titillate his senses, and in a single swig, he gulped down the remainder of the now warm liquid.

Kenzelo tipped his head to the side in response to the creaking of the kitchen door being pushed open, but he did not bother to turn. "Good morn, Your Grace," he murmured quietly as Avenor joined him at the informal table. "Still unable to rest well?" he asked after a moment.

"Mmm," grunted Avenor in response as he leaned his weapon against the table. "It seems no matter how many times I venture to Texicar, the memories never seem to elude me," he admitted woefully as he filled a mug with *koffie* before taking a seat across from Kenzelo. "I'll be grateful when Azelly and Novex arrive so we can begin the extended portion of this expedition."

"The *Sailfish*... does it sail alone?" asked Kenzelo as he leaned back in his seat. Without taking his eyes off the Khan, he watched as Avenor inspected the small, personal loaf of candied bread he had selected.

"Indeed," Avenor replied simply before tearing a piece of candied bread, submerging it in his *koffie,* and then cautiously placing it in his mouth to avoid burning himself.

"If I'm not mistaken," began Kenzelo slowly as he continued to twirl the corner of his mustache, "it takes approximately five days for the *Sailfish* to navigate from Capitalia to Harbola."

"Aye," agreed Avenor with a yawn before hastily finishing his loaf of candied bread and mug of *koffie*. "Much better than the usual three-and-a-half-week voyage," he finished while picking up his battle staff.

"Agreed," replied Kenzelo. "I anticipate General Azelly and Ambassador Novex to arrive no later than evening meal. Training again?" he suddenly asked, nodding his head slightly toward Avenor's weapon.

"Not so much training. It is more of a show of force as I challenge the soldiers to duels," replied Avenor nonchalantly.

Kenzelo grinned. "Indeed. Word has swiftly spread about how the Khan has disgraced even the most battle-seasoned warriors."

Avenor barked a short laugh in return. "Well, maybe with all of the sparring, it will dissuade any further threats of an uprising or disloyalty."

"I'm nearly certain that it will," confided Kenzelo. "With just General Manijor, General Everly, and yourself, most of the complaints from disgruntled citizens have already lessened. The farthest cities and towns will be the ones difficult to manage," he admitted with a frown.

"Indeed. We'll discuss the options once the others arrive," returned Avenor as he continued toward the kitchen's back door leading out of the palace.

"As you desire, Your Grace," replied Kenzelo with a slight dip of his head in acknowledgement before Avenor disappeared through the door only a few moments before his parents entered.

"He is already off to challenge the others?" asked Manijor as he pushed open the kitchen door to find Kenzelo sitting at the table alone.

"There is no need to answer," murmured Everly as she stepped past her husband. "The memories… even I struggle to keep them from assaulting my mind every time we are here," she said with a heavy sigh.

Kenzelo nodded his head slowly. "The others should arrive prior to evening meal. It will allow them time to prepare as we'll depart with the rising sun for the extended travel portion of the excursion," he informed the two Generals to which they both nodded in response.

* * *

"Gah!" exclaimed Dondree as he lost his footing on the loose gravel. "Argh!" he then cried out as his other knee hit the ground, and he unceremoniously began sliding down the steep path leading him farther away from the safety of the oasis. "I made it," Dondree breathed out nervously as the trail became more leveled, and the sand dunes came into his view. Once Dondree came to a halt, he tried to stand but instantly collapsed to his side. "Sssss," he hissed as the searing feeling in his knee announced itself. Looking down hesitantly, he noticed the skin – bloody and raw - from his unexpected decent. "This… can… not… be… good," he managed to stammer out as terror immediately seized him. "Please… please don't let there be any predators close," he whispered fearfully as he crawled to the nearby valley wall.

The sound of Dondree dragging himself along the ground combined with his ragged breathing mingled with the screeching of the wind as it coursed through the gorge. "Damn," he cursed unevenly once he finally managed to lean his back against the solid rock wall. With his chest heaving, he tried to calm his irregular gasping and panting; his attention was soon drawn down to the dark, crimson, blood seeping out from his stronger limb. With a frown, he grabbed a handful of dirt, and he allowed it to sift through his fingers to cover the open wound. "Mmph…" he grunted quietly in discomfort before grabbing another fistful to cover the lower portion of his injured extremity. He briefly inspected his handiwork and exhaled with satisfaction. "At least the bleeding has stopped. Maybe it won't become diseased," he hopefully pondered aloud as he staggered to his feet, using the wall to steady himself. "Keep moving, Boy…" he suddenly snapped harshly to himself, and he refused to waste any more time on his wound. "Now is not the time for fear," he continued scolding himself.

Forcing the pain of his recent injury from his mind, he unsteadily finished making his way toward the entrance of the valley. "At last," he sighed as he leaned heavily against the wall and gazed out at the wastelands; his short-lived sigh of relief was soon replaced with a shocked gasp. His eyes bulged with disbelief before he squeezed them closed tightly; Dondree could not escape the dread that coursed through him, and he finally threw his head back before wailing out.

"Only my fortune!" he sobbed in anguish, suddenly feeling defeated as he saw the sand dunes shifting and rolling. A mixture of fine and coarse gravel particles began whipping about Dondree as he shielded his face from the relentless windstorm; as each gust died down, it was inevitably replaced with another of equal intensity. "Shelter…" he whispered frantically. He quickly scanned the area; the feeling of impending doom continued to rise ever higher as the sky began to darken. "I need to find shelter," he repeated. Just as he felt hope slipping away, he spotted a small crevasse between a pair of boulders. With haste, Dondree crossed the path to the opposite side of the narrowed ravine, and he gingerly dropped to his knees in front of the entrance of the cavity; he managed to awkwardly burrow himself in the tight space, and he shifted to seal most of the opening with his back.

The wind howled as it furiously ripped through the canyon, and it commanded the sand to harshly assault every surface it touched. *"Of course,"* Dondree groused wordlessly to himself as the gales beat against his back mercilessly. *"The hunters never ventured out when the sky became an orange haze above the oasis,"* he suddenly recalled, remembering his mother's comments about becoming blinded and disoriented during violent windstorms. *"Hopefully, it stops soon,"* he continued silently while pulling the linen wrap over his head and tucking his face in the crook of his arm.

"Gugh," groaned Dondree as he shifted his weight uncomfortably after what felt like an eternity. The gales continued to shriek and whistle erratically, rattling his nerves. Pondering his options,

Dondree abruptly snapped his head up. "The elixir!" he uttered, anxiety lacing his voice, as he blindly reached out in the darkness in search of his travel pack. His hands soon settled on the leather pouch, and he shakily unbound the items. Fumbling in the dark, he finally managed to remove the flask. With trembling fingers, he struggled to remove the wooden plug that prevented the contents from spilling out.

Pop!

Immediately after Dondree removed the cork, a fetid stench filled the space he occupied and assaulted his senses. He felt his stomach churn and bile rise in his throat; his breathing became shallow as he tried to ignore the nauseating smell. Dondree raised the container to his lips with an expression of disgust fixed on his face, and he held it there. After a moment, he briskly pulled the tiny flagon away - sloshing the liquid within.

"I… I can't…" he muttered quietly while replacing the stopper. "You must…" he replied to himself as he squeezed his eyes closed. With reality finally dawning on him, he allowed himself the luxury of crying. "I'm going to… d…d… die here… or… or… or I'm going… t… t… to die… out there," he stammered between sobs. With that knowledge, he yanked the cork out of the opening, and void any hesitation, he hastily gulped down the elixir before he lost his burst of courage.

"Argh!" he sputtered, taking ragged breaths through his mouth, still attempting to lessen the rotten taste that lingered on his tongue. "Stay down," he said and swallowed hard as his stomach lurched in revolt. "Stay down," he repeated, feeling beads of sweat sprouting along his hairline as his body fought to expel the putrid concoction. The abrupt sensation of his insides being set ablaze caused the color to drain from his face.

"Gah!" shrieked Dondree, his voice laced with pain, and he soon curled himself tightly in anguish while clutching his stomach. The smoldering feeling rapidly spread throughout his body. His blood-curdling screams were swallowed by the ferocious storm behind him, and he writhed uncontrollably as pangs wracked his body. Forgetting where he was, Dondree vehemently thrashed his head from side to side.

Thwack!

The forceful and unexpected contact of Dondree's forehead with the cobblestone protuberance on the wall of the tiny grotto was enough to knock him unconscious; the following unholy echoes of Dondree's bones breaking and his flesh shredding fell on deaf ears. With a grimace of suffering plastered on his face, he remained motionless and curled in a fetal position; blood trickled out from the gash between his eyebrows, and it gradually formed a pool under his head.

CHAPTER 11

A warm breeze filtered through the trees, and it created gentle rustling sounds as it teased the multitude of branches and leaves. The serene chirping and tweeting of birds mingled with the lively chattering of otters as they played nearby in one of the many streams. The tranquility of the forest was soon disrupted by the *rickety-racketing* of carts and wagons being pulled along the river-rock paved road as the lazy *clop-clot* of zebril hooves striking against stone drowned out the humdrum shuffling of marching soldiers.

"A rider approaches," murmured Major Mykel Chevin upon hearing the faint signal - disguised as the shrill screeches of a disgruntled hawk - of one of the forward reconnaissance scouts. Without delay, he raised his right arm high above his head with his hand clenched in a fist. Avenor immediately followed suit, and he peered over his shoulder to ensure the silent command to *halt* was relayed to those behind him. After a few tense moments, a soldier wearing a sage-green Texicar tabard appeared in the distance.

Ayja leaned forward and rapidly blinked, forcing the tears that blurred her vision to spill from the corners of her eyes. Squinting to prevent them from watering once more from the wind lashing against her face, Ayja gazed ahead at the three different banners clearly displayed. Two, she instantly recognized. The sage-green banners indicated Texicar brethren. One banner, emblazoned with a maroon oak tree, indicated what she already knew; she was approaching members of *Force Oaklan*. The second foliage colored sign was embroidered with a centrally placed, golden-colored, single letter *"O"* and matching borders - indicating that the Overseer traveled alongside *Force Oaklan*.

"Oy!" exclaimed Ayja as realization finally dawned on her regarding the third banner. The final pennant, hoisted higher than the other two, displayed a single, neatly stitched, silverish-tinted crown with same shade of trim in the black fabric. "It is supposed to be *damiund*," murmured Ayja in awe of the material that appeared to shimmer in the sunlight, aware she was viewing the Khan's banner in person for the first time. "Different," she spoke to herself as she drew closer to the formation, and she noticed the Khan's flag was not solid. The fabric contained sporadic cerulean colored lines, reminding her of black marble with blue veins.

Avenor watched as the scout mechanically guided her mount in his direction, instinctively drawn toward the lavishly crafted headpiece indicating his position as Khan.

"Hail, Khan Crusendir," she greeted breathlessly as she pulled back on the reigns of her mount, bringing the zebril to a stop. Without hesitation, the soldier raised her right arm in salute, and she patiently waited until Avenor returned her salute before allowing her eyes to shift to Kenzelo. "Overseer Ozulben," she rasped out before finally turning to address Mykel.

"Major Chevin," she then said as her gaze snapped to her commander.

"Sergeant Rysik," responded Mykel gruffly, saluting the soldier in return. "What news do you bring?" he demanded while lowering his arm. His eyes narrowed with apprehension.

"It is as Overseer Ozulben has feared," replied Ayja as her mount nervously stamped the ground with his hoof. "Former Major Lanikeel…" Ayja gulped nervously - an action that did not go unnoticed by Avenor - before continuing, "no longer flies *Force Birchlan* banners," recalling her initial confusion caused by their lack of similar tabards. It was because of her tiny beast -Kalam, a pygmy Lorisidae – that she discovered remnants of the shredded tabards; the scraps had been identifiable by the broad, white, vertical stripes marred with uneven, horizontal black slashes that resembling the peeling bark of birch trees.

"How long have you known?" interrupted Avenor as he cast a sideways glance at the Aggressor Paladin riding beside him.

"Since last season, Your Grace," Mykel replied bluntly in response without taking his gaze off the trail and nearby forest; a deep crease gradually formed between his brows as he continued shifting his gaze from side to side of the road.

"Major Chevin announced his concerns without delay," interjected Kenzelo from his position guiding the first wagon behind Avenor and Mykel, drawing the attention of both men leading the expedition. "It is he who first realized the shipments of goods from Fairwood had begun to diminish," he added while twirling the corner of his mustache anxiously.

"I see... and you then relayed the message," returned Avenor as he acknowledged receipt of Kenzelo's previous transcription, drawing forth a nod from the Overseer.

"We attempted to extinguish the threat previously, but we were not prepared for the battle," admitted Kenzelo with a scowl.

"Indeed," grunted Mykel as his lips turned down with displeasure. "However, Sergeant Rysik..." said Mykel before pausing to address the rider, "fall-in with the others," he instructed Ayja curtly. "She has unfortunately confirmed my suspicions," he continued while harshly running a hand down his face. "Former Major of *Force Birchlan*, Rozalin Lanikeel... she has been preparing for at least three seasons, possibly well over a cycle now." He expelled his breath forcefully.

"Major Azriel Tamlin is commander of *Force Pinelan*. She and Major Chevin have had to spread their units dangerously thin to provide security to the whole of Texicar," admitted Kenzelo, his expression mirroring the apprehension that rolled off him in waves.

Manijor guided his mount closer to the wood line which allowed him to see toward the beginning of the formation. He dipped his head in acknowledgement to a female rider, adorned with an overcoat representing *Force Oaklan;* once she passed him, Manijor returned his attention back to the front. He shifted in his saddle uncomfortably, keenly aware they had remained at a standstill for a lengthy period; the uneasy feeling that had settled in his stomach made him physically tense. Assigned to the middle of the gaggle, he and Everly provided central support while Avenor lead from the front; Azelly with Leander secured the rear of the group. Glancing slightly over his shoulder, his black eyes collided with the emerald, green ones of Everly. A scowl contorted Manijor's expression, and he watched as her eyes darkened – using her Trapper ability of enhanced hearing - as she intently concentrated on their surroundings. The eerie stillness that gradually seemed to engulf them caused waves of apprehension to ripple throughout the troops. Without warning, a spine-stiffening shrill pierced through the silence.

* * *

Invoking his ability, the enormous beast appeared to merge with the surroundings before disappearing completely. Hidden from sight, he quietly stalked through the forest in pursuit of a vaguely familiar scent; it was one that he felt acquainted with, but at the same time, he was sure he had never smelt it before. The invisible creature lifted and settled his paws cautiously, advancing toward the curious scent while taking care not to disrupt the fallen leaves.

"Decay." The thought abruptly invaded Novex's mind. Breathing deeply though his nose, Novex felt his whiskers twitch as the

unmistakable smell of decomposing flesh assaulted his senses, bringing him to a stop mid-stride. Instantly, he flattened his ears back against his head; without a thought, his heckles raised from his neck down to the tip of his tail. He felt his lips draw back, exposing his immense fangs as a quiet rumble began reverberating in his chest. Forcing himself to take a calming breath, Novex managed to still the ominous snarl that threatened to erupt. *"There is more."* Novex flicked his tail from side to side as he felt his muscles ripple anxiously with anticipation. Instinctively, he flexed his paws and protracted his claws.

"Sickly sweet," he wordlessly said to himself in confusion as he absentmindedly crouched lower, feeling the blades of grass lightly graze his underbelly. The closer he advanced, the more his thoughts became increasingly clouded by a faint droning he failed to recognize. After a time, the continuous whirring became apparent to Novex. *"Oy! What is that humming?"* he grumbled to himself while vigorously shaking his head from side to side. As quickly as the question formed in Novex's mind, it was gone, replaced by a bone-chilling shriek that temporarily froze him in place.

* * *

Humidity thickened the air from the night's heavy downpour, and it made the usually tolerable warmth become nearly unbearable. Sweat profusely poured down the faces of the three unfortunate family members that the bandits had stumbled upon. The woman, standing between her husband and son, shed silent tears as she clung to her husband.

"What do you want from us?" demanded Steel as he took an aggressive step toward the intruders while tenderly placing his parents behind him.

"Nah uh-uh," came Akeenah's amused response as she expertly released a throwing dagger at the man's feet, effectively halting his approach. "It is much better to obey than resist," she continued sweetly.

"We will not!" snapped Kain as he peeked around his son, and he openly glowered at the Armament Trapper languidly leaning against the fence that enclosed their small farm.

"Is that so?" sneered another of the bandits as he forcefully separated the couple.

"No!" shouted Leylah as she felt rough hands grab her shoulders and tear her from her husband's protective embrace.

"Leylah!" cried out Kain as he reached for his wife.

"Api! No!" called out Steel as he spun around and grabbed his father, catching the glint of the knife held up to his mother's throat.

"Bring her here, Shane," came the melodic voice of the Trapper that appeared to be in charge.

"Aye, Akeenah," replied Shane as he dragged Leylah – wailing and thrashing – away from her husband and son.

"On your knees, my dear," said Akeenah as she met Leylah's fearful gaze.

"No!" responded Leylah defiantly before spitting a globule of phlegm in Akeenah's face.

"Well then," said Akeenah with a chuckle as she wiped the spittle from her face and flung it aside. "That's settled," she finished before making a signal with her hand. Immediately, a larger group emerged from the forest and restrained the two men while Akeenah harshly grabbed a fistful of Leylah's hair and yanked her to the side. "As I said, it would have been better to obey," she whispered against the fearful woman's ear.

"Let her go!" hollered Kain as he watched Akeenah forcefully bring a knee up to Leylah's stomach. "Stop!" he continued shouting as Leylah crumpled to the ground before receiving a kick to the face. His worried gaze snapped to Akeenah's. The daunting grin that spread across Akeenah's face sent a shiver down Kain's back.

"Ami!" Steel shouted as he fought wildly against the multiple thugs that held him restrained. His struggling ceased temporarily as he felt a metal collar fastened around his neck. "Argh!" he grunted as he pulled with all his might.

Akeenah lowered herself to a squatting position beside Leylah's limp form; carefully, Akeenah picked up one of Leylah's hands and examined her slender fingers. Without hesitation, she reached behind her back, removed a leather wrapped kit, and set it down beside her. Her cruel eyes met the terrified ones of her defenseless object as she untied her tools singlehandedly. Tightening her grasp on Leylah's hand, she felt her grin broaden to a malicious smile as she watched Leylah's expression change from fear, to curiosity, to realization right before horror became permanently etched on her face.

"No! Please don't!" cried Leylah as she squeezed her eyes shut and began tugging her arm, trying to free her extremity from Akeenah. "Oof!" grunted Leylah as a sudden weight settled over her. Opening her eyes frantically, she looked up only to realize Akeenah was now straddling her chest, effectively pinning her to the ground.

"It is too late now, my dear," replied Akeenah with a pout. "Rozalin is not known for her kindness," she informed Leylah while selecting one of her woodworking tools. "Do you know what this is?" asked Akeenah as she held up the item for Leylah to see.

"A... a... gimlet," came Leylah's shaky reply as she eyed the device, recognizing it as a handheld tool like the one Steel used for drilling small holes.

"Excellent!" replied Akeenah cheerfully as she grabbed Leylah's hand again firmly before continuing. "So, you're familiar with it?" she asked and waited until Leylah hesitantly nodded her head. "Perfect!" Akeenah squealed with delight. "Unfortunately," she said and purposely allowed her voice to trail off as she brought Leylah's hand to her chest and held it firmly in place. "I will be using it to drill a hole through your finger right here," she informed her captive as she placed the sharpened tip at the base of her thumb nail.

Tears began streaming down Leylah's face as she sensed the viciousness simmering beneath the surface of Akeenah's demented gentleness. "I'll... I'll be... g... g... good. I... pr... promise... to... obey," she whispered between sobs.

"Tsk-tsk, my dear," replied Akeenah, "weakness is also frowned upon." Scowling with distaste, Akeenah shrugged her shoulders. "Once I've drilled the hole, I will remove the nail. I'll do it for every one of your fingers," she announced calmly with an inconspicuous dip of her head to someone nearby which went unnoticed by Leylah.

Leylah frowned, suddenly feeling someone tugging her boots off; terror spurred her to action, and Leylah began wildly kicking her feet.

"Ah, that is Katena. After your fingers, I'll move to your toes," Akeenah added with a warm smile as she tightened her hold into a vice-like grip on Leylah's hand. "Shall we begin?" she asked. Without waiting for a response, Akeenah expertly shoved the gimlet through Leylah's digit, eliciting an ear-splitting scream.

CHAPTER 12

Taleena sailed high above the mass of travelers below her; periodically, she glanced down to catch a glimpse of her handler. With her red-tipped wings outstretched, she was clearly at ease gracefully soaring through the sky. Her natural speed whipped the clouds about while her keen eyesight allowed her to spot the smallest of animals nearly two miles in the distance.

"She is beautiful," murmured Iriva as she watched the magnificent bird of prey dive toward the group before sweeping upward, a lowland hare clutched in her talons.

"Indeed," agreed Betaro as he adjusted his weight in the saddle to look over at the Trapper traveling beside him. "How long have you had her, Captain Wentworth?" he casually asked.

"Since she was a new babe," replied Jaquel with a frown. "I found her, still covered in white down, expelled from her nest as I visited Serenity Springs," he said as his frown deepened. "I concluded poachers captured her parents but failed to realize there were hatchlings. I didn't find any others, nor was I aware that she was one of the rarest falcons."

"Clearly a red-tipped falcon," replied Betaro as he had remembered admiring the fiery-red ends of the bird's feathers.

"Aye," said Jaquel with a curt nod. "They can live nearly three times as long as other raptor type birds," he continued as the small group watched the bird settle on the branch of a nearby tree.

"Oy!" exclaimed Iriva. "Other raptors live between, what?" she paused briefly as she tapped her chin thoughtfully. "Between... twelve and fifteen cycles!"

Jaquel chuckled softly as he nodded his head once more. "Aye, General Jander. Taleena will be twenty cycles at the end of the season," he added proudly.

"She has served you well over the cycles," commented Overseer Mulbin with a smile as she guided her zebril alongside the others. "It is exceedingly rare for orphan falcons to survive, much less thrive, as Taleena has."

"Aye, she has," murmured Jaquel with another smile as he watched Taleena consuming the hare she had procured. As if on cue, Taleena tipped her head to the side as she observed something in the distance; without hesitation, she dropped the carcass, spread her wings, and launched herself into the air. Within moments, she released an ear-splitting screech. Jaquel closed his eyes, and he activated his Trapper ability to see through Taleena's eyes. "She has identified the concealed path," he then announced.

* * *

"We'll form a perimeter roughly a mile out from the path," Jaquel began informing his troops while the visiting Generals and Juldeyah stood back; the three senior leaders quietly listened, and they only interjected when needed to clarify details or answer questions. "The trail is camouflaged well," he said while drawing out the plan in the dirt.

"Meaning… any traveler this far out likely has knowledge of it," said Juldeyah sternly.

"Indeed, Overseer Mulbin" agreed Jaquel with a brief nod at Juldeyah before continuing. "Sedwin is the only known village in this area of Itagrio. And this is not the trail that leads there. Our mission is to capture one of these *raiders* for interrogation," he finished while dusting his hands off on his leather breeches.

"Why don't we just attack?" asked one of the soldiers standing near the back of the group.

"Because we would be blindly advancing in known enemy territory," answered Betaro impassively. His voice had unexpectedly become void of emotion as he became lost in his memories; with an ache in his heart, his thoughts drifted to a time, cycles ago, when he had agreed to banish a child to the infrequently visited fishing village.

"It is likely they have already established watch posts," added Iriva in response to the additional questions, sending a curious look in Betaro's direction as he had fallen quiet. "Depending on what information we gather will determine if we strike or just allow the *raiders* to exist away from the other towns and villages."

"If we decide to allow the *raiders* to exist, then the nearby towns and villages will be fortified in hopes it will dissuade future incidents," added Juldeyah in response to the confused expressions of the soldiers which garnered a verbalized chorus of understanding.

Jaquel signaled his patrol leaders, beckoning them to approach. "You four will be positioned here," he informed them. "Fifth patrol will remain with Overseer Mulbin, the visiting Generals, and myself." After answering last minute questions and concerns, Jaquel released his leaders to take command of their respective patrols. Once in place, the complete Unit silently waited for Taleena's signal as she calmly soared through the sky.

* * *

Peygar sat at a distance away from the encampment munching on an apple; hidden in the shadows cast by the nearby trees, he patiently waited for Lana to leave the safety of their unsteady tent. It had been just over two weeks since her bizarre transformation, and he planned to finally get some answers. The fluttering of the flap covering the entryway drew his attention, and he watched as his niece stepped out from the flimsy structure. Peygar raised the fruit to his mouth and took one last bite before tossing the remainder aside; shoving himself to his feet, he then wiped the juice from his lips with the back of his hand before heading inside.

"Peygar!" gasped Taygan, her head snapping up, as light unexpectedly spilled in from the doorway. "What are you doing? You should be out gathering supplies," she chided her brother before returning to her task of mending broken fishing nets.

"No, whot I need ta be doin' is findin' out whot da *puq* is she?" he responded quietly.

"She is your niece," replied Taygan without raising her eyes although she could feel Peygar's eyes bearing down on her.

"Whot else?" demanded Peygar quietly, his anger slowly being fanned to life at his sister's evasive answers.

"There is nothing else," answered Taygan nonchalantly.

Peygar watched Taygan as she raised a single shoulder before dropping it casually. Instantly, he felt his slow growing fury erupt into a wildfire of rage. Without warning, he stormed across the short distance to Taygan; reaching down, he grasped her linen tunic and harshly snatched her off the ground.

"Eep!" squealed Taygan in surprise. "Peygar! Stop! You're hurting me," she then cried out as she struggled against her brother's vice-like grip.

"This is yer last chance…" he warned, his voice ominous. Peygar watched as Taygan tried hard to swallow, her mouth suddenly dry, as he moved one hand to her throat and tightened his hold. "Well?" he asked and arched a single eyebrow while continuing to squeeze harder.

"Wobla…" croaked out Taygan as her eyes rolled back in her head, and her chest began to burn from lack of oxygen.

"Whot?" asked Peygar as his mouth dropped open, and he distractedly dropped Taygan.

Crumpling to the ground, Taygan hungrily gasped in shaky breaths, trying to squelch the fire burning in her lungs. "Wobla…" she said again, this time her voice harsh, before lifting her head to glower up at her brother. "She is Wobla's daughter…" she admitted while wiping the spittle from her chin and scooting back away from Peygar.

"Whot do you mean Wobla's spawn?" he suddenly demanded once the words finally registered, taking a threatening step toward his sister.

"Wobla was with child when he nearly killed her," answered Taygan honestly, knowing if she lied, her brother would undoubtedly sever her head from her shoulders without remorse. "He… Wobla… hadn't died… not right away… made promise… Kifta helped… kept barely alive… take out spawn… raised… my daughter," stammered Taygan, her mind racing clearly but the words spilling forth as gibberish.

Peygar frowned as he listened to Taygan's garbled confession; through his own recollection, he managed to piece together Taygan's recount of the events. "Wobla…" he said, his voice catching as he fisted his hands tightly at his side. "Dat coward!" seethed Peygar as he recalled how the former *Troll* chief forcibly claimed Wobla as his mate. "She was ta be my mate!" he growled out between clenched teeth. After a few moments of tense silence, Taygan noticed Peygar's expression change. "Den dat makes her Wobla…" Peygar choked on Lana's name, suddenly aware that the first part was in memory of her mother. "Woblana *Blutdrache, Regina der Drachen…*" he whispered in awed disbelief.

Taygan crinkled her nose in curiosity as she openly gaped at her brother. "What madness are you blabbing on about now?" she suddenly demanded, recognizing the sinister look slowly transforming Peygar's face.

* * *

Lighthearted chuckling floated on the afternoon breeze from the veranda just off the Dining Hall, and it created a welcoming contrast to the robust chortling and excitable squeals of playful youths. Bustling with energy from their afternoon meal, the children romped about in the quadrangle – a large, secured, open-air, section within the palace walls. With each gust of wind, the changing greenery of the trees, began losing their grip on the branch that once held them steady.

Cshhh! Cshhh! Cshhh!

Wesdin sprinted through a freshly raked pile of fallen foliage, and it erupted into a flurry of cascading leaves. "Huh-hah!" he shouted as he purposefully kicked at the heap of debris, trying to launch the contents as high as possible.

"Oy!" squeaked Laynee before giggling as she darted toward Wesdin. Not looking to collide with her cousin, she skirted just past him with her arms raised as she tried to catch the settling burnt-reddish and golden leaves.

Leandra stood at a distance, a look of concentration plastered on her face, with her arms outstretched before her. *"I command thee… fri-gee-doh…pequen-ito… tor-bay-yeeno!"* she whispered fervently. A small cyclone began to form, and Leandra radiated with pride before continuing to focus on the small, ice-cold, whirlwind she had created.

"Oy!" hollered Wesdin as he felt a shiver go down his spine; his hair began whipping about his face right before he noticed Leandra's mistral approaching him. Scampering a few feet further away, he then began his own incantation.

Geodani instantly sensed the change in the atmosphere, and he began searching the area frantically. His eyes landed on Leandra; he quietly observed her and noticed her mouthing something softly. The sudden chill that filled the air before the appearance of a tiny tornado stunned him briefly. Without another thought, he rotated his shoulders before lowering himself to a slight squatting position. In an instant, Geodani felt as if his body exploded into a puff of white powder before re-congealing.

The unexpected *poof* sound captured the attention of the nearby adults seated under the veranda.

"Ey-hey!" exclaimed Gelriz with delight as he began clapping wholeheartedly. "Well done, Geo! You've learned to control the *transformation!*" he called, his voice ringing with fatherly pride.

Geodani forcefully shook his tigal form, starting from his head down to his tail. The unintentional overuse of his strength caused him to topple over, and the action garnered an amused chuckle from his father.

"That's my boy!" sang out Baylay, her voice filled with approval to which Geodani happily chuffed in response.

Turning back to his playmates, Geodani re-focused his attention on Leandra. Lowering himself, he began the difficult task of sneaking up on the young Wizard.

"Oy!" Galhix absentmindedly exclaimed wordlessly to the others, her voice penetrating their thoughts through the common mind-link bond shared among tigals. *"He stalks Leandra!"* she continued lightheartedly. As if on cue, the entire group turned to watch the scene unfold.

Valcaly, unaware of the mute conversation, followed suite and turned in the same direction as the others.

From the corner of her eye, Laynee glimpsed a familiar black tigal with dark grey socks reaching just below the bend of his ankles and wrists, stalking toward Leandra. A mischievous grin slowly spread across her face. Without difficulty, Laynee initiated her *transformation,* and she felt herself burst into tiny silverish flecks before rejoining. To avoid detection, she quickly blended with her surroundings, knowing the other tigals could see her if they were aware of her presence and focused on her form.

"I summon thee…" began Wesdin as he held his arms out to his sides though slightly in front of him with his palms turned upward. Closing his fists tightly, he then pulled his arms in as if drawing an invisible force toward himself. To the untrained eye, it appeared the shadows moved because the branches swayed, when in truth they responded to Wesdin's command. "Go to her…" he whispered quietly and watched as the shadows crept along the ground toward Leandra.

Geodani grinned to himself as he reached Leandra, and he lowered himself closer to the ground in preparation to pounce on his unsuspecting victim.

Having mastered the *transformation* nearly a fortnight prior, Laynee effortlessly controlled her movements and slinked across the quadrangle. Trying to stifle her giggle, Laynee purposefully waited until she knew her brother was about to attack.

"Oy!" shrieked Leandra as she sensed something slithering around her body. "What is this?" she demanded hotly as her arms were pinned against her sides and she was effectively bound from moving.

"Twirl!" yelled out Wesdin as he rotated his fists, pointing them vertically - though in opposite directions- and began making motions as if twirling the air. Wesdin burst out laughing as Leandra began screaming as his shadows spun her in a circle. "Stop!" he then commanded and began cackling uncontrollably as Leandra fell to the ground in a dizzy heap.

Geodani faltered as Leandra toppled over, but he was unable to stop himself as he pushed off the ground.

Laynee timed her actions and propelled herself forward just after her brother; her execution was perfect, and she soared across the short distance. *Thud!*

Geodani released a surly, cat-like groan at the unsuspected impact in his side as Laynee crashed into him. Her force sent him sprawling away from Leandra, and he landed clumsily on his back. Geodani shot an angry scowl at his sister's black tigal, now sitting on his chest and looking down at him. He watched as she raised one of her paws.

"Too slow, Geo," she silently taunted before playfully swatting Geodani on the nose with her silver tipped feline fingers.

"Oy!" exclaimed Valcaly as she and the others began applauding the mini skirmish. "Well done!" she praised, along with the others, the children for their display of mastering different aspects of their abilities.

Leandra pushed herself to her feet and dusted off her robe; abruptly, she spun around to find two unfamiliar black tigal cubs, growling and hissing at one another. *"Geo? Layn?"* she asked curiously through the common telepathy link.

Laynee turned and met Leandra's light brown eyes with her sapphire blue ones.

"Aye," replied Laynee with a swish of her silver-tipped tail.

"Aye," grumbled Geodani as he shoved his sister off his chest.

Leandra noticed how their blue eyes matched the Chief's. *"Very pretty colors,"* she admitted with a broad smile.

"Ey!" exclaimed Laynee, her ears twitching excitedly as she realized Leandra was speaking telepathically. *"You have transformed?* "she asked eagerly more as a statement.

"Aye..." answered Leandra slowly. *"I haven't learned to control it though,"* she admitted with a frown.

"Try now!" encouraged Laynee as she began bouncing up and down in place, unable to contain her delight.

Nodding her head, Leandra closed her eyes and focused on her feline shape. In her mind, she visualized herself morphing into her cat form. Leandra's eyes snapped open as another roar of merriment erupted from the grown onlookers.

"You did it!" gushed Laynee cheerfully as she pranced around her friend, admiring her tan fur.

"Leandra!" cried out Valcaly as she rushed across the yard to the cub. "Look at you!" she exclaimed as she examined the large animal. "Your Ami and Api will be thrilled!" she informed the girl with a broad smile. "But that doesn't mean you give Trittni any trouble now, or she'll have your hide..." she cautioned sternly before softening her warning with another smile.

Wesdin's joy vanished as he watched his cousins and friend willingly transform before his eyes. *"I haven't even transformed..."* he said to himself woefully. *"I don't think I ever will..."* he continued. With one last look at the grownups - now standing around his companions – complimenting the others, Wesdin dropped his head in defeat and hastened back into the castle, momentarily forgotten by everyone.

CHAPTER 13

Peygar paced back and forth, taking three strides before being forced to turn back around in the limited space of the shelter he shared with his sister and niece. Clenching and unclenching his hands, he mumbled under his breath as Taygan watched him with a scowl plastered on her face.

"The day has ended for erudition. She'll return soon," said Taygan as she watched her brother impatiently walking to-and-fro, flatting a section of grass along the far wall of their makeshift home. At that exact moment, Lana pushed aside the flap that covered the entrance and stepped inside over the threshold. "See?" said Taygan with a smirk on her face as she tilted her head to the side, as if to say, *I told you so.*

"See what?" asked Lana, arching an eyebrow as she looked from her mother to her uncle and back again.

"Your uncle has something to discuss with us," replied Taygan slowly, still unsure of what had her brother so agitated to begin with.

"I can'no read. So, here," he said while pulling a rolled-up scroll from his tunic and holding it out for his niece to take.

Lana made a face of revulsion at her uncle while taking the scroll from him. As her hand closed around the item, she realized it was not a normal parchment scroll, but a document written on some sort of cloth to preserve the contents for an extended period.

"I sort'a know whot it says because Gulroq boasted 'bout it. I thot he was stupid. Turns out, he was tellin' the truth dis entire time." Peygar finished with a snort. "I have a plan tho," he then declared, his eyes sparkling fiendishly as he waited for Lana to read the inscriptions.

Entry 1: I was foraging with Gelriz and Galhix today when I saw some men riding up to our cozy home. They were mounted and looked like soldiers. Mother looked fearful and father looked angry. I only saw them from a distance, so I couldn't hear what they said. But it looked like father sent them away because he raised his arm and pointed back in the direction from where they came.

That evening I asked about it, but father just glared at me and said to never bring it up again. It was the first time he had ever raised his voice at me.

        Entry 2: Ever since those men came, mother and father have been acting strange. Last night, I woke up because it sounded like they were fighting. I pressed my ear against the door to the room I shared with my little brother and sister so I could hear better. I overheard mother and father talking about going home. I was confused because I thought this was our home. I kept on listening. I heard father say the King demanded he return to 'Burg der Drachen.' Father and mother taught me some of their native tongue, so I understood. But why would the King demand father return to the Castle of Dragons?

        Entry 3: Father and mother have been fighting more frequently. Gelriz and Galhix don't seem to notice. From all the arguing, I have been able to piece things together. The King and Queen are my grandparents. My father – Prince Klaus – is the firstborn male. Princess Hannah, my aunt, is the firstborn female. My father betrayed his family for love. He betrayed them for my mother, a slave, given to them from their allies – the Barbarians- as a gift. Father also did something despicable. But he can't bring himself to tell mother what it was.

        Entry 4: He admitted it! Father finally broke down! I had come back because I forgot my water flask. Before I opened the door, I heard father crying and mother consoling him. He stole something called 'the source' from Princess Hannah. Half was in his blood and half in the firstborn daughter's blood of the King and Queen. Father said he received a notice from his parents. His mother was most upset. He said his parents claimed he left Hannah mute and bedridden by forcefully taking 'the source' from her. Mother asked the questions I had. What was 'the source' and why was it so important? Father had laughed, but it was without humor. He said the Dragons were responsible for maintaining balance in nature. The Dragons were ruled by siblings – the first son and daughter born to the King and Queen. The first child, no matter if a boy or girl, would ultimately become the Alpha Dragon. Once that child married, he or she would then become King or Queen. The second child would become the Beta Dragon, the second in command, and be the one to take over if the Alpha were slain before an heir was born. Once he or she married, they would eventually become the Duke or Duchess. Mother must have been confused because father kept explaining. If the King and Queen did not have a child of the opposite gender, then the Queen could grant another to be the second carrier of 'the source.' If the Alpha ever tried to disrupt the balance of nature, the Beta could call on the Drachenian bloodline and become as powerful as the Alpha to overthrow him or her. It was how the Dragons prevented the firstborn from ever becoming powerful enough to disrupt the balance of nature. But father had stolen 'the source' from his sister by using knowledge he had gained from the Drachen Tome – the ancient tome that contained all the information about the Blood Dragons, 'the source,' how to remove it and grant it to another, and other relevant Dragon knowledge. Since father had taken 'the source' from his sister, he was not just the Alpha, he now possessed 'the Beta source' also.

104

Entry Five: We're finally settled again. Father and mother made us move even farther away from others to the Outskirts. I couldn't even imagine why we had to move so far away. Not until I overheard mother ask what would happen to us. Father wasn't sure. Since he had already married mother and had me, Gelriz and Galhix, he should have been crowned King with 'the source' having been transferred to me and Galhix. But mother was a slave, and grandfather would have never allowed father to marry her. Father feared that grandfather would come for us one day, to remove 'the source' from us bastards.

Entry Six: I've reached my eighteenth cycle. It doesn't matter though. Every cycle comes and goes without anyone noticing... At least that is what I thought. Mother and Father just handed me a tome. It looks rather old. The red leather cover is dry and cracked. It doesn't even look like the spine can hold the pages anymore. Interesting, it isn't just on parchment though. It looks like the inscriptions are on silk cloth... Ha! I just read my old entries... 'The source.' Ha! Mother and father have never mentioned anything about it to me or my siblings. I remember cycles ago when father had said the Dragons kept nature in balance. I'm not sure if it matters or not, but the water has stopped flowing as much. The land seems to be starving, or at least dying of thirst... Unbelievable! Mother and father gave me the Drachen Tome! Father said it was an entertaining relic he bought from a pickpocket. I don't know if father is lying, if he's had it this entire time, or where he got it from. I know he won't tell me about the Dragons on his own. But maybe... I can find my answers without him telling me. I don't know if it has anything to do with 'the source.' I have a feeling that the land dying and 'the source' being stollen could be the reason for such a drastic change. It's just a guess. I doubt I'll ever really know for sure.

Lana finished reading the final entry before rolling the scroll back up. Refusing to raise her eyes to her uncles, she stood there silently and tried to process the information. After what felt like an eternity, she tossed the information to her mother to read.

"Whot do ya thin' 'bout that?" Peygar asked with a sinister grin on his face.

"I think you're stupid," retorted Lana with a flip of her hair before flopping down on the mat next to her mother. "I'm tired, uncle. I do not feel like dealing with your nonsense," she finished curtly.

"Why you..." began Peygar, his voice full of rage as he took a threatening step toward Lana.

"Peygar!" said Taygan, her voice low and stern. "Gulroq mentioned having the *Drachen Tome*. Do you have it?" she then asked curiously.

Peygar glanced at his niece, hatred burning in his eyes, before he turned his attention back to his sister. Scoffing, he quickly crossed the area to a wooden trunk with his personal possessions. After rummaging around, he finally withdrew an item in a leather wrap. He then took the item and held it out to his sister to take who then passed it to Lana.

Lana laughed sarcastically before accepting the leather wrapped object. "You truly expect me to believe this is the **ancient tome** of the Dragons?" she asked, her voice incredulous.

Peygar shrugged one shoulder nonchalantly before crossing his arms over his chest. "It would make you Woblana *Blutdrache, Regina der Drachen* – Queen of Dragons," he said with a greedy glint in his eyes.

Lana frowned before arching a brow skeptically. "According to those," she began while pointing at the scrolls in her mother's hands, "that would mean I would have to rule with another."

"Not if ya steal 'tha source' from yar aunt," returned Peygar as a sinister smile slowly spread across his face.

* * *

Everly felt the hair at the nape of her neck stand on end, and she instantaneously nudged her mount with her heels while making a clicking sound with her tongue. The zebril responded without delay and carried Everly across the short expanse to join Manijor.

"Shall we?" grunted Manijor as his eyes momentarily met those of his wife before his attention was drawn toward the rear of the group at the sound of approaching zebrils. "It appears Azelly and Major Swiftpaw feel the same," added Manijor as he tugged on his mount's reins. Without waiting another moment, Manijor and Everly lightly struck their mounts, encouraging them into a gallop.

Azelly and Leander encouraged their zebrils to run directly behind Manijor and Everly; the quartet wordlessly approached their Khan. Manijor guided his mount to one side of the Khan; Everly directed her steed opposite of her husband while the other pair rode past the front of the formation. Azelly made a hand gesture at Leander, silently signaling him to stop.

"We'll go ahead. Make haste with the troop," Avenor finished instructing Mykel and Kenzelo. He then turned to his parents. "General Akeenil, take point," he instructed his mother.

"As you command, Your Grace," responded Everly with a salute. Needing no further orders, Everly prodded her mount to action.

Azelly watched the expert tracker thundering down the path followed closely by Manijor and Avenor. Azelly quickly shot a glance at her mate, and she made another silent signal to which he nodded in response.

Leander waited until the trio passed him before urging his steed to follow suit; he then peered over his shoulder to ensure Azelly joined as well, providing rear security for the small party.

106

* * *

The nearby woodlands had fallen quiet, and the uneasy stillness enveloped Novex as he sprinted through the dense thicket and trees; with his claws protracted, he gripped the earth and propelled himself faster with each stride. Novex veered toward the agonized wails as they pierced through the silence.

"Just toss 'em," whispered on the wind, teasing Novex's ears. Frowning, he slowed his pace. His ears flattened back against his head, and his lips curled back in a noiseless snarl. The aggravating whirring sound had become nearly deafening as Novex noticed a clearing in the forest.

"But Rozalin..." said a man, his voice - whiny sounding as it waivered, before being interrupted by another gruff voice.

"Oh, shut up, Lorance! We've enough food already from their livestock!" came the annoyed brusque reply.

Novex effortlessly climbed the trunk of a nearby tree and vaulted through the branches until he could see the clearing. Immediately, he felt his stomach lurch at the sight before him. A ravine – approximately fifteen feet deep and nearly three times as wide - had been dug, and it was full of corpses in various stages of decay. Novex finally recognized the whirring sound of countless flies as they swarmed the pit of death.

"Now help me unload them... unless you want to carry them back to camp yourself," finished a burly individual, clearly the owner of the deeper voice, as he uncovered the back of a wagon.

"But Axsel, can't they be used to feed the beasts?" questioned Lorance - a tall, lanky man with beady eyes.

Novex tensed as he observed Axsel drag a lifeless body from the cart and hoist it over his shoulder.

"Ugh," grunted Axsel under the weight of the dead man before turning to glower at his partner. "If Akeenah felt the need to keep these two, she would have told us. And if Rozalin desires it, we will come back and retrieve the corpses," he then snapped.

"Very well," sighed Lorance as he reached in the back of the wagon and began tugging a second body out.

Without a second thought, Novex cautiously jumped from tree to tree until he was at the edge of the clearing; he then quickly pounced down from the tree, landing noiselessly on his paws, before sprinting after Axsel.

"Too bad, kid," mumbled Axsel after he released his hold on the young man and watched his frame roll to the bottom of the pit. "What wasted potential," he added with a shrug of his shoulders before clapping his hands together as he dusted them off.

107

Novex allowed his cloaking ability to fade just as Axsel turned away from the gorge of decaying bodies and had taken a handful of steps.

"Oy!" exclaimed Axsel as he abruptly halted. "Where did you come from?" he asked as he slowly lowered his hands down by his side.

Novex pulled his lips back in a soft snarl, and he crouched lower to the ground as he prepared to lunge at the brawny man. He then flicked his tail to the side once, and his chest began to reverberate with his low growls.

"Come on, ya big beast," whispered Axsel, closing his hands around the hilts of his throwing knives. Suddenly, Axsel brought up his hands and swiftly released both blades at Novex.

Novex vaulted upward and forward a fraction of a second after Axsel threw his weapons. Novex hissed as a burning pain sprung to life in his side, but it was short-lived as he collided with the large man; the force of his attack sent Axsel sprawling backward. Moments before they hit the ground, Novex firmly clenched his jaws down on the man's neck, choking off his cries for help. Novex then robustly yanked his own head to the side, ripping out Axsel's throat. Novex dropped the chunk of flesh and bone from his mouth as blood burbled out of the gaping wound under Axsel's chin.

"Oy…" groaned Lorance as he staggered under the weight of the older man he had been tasked to dispose of. "Do we… ugh… have… to… ugh… go back?" he asked between gasps while struggling to remain upright.

Novex looked over his shoulder, and he watched as the smaller man finally fell to his knees under the weight of the corpse he carried. Turning completely to face the lanky individual, Novex emitted a menacing growl.

Lorance's head snapped up, and his terrified eyes met the sapphire ones of the black tigal approaching him. "Uh," sputtered Lorance. Audibly gulping, Lorance scanned the area. His eyes stopped on Axsel, laying lifeless in a pool of his own blood. His gaze snapped back to the tigal, finally aware of the dark red liquid dripping from his mouth and down his neck. "Nnn… nnn…. Noooo… Ppp…. Ppp… pleassssse," whimpered Lorance as he turned and scurried away as the animal stalked toward him; in his haste, Lorance stumbled and fell backward. "Ooof," he grunted as the air was knocked out of his lungs.

With a *poof*, Novex reverted to his human form. Looking down, he eyed the dagger lodged in his side. Grasping the hilt, he removed it with a quick jerk before tossing it aside. He then stalked toward the other man as he attempted to flee. "You'll come with me," said Novex tersely as he wrapped his hand around Lorance's throat, and he effortlessly hoisted the man to his feet.

"Wwwhh…" stammered Lorance as his eyes darted from side to side before resting on Novex's blood-stained face. "Yyy… yyy… you're the… the… bbb…. bbb…. beast!" he finally managed to exclaim as he noticed the shirtless man's sapphire blue eyes.

"You'll come with me," repeated Novex, his voice void of emotion, before adding, "or I'll rip out your throat as I did your companions."

"I'll do as you say!" squawked Lorance as he felt the man's hand tightening around his neck.

"Very well," returned Novex as he relinquished Lorance. "Take me to your leader. The one you call Akeenah," said Novex as he glared at the cowardly man.

"Akeenah is the mission leader. Rozalin is our commander," replied Lorance hesitantly. "We were out on a scouting mission. I can take you to Akeenah. If she isn't there, then I will take you to Rozalin," he continued shakily.

"Very well," agreed Novex as he held out a hand and said, "After you."

* * *

The vigorous pounding of zebril hooves against the river-rock, paved path echoed like thunder throughout the forest.

"There!" shouted Everly over the deafening sound of their racing mounts. Knowing the others would not understand her clearly, she reached up and made a signal with her hand. The small group simultaneously tugged on the reins of their steeds, bringing them to a slow canter.

"Up ahead," called out Everly over her shoulder, "there is a break in the tree line. It looks like a small road. Maybe leading to a homestead."

Avenor raised his arm, signaling the others to halt. "We'll dismount here," he said, beginning to get off his own zebril once the others were close enough to hear him. "We'll proceed on foot. Ami, you take point. Api, you and Azelly follow while I secure the rear." Once on the ground, he turned to face Leander. "Major Swiftpaw, you'll provide security here until Overseer Ozulben and the others arrive. You'll then take lead and follow suit," finished Avenor before guiding his mount off the road into the trees.

"As you command, Your Grace," responded Leander with a quick salute. Leander and the others led their mounts off the road and tied them close to one another. Leander returned to the edge of the path;

he then lowered himself to a crouched position, concealed between a bush and tree where he remained waiting.

Wordlessly, the others assumed the positions assigned by Avenor. Everly met her son's black eyes, and she waited until he dipped his head. Rotating her head forward, Everly mutely indicated to begin their advance toward the lesser pathway. With every few steps, Everly glanced over her shoulder; she continually swiveled her head from side to side, her senses hyperalert. "What is this?" she whispered to herself, signing for the others to stop.

Everly swiftly examined the snapped branches, crunched leaves, and displaced mounds of dirt – an invisible footpath left by the intruders' yards before the turn. Dropping to a knee, Everly crooked her neck and used various hand signals to wordlessly communicate with Avenor, Manijor, and Azelly – who had all crouched to a knee and had concealed themselves.

"More than one. Different sizes. Some main route. Some in brush. Stay. I'm going. Back in ten."

Everly hastily kicked off her boots; with her feet bare, she darted into the woods. Sensing the terrain changes beneath her feet, Everly expertly adjusted her weight, and she avoided breaking any fallen branches or leaves that would betray her presence. Using her extraordinary tracking ability, she soundlessly followed the barely detectable trail leading to a farm. After briefly observing the surroundings, she retreated to rejoin the others.

"Well?" asked Avenor as he watched his mother brush the dirt off her feet.

"It's a farm. Whoever was here is no longer, but it appears to have been recently inhabited," replied Everly as she donned her boots. "There is smoke still coming from the chimney," she added with a frown. "I advise we ensue with caution," she finished.

"As you suggest," returned Avenor with a curt dip of his head. Mutely, the group re-formed and progressed toward the homestead.

CHAPTER 14

Reeyah gradually swirled the greenish-black contents in her crude stone bowl; using her hand, she wafted the squalid odor toward her face. "Burggh!" she involuntarily retched, and abruptly clamped a hand over her mouth. The bile burned her throat before she managed to swallow it back down.

"Ugh," she exhaled and shuddered as the smell lingered in her nasal passages.

"Ree…" called out Demic cautiously as he neared the hidden crevice on the obscured plateau at the outskirt of the oasis. "It's Demic," he continued with apprehension, knowing what would happen if he startled the Lordess.

Reeyah peeked out from within the shrubs and hedges that camouflaged her secrete work location. Her eyes flashed with fury as she peered past Demic.

"I came alone," he assured her quickly as he slowly advanced toward her.

Suddenly, a pile of rocks was disturbed and began tumbling down the steep path. "Hound's piss!" cursed Dimor as he struggled to keep pace with his brother. "Dem!" he shouted once he stopped sliding down the trail.

"Alone, eh?" questioned Reeyah, anger rolling off her in waves.

"I swear!" whispered Demic, worry evident in his voice, as he glanced over his shoulder. "He must have followed me," he finished with a confused shake of his head and shrug of his shoulders.

"Dem! I saw you creep out of camp again!" hissed Dimor, confirming his brother's statement, as he lost his footing once more. "Why do you continually sneak about?" demanded Dimor as he finally crested the plateau and collapsed on his back in exhaustion.

Reeyah stood motionless as she eyed the muscular man heaving on the ground as he tried to even his breathing. "For how strong and

111

agile you are, a steep path has bested you," chided Reeyah as she shoved past Demic as he swayed from side to side, shifting his weight nervously.

"Lordess!" exclaimed Dimor as he bolted upright. Frowning, he surveyed the area. "There you are!" he suddenly said as his eyes landed on his brother. "I knew I saw you come this way!" he continued with a grin.

"And why are you following me?" demanded Demic as he crossed his arms over his own chiseled chest as he raised a brow expectantly.

Reeyah eyed the two brothers suspiciously, and she absentmindedly darted her tongue out to moisten her suddenly dry lips.

"Well…" began Dimor as he pondered the question, "because we tend to do everything together."

"Bah!" grunted Reeyah in exasperation as she turned on her heels and stormed back to her workplace, her heart pounding wildly in apprehension.

Dimor's gaze turned back to Reeyah, and he felt his eyes linger on her hips as they swayed from side to side. The unexpected smack to the back of his head jolted him out of his own wayward thoughts. "Ow!" growled out Dimor as he turned and glowered as his brother.

"She's not yours to ogle," returned Demic, his quiet voice laced with possessiveness before he hurried after Reeyah.

"What?" asked Dimor as his mouth hung open. "Ahhhhhh," he finally said with a chuckle before standing and following the other two.

"Here it is," Demic said, handing the scale to Reeyah, just as his brother stepped through the brush to join them.

"Finally!" exclaimed Reeyah as she took the rare item from Demic and clutched it to her bosom.

"Is that why you lied to the Overlord?" questioned Dimor as he watched his brother hand the treasure over to Reeyah. "So, you could give it to the Lordess?"

"He doesn't deserve to be Overlord," grunted Demic with a roll of his eyes.

"And what? You do?" retorted Dimor as he arched a brow and glared at his brother. "What happened to your honor? These people have taken us in. They've given us a home. They've…"

"No!" snapped Demic suddenly, abruptly cutting his brother off. "She deserves to be Overlord!" ground out Demic between clenched teeth.

"What are you talking about?" queried Dimor as he took a step back, confusion etched in his expression.

"Gunter wanted us all killed," Demic finally said. "It's only because of Reeyah that he allowed us to live."

"All except Ozgar," added Reeyah, her face void of emotion. "Gunter killed him because Ozgar claimed I was his mate," she said and laughed humorously. "As heavy handed as he was, Ozgar never forced himself upon me."

"How do you know this?" asked Dimor, his voice wavering dubiously.

"Why else do you think I'm now Lordess?" interjected Reeyah. "I negotiated for your lives. Little did I know Ozgar had already told Gunter I was his mate. And Gunter does not share."

"Ah, so that's why Ozgar was executed when the rest of us were released from our cages so many cycles ago. I wondered. My manhood was never large enough to investigate," Dimor admitted with a wry grin. "So, what is the scale going to do?" he asked.

"I am going to add it to this elixir," said Reeyah as she held up the bowl. "Once it has decomposed, I'll consume it."

"Do you even know what that," Dimor said as he pointed at the container in Reeyah's hands, "is going to do to you?"

"I have an idea," chuckled Reeyah as she reached into a dark cage. "Shh, come now, little one," she crooned. After a moment, she removed a small creature resembling a bat. It clung to her hand and wrapped its wings around itself to shut out the remaining light as the sun continued to set. "Here," said Reeyah as she gently retracted the flesh over the bat's claws, "are Evin's newly grown retractable spikes. And here… is his armor," she added as she stretched a wing out before pushing on the opposite side, forcing a handful of concealed scales to the surface, to which Evin screeched in protest. "Shhh, shhh. That's it. I'm done," whispered Reeyah as she placed Evin back in his unsecured cage.

"You are not afraid he'll fly away?" asked Dimor curiously as he eyed the open enclosure.

"Nay. He comes when I call. And should he escape, he will perish within a day without my blood," answered Reeyah flatly.

"I see. So, you expect me to keep all this from Overlord Gunter?" questioned Dimor as he glanced between Reeyah and Demic.

"I'll kill you before I let you reveal anything to him," grumbled Demic as he took a threatening step toward his brother.

Dimor grinned, his eyes twinkling. "Well, brother, I don't feel like dying. I'll not expose you both, unless…"

"Unless?" probed Demic and Reeyah in unison.

"Unless you do not allow me in on this plan of yours," answered Dimor enthusiastically. "I've always enjoyed a good thrill," finished Dimor as he waggled his brows impishly.

Reeyah groaned inwardly and swallowed hard, her heart suddenly pounding erratically again.

Demic allowed his eyes to slide sideways and rest on Reeyah; however, he did not utter a word.

Reeyah clasped her hands together and twiddled her thumbs as she contemplated her answer. While Dimor said he wanted to be part of the plan, he never claimed he would support her as Overlord. She chanced a fleeting glimpse at her brawny lover before directing her attention back to his equally powerful brother. "On one condition, Dimor," she finally said.

"And what is that?" Dimor asked. Languidly, he canted his head slightly to the side while leaning against the large crate that contained Reeyah's miscellaneous ingredients and concoctions.

"You mentioned you and Demic do everything together," stated Reeyah firmly and paused. Once Dimor nodded, she continued. "The one condition is that you accept me as Overlord when the time has arrived."

Demic physically tensed, uncertain of his brother's response. After what felt like an eternity, Demic watched as his sibling pursed his lips and scrunched his nose.

"Very well, Overlord Reeyah," Dimor finally answered with a slight bow. "So, how do you propose we overthrow Gunter?" he inquired seriously.

Reeyah forcefully exhaled the breath she did not realize she was holding. Inhaling deeply to calm her frazzled nerves, she then motioned for the two men to draw nearer so she could explain her plan.

* * *

Iriva half-sat and half-lounged in the shade cast by one of the few trees growing on the Flatlands; she rested with her back against the tree, and she had one leg draped over the other at the knee. Idly, she bounced her foot up and down. It had been a little over a week since they had set up for an ambush; since then, no raiders had been spotted, however, the occasional hunter or forager was observed. For security and surprise purposes, the group remained out of sight from even the common citizens.

Betaro navigated his way through the few soldiers that remained at their designated site. "You're well?" he asked a bunch of soldiers as they rested under a tan colored tent that camouflaged them with the dried grass. "You've had your fill of water?"

"Aye, General Akeenil," the soldiers replied in unison, nodding their heads respectfully.

"And you've had midday meal?" continued Betaro, asking his standard series of questions.

"Aye, General Akeenil," the soldiers answered. "And we've changed our feet hosiery," they added with impish grins.

Betaro stopped with his mouth agape before chuckling. "Very well," he returned before turning away from the men and women.

"He is an excellent leader," one of the soldiers whispered to the others. "How many truly care for their troops the way he does?"

"Aye," one of the youngest agreed. "I never even considered changin' my stockings so oft ta keep my feet dry. I hav'nt had any blisters nor foot rot this expedition!" she exclaimed while watching Betaro with admiration.

"You're well, aged hag?" Betaro asked as he approached Iriva and held out a flask of water.

Iriva tilted her head back, shaking her long silver locks in the process, and glowered up at Betaro. "Perfectly, old goat," retorted Iriva.

Betaro emitted a short bark of laughter. "Here. You need to drink before the heat causes you more damage than any raider would," he warned her sternly while tossing the flask in Iriva's lap. "Some of the younger soldiers at the other positions have already displayed signs of being sun drunk," he informed Iriva.

"Do they require treatment?" asked Iriva immediately as she sat up completely before relaxing once more as Betaro slowly shook his head.

"Nay, they've much improved with shade and consuming more water. I've instructed them to remain out of direct sunlight. If their conditions progress past heat exhaustion, you'll be the first to know," Betaro replied. "Now, drink. You're already showing the early signs." With an exasperated sigh, Betaro continued in response to Iriva's questioning expression. "You lack perspiration. You're normally deep blue skin is paler, more of a lighter hue. Your lips are dry and slightly cracked," he finished.

"Bah! Very well," grumbled Iriva as she held the flask up to her lips, hiding the smile that tugged at the corner of her lips before taking a large swallow of the cool contents. *"He truly is an exemplary leader,"* silently thought Iriva before closing the flask and tossing it back to Betaro. "You have my thanks, dried out grape."

"You are welc…" began Betaro before abruptly halting mid-sentence. Betaro's eyes narrowed as Iriva's remark finally registered. "Did you just refer to me as a… **a raisin?**" he demanded hotly to which Iriva snickered in response.

"If the boot fits," she taunted with a snort.

115

"He's not quite there yet, General Jander," added Juldeyah as she tried to stifle her own giggle. "Give him another cycle. Then he'll be wrinkled enough to be considered a raisin."

Betaro grunted. "Ladies, at least I've been referred to as a *'silver fox'* rather than an *'old crone.'* I've accepted my graceful aging," he retorted while bring his hands up to his face. With his palms downward, he rested his chin on the backs of his hands and batted his eyelashes in response.

Iriva shot a menacing glare at the younger soldiers, attempting to smother their guffaws and chuckles. "Hmph! Old crone my rear…" Iriva managed to mumble before being interrupted by a fleeting shriek from Taleena as she soared above them. "Finally!" she then exclaimed.

Betaro extended a hand down to Iriva. "We don't need you straining your back before the ambush even begins," he teased as she placed her hand in his own.

"You, General Akeenil, are a zebril's arse!" snapped Iriva, swatting at Betaro after he smoothly hefted her to her feet.

"Hah!" scoffed Betaro as he crossed his arms over his chest. "If you cannot handle the backlash, then you shouldn't dare deal out insults in the first place," he said sternly.

"Hmph!" returned Iriva as she lifted her head and turned away from Betaro before hurrying to her position for the ambush.

"Stubborn hag," muttered Betaro under his breath with a shake of his head. Glancing once more at Iriva as she hurried away from him, a smile played at the corner of his mouth.

* * *

"Patrol Sergeants… Report!" shouted Jaquel after the minor skirmish, striding through the center of the now secured ambush site.

"Patrol 1 – Amber, Green, Green," called out the Sergeant of first patrol sequentially followed in similar fashion by the next two patrol leaders.

"Patrol 4 – Amber, Amber, Green. 1 Soldier with a shallow flesh wound. He's already bandaged and ready to move," finished the Sergeant.

"Very well. Distribute ammunition as needed," barked out Jaquel in response. "And inspect equipment. It's a good trek back to Kespeda," he ordered his troops. "We don't want to be caught with our breeches around our ankles," he said, garnering quiet laughter from his soldiers. While there were no accounts of broken or malfunctioned equipment, he preferred to be prepared regardless of the situation.

Iriva crinkled her nose before leaning down to Betaro. "What are the patrol leaders going on about?" she whispered curiously.

"Hmm?" Betaro swiftly finished tying a captive's hands behind his back. Standing, he yanked the raider to his feet and passed him to one of the nearby patrol leaders for interrogation. After wiping the sweat off his brow, Betaro glanced around. "Ah," he quietly exclaimed before responding. "They are informing Captain Wentworth if there has been any loss of ammunition, if any patrols have sustained casualties, and the status of their equipment."

"How do they know? Better yet, how does Captain Wentworth know what they're talking about?" she asked in awe.

Betaro frowned as he eyed Iriva skeptically. *"Oy! That's right. She was never trained in military procedures,"* he silently reminded himself before continuing to answer her series of questions. "There are procedures which are taught in the same manner throughout the Grand Military. Therefore, if one soldier is moved to another patrol, or a patrol joins another unit, there is a seamless merger."

"That is quite intriguing," murmured Iriva as she gazed around, observing the troops inspecting their equipment for any flaws.

"General Akeenil, General Jander," interrupted Juldeyah as she joined the pair. "Captain Wentworth has sent three of his best scouts in search of the hideout the raiders claim is along the coast not far from the fishing village of Sedwin."

Betaro suddenly inhaled sharply; he opened and closed his mouth, yet no words emerged at the mention of the small town.

"Betaro? Are you ill?" asked Iriva void of any jesting in her voice.

Finally, able to breath once more, Betaro cleared his throat and replied gruffly, "Aye. Sedwin brings back unpleasant memories."

Hesitantly pulling her gaze away from Betaro, Iriva looked back at Juldeyah. "How long until they return?"

"Not long. Terror rendered the young lass incredibly compliant. She provided detailed instruction on how to locate the encampment along with the various access points," answered Juldeyah with a sad shake of her head as she peered at the frail youth tied with the other raiders. "She is no more than a child."

"If this pathetic lot says anything about the raiders as a whole, I'd wager Itagrio does not have much to fear," said Betaro as he crossed his arms over his chest. "And that lass is old enough to understand that there are consequences for her actions," he finished curtly, his voice harshly directed at the girl amongst the band of thieves and ruffians.

Juldeyah heaved a sigh and nodded her head in agreement. "We'll wait for the scouts to return before making a decision?" stated Juldeyah in a tone that relayed her question to which Betaro and Iriva silently nodded in response.

* * *

"I'd best you if I could transform too!" shouted Wesdin seconds before slamming the door to his personal chambers.

Bang!

The unexpected sound of a door being slammed caused Galhix to jump. Ouch!" she gasped and immediately brought her finger to her mouth, sucking at the freshly pierced flesh. Quietly reciting an incantation, she alleviated the discomfort before setting her embroidery work aside. Opening the door to her personal chambers, she greeted Valcaly and Aylox with a curt nod.

"Your Grace," the pair greeted her in unison before falling in beside her. Walking the short distance to her son's chambers, she eyed the two brothers.

"Your Grace," the brothers said simultaneously with a salute.

"Good eve," replied Galhix before rapping her knuckles lightly on her son's door. After a moment with no response, Galhix let herself in to find Wesdin strewn across his bed with his face buried in the blankets.

First closing the door behind her, she then crossed the distance to Wesdin's bed; gradually, Galhix lowered herself to sit beside her son. "What troubles you, my beloved?" asked Galhix as she gently ran her fingers through Wesdin's hair.

Wesdin mumbled incoherently and buried his face deeper in the covers.

"Tsk, tsk, my son," chided Galhix lightly. "Where have your manners gone?" she demanded quietly.

Wesdin gradually rolled on to his back to meet his mother's gaze. "I can no longer defeat the others in a dual since they've all learned to transform," he admitted with a sniffle and angrily swiped at the tears that spilled down his cheeks. "Why haven't I transformed?" he asked with a quiet sob.

Galhix exhaled slowly as she pulled Wesdin into a loving embrace. "Oy, my beloved…" she said quietly and lightly stroked Wesdin's back. "We do not all have the same abilities…"

"But I'm a tigal too!" he interposed, pulling away from his mother and frowning.

"Aye, this is so. However, your father is not…" answered Galhix before Wesdin silenced her mid-sentence again.

"Leandra's Ami is not a tigal… And she transformed!" returned Wesdin, still struggling to understand why he had not transformed.

Galhix scowled at her son and lightly clasped a hand over his mouth to prevent him from interrupting once more. "Oy, my beloved. You have many abilities coursing through your bloodline. Many abilities you have already mastered, even at your young age. However, I doubt you possess every ability, including the *transformation* ability."

"I don't understand," pouted Wesdin once his mother removed her hand.

Galhix tapped an index finger against her lips before exclaiming, "Ah. Think of Great-Grandapi Betaro and Grandami Everly. What color are their eyes?"

Wesdin reached up and scratched his temple as he considered his mother's question. "Umm, Great-Grandapi Betaro has blue eyes. Grandami Everly has green eyes."

"And Grandami's mother, your Great-Grandami Lukesia, also had blue eyes. You would think that Grandami Everly would then have blue eyes, correct?"

Wesdin gradually nodded his head. "Hmm, why doesn't Grandami Everly have blue eyes?" he then questioned with a frown.

"In your Grandami Everly's bloodline, there are others who possess different traits and abilities. While both of her parents did not possess green eyes, that forgotten trait became evident when Grandami Everly was born."

"Is that why I have mostly black eyes like Api and only a little bit of purple like yours?" he asked as he peered into his mother's lavender orbs.

"Your eyes, my beloved," began Galhix slowly as she stared intently into Wesdin's eyes, "are different than all the other's I've seen. There is a possibility it is because I am considered an *ancient*."

"You're one of the three ancients!" Wesdin suddenly exclaimed cheerfully before pausing to look his mother up and down. "Ami..." he whispered and paused.

"What is it, my beloved?" Galhix returned as she leaned closer, hearing the seriousness in Wesdin's voice.

"You... are... *ooooooollllld!*" he said, his eyes wide as he gaped at his mother.

"Ey!" exclaimed Galhix with a slight glare as she sat back. "It was not by choice that I aged a single cycle after every hundred cycles," she responded while crossing her arms over her chest.

Wesdin giggled to himself. "Well, Ami... you're still the most beautiful old tigal that I know!"

"Bah!" grunted Galhix as she reached out and began tickling Wesdin's sides, causing him to squeal with laughter and thrash about. After a few minutes, Galhix stopped and ruffled Wesdin's hair. "It is late, my beloved. Get some rest. I plan to as well," she said with a forced smile.

119

"Ami?" Wesdin said as he sat up, keenly aware that his mother's mood had suddenly changed. "Are you well?" he asked in a concerned tone.

"I'm fine. Just a touch of a stomach illness," she admitted. As if on cue, a dry heave wracked her body and perspiration immediately sprouted along her hairline. "Rest now. I'll see you in the morn," she instructed her son. Swiftly standing, she pressed a kiss to his cheek before hastily retreating to her own quarters.

CHAPTER 15

Valcaly rested with her back against the wall across from Wesdin's chambers; with one foot casually crossed over the other, she quietly sharpened her throwing blades.

"What damage can you even do with those little things?" taunted Aylex after he strolled the few feet to a nearby chair. Sitting, he then raised one leg and draped it over one of the oversized chair's arms. With his arms resting along the back of the chair, he carelessly lounged with his legs stretched apart. "Perhaps you'll allow me to use one. I need to pick a little bit of meat from my teeth," he finished. Making squeaking sounds with his mouth, Aylex feigned trying to remove a wedged chunk of food from between his pearly whites.

Valcaly nonchalantly turned to stare at Aylex and arched a brow. "You'd like to borrow one, eh?" she asked, her voice overly sweet.

"Why do you insist on troubling the lady?" Daylin grumbled as he stood with his arms crossed over his chest. "Don't mind him," he then said, casting an apologetic look in Valcaly's direction.

Valcaly grinned in return before mischievously winking at Daylin.

"You would truly let me borrow one of your treasured toothpicks?" asked Aylex incredulously as he allowed his head to fall back and rest on top of the seat back.

Aside from an amused lift of his brow, Aylox remained motionless as he stood posted diagonal from Valcaly. *"I wager one gold that the High Trapper will allow your brother... borrow... one,"* he silently spoke to Daylin, stressing how he said *borrow.*

Daylin began to chuckle but abruptly concealed his reaction as a cough when Valcaly's eyes narrowed on him. Clearing his throat, he then responded wordlessly to his father. *"Nay. I wager she'll not hand one over that easily,"* replied Daylin, hiding his grin by pretending to gnaw on his nail.

"Of course," replied Valcaly lightly. Fluidly and without warning, Valcaly stepped forward and let loose one of her throwing blades. The dagger whizzed through the air.

121

Thwack!

"Ey!" shouted Aylex as his head jerked up, and he instinctively scooted back in his chair. Glancing down, Aylex examined the throwing dagger, deeply imbedded in the wooden seat just below his man parts. "Really?" he groused, turning to glower at Valcaly.

A deep rumble drew Valcaly's attention toward Aylox and Daylin immediately before the two erupted into an uncontrollable fit of laughter. "You deserve it, lad!" Aylox answered for Valcaly as he wiped a tear of merriment from the corner of his eye.

"Your face!" wheezed Daylin as he clutched at his stomach. "You... should have seen... your face!" he managed to sputter between gasping for breath and chortling.

"Ha, ha," grumbled Aylex as he reached down and lightly tugged at the dagger. "Damn," he whispered to himself, realizing that the tiny blade was lodged deeply in the wood. Firmly grasping the hilt, he yanked on the throwing blade and managed to remove it after a handful of attempts.

"Well, you asked to borrow it," returned Valcaly with a mischievous snicker.

"Not by having you throw it at my... my.... **twig and berries!**" he growled, crossing the expanse to return the weapon to Valcaly.

"Now you know what kind of damage her little toothpicks can do," added Daylin as another bout of laughter shook his large frame.

"You owe me a gold," Aylox mutely reminded Daylin with his lips upturned in entertainment.

Just then, the door to Wesdin's chamber was pulled open and out stepped Galhix - her face pale and green around the gills.

"Regent Khan, you do not look well," Valcaly immediately observed and rushed to Galhix's side. Displaying no hesitation, Aylox hurried to assist Valcaly. He easily scooped Galhix off her feet; he then proceeded toward the Khantessa's personal quarters with Valcaly leading the way.

"Post!" Aylox commanded his two youngest sons wordlessly. Without delay, Aylex hurriedly joined his brother standing guard, one on each side of the Khanzito's door.

* * *

"It's late in the eve, but we'll send for the master healers to come evaluate you," said Valcaly as she pressed a cool compress to Galhix's forehead.

"I am a master healer," protested Galhix weakly.

"Aye, this is true. However, you're in no condition to treat yourself," replied Valcaly sternly.

Galhix barely had the strength to nod her head ever so slightly in agreement as she completely leaned back, resting propped up on her pillows.

"I'll send Daylin to stand guard. Aylex will remain just down the hall with Wesdin," added Aylox as he filled a glass with cool water and set it on the bedside table.

"Aylox and I will head to the sanitorium to gather miscellaneous items the master healers typically request. We'll only be gone briefly," Valcaly assured the Khantessa.

"Before you depart," murmured Galhix breathlessly, halting her two personal protectors.

"Your Grace?" asked Valcaly, waiting for Galhix's request.

"Please… the windows. The air is oppressive in here," she groaned weakly.

"As you request, Regent Khan," returned Aylox as he cast the windows wide open, allowing the cool evening breeze to filter in.

"My thanks," Galhix managed to whisper before slipping into a restless sleep.

"Let's make haste," said Valcaly quietly as she spun on her heels, closely followed by Aylox. Within moments, Daylin and Aylox were positioned in the corridor to adequately provide security for both the Khantessa and Khanzito. A handful of soldiers and palace keepers had been instructed to retrieve various master healers; at the same time, Valcaly led Aylox to the sanitorium to retrieve an assortment of equipment she knew the healers typically used in their treatments of the ailing and injured.

* * *

Wesdin tossed and turned on his bed, unable to rest peacefully with the frequent clanking and pitter-patters as different people rushed throughout the corridor. A combination of curiosity and irritation finally stirred him to action; kicking the blankets off, Wesdin hurried to the door and pulled it open just enough to peer through the crack.

"Overseer Truceran and Vice Commandant Clawbane have gone to the sanitorium," Wesdin heard someone mention as they rushed through the hall.

"Hmph!" grunted Wesdin before he closed his own door and retreated into his own room. "Ami must be doing an evening incantation with the healers," he mused in annoyance. "I won't be able to sleep tonight," he grumbled. Lost in his own thoughts, Wesdin began to sink further into despair. "Why would Ami and Api want me around? I can't even transform," he said miserably, recalling the hurtful words of other children that had experienced the *transformation*.

Wesdin pressed his fits to his eyes, forcing back the tears that threatened to spill as he recalled the spiteful comments. *"I bet you're a disappointment to your parents!" "No one will want you as a ruler when you're older!" "How can you even say you're a tigal?" "You should just run away!" "Your parents must be so ashamed of you that they don't even take you on their expeditions!"*

Sniffling, Wesdin hastily swiped at the tears that had escaped from the corner of his eyes. "Maybe they're right," he suddenly whispered aloud to himself. "Maybe it would be better if I left," he continued, the corners of his mouth downturned. Without another thought, Wesdin made his way to the changing area of his personal chambers; he shed his sleeping attire and hastily replaced them with a pair of softened leather boots, leather breaches, and a linen shirt – all in black. He then grabbed the darkest cloak he possessed —one dyed midnight blue – and secured it before draping the hood over his head to conceal his metallic grey hair.

Once done changing, Wesdin peered around his bed chamber; he quickly filled his travel pack with various snacking food items that remained on his table. He then filled a flask with water and added it to his travel pack. Lastly, he fastened a belt around his waist that held a sheathed short sword and a pair of throwing blades. Finally satisfied, Wesdin strode across the room; peering out of the window, he inspected the area before cautiously pushing it open. With his heart hammering against his chest, Wesdin took a deep breath before sitting on the windowsill; quickly, he swung his legs over and allowed the momentum to carry him out of the window.

Thud.

Wesdin landed gently in the grass below; crouching down, he held his breath and listened intently for any signs that he might have alerted the guards. Without further delay, Wesdin sprinted through the city, hugging the shadows to avoid detection.

CHAPTER 16

From her concealed position, Lana glowered in annoyance as she observed the numerous soldiers and castle workers as they hurried about.

"Damn!" she hissed under her breath. "What could they be doing at this time?" she pondered to herself in a whisper. "I best be quick. This may be my only chance," she finally muttered after a time.

Crouching down, she pressed herself against the palace wall, grateful for the clouds that prevented the light from the stars and moon to illuminate the royal grounds. Her last mission – to locate the sleeping quarters of the Khan and Khantessa - had been a success. "This should be simple enough," she mumbled. Quickly, she followed the path she memorized from her last visit to the palace.

Thud.

"Oy," she exclaimed barely above a whisper while abruptly halting by the unexpected appearance of a youth just as she was about to step out from behind a bush. Grateful that her gasp had been muffled by his landing, she remained motionless. After a moment, the boy scurried off; with a sigh, Lana continued until she stood under the open window of her target. The unexpected wail of agony caused Lana to immediately freeze in place.

"Aaaah!" wailed a woman lightly. Her quiet cry of agony was carried on the night breeze, and it was soon followed by another.

"Damn! Damn! Damn!" groused Lana silently to herself, her nerves frazzled by the unexpected cries. *"I'm this close. I can't turn back,"* Lana wordlessly encouraged herself. *"I just need to get 'the source' and get out,"* she reminded herself, suddenly remembering how their original plans had seemed to change randomly. Instead of stealing valuables from the palace, Peygar insisted she had to collect something called *'the source.'*

Taking a calming breath, Lana finally managed to slow her wildly pounding heart. *"I can do this,"* she wordlessly mumbled to herself. Without waiting for her courage to abandon her, Lana swiftly climbed the nearby tree. For a time, she eyed the distance from her position in the

125

tree to the small balcony; shifting her weight, she then gracefully launched herself forward, and she landed with a quiet shuffling of dirt as she skidded on her feet. Without wasting a moment, Lana spun on her heels and peeked through the billowing curtains. A single candle flickered and danced in the breeze on the small table beside the bed where a woman lay tossing her head from side to side.

"Aaah!" cried out Galhix as she immediately grabbed at her abdomen, a searing pain shooting through her.

Lana felt every fiber of her being tense uneasily.

"Where is she?" a voice asked softly and faintly; it still managed to draw Lana's attention to the closed door.

"Oh, no!" exclaimed Lana to herself, her eyes widening with panic as she shifted her eyes to the bed before back to the closed door. She could feel her palms becoming sweaty as her heart began frantically hammering in her chest. After a moment of hesitation, Lana sprinted across the distance. With a *click,* she locked the door. Shaking uncontrollably, she then turned back toward the bed.

"Val..." groaned Galhix as she curled on her side, waves of pain coursing through her. "I nee... need... Av... ven... or-" she managed to gasp before she was overwhelmed by another jolt of agony.

Lana shook her head fiercely. *"I don't care what is wrong with her,"* she said, her face contorted with loathing. Glancing around her surroundings, Lana noticed a glass of water. She quickly removed a vial from her pocket and added the contents; the powder turned the liquid a pale-yellow color and released a bitter aroma, causing Lana to grin triumphantly.

"Eep!" exclaimed Lana with a jump, startled by a soft knock on the door.

"Regent Khan," came a gentle voice from the other side of the door.

"Damn," hissed Lana before rushing to the side of the bed. Reaching down, she struggled to sit Galhix up. "Come on," she groaned while placing the glass to Galhix's lips. "Drink," she instructed Galhix sternly.

In a daze from the pain, Galhix tried to pry her eyes open in response to the unfamiliar voice. "Who... who... aregurggle" she tried to ask but was cut off as she felt some sort of thickened liquid spill into her mouth.

Lana grabbed a fistful of Galhix's hair and tugged her head back forcefully. "Drink!" she repeated harshly.

Unable to struggle, Galhix could only swallow the fiery liquid that burned a trail down her throat to the pit of her stomach.

"Regent Khan," repeated the voice, this time louder with a stronger knock on the door.

"She may be resting," said a gruff voice. "Just go in."

Clenching her teeth, Lana pulled away from Galhix and allowed her to fall back roughly, resulting in a groan. Lana felt beads of sweat rolling down her temples as she hastily stepped back from Galhix, now motionless on her back, though her eyes were open and darted from side to side in terror.

The sudden jiggling of the door handle caused Lana to jump, and it spurred her back into motion. Leaning over Galhix, Lana grinned down devilishly. "It's a pleasure to finally meet you, Aunt Galhix," whispered Lana. Though it was gentle, her voice was malicious. "I wouldn't normally go around killing people," continued Lana pensively. "But because of you and uncle, I was forced to live like a beggar. Because of you, my chance for a lavish life was stolen!" she vehemently said in a harsh whisper. Lana chuckled at the confusion displayed in Galhix's eyes. "My father…" she whispered while removing a dagger from her boot and holding it up for the Khantessa to see. "Is your dearest brother," continued Lana hurriedly.

"It's locked," said a woman as she tugged at the door handle once more.

"What? No one has been in there since Overseer Truceran and Vice Commandant Aylox left. And I find it doubtful that the Khantessa would have locked it," responded the same brusque voice that had spoken as the door shook again. "What the…" exclaimed the man as he rattled the door even harder, trying to open it. "Khantessa Galhix?" he called out with apprehension clear in his voice. "Khantessa!" he then shouted and began banging furiously on the door.

With a sinister laugh, Lana climbed on the bed; she then positioned herself on top of Galhix with the dagger aimed at her stomach. "Gulroq," Lana added just as she plunged the dagger into Galhix's stomach. Lana couldn't contain the small giggle that escaped her lips at the shock in Galhix's eyes before she then fiercely pulled upward, dragging the small knife through Galhix's flesh, allowing blood to gush out from the abdominal wound.

"Break it down!" shouted someone from the hall, reminding Lana she had little time left.

Taking a step back, Lana then stretched her hands out toward Galhix. Quietly, she recited the incantation she learned from reading the ancient tome Peygar had given her. Gradually, a ruby light began to emanate from Galhix's wound; the light slowly disappeared, becoming

Kimberly Evette Ortuno

muted by Galhix's flesh, and traveled from her stomach up through her chest before being drawn out of her mouth.

As soon as the glow emerged from Galhix's mouth, it illuminated the entire bedchamber in a red glow. Lana's eyes widened as she watched a grape size orb floating toward her. Suddenly, it zipped through the air and plunged into Lana's mouth.

The unexpected action caused Lana to inhale sharply; grunting, Lana stumbled back a step as she felt an exploding sensation throughout her entire body.

BANG!

Lana turned her head toward the door, her every movement seeming suddenly sluggish.

BANG!

"Oy," grumbled Lana as she watched the door appear to jump with the force of the impact.

BANG!

Feeling as though she could not hold her own weight, Lana stumbled back to the balcony. Hastily, she crawled over the side of the rail. As Lana tried to adjust her hold, she felt her hands slipping because of the blood she was covered in.

"Oof!" grunted Lana as she fell on her back, the air knocked out of her lungs. Blinking her eyes rapidly, she forced away the darkness that threatened to overtake her vision.

BANG! CRASH!

"Khantessa!" shouted a voice before a chorus of commands and shouts erupted from above Lana.

Lana rolled on her side and shoved herself to her feet. Unbridled fear gave wings to her feet, and she flew through the darkness without a backward glance. She raced back toward the hidden gate she had entered through; dragging uneven breaths in through her mouth, Lana tried to enter the water as quietly as possible. Entering the frigid water, she hastily washed the blood off before slipping through the gates once more. Groaning, she forced herself to transform. With her supernatural strength, she forced the bars back to their original position before reverting to her human form once more. With her clothes in shreds, she disappeared into the night to join her mother and uncle.

* * *

Thump, thump, thump!

Leandra jumped in her sleep, blinking her eyes rapidly in response to the sudden hammering on a door nearby; her heart was racing at the unexpected awakening. Creeping out of bed, she made her way to the nearby window. Hesitantly, she pushed it open and watched as palace workers and guards rushed around below; curious about the strange events, she folded her arms and leaned against the sill as she continued her silent observation.

"I wonder what is happening?" she quietly pondered to herself as she watched a soldier once more pound on the door across from her home.

"Maestra Fiona Smitian!" called out the guard, his voice urgent.

"Something bad must have happened for them to come in the middle of the night searching for her," thought Leandra as she waited for the master Cleric to open the door.

From the corner of her eye, Leandra caught a slight movement. Shifting her gaze, she stared intently at the shadows. *"Odd,"* she thought, furrowing her brows. Continuing to gaze into the blackness, she managed to make out various objects – a few wooden crates stacked alongside some barrels. Suddenly, she watched a familiar figure dart out from the dark and race across the cobblestone road to another shadowy area.

"Wesdin?" she whispered aloud as she watched her friend sneak along the dimly lit street. "Where are you going?" she asked quietly, suddenly aware he was heading toward the city's rear gate. "Oh, no you don't!" she exclaimed quietly. "Not without me, you don't!"

Without wasting another second, Leandra speedily slipped out of her nightgown. Instead of her usual gown, she decided to dress in similar fashion to Wesdin; she then slipped her feet into black slippers rather than boots. She then hurriedly grabbed a travel bag; making her way to a nearby table, she hastily swept all the nourishments on the small table into her sack. *"My thanks, Trittni!"* she thought to herself with a grin, grateful that her *watcher* was kind enough to provide snacks as she experienced *growth hungers*. She hastily slung it over her shoulder before quieting her mind.

Poof!

Grinning proudly to herself for learning to control her *transformation*, Leandra used her ability to fade from view. She then stealthily climbed out of her open window, pouncing from one section of her home to another until she reached the ground. Immediately upon landing, she sprinted in the direction she had seen Wesdin heading.

* * *

Avenor ducked his head as he stepped through the open door of the quaint farmhouse; it had been ransacked by whoever had raided the place. "A small family must live here," he said quietly to the empty home as he stood in the center of the living space and turned in a circle.

"Halt!" Major Chevin shouted, grabbing Avenor's attention. "Halt!" repeated Mykel, his voice louder and harsher than the first time.

Abruptly, Avenor turned; with long, confident strides, he exited the house to find out who Major Chevin had managed to detain. Immediately, he saw the man holding his hand cannon; turning in the direction the commander pointed his weapon, Avenor watched as two individuals walked around bushes and trees. Avenor squinted, sensing familiarity from one of the strangers.

"Lower your weapons," Avenor finally called out before relaxing

"Your Grace?" asked Mykel hesitantly, his eyes never leaving the strangers as they continued to walk closer. With a frown, he gave a signal for his soldiers to lower their weapons.

"It is alright," returned Avenor before walking the short distance to meet the newcomers in the center of the fenced field.

"Your Grace," greeted Novex with a salute, his hand firmly gripping the arm of the other man.

"Ambassador Clawbane," replied Avenor, raising his right arm in return. "Who is this?" he then asked, eyeing the outsider up and down.

"This coward is called Lorance, and he follows Rozalin Lanikeel," answered Novex curtly, forcing the lanky male to his knees.

Lorance dropped to his knees and buried his face in the recently plowed dirt. His voice trembled as he began to beg, recognizing the Khan as he stood before him. "Y...y...your Gr...Gr...Grace," he stammered, "I c...c.... can lead y...y...you to M...m...Major Lanikeel," he finished in a rush.

"She is no Major of the Grand Military," snapped Major Chevin before Avenor had a chance to respond. "She is a traitor!" he seethed heatedly.

"Indeed," agreed Avenor briskly as Manijor arrived to stand beside him. Taking a step back, Avenor turned slightly so he could speak with his father, Novex, and Mykel. "General Crusendir, I leave you in charge of this traitor. I expect that you, Ambassador Clawbane, and either Major Chevin or a representative of his choosing will conduct a thorough interrogation." Reaching down to Lorance, Avenor grabbed a fistful of his greasy hair and yanked his head back forcefully. "You will cooperate. If not, you will be repeatedly tortured. But you will not die until I am satisfied," finished Avenor, his voice dangerously low.

Lorance's eyes bulged at the unbridled fury he saw in the Khan's eyes. His mouth suddenly dry, Lorance swallowed hard past the lump that formed in his throat before nodding. "Aye, Khan Crusendir," he managed to whisper before being roughly hauled back to his feet.

"Move," Manijor said sternly, giving the scrawny man a shove toward the looted house.

"I will go scout the area," murmured Everly as she placed a hand on her son's back.

"Do not venture too far," Avenor said as he turned and placed an arm over his mother's shoulders in a half hug. "General Crusendir, Ambassador Clawbane and one other have gone to interrogate a traitor," he said just before various howls and cries erupted.

"Oy," replied Everly as she turned with Avenor to gaze in the direction of the house where the agonizing shrieks were coming from.

"He will break quickly," added Avenor with a mirthless chuckle. "From the information that is gathered, we will plan our attack."

"As you desire, Your Grace," replied Everly as she stepped away from her son. "I shall return soon," she said with a salute.

"Very well, General Akeenil," Avenor returned to his mother, returning the gesture before she departed.

"Khan Crusendir," called out Kenzelo as he approached Avenor, his hand at the corner of his mouth twirling the end of his mustache.

"High Trapper Ozulben," greeted Avenor in return. "Instruct the Captains to prepare their units. This way, *Force Oaklan* will be prepared to depart without delay. Major Chevin is currently assisting in an interrogation."

"I am here to serve, Your Grace," responded Kenzelo. After receiving a salute in return, Kenzelo departed to carry out Avenor's orders.

* * *

"General Akeenil. General Jander. What do you propose we do with the captives?" asked Juldeyah as she looked from one to the other.

Betaro shared a quick look with Iriva before turning his attention back to the High Wizard. "Overseer Mulbin," he began slowly. "This is your continent. While we have come to aid at your request, the discipline of these few is left for you to decide."

With a frown, Juldeyah pondered the options while reaching up to tap a finger against her lips. Without warning, her eyes lit up. "I've got it!" she said while snapping her fingers. "A stint in Sicario Prison should suffice," she finished with a dip of her head.

"Sicario Prison?" repeated Betaro, one brow arched in disbelief.

"Is that not too severe of a punishment?" questioned Iriva as she openly gawked at Juldeyah.

"They are young," returned Juldeyah as she peered over her shoulder. With a sigh, she noted the raiders sat with their heads hanging down, and their hands were tied behind their backs. "I can only hope that such a harsh punishment will deter them from continuing to walk the path they are currently on," she finished with a sad shake of her head.

Kimberly Evette Ortuno

Iriva slowly nodded her head as she agreed with the High Wizard.

"Very well," responded Betaro as he dipped his head curtly.

"Generals. Overseer," Jaquel addressed the three high ranking individuals as he neared. "My unit is prepared to depart at your notice. What shall we do with the captives?" he then asked.

"Assign the patrol with your most trusted Sergeant to escort the prisoners to Sicario Prison," Juldeyah answered Captain Wentworth. "Once we have returned to Kespeda, I will address the needed changes to increase the number of sentries assigned in this region."

"I am here to serve, Overseer Mulbin," replied Jaquel with a salute. Once Juldeyah returned the action, he departed to carry out her orders.

"That is a wise decision," commented Betaro approvingly. "This seems to be the area impacted the most by the raiders," he added.

"Indeed," replied Juldeyah. "I believe with an increase in the number of guards assigned to the small towns and villages, it will decrease the frequency of attacks." Juldeyah simply nodded her head before excusing herself to prepare for the departure.

"I am slightly disappointed," Iriva said once Juldeyah disappeared, leaving her standing alone with Betaro once more.

"Why so?" asked Betaro as he grabbed the reins of his mount.

"It has been some time since I've been required to use my abilities," she replied, her voice tinged with a hint of melancholy.

Betaro snorted, drawing a stern glare from Iriva. "Apologies," he instantly said with a cough. "I, for one, am pleased with the outcome," he admitted.

"You misunderstand me," replied Iriva as she shook her head slightly. "I am pleased that the scouts returned saying the hideout was not worth attacking," she managed to say before Betaro interrupted.

"Then what troubles you?" he asked, crossing his arms over his chest.

"Bah!" grumbled Iriva as she glowered at Betaro. "Do not give me such as a stare. I merely mean that I should practice using my abilities more, lest I become inefficient," she finished while crossing her own arms over her chest and glaring back at Betaro.

Betaro arched a brow inquisitively at Iriva with a slight tilt of his head. "Then you should visit the training grounds and duel with any number of those training," he finally said with a chuckle.

"I know this," grumbled Iriva as she snagged the reins of her mount. "But they are just juveniles," she added before placing her foot in a stirrup and mounting her steed.

132

Betaro watched as Iriva sat in the saddle pretending to pat the dirt off her gown. Abruptly, he released a roar of laughter, drawing the attention of those nearby.

"What is so amusing?" demanded Iriva once Betaro had managed to control his chortling.

"You are intimidated by the trainees and others that go to spar," stated Betaro with a smug grin plastered on his face.

"Lies!" spat Iriva, but she could not prevent the redness that crept up from her neck to her cheeks, turning her blue flesh a shade of purple. The low rumble coming from Betaro caused Iriva to clench her jaw, knowing the annoying man saw through her denial.

"Oy," said Betaro before he mounted his zebril. Guiding the animal closer to the healer, he then said cheerfully, "If you but ask nicely, I would gladly accompany you."

"Pugh!' snorted Iriva in return as she made a face at Betaro. "What good would it be to have an old goat in the sparring enclosure?" she asked, looking Betaro up and down, causing him to erupt into laughter once more.

"Very well then, General Jander," he said nonchalantly with a shrug. "Just remember, this old goat continues to lay waste to many trainees and seasoned soldiers to this day," he finished before making a clicking sound with his tongue and urging his mount forward, leaving Iriva scowling at his back.

CHAPTER 17

The last rays of light disappeared behind the mountains, and at once, the scorching heat began to dissipate. The seemingly desolate landscape gradually became alive as insects and various beasts emerged from their shelters. The coolness that came after the sun set coaxed Dondree from his heat induced slumber. With a yawn, Dondree pushed himself up and allowed his legs to drop down so that he sat straddling the large tree branch that served as his bed throughout the day. While not many creatures roamed about during the day, there were still enough dangers that drove Dondree to seek safety off the ground.

"Mmm," he quietly groaned as he tilted his head from side to side and enjoyed the cracking and popping. Next, he clasped his hands together in front of him before bringing them high above his head; remaining still for a brief time, he relished the mild burn as his muscled stretched and loosened after stiffening while he slept. "Ahh," he exhaled and relaxed his arms. Then languidly, he plucked several leaves from the tree – keeping the stems intact – and placed them in his travel pack until there was no space remaining. Slowly, he removed the stem from one of the leaves he held; glancing down, he looked at the small hole where the stem had been before bringing the leaf up to his mouth. He poured the tart, life-sustaining liquid into his mouth, swallowing quickly.

"Ugh," he said with a shudder once done drinking the sour juice. He swiftly did the same with the remaining leaves he clutched before eating the leather-like leaves. With his thirst and hunger satiated, he grabbed his belongings and effortlessly climbed down from the tree.

"What unfortunate soul will I come upon today?" he asked himself with a grin before stalking off into the night.
* * *
"Mus' be somethin' importan'," murmured one of the night lookouts as she peaked over her shoulder. From her assigned position at the rear gate, she watched the flickering torch flames as multiple individuals dashed through the empty city streets.

"Aye," agreed her companion with a brief glance over his shoulder as well.

"Wai' a min-uh'…" the female sentry said hesitantly, turning around fully so she faced the city. "Am I imagin' it?" she then asked, taking a few uneasy steps forward.

"Wha' is it?" questioned the male, shifting his weight apprehensively from one foot to the other.

Hidden in the shrubs along the wall near the back entrance of Capitalia, Wesdin looked up nervously, seeing the sentries were no longer facing the area outside of the city. *"Now…I should go now,"* he thought silently to himself. With a shaky breath, Wesdin quickly examined his surroundings before running through open gates, and he sprinted as fast as possible to the nearest bush outside the safety of the city.

"He's so fast!" exclaimed Leandra silently to herself as she charged after her closest friend. Following Wesdin's actions, Leandra hugged the wall. Leandra abruptly skidded to a halt upon hearing a concerned female voice.

"They seem ta be goin' ta homes tha' belon' ta masta' healas," voiced the lady soldier, concern evident in her tone.

With increasing anxiety, Leandra felt her hackles – the fur between her shoulders down along her spine to her tail - rise on end, making her appear larger in size, in response to the guard's statement. Peaking upward briefly, Leandra ensured the guards had still not turned about to their usual sectors of observation. Fear of losing track of Wesdin, Leandra wordlessly shouted to herself, *"Go!"* Without hesitation, she leapt forward and raced after Wesdin.

"Hurry up!" hissed Peygar as he dragged Lana along behind him, followed closely by Taygan.

"You're hurting me," whispered Lana in return, her voice harsh as she resisted her uncle's relentless pulling.

"Hush! And move quickly!" came Taygan's fretted response as she pushed Lana, refusing to allow her to slow her pace. "Whatever is happening, we're fortunate it has happened this eve."

Lana clenched her teeth together from lashing out at her mother and uncle, remembering how they had been ecstatic following the information she shared regarding the unexpected arrival of palace sentries as she removed 'the source' from the Khantessa. "Oof," grunted Lana faintly as she collided into her uncle's back from his abrupt halt.

"I am to fetch Maestro Soother Danner Pasendir!" shouted a soldier, stopping directly before the group's hiding place.

Terror rapidly seized Lana, rendering her obedient, as she felt a certainty spread through her that the guard would sense their presence. *"I can't go to prison!"* she shouted mutely in her mind.

Taygan detected her daughter's restiveness, and she instantaneously placed a gentle hand on Lana's shoulder.

"I shall accompany you," answered a nearby palace worker, hurrying to join the guard, before the pair continued to complete their task.

Remaining mute, Peygar continuously shifted his eyes from side to side, taking in the movements of various citizens as they darted through the streets. Hesitating for a blink of an eye, Peygar contemplated the best course to pursue. With a frown, he recalled the large torches - fastened outside on each side of the city's rear opening – that produced enough light to illuminate the archway and a substantial distance out. "Les' go," he finally said after the temporary pause which allowed a handful of people to zip past them.

Without another word, the trio pressed themselves as flat as possible to the stone wall that encircled Capitalia. Careful to avoid detection as the posted soldiers remained distracted, they rounded the edge of the gate opening. Moving swiftly, Peygar led the others along the stone barrier until they were no longer within the circle of light created by the torches' flames. Peygar grinned to himself, pleased they had remained undetected, as he continued leading his sister and niece away from the capital. Peygar soon relaxed and relinquished his hold on Lana. Confidently, he located one of the many trails he frequently traveled during his outings.

* * *

Like a statue, Avenor stood with his arms crossed over his chest, his long hair secured in a braid that hung down his back; his pitch-black eyes reflected the light from the roaring fire that illuminated the interior of his individual shelter. Mutely, he watched Everly drawing out the terrain on the *strategy slate* that had been erected.

After a short while, Everly took a step back to inspect her handiwork. Turning to Avenor, she dipped her head slightly

Lowering his arms, Avenor then approached the *strategy slate*. "My gratitude to General Akeenil for conducting a thorough reconnaissance. Because of her expert tracking ability, I am confident that the element of surprise is ours. Since she has had eyes on the location, she and General Crusendir will expand on the current battle plan further," he finished before nodding in direction of his parents.

"My thanks, Khan Crusendir," returned Everly before addressing the group of relevant military personnel that had been gathered to discuss plans for the pending battle. "As our Khan has stated, I too, believe we possess the element of surprise," began Everly as she looked around the area, meeting the gaze of everyone present. "However, we are at a disadvantage because the traitors have claimed the town of Fairwood."

"Information we have gathered through interrogation has revealed that not only has Fairwood been overtake, but it has also become a fortified compound," added Manijor, annoyance evident by his expression. "Not only has a wooden fence been constructed around the village, watch towers have also been established."

"Indeed," spoke Everly as she used a thin, metal rod to point to clean sections on the *strategy slate*. "Rozalin Lanikeel seems to have taken account even minor details in her planning. A substantial area surrounding the compound has been cleared, leaving open fields. This creates an obvious obstacle," she finished with a scowl.

"Our informant has provided us with everything we require regarding the watchmen's rotations. Even with the clearings, this should allow us to approach the fortress without being detected. Khan Crusendir possesses a unique ability that will grant us access when the time arrives." With his last statement, Manijor and the others shifted their attention to Avenor.

"Indeed," agreed Avenor. "However, because of the complexity of the situation, I have summoned you all to discuss strengths, weaknesses, and opinions on how best to merge the two forces with a favorable outcome," he finished while shifting his gaze between both force commanders.

Major Azriel Tamlin, her appearance still disheveled from her hasty ride to join the others, cast a sideways glance at Major Chevin. Major Chevin felt the gaze of *Force Pinelan's* commander boring into him. Turning his head, he met Azriel's stare and nodded his head. "As you desire, Your Grace," answered Mykel after turning his attention back to Avenor.

Various suggestions and discussions commenced throughout the evening; plans were made, modified, discarded, and re-evaluated countless times. The night stretched out until pre-dawn light began peaking over the horizon.

Stifling a yawn, Avenor cleared his throat and silenced the others. "It has been an exhaustive night. Get some sleep. We will resume planning after midday meal," he informed the others. A chorus of voices answered in return, acknowledging his instructions. Gradually, the others exited his personal space, leaving him alone to rest as well.

* * *

A banshee like wail ripped through the oasis causing the hair on Reeyah's nape to stand on end; savage gales screamed and howled as they greedily grabbed at Reeyah's wraps while relentlessly raging about her rigid form. From the safety of Overlook Cave, Reeyah peered up at the sky before breathing out a sigh of relief. The sky, usually dotted with countless stars resembling twinkling gems, was obscured by innumerable, miniscule, particles being whipped about in the atmosphere; no light could be detected from above, and the terrain was blanketed in complete darkness.

"Heh," Reeyah silently scoffed to herself. *"This one is welcome,"* she mutely continued thinking, appreciative of the passing sandstorm as it roared outside the protective mountains surrounding the desert sanctuary. Squinting, she pulled a dark, sheer cloth over her head to shield her eyes and skin from the fine particles that felt like needles pricking at her exposed flesh. Then, she cautiously navigated toward the farthest area within the safety of the oasis – a place where no one pitched their tents or dared settle down; even the most venerated warriors dreaded an unexpected visit from the infamous *armored culebras.*

"It is now or never. I can only hope two minutes is adequate time," Reeyah whispered into the unyielding whirlwinds as she removed a vial from the protection of her wraps. Quietly, she recited an incantation; immediately, she felt her body pulse with an abundance of energy, warding off any illnesses or sicknesses. She felt her abrasions, the ones sustained just from walking in the sandstorm, healing in response to the incantation. After swiftly removing the cover from the vial, Reeyah brough the container to her lips; the unexpected smoldering sensation made her hesitate briefly.

"No! No turning back!" she hissed audibly to herself. "This is for Dondree!" she growled, enraged at her own cowardice, before swiping at the hot tears that spilled from the corner of her eyes. Without another thought, she tipped her head back, poured the liquid into her mouth, and swallowed the burning concoction.

"Gah!" she exclaimed and instantly clutched at her rapidly swelling throat, her anxiety increasing as the wind shrilled through the veiled basin. Reeyah staggered unsteadily, battling to remain on her feet as the violent gusts continued to assault her; after struggling to ease the burning in her chest, Reeyah's eyes widened in terror as she realized that the high-pitched squealing was her own labored breathing.

"Calm down!" Reeyah mutely shouted at herself. Pursing her lips, she managed to drag in long, slow breaths which eased the ache of her oxygen deprived lungs. As her fear gradually dissipated, Reeyah managed

to rasp out another healing chant right before debilitating pain erupted over her entire body.

"Aargh!" shrieked Reeyah in anguish. No longer able to support her weight, she succumbed to the weakness that surged through her body, and she collapsed to her knees in the sand.

* * *

Far from the safety of the capital, Wesdin abandoned all caution, and he darted clumsily though the night; his ability to see as if the sun was at its highest point in the sky did naught as tears blurred his vision, temporarily blinding him. His ragged breathing along with the muted thudding of his feet as they pounded the earth silenced the nocturnal animals as he charged through the forest.

"*Oy!*" exclaimed Leandra silently as she came to a gradual stop. "*Where have you gone?*" she asked herself while canting her head to the side as she strained to listen. Just as she was about to lose hope, Leandra heard a faint cry of pain somewhere ahead of her. "*That must be you!*" she supposed excitedly before sprinting forward once more.

"Bah!" grunted Wesdin as he struggled to free himself from the thorns that snagged his cloak and scraped at his body. "What a uh... uh... uh...," he stammered while walking backward and tugging at his cloak. *Rip!* "Aagh!" he cried out in surprise as his cloak gave way, and he fell back to land on his rear end.

"What a pile of dung!" he finally growled out in frustration. Although the curse was mild, it still made his face burn with shame. Standing, he then patted the dirt off himself. Before turning away from the assaultive bush, Wesdin stuck his tongue out and made a face of disgust. "I shall uproot you upon my return!" he passionately vowed before exclaiming, "hmph!" Purposefully spinning on his heels, Wesdin caused his cloak to twirl behind him.

Leandra slowed her pace as she stalked through the quiet forest, and she tried to differentiate between the shrubbery. The light from the moon failed to completely penetrate through the lush canopy of tree branches overhead, making the various greenery appear to merge into one. "*Bah,*" she groaned and stamped a paw on the ground in annoyance. Suddenly, the scowl on her face vanished. Suspiciously turning her head and squinting her eyes, Leandra tried to determine the origin of the flapping sound that had captured her attention.

"Buffoon," groused Wesdin to himself as he absentmindedly continued marching through the dense woodlands, unaware that he had stumbled upon an inclining path.

Rotating her head from side to side, Leandra listened to the deafening silence. Just then, a single word graced her ears. "Buffoon." A

139

giddiness instantaneously bubbled in her chest, and her lips stretched into a broad grin. *"Wes,"* she whispered to herself, feeling relief wash over her, as she continued after Wesdin.

Huffing and puffing with each step, Wesdin continued his trek upward. Pausing briefly, Wesdin tossed his head back and inhaled deeply. Gradually, his eyes widened in panic as realization seeped through him. *"Someone is coming!"* he wordlessly screamed. Without looking back, Wesdin turned and scurried up the trail as swiftly as possible, occasional slipping on the dirt and loose gravel.

"Wesdin!" shouted Leandra in the common mind-link before growling with exasperation. *Oy!"* she exclaimed, realization dawning on her that Wesdin could not access the connection as he had not experienced the *transformation.*

The menacing growl behind him prompted Wesdin to quicken his already rushed steps. *"No, no, no! What was I thinking?"* he shouted in his own mind. Suddenly, the ground disappeared from under his feet, and he felt himself tumbling head over heels as he careened along the opposite side of the mountain leading to *The Forbidden Wilds.*

"Wonderful..." mumbled Leandra as she witnessed Wesdin lose his footing before plummeting down the steep trail. Gingerly skidding along the path, Leandra watched her companion as he was bounced between the high walls. With her attention solely on Wesdin, she failed to notice the numerous routes and divides in the trail, many leading to dead ends.

"Ugh," groaned Wesdin when he finally rolled to a stop. Reaching up, he placed an unsteady hand against his throbbing head.

Smelling blood coming from Wesdin, Leandra wasted no time in returning to her human form and rushing to his side. "Wes," she called softly.

"Who..." began Wesdin groggily as he blinked rapidly, trying to clear his blurred vision.

"Wes," repeated Leandra as she placed a cool hand on his forehead. "It's Leandra," she informed him quietly.

"Lea?" he said questioningly as he struggled to sit up.

"Aye," returned Leandra as she moved to assist Wesdin by placing an arm under his shoulders. "That was an incredible fall," she commented with a slight giggle.

"Hmph!" grunted Wesdin as he sat cradling his head. "It would have been better if it had killed me," he said, avoiding Leandra's face.

"Wes!" exclaimed Leandra, her expression mortified. "Why would you say such a thing?"

"Just go away," he spat angrily while staggering to his feet. "Go home," he said as he leaned against a nearby tree for support.

"You are serious?" she demanded hotly, crossing her arms over her chest. "Look at you," she jeered. "A wee bantling could best you," she taunted him angrily as her own irritation continued to rise.

"Nonsense," retorted Wesdin as he quietly recited an incantation. "These wounds of mine... regeneratetat et sanatetat." A dim, green light began swirling around Wesdin, warding off his weakness and fatigue while healing his physical injuries. "I will be fine," he said with a smirk at Leandra.

"Lies," returned Leandra with a nonchalant shrug. "I shall accompany you until you decide to return home," she then announced firmly.

"I do not need you," grumbled Wesdin between clenched teeth. Turning away from Leandra, Wesdin took a step before abruptly stopping. His movements spurred Leandra to rush to his side. "Oy," the pair simultaneously breathed incredulously, taking in the jungle-like landscape.

* * *

"Aaaah!" yawned Lana boisterously from behind her mother and uncle, stressing the sound as an attempt to express her overtiredness.

Taygan looked back at her daughter's hunched form with a furrowed brow. Reaching out, she snagged her brother's arm before speaking.

Peygar felt Taygan's light grip on his forearm, and he stopped to turn around; a gap in the canopy overhead allowed a sliver of light to splash across his face. "Whot is it?" he asked curiously.

"It grows late. We should stop and rest," Taygan answered her brother quietly. Taygan watched as Peygar's eyes narrowed, and a terrifying glower gradually transformed his expression.

"You thinks da guars will rest?" he abruptly hissed. "You thinks dey will allow whot Lana did ta go uh-n'punish'd?" Not bothering to wait for a response, Peygar spun back around, yanking his arm from Taygan's grasp. "We will no' rest until we crossed over the pass," he spat over her his shoulder.

"I am sorry," whispered Taygan as she draped an arm over her daughter's shoulders.

Lana gave her mother a half-hearted smile for even suggesting they stop. "It is not your fault," replied Lana as she openly glared at her uncle's back. "He will be the death of us," grumbled Lana under her breath so only Taygan could hear.

Kimberly Evette Ortuno

"Do not say such things," chided Taygan with a slight frown. "Let's hurry," she then said while propelling Lana along.

CHAPTER 18

Leandra felt her heart beating erratically in her chest. Absentmindedly, she slid her hand into Wesdin's and gradually let out a breath of relief as his enclosed hers; it was an unintentional response she had developed as a bantling whenever she was frightened or nervous. The young pair took slow, tentative steps as they surveyed their surroundings. Leandra was grateful that the assorted branches overhead, which were not as densely interwoven, allowed the light from the moon and stars to easily break through and clearly illuminate the strange terrain. "Where do you suppose we are?" she quietly asked although did not realize she spoke aloud, and she received no answer as her question fell on deaf ears. Continuing in silence, the two warily walked farther away from the path that had brought them to their current location.

Wesdin, 's gaze landed on what appeared to be a green tree trunk. Squinting curiously, he tilted his head back and followed the green post upward. His eyes grew larger, and his jaw dropped. "Oy," he whispered in awe. "How... what... no..." he stammered in confusion as he peered at the massive flower, easily towering eleven feet or more over them.

Leandra cast a sideways look at Wesdin; following his line of sight, she looked up as well. "Oy!" she exclaimed. "How pretty," she cooed with appreciation as a faint and pleasant smell tickled her nose. "Hmm," she whispered before inhaling deeply. At once, the wonderful scent flooded her nostrils, and she exhaled with a cheery smile on her face. The fragrance was calming and addictive. With her nose turned upward, she continued to take large breaths; soon, her eyelids began fluttering, and she allowed them to close, her eyelashes settling high on her cheeks. Unknowingly, she released her grip on Wesdin's hand, and her feet began to move on their own accord, taking her closer to the giant flower.

Bewildered by the immense flower, Wesdin continued to stare brazenly. "Wha..." he whispered as the petals began to curl. "I must have

143

hit my head harder than I thought," he said. Reaching up, he rubbed his eye before rapidly blinking. After a moment, he turned his attention back to the strange plant. "Oy!" he suddenly exclaimed.

The blossom continued to change before Wesdin's eyes. The edges of the rounded petals became serrated. The enormous stem curved and twisted.

After a while, Wesdin's eyes widened in horror. Immediately, he squeezed his hand, expecting to feel Leandra's. When his hand formed a fist, he gasped and quickly looked to his side. Bile rose in his throat, and he swallowed hard to force it back down. His gaze immediately turned forward, and he caught sight of Leandra as she leisurely approached the deadly *dulsay snapper.*

"Lea!" shouted Wesdin as he sprinted forward. His heart thundered frantically in his chest, pounding so hard it sounded in his ears. Even though the distance was short, he felt like it took an eternity to reach Leandra. Aware of the monstrous bloom ready to lower over his friend, Wesdin forced himself to run faster than ever. "Lea!" he screamed.

Just as Wesdin used all his might to shove himself off the ground, the flower unexpectedly shot downward. Wesdin forcefully collided with Leandra right before the flower petals smashed against the grass where Leandra had stood transfixed mere moments prior.

Wesdin and Leandra fell together and continued to roll a few feet. Abruptly, the ground gave way. The friends shrieked and yelled as they tumbled down a small slope.

"Aah!" cried out Leandra. It was the last sound she made before her head slammed against a small boulder, and she instantly plunged into oblivion, hidden from Wesdin's view by a large bush.

"Ugh," groaned Wesdin as he came to a stop, his face pressed into the grass under him. Hesitantly, he pushed himself up to his knees and immediately regretted the decision. "Gah!" he grunted and clutched his side as a stabbing pain in his flank made itself known. Glancing down, he noticed his hand covered in his own blood. "Better the flower got me instead of Lea," he groused to himself. Clenching his teeth, he took slow deep breaths. As the discomfort lessened, he finished rising to his feet. "Lea?" he whispered. Forgetting his ability to heal himself and others, Wesdin remained slightly hunched over as he hobbled in a circle. "Lea?" he hissed out again anxiously when she did not respond. Staggering forward unsteadily, he frantically examined his surroundings.

He felt dread spreading through his body. "Lea!" he finally shouted. His voice echoed through the darkness; once it completely faded, a nearby melodious voice captured his attention. Unable to resist, he turned in the direction of the alluring song.

"Oy... my head," moaned Leandra. Blinking slowly as she regained consciousness, she tentatively raised a hand to her head. "Youch!" she yelped as her hand grazed against the gash above her right eyebrow. Grunting, she sat up and grabbed the hem of her blouse. She then raised it to her mouth. *Rrrrrip!* Wincing, she wiped the blood from her eye before placing the strip of cloth to her oozing wound.

"Wes?" she said in manner resembling a whispered shout as she tilted her head to the side. Listening intently, she briefly heard her name before it disappeared in the distance. "Wesdin Crusendir, you answer me this instant!" she fiercely stated in the same tone. After struggling to her feet, she stepped forward and exhaled forcefully, thankful that the only agony she had was from her throbbing head. "Gah!" she suddenly groaned. "What is that awful noise?"

The continuous sound alternated between high-pitched squeals and raspy shrieks.

Leandra contorted her face and shuddered as the cacophony assaulted her senses; instinctively, she placed her hands over her ears. *"He is a dimwit at times... perhaps he has gone that way,"* she pondered to herself as she began stalking toward the unpleasant sounds.

* * *

Reeyah remained motionless on her hands and knees, her head limply hanging down, as ferocious gusts continued incessantly roaring around her. Her clothes, at the mercy of the relentless wind, forcefully shook and waved uncontrollably. Suddenly, another bone-chilling scream escaped Reeyah's lips, and her body trembled in anguish as her hands – covered in numerous fresh cuts and abrasions – tightened around various miniscule, yet pointed, objects buried in the gravely-sand.

However, the vicious gales swallowed her cry with a thunderous roar and disguised her tremors by angrily clawing at her coverings.

After what felt like forever, Reeyah finally collapsed on her side in exhaustion.

The storm had no remorse as it maintained its strength and ferocity. As if relishing in Reeyah's pain, larger items began flying toward her; incredulously, a felled sapling soared through the air and struck the entire length of her spine. Involuntarily, Reeyah arched her back as searing pain erupted throughout her entire being. The wind rapidly alternated between shrieks and whistles, as if laughing and mocking the crumpled woman, before sending forth larger sand particles that carelessly ripped and sliced through Reeyah's clothing.

As the pain finally became a bearable ache, Reeyah squinted against the tiny grains that clung to her eyelashes; mustering the little strength she could, she managed to whisper a brief chant. Suddenly, a faint, golden glow developed and began steady pulsating in front of her chest. Reeyah sighed quietly with relief as she felt the effects from the short-lived health restoring incantation. Once the restoration session was complete, Reeyah conducted the procedure again exactly as before; she repeated the process countless times until she had recovered enough to recite more complex and energy-draining incantations before finally being drifting into an exhausted slumber.

The moon had completed more than half of its journey across the night sky when Reeyah woke. With a smirk, she silently said to herself, *"Finally."* Without warning, her mouth opened wide in a yawn. *"The storm does not sound like it will end any time soon."* As she quietly pondered what action to take, she became aware of a tightness that surrounded her. Terror seized her, and she immediately froze. *"No!"* she mutely screamed. *"I should have left sooner!"* she continued to wordlessly chide herself. *"What if he made it? What if Dondree comes back? No one knows where I am! Dondree would never know I was a treat for an armored culebra!"* she woefully cried to herself.

The sand continued to shift around her, and she squeezed her eyes closed tightly, refusing to see the massive serpent before it swallowed her whole. *"Oh, my boy! I love you!"* she thought, feeling the earth shift once more.

After a tense moment, Reeyah felt the layer of sand over her head blow away. The wind continued to howl as it angrily danced above Reeyah. Reeyah winced as her covering lashed against her face, leaving a burning welt in its wake. As apprehension coursed through her, she hesitantly raised her head and opened her eyes. Reeyah dropped her head back and scoffed in self-mockery, realizing it was just a heavy layer of sand surrounding her and not a monstrous snake. After her fear dissipated, she reached up and grabbed her face covering. Carefully wiggling, she turned on her side, careful not to disrupt the sand that had settled completely around her. After finding a comfortable position, she pulled her head covering down and secured it. *"I suppose I am safe enough, concealed under the sand… at least my end will not be because I was consumed by a snake,"* she grumbled to herself before allowing the snugness surrounding her to comfort her as she drifted back to sleep.

* * *.

Wesdin continued walking slowly, stumbling every so often because his gaze had narrowed on sparkling pools of water in the distance. With his sight locked in tunnel vision, he was unable to notice as the terrain began to change, resembling swamp-lands.

Crrrooooaaaaak! A nearby *mud hopper* voiced her displeasure as she watched Wesdin advance on her position. *Crrrooooaaaaak!* The amphibian opened her mouth and curled her tongue, preparing to spit her lethal neurotoxin.

Wesdin continued to ignore the large frog, eager to find where the beautiful melody was coming from.

The *mud hopper* finally relaxed after watching the intruder who had not once glanced toward her; however, she knew she would be safer in the murky, swamp waters.

Splash!

"Eep!" squealed Leandra quietly with a jump, startled by a nearby splash. "Wes!" she whispered in a hushed shout. "Bah…" she said in exasperation while squinting her eyes. "If only I could see…" she began but cut herself off. "You are a dolt!" she exclaimed to herself. *Poof!* Leandra grinned to herself and shook out her fur. Intimidated by the swampy surroundings, she willed herself to become camouflaged. With her heightened senses, Leandra listened to the various noises.

Splash!

Tensing as she heard the water disrupted once more, Leandra turned. Far ahead of her, she watched as Wesdin scrambled back to his feet. Knowing he could not hear her in her tigal form, she began cautiously following him. *"Don't run,"* she reminded herself uneasily. *"Surely, there are creatures here that may be able to see through my concealing ability."*

Wesdin reached up to the closure at his neck and unclasped his cloak; the cloth, now heavily saturated, slowed his progress. Absentmindedly, he allowed it to drop in the water that he continued to slosh through.

Leandra nervously sliced through the hazy pond, creating gentle ripples in her wake. Glancing from side to side, she caught sight of a handful of fallen logs, and she approached the closest one. After sinking her claws into the wood, she pulled herself out of the water. Now able to maneuver better, Leandra hurried across the log and lunged to the next. The stump dipped with her weight and sent forth a series of larger waves but did not make any other sound.

With her eyes fixed on Wesdin, Leandra paid little attention to the logs under her feet. As she jumped to the next, she struggled to pierce through the substance under her paws.

Suddenly, the log's front raised up and turned.

"Hissss!" left Leandra's mouth as she pulled her lips back, exposing her fangs, at the dangerous lizard.

The *swamp thrasher* heard the feline-like hiss and felt multiple sharp pricks along its back, but upon looking, saw nothing. Opening its jaws, exposing its own monstrous fangs, the crocodile angrily hissed in return before violently snapping its mouth closed.

Leandra hastily looked around, unsure of where to go. The sudden appearance of additional *swamp thrashers* rendered her immobile as fear seized her. Another snap from the creature she stood on broke through her terror. *"Run!"* she silently shouted to herself. With the advantage of being invisible to the large lizards, she leapt from one to another; she was careful to avoid the thrashers' quickly opening and closing jaws.

Wesdin approached the crystal-clear, interconnected, spring-fed pools of water of varying heights; the uppermost one had a small waterfall which gently cascaded into the next two, side by side, slightly below it. Those, in turn, did the same, which created four more miniature ponds below it; finally, the four all spilled out to form a single, shallow, lake that narrowed at the end to create a fresh-water stream.

Leandra managed to escape the *swamp thrasher* lair unscathed, however, the shock that possessed her left her tremoring uncontrollably.

Wesdin tilted his head to the side, motionlessly watching as the most gorgeous woman he had ever seen, emerged across from him. Her lips continued to move, singing the fascinating melody that had captured Wesdin's attention, as she gracefully swam through the water toward him.

As the shock released its grip on Leandra, she shook her head to clear her thoughts. Taking a calming breath, she then frantically surveyed her surroundings to find Wesdin. Her eyes widened as she caught sight of her friend, leaning over the edge of a pool of water; however, what startled her most was the gruesome half-beast and half-human – the creator of the dreadful ballad – that had wrapped its tentacles around Wesdin, and was gradually pulling him into the water.

Without hesitation, Leandra sprinted across the distance to her friend. Hastily, she reverted to her human form. *Poof!* "Wesdin!" she shouted a few feet from her friend. The hideous creature turned to Leandra, roared thunderously, and began pulling Wesdin over the rocky ledge into the sparkling water.

"Argh!" cried out Leandra, immediately raising her hands to cover her ears. *"Wesdin!"* she silently shouted before beginning an incantation. Leandra frowned, though she continued her chanting, as she watched the aquatic fiend settle her hands on Wesdin's upper arms. Just as Leandra finished, a *blizzard* encompassed her friend and his assailant, slowing their movements.

Not waiting for another moment to pass, Leandra charged across the short expanse. In mid-stride, she changed to her feline self, and she instantly grabbed ahold of Wesdin's tunic with her teeth. Ensuring she clamped down on as much fabric as possible to prevent tearing, she then pulled back with all her strength. She sank her claws into the soft flesh of the tentacles, scratching and slicing away their hold on Wesdin.

The creature released an ear-splitting shriek as she felt Wesdin slipping from her grasp. She tried to tighten her hold, but it was in vain as her fingers barely closed an inch. Screeching again angrily, she continued trying to strengthen her grip on her prey.

Wesdin blinked slowly, his vision clearing; the hypnotizing song produced by the beautiful woman that had enraptured him had been replaced by a hideous part-woman and part-octopus. "Aaaaaaaah!" he instantly screamed as she turned her murderous glare on him, and her needle like nails pierced through his skin. "Let me go!" he shouted before he cried out in pain once more, feeling the beast sinking her nails deeper into his muscles. "Gah!" hollered Wesdin in agony as the beast tore away sections of his flesh.

Rip! Thud!

Wesdin heard a ripping sound before feeling the sleeves of his tunic drawn from his arms and the sound of his travel pack falling to the ground. As his arms slipped through the sleeves, he felt his back collide with whatever was behind him.

Leandra refused to relinquish her hold on Wesdin, and she continued her hasty retreat, hauling Wesdin away from the furiously screeching beast.

Wesdin gradually became aware of being dragged along by his tunic from behind. *"What has got me now?"* he wordlessly thought as his eyes widened and his heart began hammering frantically against his chest. *"Leandra? Where is she? I have gotten her killed! I am going to die too! Why did I leave?"* his mind tossed questions and statements around in a tizzy, unaware he was no longer moving.

"Let me see you," came a familiar voice, quietly easing through Wesdin's irrational thoughts.

"Huh?" mumbled Wesdin with a baffled expression on his face.

"Oy," grumbled Leandra as she reached for one of Wesdin's arms. "You are wounded," she said sternly. "You must heal."

Wesdin looked down at his arms, though he failed to comprehend what his eyes saw; sections of his flesh and muscle had been gouged away from his shoulders down to the bend of his elbows. The wounds, deepest in the muscles surrounding his shoulders, exuded blood at a rate that if not ceased, would leave him dead within minutes. Absentmindedly, he tensed.

"Heal, Wesdin!" commanded Leandra, noticing the gloss-eyed look in her friend's eyes and the confusion on his face. "You must heal yourself!" she repeated harshly.

Wesdin's eyes snapped up to Leandra's. The concern etched on her face softened his sudden wariness. "What?" he said after a few stressful moments.

Leandra sighed and shook her hands out beside her in exasperation. "Heal, now!" she hissed at her friend, feeling desperation seeping through her every fiber.

"I see," mumbled Wesdin once understanding registered. After closing his eyes, he frowned. The scowl continued to deepen until Wesdin finally whispered a brief incantation. With his life force pouring out from the injury, his energy was completely depleted, and he began slipping back.

"Oy!" gasped Leandra as she reached out and steadied her closest companion. "Wes?" she questioned softly to which he opened his eyes to mere slits and mumbled incoherently in return.

"Hmm?" was all Wesdin managed to say.

"Why haven't you healed further?" she asked, her tone implying as she arched her brow.

"No energy," he returned quietly before allowing his eyes to close.

Hastily, Leandra reached up to a sealed section of her tunic; she removed a small flask and removed the stopper. She then pressed the opening to Wesdin's mouth. "Drink," she said sternly.

Without opening his eyes, Wesdin swallowed a few mouthfuls of mildly-bitter, gritty-textured pudding-like substance. "Meal mush," he croaked after he downed the last of it.

"Aye," returned Leandra. "Wait a handful of minutes. You must heal more. I feel you have lost too much blood," she quietly informed Wesdin. "Do not leave from here. I am going to retrieve your travel pack," she instructed.

Wesdin dipped his head ever so slightly; a sudden *poof* sound followed by quiet pitters-patters told him that Leandra had already left him. After a moment, he recited another brief chant. "Oy," he grunted softly as he leaned back, grateful Leandra had moved him to a tree after he healed the first time. Wesdin managed to heal his injuries a total of three times before he slipped into oblivion.

Leandra cautiously edged her way to the crystal-clear water. *"Bah,"* she grunted to herself. *"Why **right** there?"* she grumbled, eyeing the leather sack at the stony edge. Snorting to herself, she sprinted to the pond's border, snatched the bundle from the ground – unintentionally dropping a couple of items - and dashed away without a second glance.

"Wes?" Leandra called out softly immediately upon her return. "Wes? Are you okay?" she asked as she gently shook him. Leandra frowned as she watched Wesdin's slight nod and unintelligible grumble. "You better be!" she said in a commanding voice to conceal her worry. "Phew!" she exclaimed with a sigh of relief as her eyes landed on Wesdin's fresh wounds which were no longer oozing. "You managed to heal," she whispered before snuggling against his side and drifting off to sleep.

* * *

'They'll be tha death o' me,' Peygar quietly admitted to himself after glancing back at his sister and niece as they reached the peak of the mountain path. Removing a crude sled from his back, he set it down. "Sit," he callously instructed the other two and tightly strapped them to the wooden slab.

Too tired to object, Taygan and Lana collapsed and clung to one another; Peygar wasted no time in wrapping a rope around them and securing them to the makeshift sleigh.

"Wha... what... are you doing?" Taygan managed to ask warily.

"Lowerin' ya two down tha path. I dun feel like havin' ya both kill us," he replied with a snort. "Yer neer'ly sleepin' on yer feet," he grunted as he cinched the opposite end of the rope around his waistt. Not caring to answer any other questions, Peygar lessened his grip on the rope. The improvised sled slid down the trail, following the natural course with least resistance. Once the rope became taunt, Peygar removed two mining picks for his own safety and carefully began the decent. After a significant time, Peygar felt the weight around his waist lessen. Hastily, he lowered himself the remaining distance before examining his sister and niece.

Taygan and Lana snored quietly as they slept peacefully embraced in each other's arms.

Peygar rolled his eyes and shook his head with annoyance. Grunting, he looked up and his eyes widened in awe. "Oy," he exclaimed in a breathy tone. "Wha' a place," he said before yawning. "Es'plorin' will hav'ta wait," he groaned while reaching toward the sky, stretching his aching muscles. Not bothering to remove the rope from around his waist, he pulled the slab to a nearby crevice between two boulders. Stepping forward, Peygar inspected the moderate area for any critters. With a sigh of relief that they would not meet any hostile creatures, he tugged the sled with his sleeping sister and niece alongside of himself. Laying down on the grass, Peygar finally allowed his consciousness to slip away.

* * *

"Save her or it will be all your lives!" threatened Valcaly as every master healer assigned to the palace recited various incantations.

Aylox stood motionless, except for his rapidly rising and falling chest, with his arms crossed. A muscle in his jaw jumped as he clenched and unclenched his teeth as he watched the healers fighting to save the Khantessa's life.

Valcaly stormed across the crowded chamber and stepped out into the corridor; scanning the area, she quickly located a guard. "You," she said, her voice dripping with malice, as she raised her hand.

Aylex and Daylin exchanged nervous glances after seeing the rage swirling in Valcaly's eyes, but the brothers remained silent.

"Overseer?" returned the soldier with a hesitant salute. His brows drew together as he waited, unsure of how to address Valcaly as she pointed at him.

"Major Jonetal Teyio. Here. Now," spat Valcaly harshly.

The guard quickly saluted Valcaly after exhaling the breath he unknowingly held. "As you command, Overseer," he returned, aware her curtness was due to the grave situation.

Valcaly grabbed another soldier by the arm as he tried to scurry past her. "You," she snapped and tightened her grip on the guard's arm. "Captain Weelton. Make sure the Khanzito is with Commandant Clawbane," she hissed before relinquishing her hold with a shove.

"As you command, Overseer," grunted Kalven Weelton as he staggered back slightly. Rendering the proper salute, he rushed to the Khanzito's personal quarters.

Spinning on her heels, Valcaly stalked back to check on the Khantessa's condition.

Aylex stiffened his posture as the sentry approached him. "What business do you havve?" he demanded with his arms crossed over his chest.

"Overseer Truceran has instructed me to guarantee that Khanzito Crusendir is in the safety of Commandant Clawbane," Kalven announced sternly.

"Very well," grunted Aylex, stepping to the side to allow the captain to pass.

Eyeing the tigal warily, Kalven entered Wesdin's personal quarters. After searching the area, only to discover it was empty, he scowled with confusion. Scratching his head, he exited the Khanzito's chambers.

"Well?" demanded Aylex with an arched brow, wondering why Wesdin had not accompanied the shorter man.

"I shall go to the Commandant," retorted Captain Weelton. Without waiting for a response, he turned away from Aylex and rushed down the hall.

"Captain Weelton," called out a palace worker as the soldier approached. "May I assist in any way?" she asked lightly.

"No…" Kalven began slowly before stopping. "Actually," he said slowly, recalling the other tasks that the Vice Commandant had order he complete. "Aye. Aye, I would appreciate your assistance," he finally said with a nod. "Khanzito Crusendir should be under Commandant Clawbane's protection. Verify this, and return to me," he instructed her.

"As you desire, Captain," replied the palace keeper. Kalven watched her disappear around the corner before hurrying to complete his own tasks.

As the palace keeper rushed through the palace, she passed along the message. The message continued to be passed along until a guard finally arrived at the quarters where the visiting allies were resting under the protection of Commandant Mikela Clawbane.

A knock at the door drew Mikela's attention, and she looked up from the tome she was reading to pass the time. Setting it down, she took long, even strides to the entry. Quickly, she turned the handle and drew the door open wide. "What news do you bring?" she immediately demanded.

"Commandant Clawbane," began the sentry with a salute. "I was requested to inform you that Khanzito Crusendir remains safe during this time," he reported.

"Very well," returned Mikela with a curt nod. After dismissing the guard, she closed the door.

The soldier then reported he had completed the undertaking to the person he assisted. In reverse order, the various people repeatedly reported that the assignment had been carried out to those they had accepted the task from. However, unknowingly to each of them, the message had progressively been unintentionally changed until the ordered mission had been entirely altered.

* * *

Betaro cleared his throat nervously as he peeked sideways at Juldeyah as they guided the troop; after a circle had been formed, Betaro gracefully dismounted – the signal for the others to follow suit and begin making camp for the evening. The sun had already dipped under the horizon, however, a faint glow remained. The light would not completely disappear for another half-hour.

Betaro strolled through the encampment and easily found the tent he sought; the banner, proudly waving in the wind, indicated Overseer. Coughing quietly, he then rapped on the wooden post at the entrance. "High Wizard Mulbin," he called out and waited, listening to the shuffling within the tent.

"General Akeenil," greeted Juldeyah as she pulled back the flap. "What do I owe for the pleasure of your visit?" she asked curiously.

"Nothing so serious," he returned with an anxious chuckle. "May I enter?" he asked with a slight dip of his head suggestively.

"Of course," returned Juldeyah as she took a step back to allow Betaro to enter. "Please," she continued with an outstretched hand, "take a seat." She let the flap drop closed as he stepped over the threshold before joining him at the table. "What troubles you?" she asked while pouring two glasses of *lavendia* tea.

Betaro ran a hand through his already disheveled hair, and he paused to massage the nape of his neck. "It has been many cycles," he began slowly. "I understand Knight and Cleric Wynox returned to Itagrio after their daughter's disappearance," he continued in a strained voice.

"Aye," returned Juldeyah, her eyes becoming cloudy with unshed tears. "It was exceedingly difficult for them both, especially Bebelyn," she admitted woefully.

"Where are they now?" pressed Betaro. "Since my business in Itagrio is complete, I feel it necessary that I should pay my respects," he said quietly.

"Oy," gasped Juldeyah and pressed a hand to her lips as a single tear escaped the corners of her eyes. "They are gone," she finally murmured.

"Gone?" repeated Betaro incredulously, his face contorting in disbelief. "What do you mean?"

"From the whispers I have heard," she said with a sniffle, pausing to wipe away her tears, "not more than a cycle after their return, Bebelyn forced Josegos to abandon everything and return to Savenius." She paused for a moment, and her brows drew together as she frowned. "I suppose at that time, the land was still considered the *Feral Unknown*. Whatever the case, it was whispered that they returned to continue searching for Sedria," she added with a sad sigh.

"You are certain?" asked Betaro in a tone indicating he still did not believe the High Wizard.

"Aye," she nodded fervidly once before adding, "when I sent soldiers to investigate their assigned quarters in the palace... their belongings had been hastily tossed about. Whatever did not appear relevant was abandoned," she said, again wiping away a stray tear. "I have not heard from them since."

"At that time..." muttered Betaro under his breath, his mind racing, "Feralia was the capital. They would have passed through. Surely, someone would have recognized them immediately upon disembarking."

"Aye," agreed Juldeyah with a slow nod of her head. "Oy," she whispered, and her eyes widened. "It makes sense now!" she then exclaimed. "The guards had reported finding copious amounts of discarded hair. I surmised it was to reduce the need of washing while traveling..." she finished, allowing her voice to trail off.

"Oy," groaned Betaro, his eyes suddenly misty. "They passed through the city without ever being detected because their appearances had changed!" he finished and tossed his head back, staring at the leather ceiling. After a short time passed, Betaro cleared his throat once more and stood up. "You have my thanks," he said gruffly. "I shall take my leave," he announced before turning, leaving Juldeyah seated at the table, and letting himself out of the tent; both remained lost in their own thoughts.

* * *

Still standing like he was made from stone, Aylox remained in the same position as when Valcaly had stomped away from the chaos surrounding the bed where Galhix lay in blood-soaked linens. With his eyes locked on the scene in front of him, he caught sight of Valcaly with his peripheral vision. Just as she was about to storm past him, he reached out and firmly clamped his hand down on her forearm.

"Unhand..." began Valcaly as she turned and tried to wrench her arm free, but she abruptly stopped when she realized who had stopped her.

Aylox finally shifted his gaze, and he peered down at Valcaly. "Calm down," he said, his voice low and threatening. "They," he paused momentarily, jerking his head in the direction of the healers, "do not need you threatening them each time you stalk by," he finished, his eyes flashing angrily.

Valcaly pried her arm free before placing her hands on her hips defiantly. "It will be your life and mine if she should pass," hissed Valcaly under her breath so only Aylox could hear.

"Aye," he agreed while clenching and unclenching his jaws, trying to control his fury. "But shouting at them does no good," he finished before grabbing ahold of Valcaly once again as she turned to leave. Placing his hand sternly on her shoulders, he refused to let her move away.

155

Valcaly looked over her shoulder, her eyes glinting with rage, and glared at Aylox; she opened her mouth to lash out in return, but instantly snapped it closed, knowing she would regret her words if spoken while her emotions were in an upheaval.

Not long after, Jonetal entered the royal quarters. His eyes met Aylox's, and the two men shared a look of mutual understanding. Without a word, Jonetal took ahold of Valcaly and wrapped her in his embrace. "Khantessa Galhix will not surrender. She is strong. She will recover," he whispered reassuringly in her ear, but Valcaly was lost in her own muddled thoughts. Sometime throughout the night, Jonetal sent for various members of his *Force*.

"Find out how this happened," commanded Jonetal in a steely tone as Captain Holdir stood at attention.

"As ya' com'mand, Major," replied Eezien, bringing his forearm to his chest in salute before exiting the cramped area.

As morning approached and the sun began to rise, a warm glow crept in through the open window.

Jonetal sat holding Valcaly protectively on his lap, her head resting on his shoulder and her forehead pressed against the side of his neck. He lightly massaged her back, easing the knots from her tense muscles. While she had relaxed as the night progressed, he knew she had not slept throughout the ordeal.

From her position, Valcaly watched as the various flashes of colorful lights from the multitude of incantations gradually ceased as the healers stopped their treatment. Immediately, Valcaly bolted upright out of Jonetal's arms.

Sensing her jump to her feet, Aylox instantly turned and cast a warning glare at Valcaly, preventing her from advancing or saying a word.

"Overseer Truceran," finally said one of the master clerics, her voice strained from the relentless chanting throughout the night.

"Speak," returned Valcaly brusquely. The fatigued healer flinched as if Valcaly had physically struck her, and Valcaly winced to herself upon realizing her voice was harsher than she intended. "Speak," repeated Valcaly, her voice softer.

"She will survive," breathed out Maestra Fiona Smitian, her shoulders slumped with exhaustion.

"Glory be to the divine," replied Valcaly in a rush as she forcefully exhaled.

"Soother Danner Pasendir took leave earlier to recover," Fiona quietly informed Valcaly and the others present in the crowded space. "We have already assigned specific periods where each of us will remain with the Regent Khan."

"Very well," replied Valcaly as she dragged a hand down her face, trying to erase the tiredness she knew transformed her expression.

Just then, a slender Shadow Runner stepped through the open door and walked directly to Valcaly.

"Maestro Pasendir," mumbled Valcaly drowsily.

"Overseer Truceran," returned the blue-skinned healer with a salute. "I have volunteered for first watch," he reiterated what Fiona had said only moments before.

"Very well," sighed Valcaly. "Wake her should condition change me," she incoherently informed the master Soother. "Vice Commandant and Aylox there I will remain," she stated while pointing to a corner where travel cots had been prepared.

"As you command, Overseer," replied Danner with a cough to conceal the smirk on his face after effortlessly unscrambling Valcaly's instructions. He then saluted before turning to join the other healers before they gradually departed to seek refuge and rest in the sanitorium.

"Rest well," murmured Jonetal after he placed a gentle kiss on Valcaly's forehead. "I have already instructed my troops to begin investigating and searching for the assailant."

"You will discover me anything wake up?" she asked, blinking her bleary eyes.

"Aye," said Jonetal with a soft chuckle. "Rest, now," he then instructed her gently.

Valcaly grumbled under her breath incoherently before lowering herself to the makeshift bed with a groan; within seconds of laying down, her eyes fluttered closed, and she allowed herself to slip into oblivion. Not far behind, Aylox felt his eyelids grow heavy as he settled on his own cot. Shutting his eyes, he inhaled deeply; before he could exhale completely, he was already sound asleep.

* * *

Tweet... Cheep... Reeyah blinked her eyes in confusion. *Tweet, tweet.*

"Ugh," she groaned softly as she shifted from her side to her back, and her muscles screamed in protest as she struggled against the sand that weighed her down. Her shawl fell from over her head, and she closed her eyes halfway against the dim morning light – the light before the sun completely emerged from below the horizon and chased away the night.

From her back, Reeyah stared up at the trees and watched as a small flock of sparrows cheeped and tweeted to one another as they gazed down at her. A handful of males, evident by the black smattering of feathers on their chests, hopped from one branch to another as they repeatedly released angry *chiiiirrrrp* shouts.

"Well, aren't you some fat ones," noted Reeyah as she made a face at the birds. After unburying herself, she immediately began an incantation. Once she finished, the discomfort in her muscles vanished, her remaining injuries healed, and she felt her energy restored. "Oy," she exhaled cheerfully while reaching her hands upwards, stretching her stiff muscles. She then stood and patted the remaining sand from her trousers and tunic. Lastly, she picked up her shawl, vigorously shook it out, draped it over her shoulder, and secured the closure at her throat before beginning the trek back to Overlook Cave.

"He'll be awake by the time I return," muttered Reeyah as she trudged through the sand. "Ah!" she suddenly exclaimed with a grin. Ahead, she discovered another of the rare, stunted – an effect as they adapted to the subtropical environment of the oasis – tress. The dwarf tree produced plentiful, red, oblong shaped berries. Reeyah grabbed the hem of her shawl to create a container, and she set about collecting the delicious mulberries to take with her. Once satisfied, Reeyah began her trek again while consuming a berry sporadically along the way.

Demic nervously scanned the encampment, skipping over every head with black or brown hair. His eyes clashed with Dimor's as he too surveyed the area along with the others in the camp.

"Anything?" roared Gunter loud enough to be easily heard in every tent in the oasis. Only the crackling and snapping of the bonfire and the gurgling of the natural spring before it cascaded over the ledge of Overlook Cave answered him. "Well?" he continued, his voice like thunder.

"Overlord," said Sordun as he approached Gunter.

Gunter's gaze shifted to the man, hunched over farther that usual as he ungracefully bowed. "Speak," spat Gunter.

"Word spreads that Lordess Reeyah is returning from the direction of the Arid Mountains," replied Sordun without moving.

With a snarl, Gunter sprang forward from the outer ledge of the cave overlooking the encampment below. His powerful muscles bulged with raw strength as he seemed to fly from the ledge down to the large clearing beside the roaring fire.

Thud!

"Eep!" yelped Maba and Kifta in unison from their places beside the massive flame before spinning around at the unexpected appearance of Gunter as he landed beside them in the grass. Trembling in fear, the two women remained motionless.

Gunter slowly straightened himself from the half-crouched position in which he landed; his perfectly chiseled muscles rippled with every movement. The glossy sheen that covered Gunter's broad chest was evidence of the warmth that already spread throughout their desert sanctuary even though the brutal sunrays were blocked by the leaves overhead. He purposefully took his time in rotating his shoulders back, and the act stretched the countless scars that marred his chest, making them appear larger and more intimidating. He silently stood proudly with his back straight, sensing the anxiety grow around him. Finally, he turned sideways and stared at the two women clutching buckets of lard used to feed the inferno. "Carry on," he said, his voice dangerously low.

"Overlord," they replied simultaneously with a slight bow. Without delay, Maba and Kifta returned to their morning chore.

Just then, a lively whistle fluttered through the camp. Everyone turned to see who dared to disrupt the Overlord.

Reeyah whistled cheerfully as she nonchalantly half-walked and half-skipped between the tents. "A basket, please?" she said, pausing only to request a container for her freshly picked berries.

Doko, uncertain of what to do, frowned and remained still.

"Oy," muttered Reeyah in mild annoyance. "Doko… a basket," she repeated, her voice becoming stern.

The man, one of the few individuals she had fled with cycles ago, turned with apprehension, and he picked up a container woven out of reeds. He then held it out to Reeyah.

"My thanks," she said as she carefully filled the basket with her morning harvest. Taking the basket, she turned and collided with a wall of muscle and stumbled back. "Oy!" she exclaimed in surprise.

"Where have you been?" demanded Gunter, his tone livid.

"Exploring," she replied simply. Shrugging one shoulder, she stepped around Gunter and continued her carefree stroll back to the center of camp.

"You dare defy me?" growled out Gunter between clenched teeth, his fury increasing with each passing moment.

"Defy you?" repeated Reeyah, tossing the question over her shoulder rebelliously. "Never," she then said as she stepped into the clearing where every person within the oasis gathered to share all meals. "Kifta. Maba," she curtly greeted the two women. "Freshly picked," she added as she set the basket of berries down.

"Much appreciated, Lordess," whispered Kifta as Maba dipped her head ever so slightly.

"Argh!" groaned Reeyah in surprise as she felt a large hand grab a fistful of her hair and yank her head back.

"Overlord," began Sordun tentatively, disgusted with Gunter's heavy handedness with women, but was instantly silenced.

"Hold your tongue or I'll feed you to the scorpions!" fumed Gunter and tightened his grip on Reeyah's maroon locks.

Demic and Dimor shoved their way to the front of the crowd that had formed around the clearing. Dimor instinctively placed a hand on his brother's shoulder, knowing he would charge into the fray. Demic shot his brother a scowl, huffed irritably, and crossed his arms over his chest.

"Oof!" gasped Gunter in surprise as he doubled over from the unexpected blow Reeyah landed in his midsection.

Seizing the opportunity, Reeyah then used all her might to forcefully extend her arm and struck Gunter in the groin with her fist.

"Ugh!" groaned the Overlord, his grip on Reeyah unintentionally lessoning, as he reached down to protect his sensitive man-bits.

Reeyah spun out of her abusive mate's slack grip and retreated a few steps before turning to face her abuser as he fell to his knees.

"I shall enjoy pounding you to a bloody pulp," muttered Gunter under his breath, trying to ignore the debilitating agony between his thighs.

Reeyah stood glowering down at Gunter and scoffed. "Overlord Gunter," she said boldly, her clear voice heard by the entire gathering. "I challenge you."

Gasps and whispers instantly exploded through the crowd. Murmurs of disbelief and mutters of bewilderment quickly spread as neighbors exchanged astonished expressions and those of horror.

A deep, humorless chortle gradually silenced the incredulous people. "You?" Gunter finally scoffed as he staggered to his feet before adding with a sneer, "Challenge me?"

"To the death," added Reeyah. Her ice-cold glare pierced through him, and her face was void of emotion.

"Very well," Gunter finally consented. "My weapons," he called out brusquely. One of the nearby hunters retrieved a double-stacked set of identical wavy swords, and he placed the hilt in Gunter's open hand. Gunter brought his hands in front of his chest before gripping a wooden section in each hand; when he stretched his arms back out to his side, a perfectly forged *kalis* gleamed dangerously from both of his hands.

As Gunter waited, Reeyah unhooked her shawl and dropped it at her side. From around her wrist, she unfastened a leather strap; she then expertly used the rawhide tie to bind her hair to prevent it from whipping into her eyes. She locked her eyes with Gunter's; without breaking the contact, she muttered under her breath. A crimson silhouette progressively developed around her until she was completely engulfed by the transparent glow.

A flicker of uncertainty flashed in Gunter's eyes but was instantly replaced with fury; his nose crinkled as his lips curled in a throaty snarl.

Reeyah absentmindedly opened her mouth, exposing fangs she had never had prior to that moment, and she instantly returned a snake-like *hiss*.

Another wave of whispers rolled through those gathered as fear and awe gripped them.

Shifting her stance, Reeyah swiftly found her balance and center of gravity. She then muttered under her breath. Immediately, she grimaced as every inch of her flesh burned with searing pain. After a moment, the discomfort dissolved.

"What the..." stammered Gunter as he examined Reeyah. Her skin, while still her normal color, was no longer tender flesh; as Gunter squinted, he noted her body was now covered in what resembled the scales of the enormous serpents – the *armored culebras*.

Reeyah gave Gunter a devious wink before chuckling wickedly.

A cruel sneer distorted Gunter's face before he announced, "Let us begin." Without another word, Gunter unleashed a flurry of stabs, slices, and thrusts as he beautifully whirled with the two deadly swords. His movements were precise, and his skill was unmatched.

Reeyah moved swifter than the lethal dancer; she effortlessly evaded and dodged his every strike.

Clink!

"Ah-ha!" exclaimed Gunter triumphantly upon feeling his blade slide over Reeyah's shoulder. However, his delight soon faded as Reeyah stood unharmed across from him.

"My turn," she then whispered. Gunter's eyes widened in disbelief as he watched Reeyah's feet. He eyed them intently, observing how they never left the ground and appeared to glide over the grass, as if slithering from side to side.

Reeyah used Gunter's distraction to her advantage; in her superior form, she crawled up his body. She wrapped her legs around his neck, and she wasted no time in locking them in place.

The tightening around his neck jolted Gunter out of his own thoughts; he managed to inhale, the sound a wheeze as it squeezed through the narrow opening of his throat.

"Hmph," grunted Reeyah as she clenched her thighs together tighter, completely obstructing Gunter's air flow.

Gunter dropped his wavy blades and reached up to furiously claw at Reeyah's legs; however, it was to no avail. His fingers and hands became bloodied as they scraped against her razor-sharp armored skin.

As his vision began to blacken, Gunter threw himself backward in hopes of dislodging his assailant.

"What is it, my loving mate?" Reeyah taunted as she reached down to caress Gunter's disfigured cheek. "Would you like me to let you go?" she asked, her voice sensual.

Gunter managed to nod slightly as his eyes bulged from their sockets; saliva dribbled from his open mouth. His face contorted with misery as his chest screamed for relief.

"Tsk, tsk," Reeyah finally said sweetly before unlocking her legs. She then stood above her fallen mate.

Instantly, Gunter sucked in ragged breaths as he tried to satisfy his starved lungs. He glowered up at Reeyah as he continued to gasp harshly with one hand massaging his aching neck.

"It is time for you to go," she then murmured with a pleasant smile. Void of any sign of remorse, Reeyah began incanting loudly with her hands outstretched to Gunter. "Tuyom lifexia et soulexia sar meyah!" she recited fervently. At once, a scarlet specter sprung forth out of her palms and surged into Gunter's mouth, down his throat and throughout his body. A malicious smile crept across Reeyah's face. Gunter's excruciating screams sent waves of shock and terror throughout the encampment as his lifeforce was drained by the ghostly apparition and transferred to Reeyah.

A warry stillness followed Gunter's last tormented cry. After what felt like an eternity, Demic finally shouted, "Hail, Overlord Reeyah!" His boisterous chant was then repeated by Dimor before the entire oasis hailed and cheered for the new Overlord.

CHAPTER 19

There was no moonlight in the darkness that engulfed the lands; what little lighting the stars provided only increased the shadows which were then turned into daunting illusions by the over-active minds of apprehensive soldiers. In the center of the forest, a significant area had been cleared around the traitorous encampment. Flames from numerous torches blatantly raged at the guard towers; the brazen fires hungrily licked at the oil-dipped wicks that had been fastened to metal tridents with miniature staves. The shortened staves had been heated before being allowed to burn through wooden clubs, providing a snuggly set safety barrier for those holding the torches.

From their positions, concealed within the surrounding trees at the clearing's edge, the two-remaining loyal Texicar Forces waited anxiously.

Manijor placed a firm hand on Avenor's back, drawing his son's gaze. Leaning forward until his mouth was close to Avenor's ear, he then questioned, "are you ready?"

Avenor grinned half-heartedly and scoffed quietly. "Is anyone ever ready?"

"Your mother. She is a battle-hardened warrior and lives for the thrill," returned Manijor, causing Avenor to snicker. "But do not tell her I have said so," he said before clapping Avenor on the back lightly and joining the stifled laughter.

Just then Everly approached; as she drew nearer, she immediately noticed the mischievous smirks plastered on her husband's and son's faces. "Do I care to know?" she asked softly.

"Know what?" returned Manijor, feigning innocence.

Everly scowled and arched a brow before crossing her arms. "Hmph," she snorted before turning to Avenor. "Your Grace, everything is set."

"Very well. Ambassador Clawbane has also indicated he is prepared," said Avenor after shooting an impish grin at his father.

Kimberly Evette Ortuno

"Indeed," Novex said, appearing out of thin air and startling both Manijor and Everly.

Everly's gasp was the only sound she made before gracefully drawing a sword and pointing it at Novex's throat. "Goat's piss, Novex!" she hissed after a moment. "Do **not** do that!" she continued to chide him. "It is not safe for you to appear out of nothingness like the divine spirit! Especially when I am prepared for battle as is."

Avenor and Manijor suppressed their chortles while Novex smirked before leaning down and placing a kiss on Everly's cheek. "Awe... did I startle you?" asked Novex with a chuckle before repeating, "like the divine spirit?"

Everly shoved the tall man after re-sheathing her weapon. "Aye and aye," she grumbled in return, glowering at Novex.

"Now that would be a notable feat," added Novex with another titter. "And do not stare at me like so. We are all aware that you still adore me," he finished, waggling his eyebrows playfully.

"Pugh! Do not try to butter up now!" retorted Everly as she glared first at Novex, then at Avenor and finally at Manijor. "The lot of you," she grumbled, causing the three men to shake uncontrollably as they fought to silence their laughter.

Avenor took a step forward and wrapped his mother in a fierce hug; he then swiftly exchanged a kiss with her, each placing one on the other's cheek. "Take your positions," he somberly instructed his parents after he released his mother, the lighthearted mood gone.

Poof! Novex shifted to his tigal form and stood patiently, watching his *hamigo* – best friend - share last minute words of reassurance with his parents. As he waited, he could not help but admire Avenor's iridescent armor. It had been cycles since Novex had last seen Avenor wear his battle attire. Avenor's phenomenal blacksmithing ability could not be compared to, not even by other *mayvens* in the craft. As he inspected Avenor's armor, created to resemble scales on a fish, he felt his whiskers twitch in appreciations before slightly nodding his head in approval. "*Ey! Look at those!*" he said to himself, admiring the added gems that reflected the scant light from the stars. "*I shall have to beg his assistance in crafting my armor.*"

Avenor finally turned and grinned at Novex. "*No begging is required,*" Avenor spoke silently to Novex.

"*Bah!*" exclaimed Novex with a sheepish grin. "*I had not intended to share my thoughts,*" he admitted with a chuff before shaking his head from side to side briefly.

Avenor smirked as he reached out and firmly pat Novex's sided. *"Intended or not, there should be no doubt in your mind that I would gladly craft suitable armor and weapon for my hamigo,"* he said warmly.

Novex placed his head against Avenor's chest and gave him a gentle nudge. *"Yea, yea,"* returned Novex lightly. *"Don't be getting sentimental on me now,"* he said, his eyes twinkling.

"Of course not," replied Avenor as the corner of his mouth turned up slightly. *"Shall we?"* he then mutely asked.

Novex dipped his head and purred deeply, the sound barely audible as it reverberated through his massive chest.

Avenor felt the rumble travel through his hand that lingered on his friend's side. He then nodded in return before wordlessly saying, *"follow me."* Without hesitation, Avenor quieted his mind and became one with the shadows.

"Lead the way," returned Novex as he faded from view as well.

"My boys... may the speed of light be with you," muttered Everly as she watched Avenor and Novex disappear before her eyes.

Manijor heard the distress Everly tried to conceal; stepping behind her, he then wrapped his arms around her waist before whispering, "no harm will befall them."

"This, I know. But a mother always worries," she responded before turning slightly so she could look up at Manijor. "It is time," she then said after they shared a brief, yet passionate, kiss.

* * *

Jonetal routinely assumed command once Valcaly laid down to rest, and the remainder of the day passed relatively quietly after the healers dispersed from the noble quarters. His first task had been to assemble everyone, both workers and guards, to conduct detailed interrogations.

Before the sun traversed halfway across the sky, word of the assassination attempt on Galhix had already spread like wild-fire, and nerve-wracking anxiety so thick it was nearly suffocating seeped throughout the city. Citizens and soldiers employed within the castle were not spared from the overpowering tension. Their minds were invaded with apprehension and suspicion; accusatory glances were exchanged without merit. Fear of being unjustly charged with the failed effort of slaying the Khantessa made even the most battle-hardened warriors uneasy.

After the interviews, when no information was garnered, Jonetal instructed Captain Holdir to lead the search of every crevice in the palace and around the castle grounds for anything abnormal.

Entertaining the notion that he would soon be preparing for war, Jonetal hastily returned to the home he shared with Valcaly. He quickly walked toward the standing wardrobe where his battle attire was stored.

"All in serviceable condition," he mumbled under his breath after he set his helm down. "No repairs needed," he then said after inspecting his shield and spiked *morningstar*. Satisfied that his armor, shield, and weapon were suitable for combat, Jonetal gradually closed the double-doors of the armoire.

"Oy," he groaned to himself as he exited the modest-sized family lodge across from the castle. "It is time to pay the piper," he grumbled under his breath.

* * *

"Ey," called out Novex without a sound, turning his head slightly, as he raced across the open field alongside a dark figure of similar size to Avenor.

"Ey, what?" returned Avenor curiously reducing his speed, unaware of how fast he traveled while merged with the shadows.

"I can only go so fast," replied Novex in a huff.

"Ah, you prefer slow and steady?" jested Avenor. Even though speaking in each other's minds, he heard the breathlessness of his friend.

"If you are that curious..." panted Novex with a brief pause before continuing. *"I appreciate thorough... preparation... followed by... an abrupt... com...mence...ment... then increasing... tem...po... be...fore fin.... ishing... swiftly,"* he ended in a rush.

Avenor openly laughed in response and reduced the pace to a moderate canter, allowing Novex to steady his breathing. *"You have let yourself go, dear friend. You are certain you are still lethal?"* he teased after a moment.

"Oy," grumbled Novex. *"When has it become a crime to entertain my feline ways by lounging about? Aye, I am still lethal..."* he said, intentionally stopping before adding, *"enough."*

Avenor allowed his hearty laughter to be heard by Novex. Once they arrived at the barrier surrounding the encampment, they forced their erratic breathing to calm and willed their frantically pounding hearts to slow. *"A serious matter though,"* said Avenor as he placed a hand on Novex's side.

Novex turned to face Avenor, and he placed one of his front paws on Avenor's shoulder.

"It is an honor to have you at my side, Brother," Avenor said somberly.

"As it is an honor to be at your side, Brother," returned Novex as he pressed his head against Avenor's malleable skull. After a few moments, the pair separated.

166

Gradually, a faint, repetitive *thudding* sound became evident to Avenor and Novex. As they waited, they listened to the foot-steps drawing closer; within moments, the boot-clad stranger was ambling over them on the walkway of the wooden boundary.

"Change of watchmen," said a surly voice.

"And none too early," returned another voice laced with annoyance.

Avenor silently pat Novex's side and took a step back. *"Shall we?"*

"Ready when you are, Your Grace," replied Novex with a flick of his tail.

* * *

Jonetal navigated his way through the empty hallways of the palace; it appeared no guards were on duty, but in truth, a sentinel was posted at every window and entrance to the castle. Jonetal gently eased the heavy door open, trying to make the least amount of noise as possible.

"Halt!" immediately called out a guard in a hushed manner upon hearing the slight creaking as the door was pushed open.

"Stand down, Sergeant," instructed Jonetal as he entered the chamber.

"Apologies, Major Teyio," responded the soldier with a swift salute.

"No apologies needed," replied Jonetal while returning the respectful act.

The guard nodded once before turning back to the open window where he keenly surveyed the exterior grounds of the castle.

"Major Teyio," greeted the master healer on duty from her position seated in a chair beside the bed, on the side closest to the Khantessa.

"Maestra Smitian," said Jonetal with a curt nod. "How is she?"

"She is stable," Fiona answered quietly. "But she has yet to waken," she finished, answering Jonetal's unspoken question.

"I understand," returned Jonetal. Turning, he then walked across the distance to where his wife still slumbered. Reaching down, he placed a hand on her shoulder and gentle shook her. "Val," he called out softly so as not to startle her.

"Hmm... s'too urrly," mumbled Valcaly as she brushed away Jonetal's hand and rolled over.

Jonetal refrained from chuckling and reached out once more. "Val," he repeated, although his tone had become stern.

Valcaly's expression changed as her husband's voice registered in her sleep-boggled mind. Squinting against the light, she then rotated herself before sitting up. "Jon," she said upon seeing her husband standing over her. "What hour is it?"

"It is nearing time for evening meal," he replied with an outstretched hand.

"Ugh," she groaned in response while taking his hand. "Thank you," she then said after he had effortlessly assisted her to her feet. A loud roar startled her, and she looked to her side only to see Aylox resting motionless except for the steady rise and fall of his chest as he snored peacefully. "Vice Commandant," called out Valcaly, and she extended her foot to nudge the cot he slept on.

"Aye," he responded and jumped to his feet, swaying precariously.

"Easy," said Jonetal, placing a hand on the larger man's shoulder to help steady him. "Alright?" he then asked.

"Aye," Aylox replied before yawning.

"I have much to divulge," said Jonetal, his expression sour. "I thought it best to do so during evening meal."

"Evening meal?" replied Aylox with a frown. "Why wait so long?" he then asked as he tipped his head from side to side, easing the ache that had developed as he slept.

"It is time for evening meal now," interjected Valcaly with a cynical grin.

"What?" exclaimed Aylox as he turned to look outside.

"Indeed," returned Valcaly as she began walking with Jonetal and Aylox. "Do not make us wait any longer," she then said, peering sideways at her husband.

Upon entering the hall, Aylox saw his sons sleeping in cots across on each side of the royal chambers. "Aylex... Daylin..." he said sternly. The two younger tigals sprang to their feet.

"Father," the brothers both replied in unison.

Without speaking another word, Jonetal and Valcaly led the way followed closely by Aylox, Aylex, and Daylin.

"No matter. Five settings," replied Valcaly in response to a palace keeper's question as they entered the otherwise empty Dining Hall.

"Very well," replied the palace keeper before disappearing through a door.

Not long after the group had seated themselves, three palace keepers entered carrying platters and flatware. Every plate was the same; another palace keeper emerged with a large flask and mugs. Once the serving was complete, the palace keepers retreated to the kitchen. Only one remained, and she stood far enough away so as not to be intrusive of the conversation.

"What have you discovered?" Valcaly immediately asked, her attention focused on Jonetal.

"Disturbing information," replied Jonetal with a scowl. "Captain Holdir found the courtyard gate…"

"The one concealed with shrubbery?" interjected Valcaly to which her husband simply nodded.

"Initially, nothing appeared amiss. However, when he inspected them closer, he noticed they were oddly misshapen," continued Jonetal.

"How so?" asked Aylox around a mouthful of meat and bread.

"The rods for the gates are all straight. *Mayven* blacksmith crafted them," answered Jonetal slowly. "The ones that allow the stream to pass through the gate… they were slightly curved… almost as if they had been pulled apart before being pushed back together."

"How is that even possible?" murmured Valcaly with a frown. "Not even General Crusendir nor General Arteno possess the strength to do such a thing," she said of Manijor and Azelly.

"Indeed. I refused to acknowledge it at first," replied Jonetal while rubbing his chin. "However, after following the tracks, it is the only sign we have discovered."

"Oy," groaned Valcaly somberly. "Oy!" she suddenly repeated with a horrified expression.

"What is it?" asked Jonetal with concern.

"I failed to even ask. Khantessa Galhix?" she then said as she began to stand up.

"She is alive," returned Jonetal quietly as he grabbed his wife's forearm and pulled her back down to her seat. "She has yet to waken," he finished in a whisper, barely audible by the others.

"*Puq*," cursed Valcaly, her brows drawing tighter together. "I must go to Avenor," she then stated after a time.

"She will teleport," muttered Jonetal in response to the confused glances from the three tigals.

"Aye," agreed Valcaly as she shoved a section of buttered bread into her mouth followed by a slice of braised bear meat. Grabbing her mug, she hastily downed a swig of her honey-wine. Setting the mug down, she then raised her hand and gestured for the palace aid to approach.

"Overseer," said the woman as she approached the table.

"Bring me a short mug of *koffie* and a mug of *restoradria*," instructed Valcaly sternly. "The *koffie*… not too hot! And be quick!" she snapped.

"Aye, Overseer," responded the lady before hurrying off to the kitchen to fetch the two beverages.

169

"*Koffie?*" repeated Aylox with a raised brow.

"Mmm," returned Valcaly as she masticated a mouthful of sustenance before swallowing the half-chewed food. "I would rather be alert and prepared for battle than not," she then answered before lifting a chicken leg to her mouth.

"And what is *restoradria?*" probed Daylin with a perturbed look.

"It is a beverage that the Khan's grandmother, Grand Priestess Lukesia, developed cycles ago before she passed. It is a blend of fruits and greens that prevents muscles cramps and assists in recuperation after intense physical activities," offered Jonetal as Valcaly continued eating. Glancing at his wife, he shook his head from side to side. "Slow down lest you inhale the chicken," he jested though his words rang with truth.

"Bah," grunted Valcaly in return with a glower. As soon as the palace keeper returned, Valcaly gulped the contents down. She then wiped the back of her hand across her mouth before standing. "Take command," she said as Jonetal stood beside her. She then stood on her toes and gave him a brief kiss.

"As you desire, Overseer Truceran," he replied quietly.

Turning, Valcaly dipped her head to the other three men. "I shall return soon," she then said. Without another word, Valcaly hurried from the palace to her dwelling place. She hastily changed, donning her war attire. For the sake of saving time, she decided not to bother going to the *teleportation tower* as it was only for show. Taking a deep breath to try and calm her racing heart, she then whispered, "Khan Crusendir, I join you, fragments rejoined." Immediately, she felt her physical form begin to fade as she was transported across the continents to join Avenor.

CHAPTER 20

As the sun began to set, a warm breeze fluttered throughout the *Forbidden Wilds*, and it whisked a lock of metallic grey hair across Leandra's face. Leandra squinted her nose in her sleep and lightly flung her head from side to side as the random strands pranced playfully across her eyes and lips. With annoyance etched in her expression, she reached up and swatted at the pesky hairs.

"Gah!" Leandra suddenly exclaimed while flinching. Tentatively, she opened one eye against the light from the disappearing sun, and she examined the hand that brushed against the wound on her face. "Wonderful," she grunted sarcastically while openly glowering at the blood smeared on her fingers. Although it was not the blood that disturbed her.

"Oy," grumbled Wesdin as he pushed himself to a sitting position. As he fully roused, the ever so faint glowing of his silver locks faded along with a scarcely perceptible thrumming from his unconscious ability that protected him and Leandra as they slept.

"Oy!" gasped Leandra as she twisted at her hips to look over her shoulder at Wesdin. "Wes!" she said, equally excited, as she rotated her legs around and propelled herself into his embrace. "You are awake! You are awake!" she whispered between sobs as she clung to what remained of his tattered tunic.

"Aye," he said weakly as he gently patted her on the back. "And why would I not?" he then asked, his voice hoarse as he expressed the confusion he felt.

"Have you forgotten?" she asked, leaning back so she could stare up at him with her mouth agape.

"Forgotten what?" he returned curiously. Just then, the last bit of light faded and cast the terrain into darkness. "Oy," whispered Wesdin as he peered around. A distant howl made the hair on his nape stand on end. At that moment, he whispered an incantation. An invisible shield formed and engulfed both Wesdin and Leandra within its protective barrier.

"Drink," Leandra said as she held out the container with the remaining meal mush and lightly tapped Wesdin on the arm with it. "I am glad to see you are better…" she paused for a moment, "but you… I do not think… you are still not fully recovered."

Wesdin accepted the flask and brought it up to his nose. "Ack," he muttered as he contorted his face in disgust, "meal mush. Always meal mush." Taking a breath, he then forcefully swallowed two mouthfuls. "Ugh," he said with a shudder as he replaced the stopper. As he cleared the gritty texture from his teeth with his tongue, his eyes widened as his memories came flooding back. "Oy," he then whispered quietly as he inspected his own wounds before turning to examine Leandra. "I remember," he stated flatly, his eyes void of emotion. He fully recalled the intermittent bouts of consciousness where he managed to heal himself; they were often followed with Leandra forcing him to consume any amount of meal mush as possible before he succumbed to his subconscious once again.

Leandra smirked and rolled her eyes. "So, are you well enough to perhaps donate some energy to a poor, heal…less, comrade?" she then asked, ending the awkward silence.

"Say again?" repeated Wesdin with a shake of his head before turning to stare blankly at Leandra. He then blinked as her expression changed from playful to serious.

"Wes!" she exclaimed as she crossed her arms over her chest. "A heal, please!" she huffed with exasperation as she unlocked one arm before pointing vehemently at the oozing gash above her eyebrow.

"Oy," exclaimed Wesdin as if seeing Leandra for the first time. "Of course," he then said sheepishly as he eyed the angry, inflamed injury. He first extended his open palms out toward Leandra, and then he closed his eyes while focusing all his attention on her. As he began whispering, a pale, green light began radiating from his outstretched hands. As Wesdin continued his incantation, the light brightened to a translucent green and grew until it abruptly exploded into innumerable ant-sized orbs. The tiny spheres danced and twirled across the distance between Wesdin and Leandra.

Leandra watched in amazement as the miniscule, luminous, green bubble-like globes began swirling around her. Looking upward, she observed as they teased every strand of her hair before spinning faster and faster around her. Squinting her eyes to shield out the sand, she felt the whirlwind travel down the length of her body; she felt a heaviness being removed out of her body, from her head down to her toes and back again.

Droplets of sweat emerged along Wesdin's hairline, and they immediately began pouring down his face and neck; his tunic became drenched as it absorbed the salty fluid from his chest and back. The scowl on his face deepened as he strained to remain focused on his curative incantation. He could sense the contamination, being carried by her own blood, as it traveled throughout Leandra's body. As his strength began to wane, his silver highlights began glowing and a faint whirring noise vibrated in their ears. Wesdin instantly felt a surge of energy course through him, granting him the fortitude to complete the incantation.

Leandra's eyes widened as she felt a thick substance draining from her wound; the yellow-green, putrid liquid was instantly coated by the lively orbs. As Wesdin finished the incantation, the spheres shrunk in size until they completely vanished, eradicating the contaminated material with it.

Thud.

Leandra's gaze snapped to Wesdin, now crumpled over in the grass. "Wes!" she exclaimed and reached out to him. She tugged on his torn top and pulled him upright. "Wesdin!" she repeated sternly with a slight shake. "Wake up, you dimwit!"

"Why must you call me names?" he finally grumbled with displeasure.

"I only state the truth!" retorted Leandra with a slight giggle that soon turned into a stifled sob.

"And now with the blubbering," he said, forcing the irritation out of his voice and replacing it with amusement.

"Shut it," snapped Leandra as she fisted her palm and jabbed Wesdin in the center of his chest.

"Oof!" grunted Wesdin as his breath was forced out of his lungs. "If not something out there," he muttered with a dip of his head, indicating out to the forest and beyond to the desert, "then **you** will surely be the death of me!" stated Wesdin with an accusatory glare.

"Hah!" snorted Leandra. "You would surely be dead if it were not for me!" she returned furiously.

The two sat glowering at one another until a ferocious snarl drew their attention. Wesdin grabbed at Leandra's cloak, shoving his hand around absentmindedly.

"Wesdin!" hissed Leandra as she batted at his hands. "What has possessed you?" she asked in her whisper-like shout.

"Meal mush," he said quietly with his hand outstretched.

173

"Now? You are serious?" she returned, her mouth falling open incredulously.

"Energy, Lea," he simply replied without moving. His eyes remained fixed on something in the distance.

"Oy," replied Leandra with an embarrassed look. "Right. That," she added as she fished out the container. Cautiously, she placed it in Wesdin's palm.

Wesdin, intentionally controlling his movement, removed the plug and raised the flask to his mouth. He quickly consumed the remaining amount of meal mush. Closing his eyes, he then recited a brief incantation to restore his energy and stamina. He then repeated the short chant on Leandra, replenishing her energy and stamina equally.

"Have you ever heard stories of the *Forbidden Wilds?*" he then asked softly just before the creature in the distance tossed its head back and released a long, spine-stiffening howl.

"N... no," stammered Leandra, sliding her hand into Wesdin's and clutching it tightly. "You?" she whispered nervously. Without him responding, she somehow knew what his answer would be. She also knew, she would not be thrilled to know them herself.

* * *

Peygar lifted a flask to his lips and relished the warm liquid as it poured into his parched mouth. He swished the water around before swallowing it rather than spitting out the life-sustaining substance; after untying his sister and niece earlier, he had explored the strange terrain while they slept. Without peering down, he kicked out his foot; the wooden plank Taygan and Lana remained sleeping on throughout the day was abruptly jolted.

"Ugh," moaned Taygan as she darted her dry tongue out, attempting to moisten her cracked lips. "Where are we?" she managed to rasp out as she lifted a hand to shield her eyes from the last rays of light before the sun dipped below the horizon.

"In a blacksmith's forge," grunted Lana as she struggled to sit up. "I am certain of it."

Peygar scoffed in amusement. "We 'ave made it ta tha Fo'bid'en Wil's," he then said before tossing a flask to both Lana and Taygan. "Drin' an' dun waste none," he added harshly.

Lana picked up the leather pouch and hastily removed the stopper; without hesitation, she brought the container to her mouth and began gulping down the stale-tasting water. The disapproving grunt from her uncle drew her attention, and she instantly slowed her frenzied drinking before stopping completely.

Taygan carefully swallowed two mouthfuls before replacing the wooden plug. She pressed a hand to her temple and complained quietly, "my head throbs."

Peygar grunted in acknowledgement. "Tha sun has drained ya," he stated with a frown.

"Water," replied Taygan quietly as she tipped the flask in her hand from side to side. The *sloshing* sound alerted the trio that they were low on the precious resource.

"Drin' it," instructed Peygar with a reassuring nod. "Ya' as well," he said with a glance at Lana as she cradled her own head. "W'ill replenish in'a bit."

Taygan and Lana exchanged dubious glances but obeyed Peygar none the less.

"Eat," commanded Peygar as he dropped an apple-sized burlap sack in both women's laps. "We moves when da sun sets fully," he informed them.

The two readily opened the small bags. Taygan broke off a section of dried razorback and began chewing thoughtfully. Lana, already salivating, tore a piece of candied bread from the quarter-loaf in her sack along with a chunk of dried cheese from the wheel; she mashed them together before shoveling them into her mouth. "Mmm, so delicious," mumbled Lana around the mouthful of food. The two finished the remainder of their portions in silence.

"It has begun to wane," sighed Taygan as the ache in her temples diminished.

"As has mine," added Lana with a nod of her head.

"Ver' good. Den pack up," replied Peygar as he finished his portion of extra-salted, preserved meat. Taygan and Lana grabbed their travel sacks and slung them over their shoulders; they then accepted the spears Peygar extended to them. "Don' tuch nu'thin," he said sternly as the last light of day faded, leaving the terrain in a faint glow as the stars began twinkling above.

"Do you think we will find fresh water?" whispered Lana as she clung to her mother's arm.

"Nothing is certain," replied Taygan as she followed closely behind her brother. "But your uncle appears to know where he is going," she added as Peygar led them away from the desolate desert back toward the lush greenery.

"Dere," said Peygar after a while.

Lana tilted her head to the side to gaze past her uncle. Ahead of him was a slow-flowing stream, sparkling like the stars above as it reflected their light. "Fresh water?" asked Lana as she looked at her uncle once she was standing alongside him.

"Mmm," grunted Peygar as he nodded his head. "Tread wit' caw'shun," he added before continuing to lead the others. Peygar removed two staves from his back, holding one in each hand, and he used them to jab at the ground before taking a hesitant step. Eventually, the small group reached the edge of the stream. Without needing guidance, Taygan and Lana dropped to their knees and began refilling their empty water bladders.

Peygar knelt, cupped his hands together, and then lowered them into the chilly brook. He then brought his hands up to his chapped lips and drank until his thirst was sated. A thought entered his mind as the excess water spilled from the sides of his mouth. He dipped his hands back into the stream, and he then splashed the cold water on his head, face, and neck. "Ahh," he sighed to himself, appreciating the refreshing coolness as it eased the ache of his baked flesh - the result of his short trek through the desert after the sun peaked over the horizon. Remembering his own empty flask, he removed it from his belt and replenished. Before standing, he removed three more empty containers and filled them as well.

"I have to relieve myself," announced Lana as she shifted her weight uncomfortably from one foot to the other.

Taygan turned and witnessed her daughter uncross her legs before locking them back together, only the opposite leg on top, and squirm from side to side. "I shall accompany you," offered Taygan as she finished securing her items. "We will be here, behind this bush," she called out quietly to Peygar.

Peygar glimpsed fleetingly over his shoulder before waving indifferently in response. "I'll be dere," he returned with a nonchalant gesture to another group of shrubs after he had slung his secured travel bag onto his back. As he neared the small thicket, he used his wooden stakes to thump against the bushes. He then pierced through the dense branches and poked toward the ground, clearing the bottom area of any creatures.

Croak!

A *mud hopper* expressed her surprise at the abrupt spearing of the earth around her; with another angry cry, she leapt out from her mucky hovel. Her eyes narrowed on the intruder as he continued stabbing the boggy area where she had been moments before.

"Agh!" exclaimed Peygar at the unexpected appearance of the large amphibian, and he openly glared at the brown creature with dark green spots.

The *mud hopper* opened her mouth and curled her forked tongue.

"Be gone!" Peygar suddenly spat while stretching his staff out and stabbing at the beast.

The rotund animal swallowed and puffed out its chest before acquiescing silently, hopping away from her assailant.

Peygar turned his back on the *mud hopper* and reached for the closure of his trousers.

Crrrooooaaaaaak!

The hostile *mud hopper* voiced her irritation as she witnessed the intruder relieve himself over her concealed refuge.

"Oh, shu'up!" grumbled Peygar, his voice laced with exasperation as the animal emitted her harsh cry of protest again. "Goat's piss," griped Peygar as he pulled his trousers back up.

"Peygar..." began Taygan hesitantly as she watched the unusual animal cautiously approaching her brother; Peygar, hearing the apprehension in her voice, turned to face his sister. *"What sort of hoppity beast are you?"* Taygan silently pondered as the creature opened its mouth and curled its tongue. As Taygan watched, the irate amphibian released a perfectly aimed flow of venom; the liquid landed on Peygar's face, entering his eyes and mouth.

"Whot da..." roared Peygar as he dragged a hand down his face, wiping away the stinging substance. He instantly spotted the *mud hopper*. With a murderous look in his eyes, Peygar took an ominous step forward with his staves raised; however, before he could attack, he felt a searing sensation in his eyes and mouth. "Agh!" screamed out Peygar as the poles dropped from his hands. He stumbled forward before dropping to his knees directly in front of the enraged beast.

"What is it?" exclaimed Lana as she rushed to her mother's side, but immediately halted as her mother grabbed her.

"No!" Taygan shouted as she tightened her grip on Lana's arm. "There," Taygan mumbled and extended a finger, pointing to the slimy animal near Peygar.

No reluctance in her actions, the furious *mud hopper* spit another stream of neurotoxin toward the shrieking man; nearly every drop entered his mouth as he screamed in misery before the *mud hopper* turned and disappeared.

"Oy," gasped Lana as she watched her uncle clawing at his own eyes. Blood spilled down his face; a mixture of a white frothy substance and his life's essence poured out of his mouth. Suddenly, he arched backward and spasmed uncontrollably as a series of violent convulsions contorted his body before collapsing in a motionless heap.

"We must go," mumbled Taygan after a time.

"Do we leave him?" asked Lana with a jerk of her head, pointing at the lifeless form of her uncle. "Aye," responded Taygan, her voice barely audible. "Grab the supplies. Take care not to touch the venom," she managed to say.

"Very well," groaned Lana, making a face at her mother.

"Be hasty!" Taygan abruptly spat. "We are not safe! His screams have enticed what dangerously lurks beyond," she hissed at Lana.

Lana's eyes became as wide as meal platters when her mother's words finally registered; turning, she barely discerned the shapes of the enormous lizards in the darkness, crawling on their bellies, as they sought out the cause of the commotion that disturbed the silence of the night.

* * *

Like clockwork, the sentries grumbled amongst themselves as they greeted one another, and they inquired about any concerns or reportable occurrences. Once the first set of guards exchanged what little pertinent information they had, the departing guard initiated the signal for the next pair of soldiers.

Bang! Bang!

The next pair of watchmen followed suite until every tower had changed guards for the remainder of the night.

Avenor waited until after the last sentinel had pounded his sword against his shield twice before nodding to Novex. *"Go,"* he instructed his friend mutely. Avenor rushed to the right while Novex raced to the left of the barricade. Avenor's shadowy form effortlessly ascended the wall that supported the watchtower, and his camouflaged darkness instantly melded with the dancing shadows behind the guard.

Novex protracted his claws and stood on his hind legs; cautiously, he placed one of his rear paws against the dense logs and pressed downward. He felt his knife-like nails slice through the wood akin to butter. Quietly, he began climbing up the wall, careful not to yank his claws which would splinter the wood and betray his presence. Not long after Avenor, he too, crouched in the shadows behind one of the evening watchmen.

"Ready, when you are, Alpha Lord," called out Novex across the way to Avenor.

"Alpha Lord?" retorted Avenor, momentarily forgetting the situation they were in.

Novex allowed Avenor to hear his snicker. *"Aye. As in the one in charge. Hmm... similar to..."* Novex paused to try and find a way to express the phrase. *"Ah... as in Boss Man."*

Avenor chuckled as he shook his head to himself. *"Boss Man, eh?"* he then repeated with a grin. *"Well then... Alpha Lord says move on three."*

"Understood," replied Novex before abruptly adding, *"Wait, wait... On three as in... one, two, move? Or as in... one, two, three, move?"*

Avenor moved with the shadows until he could glower down the walkway; his gaze was drawn to Novex, and he watched as the large feline bobbed from side to side as he tried to locate Avenor. *"You are seriously clarifying this* **now?** *Right* **now?"** Avenor seethed.

"Ey, I am not the only one at fault. You, mighty Alpha Lord, failed to mention it earlier," retorted Novex, his tail flicking irritably from side to side. Without making a sound, he drew is lips back and bared his teeth.

"Oy," groaned Avenor as he dragged a hand down his face. *"Fine! We move on three... as in one, two, move,"* he answered, his voice tinged with exasperation.

"Understood," replied Novex. Just as he sensed Avenor was about to begin his count, he said, *"Wait, wait..."*

"Goat's piss, Novex!" exploded Avenor as he threw his hands up.

Novex snickered and stifled his guffawing. *"I jest! I jest!"*

"For puqs..." began Avenor heatedly but was abruptly interrupted.

"Ey, ey, ey! Foul language is not necessary, Brother," chided Novex.

Taking a deep calming breath. Avenor closed his eyes and counted to five to ease his frustration.

"Aye, breath, Brother... Breath," coached Novex playfully.

"Oy, lock it," snapped Avenor. *"We move on three."* Without waiting for Novex to taunt him any longer, Avenor completed the brief count.

With an amused twinkle in his eye, Novex waited to pounce until the correct moment. Simultaneously, Novex and Avenor subdued the guards; Novex instantly switched to his human form, and they then removed the tabards and helms before donning them. Needing no further discussion, the two hastily executed the remainder of the plan. Removing the coils of rope from about their chests, they tied them to the wall before hoisting them over the side.

After Avenor tossed the tail end of the last rope over the side, he turned and punched Novex squarely in the chest.

"Oof," grunted Novex in genuine surprise. *"I suppose that was warranted,"* he mumbled quietly to Avenor wryly.

"Indeed," replied Avenor with a curt nod. *"Three minutes,"* he then added before signing for Novex to make his way back to the watchtower he had invaded. Avenor then turned and made his way back to opposite side of the walkway.

Novex waited patiently until he saw Avenor grab the torch from the stand in the center of the tower before grabbing the one he stood beside. In unison, they casually walked to the left side of their respective towers; they then waved the torch before walking back and forth from one side to the other a series of three times before replacing the torches.

"Now we wait," Avenor stated simply as he watched the troops emerge from behind the trees and begin their restrained advance on the fortified compound.

* * *

Kenzelo reached up and twirled the end of his well-groomed mustache nervously at the corner of his mouth; glancing sideways, he barely made out the forms of the three visiting Generals and Major Swiftpaw of Savenius. Turning his head, he managed to see Major Chevin and Major Tamlin, his two *Force* leaders. The eerie silence was suddenly broken by Everly's sullen voice.

"There," stated Everly flatly with a slight dip of her head in the direction of the barricaded city. "Onward, march!" she hissed out; the command was repeated down the long line of troops in opposite directions until every soldier began the anxious trek across the grassy clearing. The advance took no more than five minutes, but to Everly, it felt like an eternity.

As the combined *Force* members began scaling over the wooden barrier, an unexpected visitor wandered into their mist.

"What is this?" muttered the female sentry as she casually strolled along the outskirts of the town fence, deciding to walk the compound as she could not sleep. Frowning, a faint clinking sound drew her attention; looking upward in the direction the sound had come, she watched as numerous invaders continued entering the encampment; suddenly, realization dawned on her. "We're under attack!" she hollered at the top of her lungs. "North face! Defenses breached!" she shouted as she ran. Grabbing a torch, she hastily set a massive pyre ablaze before hurrying to another, allowing the compound to be illuminated.

"Charge!" shouted Avenor, his command ringing loud and clear throughout the invading warriors. No further instruction was needed as every person knew the objective: Only keep Rozalin Lanikeel alive.

With a *poof,* Novex changed to his tigal form. He remained invisible and leapt from the catwalk down to the ground; he prowled to a nearby group of traitors as they fumbled grabbing weapons. With one swipe of his razorblade-like claws, he felled three of the five and mortally maimed the other two.

As the invaders continued pouring into the camp, the unfaithful soldiers screamed and cried out in fear and surprise.

A group of youths eyed Manijor with a sneer. "Better to surrender now, old man!" they jeered at him. "You are no match for us," they continued to taunt him.

"If that is the case… you should have no trouble subduing me," he returned with a grin as heopenly flexed his hands around his battle-hammer. The light from the nearby bonfire illuminated his gem, embellished weapon which added unbridled strength, stamina, and health to its handler.

"Get him," one of the older of the group then spat out angrily. As the group charged toward Manijor, he took a step forward before spinning violently; his weapon, practically weightless, connected with the closest lad.

Crack!

"Agh!" cried out the young man as his shoulder was crushed upon the impact of Manijor's hammer. It then proceeded to break his collar bone as Manijor's ferocious attack carried him into the others.

Without hesitation, Manijor completed a series of bashes and swings. Not long after, the handful of eighteen- and nineteen-year-olds writhed in the dirt, wailing in agony.

Everly perched herself on the ledge of one of the watchtower; she hastily unsheathed her identical throwing blades. *"To his head!"* she silently instructed one sword before letting it loose. The blade whirred through the air and landed with a *thwack!* With a satisfied grin, Everly called back her weapon. Watching as an archer aimed at Novex, Everly threw her opposite sword with expert precision. Mutely commanding her weapons, Everly downed the archer. From her position, Everly continued to subdue the various ranged attackers.

Avenor closed his eyes; he appreciated the blazing infernos as they created immense amounts of shadows throughout the battleground. Motionlessly, he summoned the darkness that surrounded him. His dark form began to swell and grow to a monstrous size. A shrill scream caused Avenor's black, soulless appearing eyes to snap open. Turning the full force of his attention to her, Avenor instructed the shadows to wrap around her. Avenor sensed another traitor rushing toward his dark mass from behind; turning slightly, he then extended his hand toward his assailant before abruptly clenching his hand in a fist. Shadows surged forth and encircled the man before hastily rushing forward and fatally crushing him. Avenor absentmindedly released the woman from his ethereal hold, and her crumpled lifeless form instantly fell to the ground.

Azelly powered through each new wave of youthful soldiers alongside of Leander; the pair were relentless as they brutally struck down the poorly trained individuals. Azelly, using only her iridescent gauntlets as weapons, spun in a circle with her arm outstretched, and she grinned as she backhanded one attacker. The youth's jaw was dislodged, and he fell unconscious to the ground. Ducking under his collapsing form, Azelly then charged passed Leander.

"Oof!" grunted a soldier as Azelly collided with him and simultaneously lifted him off the ground. Before he could react, Azelly had raised him upward before slamming him down on his back. "Ugh," he then exclaimed as the air was forced from his lungs. As Azelly raised her arm back, the man raised his hands. "I surrender!" he then cried out, knowing he would be killed if he did not.

Azelly glowered at the man in disgust. Without a word, she hastily forced him onto his stomach and secured his hands behind his back.

Leander guarded his wife as she tied down one of the traitors. As he glanced over his shoulder, an honor-hungry lass sent forth her badger. The vicious creature charged at Leander, snarling angrily as froth foamed in its mouth.

Poof!

Leander emitted a roar that reverberated throughout everybody in the compound. The badger's fearless charge instantly halted; as it eyed the crouched tigal, ready to spring at him, the animal deserted its master. Watching the direction the animal fled, Leander discovered the offender cowering away from him. Without hesitation, Leander sprung forward. As she tried to kick him, Leander sunk his fangs into her knee and bit down firmly. Her scream of anguish only infuriated him more. He then jerked his head back, ripping out the bones of her joint, leaving the remaining of her leg attached only by the flesh behind her knee.

Valcaly's eyes widened in dismay, and she abruptly crouched down. "*Puq!*" she cursed, not caring she swore in an unladylike language before unsheathing her throwing blades. "*Puq!*" she exclaimed again as she tried to make sense of the carnage. "*Puq, Puq, Puq!*" she continued to chant, not sure who was friend or who was foe. Suddenly, she heard someone shout behind her; instantly, she swirled around and heaved a sigh of relief upon finding Avenor's dark form standing only a few steps behind her.

"Get him!" came an ear-piercing shriek from the South side of the city.

Turning, Avenor felt his lips curl in disgust as his eyes settled on Rozalin Lanikeel, her arm raised as she pointed at him. "Rozalin," he spat her name as if it were vile in his mouth.

Rozalin began to incant hurriedly; within moments, she felt her insides swell with continued health. While she had sustained no injuries, her incantation would heal her if she received any wounds within the upcoming five minutes. Turning her attention back to Avenor, she then began to chant vehemently. As a *Purification Priestess,* she had been taught her role was to cure diseases; however, as her mind twisted, she discovered she could also cast debilitating curses on others. While it was short-lived, it could still be fatal. Some curses continued to injure the afflicted for a full day before the effects faded.

Avenor frowned as he felt an odd sensation settle over him; his frow deepened into a scowl as the strange feeling then seemed to spread through him.

Valcaly effortlessly flipped her blades around before letting them loose in rapid succession, one after the other, at the traitors rushing toward Avenor. She then removed two more, sending them toward the charging mass of soldiers as well. Each dagger found its mark and stopped its target mid-step.

Avenor's scowl of disapproval turned to one of confusion as he recognized the pattern the throwing blades were thrown in as they whizzed past him. Turning, he watched as Valcaly came to his side. "Valcaly?" he said questioningly.

"Your Grace," she grunted as she parried from an attack; stepping beside the attacker, she then tripped the individual. Immediately, Valcaly grabbed a fistful of hair as she kneeled on the fallen woman's back, and she simultaneously removed a *kris* from its sheath on the outside of her boot. Without hesitation, Valcaly forcefully placed it at the corner of the traitor's neck and sliced her throat open from one side to the other. Wiping the blood on the outside of her thigh, she then replaced the weapon.

"Your Grace," she repeated, this time her tone rang with unease as she eyed him curiously. "Avenor," she said, unaware she addressed him so intimately, her curiosity quickly becoming concern. "You..." she said in a whisper as she took a step closer. "You... are... **diseased**!" she gasped and absentmindedly took a wary step back.

"Say again?" asked Avenor with a slight shake of his head, his thoughts gradually becoming cloudy.

"Cure yourself! Now!" she hastily instructed him.

Avenor struggled to maintain his focus as Valcaly's face split in two before blurring completely. "*Onia,*" he whispered quietly, trying to make sense of what Valcaly was yelling. "Cursed! Heal!" he managed to decipher.

A depraved cackling pierced through the fog that muddled his brain, bringing with it a moment of clarity. Avenor subconsciously recited various incantation; first, he warded off the mayhem as it threatened to consume his mind once more. Next, he repelled the nausea and weakness that fought to bring him to his knees. Then he recited numerous curative incantations before finishing with one to regenerate his health.

As their fort was overrun, the remaining defenders understood their continued resistance was futile. Gradually, they began to drop to their knees in submission.

Rozalin had not seen Avenor's performance of self-preservation; she only saw the cowardly remnants of her army falling like flies. "What are you doing?" she fumed. "I did not order a surrender!" she yelled with hostility. Just then, a large figure teased her peripheral vision. As she turned, her eyes widened in terror as she watched the Khan's shadowy figure stalking toward her, his gaze murderous.

CHAPTER 21

Wesdin pulled Leandra closer against his side protectively. Another single, forlorn howl teased Wesdin's and Leandra's ears; however, the lonely call stirred an unfamiliar reaction from the depths of Wesdin's core. In the dark, Wesdin tilted his head to the side, and he watched the deep, wine-red *fire hound* as its wolfish cry came to an end. However, his back stiffened not long after it ended.

"Oy!" exclaimed Leandra as the beast's call was soon returned by a chorus of others. Leandra clutched Wesdin's hand tighter as she frantically looked in every direction. "Wes!" she whispered anxiously. "What do we do? What…" she asked as her anxiety gradually became fear.

"I am not certain," he muttered under his breath. "I doubt my shield will protect us long," he admitted with a frown.

"We will surely die!" cried out Leandra quietly as she pressed her face against Wesdin's shoulder.

"What?" mumbled Wesdin as he watched two figures rushing out from the jungle-like cover toward the desert.

"We will surely die!" repeated Leandra.

"Huh?" grunted Wesdin as he briefly glanced at Leandra before responding. "No, that," he then said and pointed at the individuals that had emerged.

Leandra frowned as she lifted her head and squinted, looking in the direction that Wesdin did. "Who are they?" she then asked curiously, only able to discern the outline of two people.

"Lea… I think… it… it looks like… it is Lana!" he stammered in disbelief.

"Lana…" repeated Leandra as her brows slowly drew together. "Lana… Lana from erudition?" she asked incredulously.

"Aye," replied Wesdin as he watched the girl hurrying along behind a woman. "That must be her Ami," he murmured.

Taygan slowed her pace, and she reached out to take Lana's hand. "Hurry!" she encouraged her daughter as they tripped over their long cloaks.

"Oy," grunted Lana as she stumbled, this time falling completely to the ground. "Ah!" she loudly cried out in surprise.

The unexpected shriek instantly drew the lone wolf's gaze, and he viciously snarled as his eyes discovered the source of the noise. Without hesitation, the *fire hound* tossed his head back and released another howl.

"L... L... Lana!" stammered Taygan as she watched a reddish beast standing on the crest of a dune, its head back as it cried into the night. "We must find a place to hide," she said in a rush.

Lana sensed the urgency in her mother's voice; scrambling to her feet, she immediately saw a massive dog-like animal as it slid down the sandbank and began stalking toward them. Lana felt an odd drawing to the creature as fear began bubbling inside of her; the strange attraction was soon forgotten as a series of calls returned to the lone beast. Lana and Taygan clutched their spears as they fearfully watched the hound approaching them.

"Stay back!" shouted Taygan as she jabbed her stake at the large animal. "Get away from us!" she continued shouting, unaware her boisterous hollering guided the other hounds in her direction.

The beast continued to draw closer; suddenly, the animal clamped its massive jaws on the wooden pole and yanked it from Taygan's grasp.

"Ah!" shrieked Taygan as the creature then lunged and sunk its fangs into her calf as she turned to run. Jerking its head back, the wolf ripped a portion of muscle from Taygan's leg. Taygan fell to the ground as she continued screaming.

"Get away!" screeched Lana as she swung her spear and pounded the animal on its back. The hound spun around and growled menacingly.

Just as the animal sprung toward Lana, she cowered and covered her face. However, the attack never happened. Frowning, she looked back at the creature, and realized it was frozen in place.

"What?" Lana gasped as she gazed at the animal in confusion.

"Lana!" shouted Wesdin as he and Leandra rushed toward her.

Frowning, Lana turned and watched as Wesdin and Leandra sprinted across the distance toward her and her mother.

"Hurry!" exclaimed Leandra as she eyed the massive canine.

Extending his hands, Wesdin hurriedly incanted a brief healing chant to heal Taygan's wound. "Her wound is healed!" he called out.

"Here!" he continued as he removed the leather belt from around his waist that held his sword and throwing daggers, tossing it toward Lana, before turning around to face the frozen beast.

"Oy," gasped Leandra as she reached out and shook Wesdin. "There!" she nearly shouted in terror.

Turning, Wesdin watched as a pack of *fire hounds* stood motionless at the top of the shifting ridge, sand sliding down the side under their weight. "Oy," he whispered uneasily as one finally took a step forward.

Lana instantly repeated her incantation, refreshing the length the first beast would remain frozen. "We haven't long," she muttered under her breath.

Taygan struggled to her feet and nearly collapsed.

"Help her!" snapped Wesdin as he glared at Lana. "She has lost much blood!"

Wesdin's harsh instruction snapped Lana out of her daze; without hesitation, she knelt beside her mother and assisted her to stand, but she failed to remember to grab the belt Wesdin had tossed toward her.

"We won't be able to hold them long," Wesdin said sternly.

"As they near, I'll produce a *blizzard* to slow their movements," announced Lana as she watched the animals gracefully slipping down the face of the hill.

"I'll send forth the shadows," added Wesdin uneasily. "Go, there!" Wesdin instructed Lana as he pointed to a large tree behind them in the desert.

Lana nodded once as she supported Taygan's weight. "Come, mother," she grunted as she assisted her mother.

"Leave me," groaned Taygan as she eyed the approaching creatures. "I'll never be able to get up there," she answered the unasked question.

Suddenly, the immobile hound broke free from its frozen vice and issued a series of barks before howling once more. After ordering his pack, the leader surged forward. However, instead of charging the two children, the beast charged toward Taygan.

As if in a trance, Lana stood frozen and watched as the hound lunged at her mother. The force of the attack sent Taygan flying out of Lana's grasp.

"Run!" yelled Taygan as she began wildly thrashing and shrieking as the vicious canine sunk his fangs into her arm and violently shook his head from side to side. "Aa..gmmllph!" screamed Taygan but her cries of agony became muffled as the creature clenched its jaws down on her

187

neck. With a firm grip, the beast yanked its head back and ripped out Taygan's throat.

After dropping the chunk of flesh from its mouth, the *fire hound* howled once more. As the remainder of the pack began rushing to their leader, Leandra sent forth a blizzard, slowing the movements of the feral animals.

"Run…" whispered Wesdin as he turned with Leandra. "Run!" he repeated in a shout, his voice spiked with terror.

Leandra, followed by Wesdin, turned, and they sprinted toward Lana. The trio struggled to run up the sandy embankment. As they crested the dune, a sudden gust of wind blinded them with fine particles; the unexpected gale forced them to slow their retreat. Their eyes instantly watered, trying to clear the sharp bits from their vision. As the small, temporarily blind, group clung to one another, an unexpected savage roar erupted from behind them.

Suddenly, a fearless stranger charged past the terrified children; with little effort, he commanded his body and abruptly changed from man to half-beast. His teeth instantly elongated into fangs as his fingers became claws; the stranger gave a brief grunt of discomfort as an unholy sound of bones breaking and skin shredding resounded around him.

The *fire hounds* abruptly halted their advance in confusion before sniffing the familiar scent coming from the newcomer. An angry snap from their leader disrupted their thoughts, and the dangerous creatures resumed their approach.

Without hesitation, the half-hound rushed forward into the pack of wolves. Snarls, growls, and cries of pain rang out around the mortified trio.

Wesdin blinked one eye open, managing to glimpse the stranger that defended them from within the center of the fray. Concentrating on the other male, Wesdin recited a chant and healed the other's wounds. After, Wesdin closed his eyes and wrapped his arms around the girl clinging tightly to him.

From his position, the alpha hound observed the outsider's injuries mending. With a growl, he turned in Wesdin's direction; sensing an unusual connection with the boy, the alpha decided on a plan. After wordlessly instructing the others, the leader silently neared Wesdin and the girl he held from behind. Standing on his hind legs, the wolf then headbutted Wesdin fiercely; the strength of the act caused Wesdin's head to swing sideways and knock against the girl's. The pair instantly fell unconscious and collapsed. The alpha then snagged the cloaks of the two limp bodies, and he lifted them off the ground effortlessly. Without hesitation, the single wolf dashed through the desert toward the hidden castle – *Burg der Drachen* - of a forgotten and desolate empire.

"Argh!" groaned the stranger as a wolf sank its teeth into the soft area under his neck as it connected to his shoulder. Reaching up, he grabbed the animal's head and forcibly pulled it away; with no hesitation in his action, the hybrid beast grabbed his assailant's jaws and ripped them apart only to drop the lifeless corpse to the ground.

"Is that all you've got?" taunted a malicious voice, unaware that only one of the three children remained. Glowering at the remaining pack members, he stood protectively in front of the cowering child, hiding under her cloak. His eyes narrowed as the wolves encircled him slowly, their teeth bared as they snarled in return. "Let us finish this," he then said confidently. Just as the newcomer took a step forward, a deafening screech pierced through the night.

Sssssrrrrrrrrraaaa!

Scowling, the adolescent turned his head slightly in the direction of the easily recognizable shrieks of a *desert scorpion*. *"What is it doing this far South?"* the juvenile asked himself silently in confusion.

Rrrraaaaak. Trrraaaak.

The hostile cries, sounding closer than moments ago, unsettled the *fire hounds*. As the ground began to rumble, the wolves' ears flattened in fear. Just as the pack turned, a handful of the colossal creatures appeared on the ridge of a nearby dune.

"Hound's piss!" wordlessly exclaimed the youth. Spinning around, he knelt beside the trembling child; only then did he realize the other two were missing. With no time to spare searching for the others, he immediately scooped the girl off the ground and held her securely against his chest. "I will not harm you," whispered the stranger.

Abruptly, one of the wolves turned and lunged for the two youngsters as the half-beast began to flee.

"Ugh!" grunted the boy as he fell backward, his ankle firmly locked in the jaws of a wolf. Kicking violently, he tried to dislodge the canine. As he struggled, a crimson glow from behind the dog-like animal drew his attention. With his eyes wide in disbelief, the boy watched as a blood-red specter appeared to fly over the terrain. It entered the attacking animal's body through the sides of its mouth as it remained clamped down on the youngster's ankle.

Unexpectedly, the animal released his prey with a whimper. The animal took a hesitant step back before falling to its side. The wolf began to writhe in pain and an agonizing howl escaped from its mouth. The excruciating cries of their fallen brother sent a ripple of unbridled fear through the others, and the remaining wolves fled without turning back.

"Tut!" someone suddenly called out from the same direction as the giant beasts.

With his foot injured, and the child still firmly in his grasp, the boy could only watch and wait. Frowning, he soon noticed silhouettes of people on the massive scorpions' backs as they neared. *"Only the fearless tame…"* he mutely pondered to himself before his thoughts were interrupted.

"Dondree?" called out a soft yet hesitant voice. "Is it truly you?" continued the voice.

The injured boy's expression instantly changed to one of surprise upon hearing his name. "Who is curious to know?" he demanded in response uneasily as he watched a figure gracefully dismount.

"Who else…" began the woman, purposefully pausing as she took confident steps toward the older child, before finishing as she halted directly in front of him, "but your Overlord."

Dondree openly glowered at the individual before snarling aggressively. "What nonsense…" he replied but was instantly interrupted.

"Overlord Reeyah," Reeyah suddenly announced as she removed the protective wrap that was used to keep the abrasive sand from her eyes and face.

Dondree's glare gradually diminished as he eyed the woman standing before him. As he scanned the familiar features, his eyes widened in incredulity. "Mother… how… why… where…" he stammered. Dondree shook his head as he tried to make sense of his jumbled thoughts.

Reeyah covered her stifled sob with a chuckle as she dropped to her knees and pulled Dondree fiercely into her embrace; she then heaved a sigh of relief as she felt his arms wrap around her tightly. Just then, Reeyah remembered the strange bundle in her son's arms. Leaning back, she peered down inquisitively. "What is this?" she then asked.

"Oy," exclaimed Dondree quietly as he timidly uncovered the girl's face. "I defended her from the hounds," announced Dondree as the terrified girl glanced from one to the other. "You are safe," he softly informed her.

"Wes…" whispered the girl. "Where is Wes?" she asked before losing consciousness.

"Come. Let us return home," said Reeyah with a gentle smile. After watching her son squirm uncomfortably, she remembered his injured ankle. Reciting an incantation, Reeyah felt her power surge and flow out from her hands as she mended Dondree's wound.

"You have my thanks," murmured Dondree.

"Hand her…" began Reeyah as she extended her hands out to take the stranger from Dondree. However, she instantly snapped her mouth shut and retracted her outstretched hands at her son's hostile glare.

"No need," replied Dondree. Without relinquishing his hold on the girl, he hastily rose to his feet. Mutely, they joined the others; once seated atop the scorpions, the mounted warriors began the journey back to the Veiled Oasis.

* * *

Gelriz sat beside the bed staring at his younger sister's pale face; even though the healers had assured him she would live, she remained unresponsive. He gently held one of her hands in his, and he mumbled incoherently under his breath.

"Still nothing?" asked Baylay as she strode across the noiseless chamber to her mate's side. As she waited for a reply, she placed a hand on Gelriz's shoulder supportively.

"Nay," replied Gelriz in a barely audible whisper. "Not a moan. Not a flutter of her lashes. Nothing."

"Is there nothing you can do?" she asked, a crease forming between her brows.

"I never anticipated this," said Gelriz as tears welled up in his eyes. Clutching his sister's cold hand, he silently sobbed.

Baylay took the few steps to the head of the bed, and she sat beside Galhix; she then reached out and smoothed back the few stray locks from Galhix's brow. "Come back to us," whispered Baylay, her voice sorrowful.

A soft knock on the open door drew Baylay's attention. "Enter," she instructed quietly.

"*Nahm-Aztey* Chief, Chieftess," greeted Mikela as she approached her leaders. "Any improvement?" she inquired in a concerned tone.

Aylox sat wordlessly on the cot that had been set up for him. His mate's question penetrated through his thoughts and brought him back to the present. Standing, he walked over to join the others.

"*Ahz-sulam oo-laikim*, Commandant. Nay," replied Baylay with her gaze downcast. Furrowing her brows, she then looked up at Mikela. "The cubs?"

"Chiefuno and Chiefuna have already laid down to rest. Aylex and Daylin are guarding them," answered Mikela.

Baylay dipped her head slightly in acknowledgement but said nothing else, her attention returning to her unconscious second-sister.

"And what of the Khanzito?" asked Aylox in a whisper against Mikela's ear as he wrapped his arms around her waist.

191

Mikela's expression became perplexed. Arching a brow, she leaned to one side and peered over her shoulder. "What do you mean?" she then asked.

Aylox tilted his head as he leaned to the side, his face reflecting the same confusion as Mikela. "Khanzito Wesdin..." began Aylox nervously, "he is not with you?" he finished.

"Nay," replied Mikela, her response slow.

"Damn!" exclaimed Aylox as he dropped his arms from around Mikela. He then grabbed her hand and practically dragged her into the corridor. In a rushed whisper, he explained the situation to his mate.

As she listened, Mikela's eyes widened incredulously. Without hesitation, she gave a curt command to Aylox before striding through the palace with a fierce expression of determination plastered on her face to find information regarding Wesdin.

* * *

Valcaly reached out and grabbed ahold of Avenor's arm before he could reach Rozalin, and she gave him a firm tug to prevent his advance. Realizing they were surrounded by others, Valcaly waited until Avenor turned to face her.

"What is it?" Avenor snapped irritably as he shifted his attention to the person who had taken his arm. Immediately, he froze upon realizing it was Valcaly. "Why are you here?" he asked abruptly.

Taking a deep breath, Valcaly closed the distance between them and stood on her toes while simultaneously pulling Avenor's head down. "Khantessa Galhix..." she began quietly, "An assassination attempt was made on her life. Her condition is currently unclear."

"How can this be?" Avenor demanded in confusion after he straightened back to his full height. "Why was she not guarded?" Someone snickering nearby caused Avenor to sharply turn his head. His expression instantly darkened as it landed on Rozalin.

"It appears someone has beat me to it," taunted Rozalin mercilessly after overhearing Valcaly.

Fury instantly raged within Avenor, and he took the last few remaining steps toward Rozalin. Void of hesitation, Avenor reached out and wrapped his hand around Rozalin's neck and effortlessly hefted her off the ground. "You dare threaten my wife?" he thundered.

"I am thrilled to know she lives," sneered Rozalin. "I was saddened to think that I would not be the one to send her from this world to the next," she finished before cackling manically.

Instead of a verbal reply, Avenor clenched his jaws together as he tightened his grip around Rozalin's throat. He watched the mirthful look in her eyes gradually be replaced with fear as he prevented her from breathing. Avenor smirked without humor as he watched Rozalin's eyes begin to bulge, and her hands reach up to claw at the vice around her neck.

"Release her," muttered Novex as he clapped Avenor on the back firmly. "Death is much too kind. Send her to Sicario Prison for the remainder of her life," he then suggested.

After careful consideration, Avenor forcefully threw Rozalin to the side, and she instantly collapsed to the ground in a crumpled heap. "Ambassador… deal with her," he instructed Novex coldly while glaring down at the gasping woman. *"I must return to Capitalia. Galhix… there was an attempt on her life,"* he silently informed his *hamigo*.

"Shall I accompany you? Or should I personally escort the traitor to Sicario Prison?" questioned Novex with a sideways tilt of his head at Rozalin.

"I believe Major Chevin would enjoy the opportunity," answered Avenor. *"I would appreciate if you would join me once the remaining prisoners have been delt with as well."*

"As you desire, Your Grace," replied Novex with a salute.

"And if you would, inform my parents," Avenor then said with a hasty look around to which Novex nodded his head briskly. *"My thanks, Brother,"* Avenor replied with a small smile before turning to Valcaly. "Return to Capitalia," he instructed her sternly to which she nodded her head in acknowledgement. Not wasting another moment, the two recited the incantations and felt their bodies fade as they were transported back to the capital city of Savenius.

* * *

"Nahm-Aztey Khan Crusendir and Overseer Truceran!" greeted the sentinels instantly as Avenor and Valcaly materialized beside the pink boulder within the *Teleportation Tower*.

"Ahz-sulam oo-laikim," the two leaders replied in unison before expertly navigating through the intricate obstacles until they reached the ground.

"Details," demanded Avenor as he took long strides toward the palace with Valcaly trotting alongside of him.

Knowing the single word was directed at her, Valcaly began explaining the situation to Avenor. At the rear entry, the guards greeted the pair and rendered the appropriate salutes, however, they were not returned. Without a word, the two guards exchanged knowing looks that the Khan was deep in thought regarding his wife's condition. After Avenor and Valcaly entered the palace, one soldier raced to the top of the palace and hoisted the Khan's banner to indicate his return.

"How is she?" demanded Avenor instantly as he walked into his personal chamber. Upon entering, he halted abruptly, causing Valcaly to

193

Kimberly Evette Ortuno

collide into his muscular frame. The sight of his wife laying pale and motionless froze him in place.

"Oof," she grunted at the sudden impact and nearly fell backward. However, a set of strong arms wrapped around her waist to steady her.

"Careful now," came a quiet voice that sent tingles of awareness down her spine.

"Daylin," she absentmindedly thought, recognizing the familiar sensation his voice stirred within her. Glancing over her shoulder, her eyes met the sincere ones of Novex's brother. Feeling her face flush, she stepped out of his embrace and dipped her head slightly. "My thanks," she said before turning to give Avenor a gentle shove forward. "Go to her," she grunted, unable to move the mountain stand motionless in front of her.

Feeling a pressure on his back and Valcaly's prompt, Avenor broke free from the shock and ran to his wife's side.

"Your Grace," greeted Baylay from her seated position opposite of Avenor. "She has not responded," she then said in a pitiful whisper.

Avenor pressed his forehead to his wife's and spoke gently to her, begging her to wake up. However, she did not answer him. After a while, rage began to bubble up from within Avenor. Absentmindedly, Avenor called to the shadows, and they began to converge in the silent chamber.

Valcaly's eyes widened as she watched the increasing darkness begin to surround Avenor. Hurriedly, she joined Avenor beside the bed and wrapped him in her embrace. "Avenor," she whispered while caressing his back in a motherly gesture. "Avenor, do not allow the rage to consume you," she begged quietly. "You must remain strong for Galhix and Wesdin!" she hissed, trying to break through the frenzied fury that began to possess him.

The muscles in Avenor's jaw jumped as he clenched and unclenched his teeth as he fought for control of his emotions. Gradually, the shadows began to disperse. "Why, *Onia?* Why?" questioned Avenor so only Valcaly could hear him as he fiercely hugged her in return and allowed tears to spill down his cheeks.

"Brother," said Gelriz, as if finally realizing Avenor had arrived. He stood and walked to stand beside Avenor. Looking down, he noticed Avenor's tear stained face and expression of despair before pulling Avenor up into his embrace. Wordlessly, the two men consoled one another.

194

As they stood in silence, a foggy memory made its way to Avenor's current thoughts. Pulling back slightly, he eyed Gelriz. "Brother…" he began tentatively.

"Aye?" replied Gelriz curiously as he studied the hopeful expression on Avenor's face.

"Do you suppose…" Avenor said as he broke free from Gelriz and turned back to Galhix. "She is trapped in the Dream World?"

Gelriz turned and frowned as he peered down at his younger sister. Tentatively, he nodded his head. "It is a possibility," he finally answered. "Why do you ask?"

Avenor swallowed hard before turning to look back at Gelriz. "Would it be possible… could you… I remember…," he stammered, unsure how to ask the question that probed at him.

"Spit it out already!" grumbled Gelriz impatiently.

"Can you find her in the *Melded Dream Realm?*" Avenor finally asked in a rush.

"Oy," gasped Gelriz quietly, his eyes widening in understanding. "I had not even considered it. It is possible…" he said, his gaze suddenly becoming distant. After a moment, he finally nodded. "It can do no harm in trying."

"Do it," instructed Avenor flatly.

"Very well, Your Grace," replied Gelriz. Without wasting time, Gelriz instantly began instructing the others.

Avenor ever so gently rolled Galhix on her side, and he angled her head to expose the back of her neck. Once she was positioned, he laid down beside her and placed a tender hand upon her cheek. "I will see you soon," he whispered hopefully.

Avenor ignored the *poof* that sounded nearby and briefly glanced at the black tigal that appeared behind his wife, knowing it was Gelriz.

"Bring her back," pleaded Avenor as he met Gelriz's eyes over his wife's shoulders as the tigal climbed on the bed.

"I shall do my best," Gelriz assured Avenor. After speaking those words, Gelriz opened his massive mouth and sunk his fangs into the back of his sister's neck. Clamping down, Gelriz penetrated through Galhix's flesh until his fangs reached the fluid that traveled to and surrounded her brain. As she was not awake, Gelriz was unable to control the dream and was forced to enter his sister's unconscious thoughts.

CHAPTER 22

"Oy," groaned Wesdin as he placed a hand on his throbbing head and sat up. Reciting an incantation, he eased the discomfort he felt. He then opened his eyes and glanced around. "Where am I?" he asked aloud to himself. A shuffling sound nearby drew his interest.

Lana moaned as she pushed herself to a sitting position. Blinking her eyes, she tried to inspect her surroundings.

"Lea?" questioned Wesdin as he eyed the unfamiliar cloak around the girl across from him.

Lana recognized Wesdin's voice and immediately turned to glower at him. "Wesdin," she said his name, trying to conceal her hatred for him.

"Lana?" replied Wesdin in confusion. "Where is Leandra?" he then asked, trying to recall how he had ended up with Lana. He had been certain he had protectively hugged his friend rather than Lana.

"I do not know. Nor do I care," she replied indifferently as she peered around in the darkness. An eerie silence surrounded them, and at that moment, she decided she needed Wesdin.

Wesdin made a face of disgust at Lana, feeling hostility rise in his heart for an unknown reason. He could clearly see Lana's expressions, but it was clear to him that she could not see him. Just as he was about to leave her, she called out to him.

"I'm sorry," she tried to sound sincere. "It's just... my mother," she then said, forcing herself to hiccup and feign a sob. In truth, she felt no remorse, knowing fully that Taygan was not her birth mother – a secrete she had discovered from Peygar.

Wesdin crossed his arms over his chest and arched a brow incredulously, watching the deceitful expressions betraying Lana. *"She lies,"* he grumbled to himself as he glanced around once more. *"But... I suppose it is better than exploring alone,"* he finally conceded silently. "I understand," responded Wesdin as he tried to keep his voice neutral. Pretending to be unable to see, he then asked, "Where are you?"

"I am here," said Lana as she tried to follow Wesdin's voice.

Wesdin walked straight to Lana and waved his arms around as if he were blindly searching for her in the dark. After a moment, he allowed their hands to awkwardly find one another. "Can you remember anything?" he asked her as he realized they were in some sort of stony chamber.

Lana contorted her face as she tried to recall the events prior to waking. "Only being carried away by some sort of beast," she finally answered, remembering she had woken up only to find herself flying over the desert, dangling precariously from a hound's mouth. She had fallen unconscious out of sheer fright at the sight.

"Same," muttered Wesdin as he tugged on Lana's hand. "Come," he said and guided her toward the only opening.

"Youch!" exclaimed Lana as her knee bumped something hard. "How do you know where you are going?" she suddenly demanded. "I cannot even see my own hand before my face," she complained.

"I cannot see. I am just feeling my way," he quickly lied. Guiding her to a wall with a torch, he pretended to have stumbled upon it. "Hmm, what is this?" he asked, letting go over Lana's hand.

"What is it?" she asked, her voice anxious. "Wesdin?" she said as she heard a scraping sound.

"It feels like a torch," he said with a roll of his eyes. "Do you have kindling and a striker?" he asked quietly, not caring to divulge his full powers to her.

"Aye, in my pack," she replied as she reached for the strap on her shoulder. "No," she suddenly whispered.

"What?" asked Wesdin as he peaked over his shoulder at Lana, curious to know why her voice had trembled.

"My pack... it's gone," she admitted and plopped to the ground in dismay. "My tome..." she unintentionally whispered aloud.

Wesdin looked back to the spot where he had first seen Lana and saw the leather pouch on the ground. "I have fou..." he began but suddenly snapped his mouth closed. *"Oy, that was close,"* he mutely thought.

"You have what?" Lana asked quietly, aware that Wesdin was about to say something.

"I, uh... I may have my own," he stated uneasily. "Give me a moment. I will try and search through my belongings," he informed her as he crept back to grab Lana's bag. Sneaking back to her side, he then sat down a few feet away from her so she could not reach out and touch him. Dumping the contents out, he was instantly attracted to a ragged looking tome. *"Is this the tome she mentioned?"* he pondered to himself.

"Well?" snapped Lana impatiently.

"Patience!" spat Wesdin in return, trying to find a way to dally. "I cannot see in the dark either," he sneered irritably.

"Hmph," snorted Lana, sensing the hostility coming from Wesdin.

As Wesdin shuffled through various items to create random sounds, he hastily opened the tome and was greeted by a cloth item. Cautiously, he unfolded it. Reading the entries swiftly, a frown contorted his child-like features as his mind raced. *"Gulroq is Ami's older brother... He tried to kill Ami before... My Grandapi was the Prince... I am so confused,"* he admitted mutely as he scratched the side of his head. Setting the few entries aside, he thumbed through the tome briefly. He learned about "the source" and how to invoke the *Drachenian* bloodline. His interest triggered, Wesdin momentarily forgot where he was.

"Anything yet?" groused Lana, startling Wesdin.

"Uh... aye... I have found my kindling," he stammered as he hastily packed Lana's belongings. He then shoved her pack into his own. He then removed the items needed to start a fire. "Finally!" he said in feigned excitement. "I've found it!" Absentmindedly, Wesdin lit the torch before placing the fire starting items back in his bag; he then placed it over his head and angled it across his body. "Let's go," he mumbled flatly and began casually strolling away from Lana.

"Ugh!" exclaimed Lana, disgruntled because Wesdin had not offered to assist her to her feet before walking off without her. Afraid to be left alone in the dark, she bit her tongue; she then quickly jumped up and hurried after him while glaring daggers at his back.

* * *

Gelriz blinked his eyes repetitively as he glanced around, trying to discern where he was. As he watched, various scenes unfolded before him. *"She controls this dream,"* he acknowledged to himself, not surprised as it was only his second time to ever use his ability.

"Galhix?" called out Gelriz as he tried to find his younger sister trapped in her own mind. Suddenly, a little girl appeared before him.

"Hello, Handsome Sir," greeted the child with an ethereal like voice. "Will you come play with me?" she asked innocently before cheerfully skipping away from him.

Gelriz frowned as he watched the faintly familiar cheerful cherub disappear from him. "Galhix?" he asked as he began walking in the direction she had gone. The clarity of the image suddenly became hazy, and Gelriz knew her dream was changing.

A child's cry guided Gelriz as he approached a wooden cabin; pushing open the door, he discovered Galhix sitting in a pool of blood.

The despair in her eyes was evident as she rocked back and forth while hugging her knees to her chest. Stepping inside, Gelriz gasped as realization struck him like a lightning bolt. "Mother... father..." he said in a tone that was barely audible. His sister's sobs reminded him she was present. "Galhix," he said her name softly. "Come with me," he pleaded with her.

"Go away!" she wailed before bolting to her feet and darting past him through the door.

"Galhix!" he cried out as he spun around to follow her; stopping with a groan, he closed his eyes as the environment became foggy once again. Opening his eyes, he found himself in the corridor outside of the personal chamber she shared with Avenor. "Who are you?" he heard Galhix demand. Pushing the door open, he watched as an adolescent outstretched her hands toward his sister. In horror, he watched as the girl sliced open his sister's abdomen. The girl appeared to draw a glow from Galhix before escaping through the open window.

"Galhix!" shouted Gelriz as he sprinted across the chamber to her side just as the door burst open. Quiet sobbing droned out the other sounds in Galhix's dream and caused Gelriz to turn. In a far corner, his recognized Galhix's slender frame. "Galhix?" he said gently as he approached her.

"Leave me," she mumbled gruffly.

"I cannot," replied Gelriz as he knelt beside his sister. "I beg of you... please... come back."

Sniffling, Galhix turned and met her brother's worried gaze with her swollen, red eyes – evidence of her uncontrollable crying. "She took her..." she admitted to her brother before erupting into an inconsolable weeping mess once more as she clutched a bloody bundle to her chest.

His face a mirror of his internal puzzlement, Gelriz reached down with a shaky hand and pulled the blanket back. His face instantly became pale and contorted in disbelief as he discovered a faceless infant.

"How could she take my baby!" wailed Galhix as she rocked back and forth with her face pressed into the bloodstained wrap.

"Oy, Galhix," murmured Gelriz, not knowing how to soothe his sister. "I cannot even begin to fathom the pain you feel," he acknowledged as he dropped to his knees and pulled his sister into his embrace. After a long while in silence, Gelriz gently caressed the lifeless child. "I know it is difficult," he whispered before swallowing hard and continuing to remind her, "but Wesdin still needs his Ami."

Gradually, Galhix turned to face her brother, as if coming out of a trance, and she stared into his concerned eyes. She then looked down at the unborn child she would never meet as her brother's words continued to resound in her mind. "Wesdin," she finally said, remembering her son. "Ami is so sorry, my beloved," she whispered as she gently caressed the tiny corpse. "I was not able to protect you," she admitted with another sob. After a while, she said, "I wish to remain, but your brother needs me." Taking a moment to ponder something, she then turned to look at Gelriz. "She will have the proper ceremonial burning," she announced quietly.

"Of course," agreed Gelriz with a single nod.

Once she finished carefully cleansing the baby's body of blood, Galhix wrapped her in a white, silk blanket. She then placed the deceased child in a basin before setting it ablaze.

Gelriz stood beside his sister during the brief *ceremonial burning*, sending the child to the next world in peace. Eventually, he took his sister's hand and guided her to the bed where her physical form remained, and he anxiously watched as she extended a hand. Just as her hands touched, his mind went blank.

* * *

"Kenzelo," said Manijor as he wiped blood from his face while seemingly distracted, "do what you feel is appropriate with the footmen and peons."

"Aye, General," replied Kenzelo as he watched Manijor surveying the area. "Is there anything else?" he suddenly asked.

"Hmm," hummed Manijor as he finally met the Overseer's concerned eyes. "Have you seen General Akeenil?"

"Now that you mention it…" began Kenzelo as he turned but was soon interrupted by Novex.

"General Crusendir," greeted Novex in a serious voice.

"Ambassador. What is it?" inquired Manijor, sensing the negative energy coming from the tigal.

"His Grace has returned to Capitalia. Action was taken against the Regent Khan in his absence," Novex informed Avenor's father.

"What?" roared Manijor as his black eyes appeared to darken even further. He then canted his head to the side and shifted his attention back to Kenzelo. "Handle the traitors as you deem appropriate," he announced firmly. "That wench…," he began as he turned to look at Rozalin, but he was interrupted by Novex before he could finish.

"His Grace has instructed Major Chevin to escort the traitor, Rozalin, to Sicario Prison where she will stay for the remainder of her miserable life," said Novex with an apologetic nod toward Manijor.

"Very well," replied Manijor and Kenzelo in unison.

With a scowl on his face, Manijor turned to search for his wife. As he walked through the center of the fort, he listened to the casualty count, satisfied that Texicar had not sustained many losses. As he passed a familiar face, he stopped and called out to her, ""Sergeant Rysik."

"General Crusendir," Ayja returned with a salute. "How may I assist?" she asked respectfully.

"Do you know the whereabouts of General Akeenil?" inquired Manijor as he continued glancing around the area.

"Nay," replied Ayja hesitantly as she turned in the direction where she had last seen Everly. "Last I saw, she was atop there," she finished and pointed toward a watchtower.

"My thanks," replied Manijor as he hurried toward the pillar anxiously. As he bounded up the stairs taking two at a time, Manijor called out, "General Akeenil!" An uneasiness began to spread throughout his body when Everly did not respond. "Everly!" he called out again before finally shouting, "Everly!"

The frantic shouting of Avenor's father drew Novex's apprehensive gaze; without hesitation, he burst into action and chased behind Manijor. Novex diminished the distance between himself and Manijor briskly and followed closely on the older man's heels.

A soldier jumped up as the sound of pounding footsteps thundered along the wooden walkway. "General Crusendir," said the burly warrior as he tried to slow Manijor's progress.

Manijor saw the dismay in the other man's eyes, and he forcefully tried to push the soldier out of the way. "Move!" growled out Manijor. Just as Novex was about to intervene, Manijor managed to shove the sentry aside; Manijor stormed passed the warrior with Novex following close behind. Manijor's steps abruptly faltered, causing Novex to crash into his back, but he failed to notice. His unwavering gaze landed on a familiar figure, face down, wearing his wife's armor. An arrow protruded from the felled soldier's back. "Everly," he choked out as tears instantly sprung into his eyes. "It cannot be," he mumbled as he staggered forward and fell to his knees beside the motionless warrior. With his heart thundering frantically in his chest, he fearfully reached out and turned the woman over. His black orbs were instantly met with Everly's emerald, green eyes; her once bright and sparkling windows to her soul were now dull and void of life. His breath hitched and caught in his throat as a heart wrenching sob escaped from his mouth; with tears cascading down his face, he forcefully pushed the serrated arrow forward through her back and out through the front of her chest before casting it aside. Cradling his wife's body to his chest, he sobbed uncontrollably without care of who witnessed his grief.

* * *

"*Nahm-Aztey,* Ambassador Clawbane!" greeted the sentinels at the *Teleportation Tower* as Novex appeared just as the sun had peaked over the horizon.

"*Ahz-sulam oo-laikim,*" replied Novex with a stony expression while returning their salutes before smoothly easing his way down from the arrival platform. Without another word, he reverted to his tigal form and dashed to the palace. As he neared, he caught sight of two individuals bickering as they walked side by side. "***Rawr,***" growled Novex once he was directly behind the pair.

"Oy!" exclaimed Betaro as he spun around, preparing to bash the attacker with his shield. Suddenly, a grin spread across Betaro's face.

Iriva squealed in surprise and jumped a foot off the ground; she then twirled and glowered furiously at the tigal behind her. "Damn, you, Novex!"

Novex's eyes twinkled in merriment briefly before he changed back to his human form. Hastily, he then said, "apologies, General Jander, but I am in a rush... as you both should be also."

"What do you mean?" asked Betaro worriedly.

"I shall explain as we go," replied Novex as he extended a hand, indicating for the two Generals to proceed before him.

"What of Everly and Manijor?" asked Betaro after Novex finished explaining the situation regarding the Khantessa.

"General Crusendir has remained with General Akeenil in Texicar until the traitors have been punished as deemed appropriate by Overseer Ozulben. The leader, Rozalin Lanikeel, has been sentenced to life imprisonment at Sicario Prison," Novex finished informing Avenor's grandparents just as they arrived to see Galhix stirring. Novex gnawed on his bottom lip nervously, expecting Betaro to press for more details, but eventually sighed in relief when Betaro simply nodded. *"Now is not the time,"* he silently said as he watched Betaro nervously.

Gelriz opened his eyes groggily and licked the puncture marks on the back of his sister's neck, ensuring the wounds would heal without any adverse effects. He then changed back to his human body.

"Were you able to find her?" asked Avenor upon seeing Gelriz awake.

"Aye," replied Gelriz quietly. Nodding his head slowly, he then added, "She is mourning." Noticing the confused look plastered on Avenor's face, he tried to explain what he had witnessed in the dream realm. "Her assailant... Galhix... the child... ceremonial burning," stammered Gelriz as he reached up to press his fists to his eyes.

Avenor jerked his head back as if his second-brother had physically reached out and struck him. "A child?" repeated Avenor incredulously. "She was with child?"

"Oy," whispered Valcaly, "it makes sense. She had been feeling ill the few days after your departure, Your Grace."

"Av… Avenor," came a weak voice from the bed.

"Galhix!" exclaimed Avenor as he pulled his frail wife into his embrace. "You are awake!" he breathed a sigh of relief as he rained tender kisses over her face.

Galhix leaned her head against Avenor's chest, hiccupped once, and allowed silent tears to spill down her cheeks.

"I am sorry," whispered Avenor as he kissed her temple. With his face buried in her hair, he added, "I am sorry we will never meet our unborn child." Avenor felt Galhix tense in his arms before she leaned back to peer into his eyes. "Gelriz informed me," he answered her unspoken question.

"I see," was all Galhix said as she snuggled closer into Avenor's embrace.

"Do not scare me like that again!" scolded Gelriz lightly before leaning forward to wrap both Avenor and Galhix in a hug. "It is good to see your lavender eyes again," he whispered before stepping back.

"Aye, you cannot be doing that to us," added Valcaly as she walked toward the bed. She then bent down to press her forehead against Galhix's briefly; after a brief time, she straightened herself and saluted as she moved out of the way.

Iriva said nothing as she watched the exchanges, relief washing over her upon seeing the Khantessa awake. Extending her hands, she recited multiple complex incantations that were only audible to herself; however, the chants were directed at Galhix, and they completely revitalized Galhix's health, erased her fatigue, and rejuvenated her energy.

The ragged breathing behind him caused Betaro to arch a brow and slowly turn; the sight of Iriva leaning against the wall in exhaustion jolted Betaro. Once the shock waned, he rushed to Iriva's side and scooped her up in his arms. "Oy," he said quietly with a slow shake of his head. "Why is it that I frequently find myself rescuing a Soother in distress?" he asked in a teasing manner.

"Shut it," replied Iriva weakly as she hesitantly wrapped her arms around Betaro's neck. "Galhix is physically well," she whispered before allowing herself to be claimed by exhaustion and drifting into oblivion.

Novex heard the exchange between Betaro and Iriva, and he turned to watch as Betaro scooped up Iriva. Meeting Betaro's gaze,

Novex simply nodded in acknowledgement as Betaro carried the unconscious Soother to her personal chambers to recover.

"Your Grace," said Novex as he walked further into the Khan's personal chambers. "I suggest you bathe before continuing to comfort Khantessa Galhix," he said lightly, causing all those present to chuckle which helped ease the tension.

"Indeed," agreed Galhix with a smirk. "You reek of blood, sweat, and zebril."

"Hmm," said Avenor with a slight cant of his head to the side. "So, you are saying… I smell like a man?" he said with an amused arch of his brow and questioning tone.

"Aye," replied Galhix with a giggle as she added, "women warriors always smell of roses."

"Aye," said Valcaly before purposefully making a face of disgust and pinching her nose before smirking. "Then, we shall leave you to it," announced Valcaly as she turned and ushered the others out of the Khan's personal chambers. "I shall send the palace keepers to prepare your bath," she said before closing the door behind her.

* * *

Heat from the rising sun began to make itself known as the surroundings were covered in greyness as pre-dawn arrived.

"Overseer Reeyah," called out Dondree from behind his mother, causing her to glance over her shoulder.

"Aye?" she shouted over the *clattering* of the scorpions as they crossed the desert with ease.

"We near the oasis," stated Dondree loudly. "I have yet to complete my hunt," he announced tentatively.

Reeyah tossed her head back and gave a short bark of laughter. "You have survived this long. And you say you have not completed your hunt?" she said incredulously. "I do not believe it!" she finally said with another chortle.

Dondree raised his brows in unison, clearly surprised by his mother's reaction, but he refused to return without a proper kill even if she was correct. "I will not return unless I arrive with a carcass to prove my worth as a hunter," he stated firmly.

Grinning, Reeyah glanced over her shoulder before nodding. "Very well," she answered. "Tell me when you desire to dismount."

Dondree saw the Arid Mountains rising in the distance as they approached the Norther terrain. Turning to the right, he clearly saw the life-sustaining trees and the Salt Flats beyond. Not long after, he saw the trail leading to the Veiled Oasis. *"Finally… home,"* he silently sighed to himself. At that moment, an angry shriek from his left made him turn in that direction. *"Deaf Raptor."*

Reeyah glanced to her side and watched as the disgruntled reptile arched its head and gave another shrilly scream as it roared. Instantly, she reached up and covered her ears as did the others traveling alongside her. Just then, she felt a tap on her shoulder. Turning, she saw her son indicating he wanted her to stop. "Surely you jest?" she demanded with a scowl only to have Dondree grin mischievously at her as his response. "Oy, very well," she said after realizing Dondree was serious. Raising her arm, she signaled for the group to halt.

Dondree handed the unconscious girl to Demic before he jumped down from the back of the monstrous scorpion. Glancing back, Dondree recognized the familiar faces of the hunting party who were also battle-hardened warriors. *"Time to prove your worth,"* he silently encouraged himself. During the trek across the desert, he had dismissed his beastly form. Now, however, he initiated the transformation once more as he would not live long against a raptor otherwise.

Reeyah watched in awe as Dondree changed before her eyes; in an instant, he grew nearly three times his normal size. The ghastly sound of his bones snapping and breaking echoed through the desert while maroon fur sprouted over most of his body. His hands transformed to paws, however, his fingers remained but lengthened into deadly claws with razor-sharp nails. Looking at her son's face, she realized he looked more like a *fire hound* than he did a human. Smirking, she knew he had consumed the elixir which is why he had survived.

Grrrrr. Grrrrrr. Grrrrrrrrrrrrrr!
Shhhhrrraaaaak!

Demic and Dimor exchanged baffled looks before turning back to watch Dondree growling as the *Deaf Raptor* shrieked defiantly. Sordun tensed nervously as he watched his trainee crouched with all four extremities on the ground.

"Do not assist!" hollered Reeyah as she saw the uneasy looks from the others. "He desires to complete his hunt."

The gigantic reptile stomped the ground furiously with one foot, and it lowered its spiked head at Dondree. Locking its eyes on its target, it then snorted loudly.

Dondree lunged forward at that instant and charged at the lizard. The raptor stood motionless, stunned as it eyed the single hunter rushing forward – something the apex predator had never experienced. Dondree took advantage of the situation, and he sprang off the ground.

The raptor took a step back just in time to avoid Dondree's jaws from clamping down on its neck; however, it was unable to avoid the nails that pierced through its leathery flesh on its side. With a cry, the beast swung its tail violently and dislodged its attacker.

Dondree flew off the creature, and he landed on his paws only a few feet away. Snarling, the novice hunter and his prey circled one another warily.

Just then, the animal rushed toward Dondree; at the last moment before impact, the raptor spun around, trying to swipe Dondree off balance with its tail. However, Dondree was too swift, and he bounded straight up in the air and landed on the surprised beast's back.

Reeyah grinned as she crossed her arms over her chest and watched the deadly dance between her son and the raptor. As the raptor spun in circles frantically, she saw her son ferociously lower his head and sink his fangs into the side of the beast's neck.

Dondree felt blood gushing into his mouth, and he swallowed the warm liquid. Securing his grip on his prey's neck, he then used all his might to shove himself forward over the raptor's shoulder.

Rrriiiip!!

The sound of the beast's thick hide shredding apart sent a disgusted shudder through those watching.

Dondree stood motionless with a chunk of raptor in his mouth while blood dripped from the sides of his mouth. Not bothering to look back, he heard the massive animal collapse behind him. With a *snap,* Dondree repositioned the raw portion of meat in his mouth and hastily devoured it.

An unexpected uproar of praise and cheering startled Dondree, and he turned his head to see his mother sitting with a proud smile on her face. "Retrieve it," she said with an approving nod, "and return home." Not waiting, Reeyah and the others urged the scorpions forward and completed the remainder of the journey ahead of Dondree.

Without hesitation, Dondree hefted the carcass over his shoulders and carried his kill back to the Veiled Oasis. As he approached, the slow clapping sound intensified until the entire encampment surrounded him as he dropped the dead raptor beside the raging bonfire. With a triumphant grin, he turned and waved until he met his mother's proud eyes.

"We welcome you home, Lord Dondree," she then announced in a boisterous voice so that the entire camp heard his title.

CHAPTER 23

Avenor sat behind Galhix dragging a comb through her long, lustrous hair absentmindedly with a frown on his face. Galhix remained quiet as she studied his expression in the mirror. It had been some time already, and Avenor was still easily sliding the comb through her damp locks.

"She was almost lost to me," ruminated Avenor as his heart began beating faster at the thought. *"Our child was taken from us."* The thought caused him to clench his teeth together as fury flashed in his eyes.

"I desire to go to the Dining Hall for evening meal," said Galhix suddenly, drawing Avenor out of his own gloomy thoughts.

Avenor met Galhix's soft gaze in the mirror, and the frown on his face deepened into a scowl. "We shall share evening meal here," he answered her flatly.

Galhix grunted in annoyance before turning to face Avenor. She took the comb from his hands and set it on the vanity before standing. "I have no desire to remain confined to these walls. The scent of blood lingers, and the memories are still painful," she finished saying. "I would appreciate if you would accompany me and Wesdin," she said firmly.

Avenor took a calming breath before standing. "Very well. I shall accompany you," he responded hesitantly, still uneasy that someone managed to enter the palace and dared attempt to take her life. Without another word, Avenor tucked Galhix's hand in the crook of his arm and escorted her to the Dining Hall. Immediately upon entering, the two noticed there was no one else present.

"Odd," stated Galhix as she took her place at the table beside Avenor. "Where are the others?" she suddenly asked.

"Hmm. Odd, indeed," added Avenor before turning to a nearby palace keeper. "Where are the others?" he asked bluntly.

The server shifted uncomfortably from one foot to the other, and he avoided meeting the Khan's probing gaze. "Y…our Gr… Grace," stuttered the worker as he peered everywhere else besides Avenor's face. "The others… they… they are…"

Just then, Mikela strode into the Dining Hall and halted directly in front of Avenor and Galhix.

"Good eve, Commandant Clawbane," greeted Avenor warmly. "We were beginning to wonder where our allies were."

"Aye," agreed Galhix, smiling up at the intimidating tigal. Realizing Mikela was alone, Galhix turned and looked toward the door. "Wesdin? The others?" she asked with an arch of her brow.

"Your Graces," began Mikela in a tone that relayed the urgency of her message. She paused and swallowed hard, knowing she had to divulge the truth sooner rather than later. "Khanzito Wesdin 'as fled from the palace." Mikela stood motionless as she watched Avenor's expression become dark while Galhix's face reflected the disbelief she felt.

"Explain yourself," growled out Avenor as he clenched his hands.

"I believe he fled the night Khantessa Galhix was attacked. I cannot be certain though," replied Mikela as she balled her fists at her side. While her charge had not been Wesdin, she was the *Apex* leader, and therefore responsible for the success or failure of those she led. "He has left to the *Forbidden Wilds,*" she admitted quietly.

Avenor sat motionless for a moment as he contemplated what Mikela had just divulged. He then turned as Galhix grabbed his arm and began shaking him frantically.

"Summon him! Now!" Galhix pleaded with Avenor.

"Aye," he replied to Galhix before immediately reciting *'The Call'* that would summon Wesdin to him. "Wesdin… To me I summon, fragments made whole." A frow gradually appeared on Avenor's face when his son did not appear which meant only one of two things. Wesdin's shard had somehow been removed from his flesh or he was deceased.

"It cannot be!" gasped Galhix as she pressed her hands to her mouth in horror as she turned to look pleadingly at Avenor. "Tell me I am still dreaming," she begged him.

Avenor stood forcefully, the abrupt action knocked the chair over behind him, and he glowered at Mikela before finally snarling, "Gather the others. We depart at once!"

"I am traveling as well," announced Galhix as she shoved back from the table. Looking at the palace keeper, she instructed, "Prepare multiple vessels of meal mush, flagons of *restoradria,* and water."

"As you desire, Your Grace," replied the castle worker as she dipped her head respectfully. "I shall have it prepared shortly," she added before disappearing through the doors leading to the kitchen.

"I forbid you to come along," grumbled Avenor as he stormed down the corridor along with Galhix.

Galhix turned her head sharply and openly glowered at Avenor. Grabbing his arm, she then halted abruptly. "You will **not** prevent me from searching for **my** son!" she snapped harshly. "I carried him within my womb! You dare try and forbid me to assist in his rescue?" she continued, her voice becoming a thunderous roar with each word. "I shall take the life from you if you attempt to prevent me from embarking on this expedition!" Her words reverberated throughout the palace as she stormed away from Avenor, stunned in place with his mouth agape, as he stared at her back.

* * *

Notification of Wesdin's disappearance circulated swifter than the attack on Galhix. Betaro hastily inspected his armor, satisfied the damage was not severe from his mission in Itagrio. Upon departing his personal quarters, he encountered Novex pacing to-and-fro as if he had been waiting for him.

"Ambassador Clawbane," Betaro said as he approached Novex.

"General Akeenil," replied Novex softly with his eyes downcast.

"What concerns you?" asked Betaro apprehensively, sensing the usually lighthearted tigal was troubled by something.

"You should remain in Capitalia," said Novex as he massaged the back of his neck nervously.

"Why would I not aid in the search of my grandson?" inquired Betaro with an arch of his brow as he crossed his arms.

Novex swallowed hard multiple times, the *gulp* sounds audible in the tense silence. "General Akeenil..." he finally began in a strained whisper, "has passed." The pain in his chest prevented him from saying any more.

Betaro scrunched his nose and contorted his face while tilting his head to the side. "Where have I passed to?" he asked in confusion. After a moment, he then clarified, "General Akeenil... you mean to say Everly?" Betaro grabbed Novex's tunic and shook him, but Novex refused to meet his probing gaze. "She has passed what? Passed where?" he asked frantically, feeling dread seeping through him. "Novex!" he suddenly hollered. "Explain yourself!"

"I offer my sincerest condolences," was all Novex could muster.

Abruptly, Betaro released his hold to turn away from Novex, and he placed his hands on the sides of his head as he struggled to accept what Novex had said. Without warning, he spun back around to face Novex; he then drew his arm back and delivered a single blow. "You lie!" spat Betaro vehemently as his fist connected with Novex's face in a dull thud.

Novex's head involuntarily turned with the force of Betaro's punch, and he winced at the discomfort but made no move to retaliate. Instead, he grabbed Betaro and drew him into a fierce hug as heart-wrenching sobs wracked the older man's burly frame. Soon after, Betaro pulled away from Novex.

"Is Manijor aware?" Betaro questioned mournfully before continuing after Novex nodded. "Avenor?" Betaro watched as Novex hesitated briefly before shaking his head from side to side. "Let it remain as such until Wesdin has been recovered," Betaro then said as fresh tears filled his eyes once more. Before Novex could leave, Betaro reached out and placed a hand on his shoulder. "Ambassador... my apologies for my brutish reaction," he mumbled as the tears finally escaped from the corners of his bloodshot eyes. "You have my thanks," he then quietly added before dropping his hand and retreating to his assigned chambers.

* * *

Dondree sat on the ground in his personal hollow staring admiringly at the fair-skinned girl sleeping peacefully in his bed. He had not left her side since his return to the oasis, and he began to worry as she mumbled incoherently in her sleep.

"What is your name, girl?" he softly asked as she slumbered. "Where are you from? Who were the others with you? What is your age?" The longer Dondree sat there and pondered about who the mysterious girl was, the more intrigued he became and wanted to know every detail about her.

A shuffle just beyond the entryway to his hovel disrupted Dondree's thoughts. "Overlord Reeyah," he said after peering over his shoulder. Quickly, he sprung to his feet before turning to face his mother.

"Lord Dondree," replied Reeyah with a smile before tilting her head to the side so she could peer around her son. "Any improvement?"

Dondree turned around to face the girl once more. "Nay," he answered with a frown. "Where do you suppose she is from?" he pondered aloud.

Reeyah crinkled her nose as she inspected the child intently; something at the back of her mind kept insisting she recognized her, but Reeyah knew she had never seen the child before in her life. "Perhaps a nomad?" she finally offered with an indifferent shrug.

"Perhaps," muttered Dondree as he sank back down and sat with his legs crossed.

Reeyah smirked to herself knowingly after listening to Dondree's expressive sigh; his behavior clearly indicated he was smitten with the stranger. "Will you attend the feast?"

"Hmm?" murmured Dondree, becoming aware his mother had asked him a question but could only stare at her blankly.

"Feast?" repeated with an amused tone. "Will you attend?" she added before chuckling.

"I would rather not," he answered honestly. "I desire to be here should she wake."

"Very well," said Reeyah with another grin before adding, "I shall send a *lowling* with a platter of nourishments." Snickering to herself, she left Dondree in an enamored daze and joined the others for the evening feast.

* * *

Wesdin and Lana walked around aimlessly; as they explored, Lana discovered a lamp which Wesdin gladly placed his own flame against. The added light expanded the illumination around them, intensifying their trepidation instead of easing it.

"It feels as if we are going deeper," grumbled Lana as she raised her light high above her head.

"You can guide us then," spat Wesdin in annoyance, sensing they were lost in a series of what he could only assume was underground tunnels.

"Perhaps we should just go our separate ways," she snapped back hotly. "It is not as if we are friends," she then sneered.

"That is true," agreed Wesdin with a look of disdain. Even though he disliked Lana for some unknown reason, he still could not hope misfortune upon her. "*Gahn-baht-teh,*" he said quietly through clenched teeth, not caring if she heard him say 'good luck to you.'

Lana canted her head to the side slightly in response to Wesdin's whisper, but she could not understand what he said. Her lack of understanding made her despise him even more. Instead of responding, she scoffed and flipped her hair over her shoulder before selecting a random tunnel to explore on her own.

"Phew," breathed Wesdin in relief once the faint glow of Lana's lamp had completely disappeared. Without hesitation, he then extinguished his torch and placed it in his pack, preferring to hide in the pitch-black darkness where he was still able to see clearly as though the entire place was completely illuminated. "Oy," he breathed out in wonder as he examined the intricate carvings and statues he had purposely ignored when Lana was alongside him. Just then, the scattering of loose pebbles nearby startled him. "Hello," he called out softly as his heart pounded erratically.

Wesdin listened to his own voice echo a handful of times before finally fading; remaining motionless, he strained to hear a response. As he began turning away, another sound stopped him.

Click, click, click, click.

"Hello?" repeated Wesdin, his voice louder than the first. "Who are you?" he then asked after receiving no response. Contemplating his actions, he finally decided to follow the sound.

From a concealed location ahead of Wesdin, a pair of bewildered eyes watched the blue-skinned boy approaching. From his watch post earlier, he discerned that the child was fully capable of seeing in the dark. As such, he made certain to remain camouflaged. Deciding the newcomer was close enough, the hidden observer began moving once more, ensuring his nails *clicked* against the stone ground with every step.

"Oy," groused Wesdin in confusion as he twirled around in circles, trying to discover what was producing the repetitive *clicking* sound. After a while, Wesdin realized he was in an enormous cave. "Oy!" he repeated, but instead of confusion, his voice was full of astonishment.

Thud!

"Oy!" he exclaimed again in response to the sudden noise of a heavy door closing. Spinning around hurriedly, Wesdin saw two solid wooden slabs that reached from the ceiling to the floor of the vast grotto. With admiration and awe in his eyes, Wesdin inspected each section of wood; both doors had intricately carved images of a dragon on them facing one another with their heads bowed. With the doors closed, the creatures were depicted with crowns atop their heads while standing on their hindlegs; the claws of their forelegs were touching, their foreheads were pressed together, and their wings were extended proudly behind them. "Beautiful," sighed Wesdin breathlessly in admiration. Gradually, his gaze was drawn back to the monumental cavern.

"Remarkable," he murmured to himself as he wandered around the area. His eyes immediately widened when he noted four giant looking seats. Each was constructed from solid *damiund*, but they were adorned with different gems. Emblazoned on the back of them were different symbols. Unexpectedly, a low rumble caused Wesdin to tilt his head uneasily in the direction of the closed doors.

* * *

A low-pitched growl reverberated threateningly from within the cavern on the opposite side of the dragon engraved double doors.

"For what reason have you dared disturbed my slumber, Amaruq?" asked a savage voice from the farthest corner in the dark.

The alpha *fire hound* whimpered and cowered in response to the harsh tone of the lone, remaining master's question. Suddenly, a hostile pair of crystal-like sparkling, yellow eyes appeared in the blackness.

"Lord Ignahzel," greeted Amaruq mutely with his head lowered and tilted to the side in complete submission. *"I believe I have discovered the lost lineage of Regina Elemperia."*

"Impossible!" snarled Ignahzel from his resting place. "Where have you discovered such persons? It has been over five centuries since her lineage ended! Over five-hundred cycles since balance was obliterated!" he seethed, his eyes beginning to smolder as smoke escaped from his nostrils with each furious breath.

"What I speak is true, Lord Ignahzel!" exclaimed Amaruq. *"I have brought two children here! Here, to Burg der Drachen!"* he finished, his voice trembling while he visibly shook with fear.

Ignahzel glared down at the recoiling canine skeptically before scoffing coldly. "If the words you speak are true, Amaruq…" he finally said coldly, "lure the supposed *Blutdrache* to the Ring of Blood."

"Aye, Lord Ignahzel. As you command," replied the alpha *fire hound* before scurrying away from the brooding *Feuerdrache.*

* * *

The day had come and gone, leaving the desert haven in darkness aside from the occasional flame dancing in the wind as someone walked between the tents. Reeyah refused to stay in the hollow she previously shared with Gunter; instead, she erected a tent for herself alongside the one Demic shared with his brother.

Dondree absentmindedly picked at the various items arranged on the stone slab a *lowling* had delivered earlier that evening. Without conscious thought, his fingers landed on a juicy piece of meat; he glanced down as he picked it up, and he inspected it closely. "Deaf Raptor meat," he finally said with realization before tossing the tender morsel into his mouth. "Mmmm," he moaned in pleasure as the fire roasted taste, enhanced with salt mined from the Salt Flats, assaulted his tongue and *flavorbuds.*

Leandra opened her eyes to slits, just enough for her to watch a boy sitting on the ground beside a small fire. *"Oy, I am famished!"* she groaned to herself in discomfort as she watched him savoring the food he was in the process of consuming. *"Gah!"* she silently cried out to herself in dismay as her stomach rumbled with such an intensity that it startled the adolescent.

Dondree's head instantly snapped up; aside from a frown that slowly formed, he remained motionless as he inspected the girl. "Girl…" he said quietly after a while. "Girl… are you awake?"

213

Leandra continued to pretend she was asleep, but the soft gasp that escaped her lips as Dondree stood betrayed her. Finally building up her courage, she allowed her eyes to flutter before opening completely.

"Uh... are... hmm... uh... I..." stammered Dondree when he noticed the girl had opened her eyes.

Leandra stifled a giggle and pulled her lower lip in between her teeth as she watched him shuffling uneasily. "Hello," she said to ease the tension that filled the small grotto.

"Hello," Dondree said in a rush as he exhaled simultaneously. "I am Dondree," he announced quietly.

"I am Leandra," she then returned as her gaze unintentionally shifted to the platter of food on the stony floor.

"You must be hungry," Dondree immediately said as he followed Leandra's gaze. "Here," he said, bending down to pick up the slab and walking the short distance to stand in front of her.

Leandra abruptly sat up and pushed herself as far away from Dondree as possible, her eyes flashing warily.

"I will not harm you," said Dondree in a disheartened manner, aware that the adorable stranger feared him. Setting the platter down beside Leandra, he then turned and began walking away. "I shall return shortly. You are safe here," he informed her before leaving her in solitude.

Leandra studied the strange items for a long while, unsure what they were. "Surely they are edible," she said to herself with a brow arched. "Berries?" she said in a questioning voice as she crinkled her nose and contorted her face. "Squishy like one," she mumbled while gently squeezing an oblong shaped food between her fingers. "Well... down the hatch it goes," she decided and popped the fruit in her mouth. "Mmm, it is pure deliciousness!" she exclaimed happily before consuming the remainder. Fear thrown to the wayside as her hunger took over, she then devoured every single edible piece set beside her.

"Hmm, would you like more?" Dondree asked with a smirk as he leaned against the entryway. "Here is some water," he said as he held a flask out to her. He suddenly laughed as Leandra nodded her head enthusiastically. "Very well. I shall return again soon." With one last smile, Dondree disappeared.

* * *

Azelly sat with her arms resting on her knees, staring blankly into the crackling inferno, as it greedily licked at the logs within its reach; there had been few casualties during the raid. Nevertheless, there was one that was most difficult for her to accept. The death of her brother's mother.

214

"You should rest," said Leander as he came to sit beside her, extending a mug of steaming *lavendia* tea.

"You have my thanks," she whispered in return as she accepted the stein and inhaled the soothing fragrance before taking a cautious sip of the scalding contents. "However, I cannot bring myself to rest," she admitted pitifully.

Leander nodded his head in understanding but remained silent otherwise.

"I should be at my brother's side during this time," mumbled Azelly uncomfortably. "Everly and I... we had a strained relationship. She disliked me because I have been at Avenor's side longer than she has as his mother," she informed her mate quietly.

"Aye, I remember," Leander replied, knowing his wife simply needed someone to talk to. After a while, he turned so he could place a comforting arm around Azelly's waist as they sat side-by-side. The two remained unspoken, but Leander had his face distorted in contemplation. "You should return ahead of us. I shall offer my support and companionship to Manijor on the voyage to Capitalia," he suggested sympathetically.

Azelly turned and lifted her hopefully eyes to her mate. "You are certain? You will not be angry?" she asked in return.

"Aye, and I have no reason to be upset," he responded with a loving smile. "He is your brother. It is always best for family to support one another in their times of distress," he added to put her mind at ease. "Come," he said after standing. He extended his hand out for Azelly to take it, and she immediately placed her hand in his. Leander then assisted her to her feet. "I shall escort you to our tent so you can gather your armor before you return."

Azelly sighed as a heavy weight seemed to be lifted from her shoulders, and she stepped in time with Leander, their fingers interlocked, back to their temporary lodge. Once she donned her armor, she gave her mate a passionate kiss. "I love you," she murmured with her lips against Leander's which he instantly repeated. After stepping out of his embrace, Azelly then said the phrase that teleported her to Capitalia.

* * *

"Captain Quilaro... Have five more readied!" instructed Major Teyio as he cinched the strap of his saddle around his personal zebril. "The *Apex* will accompany us," he informed the palace Stable Master.

"Aye, Major Teyio," replied Everita with a hasty salute before turning to shout orders at the soldiers under her command. "Ready Drayd and Pylo!" she called out regarding the Khan's and Khantessa's personal mounts. "You, there!" she then said sternly at a group of soldiers standing on the wayside waiting for instructions, "Ready five of the Military zebrils... nay... five of the *ephalants* for the *Apex* members," she then decided, recalling how large the family of tigals were.

"Oy!" exclaimed the soldiers in unison, dumbfounded Everita had instructed they prepare the exotic creatures. The immense greyish-purple mammals were remarkably strong, stood nearly twice as tall as the royal steeds, and were just as swift as the twin jaguars due to their long legs.

Jonetal stopped instantly, recalling how zebrils were not as hasty as the *ephalants* or any of the jaguar steeds. Zebrils were more plentiful, thus providing for the *Mounted Detachment*. Unfastening the saddle from his steed, he then turned. "Captain Quilaro," Jonetal called out suddenly.

"Aye, Major?" Everita answered in a questioning voice.

"Leave the zebrils. Ready twelve *ephalants*," he said sternly. "I am uncertain who all will join in the search," he then said, answering the unmentioned question in Everita's eyes.

"As you command, Major," Everita then replied with a salute before hollering out the new directives to her soldiers.

Azelly gradually came to a halt as she peered around the bustling city; while there were no citizens on the street, soldiers were frantically hurrying from the palace to the stables. As a soldier came running in her direction, she grabbed the front of his tabard and hoisted him into the air.

"What is the current situation?" she inquired curtly, jerking her head to the side to indicate the mayhem that currently existed.

"Gen... Gen... General Arteno," replied the soldier apprehensively before answering, "The Khanzito is missing. The Khan and Khantessa depart shortly for the *Forbidden Wilds*," he informed Azelly hurriedly.

Azelly's curious expression instantly converted to a dark scowl. "The *Forbidden Wilds*?" she repeated incredulously.

"Aye, General," replied the soldier as he clutched at Azelly's hand holding him a foot off the ground.

"Carry on," she suddenly replied as she dropped the soldier back to his feet. Without waiting for an answer, she spun on her heels and marched straight to the stables.

"Major Teyio!" roared Azelly as her eyes landed on one of the Savenius *Force* commanders.

"Aye?" replied Jonetal as he raised his head after settling his saddle on the back of an *ephalant*. "Oy! General Arteno!" he then exclaimed before jumping down from the wooden step ladder required to prepare his steed.

"Is it true?" she demanded as she strode purposefully across the busy building until she stood directly in front of Jonetal.

"Unfortunately, it is," he responded quietly with a curt nod. Silently, he watched as a series of emotions flashed over Azelly's face as she clenched and unclenched her teeth.

"I will join in the search," she then said sternly. Just as she was about to turn, she felt a hand on her forearm.

"General," said Jonetal and waited until Azelly turned to look at him. "*Ephalants* are already being prepared," he said.

Azelly dipped her head once in acknowledgement. "Are you aware of any healers that will join us?" she then asked.

Jonetal tipped his head to the side slightly in thought; eventually, he shook his head from side to side. "Aside from our Khantessa, I do not believe so," he answered truthfully.

"Very well," said Azelly with a pensive look plastered on her face. "Send for Senior Sergeant Agoreena and Senior Sergeant Samsedir. They are both assigned to *Force Tohunga*. Inform the master healers their presence is demanded by General Arteno," she said firmly, recalling two of the best healers under her mate's command that had warranted a new rank be established for.

Azelly heard Jonetal's hasty reply. She returned his hurried salute with one of her own, and then she stalked to the back of the stables where the steeds were being fitted with suitable equipment for the impending journey.

* * *

Dondree dashed out of Overlook Cave down to the waning blaze where the remaining feast items were guarded from scavenging beasts.

"Lord Dondree," said one of the *lowlings* that sat beside the table of remnants in a giddy tone. "Your appetite is far greater than when you departed," she noted with a giggle.

Dondree grinned in response as he picked up one of the small reed baskets and began piling food inside. "Not as much as you would assume," he replied casually. "The girl has finally woken."

"I understand," replied the *lowling,* her teasing voice suddenly becoming cold. "Remember to replace the covers," she then snapped before turning her back on Dondree indifferently.

Dondree did not sense the change in the *lowling's* behavior, and he simply nodded in return as he placed the covers where they had been. Satisfied with the selections, he then returned to Leandra.

217

Leandra heard the *pitter-patter* of approaching footsteps and looked at the entry expectantly; not long after, Dondree appeared carrying a reed container, and he walked directly to her.

"Here," said Dondree as he placed the basket beside Leandra then stood shifting his weight from one foot to the other nervously.

"Please, sit," said Leandra as she scooted over to one side of the bed where she had remained sitting. She smiled when Dondree finally sat next to her apprehensively. "Where are we?" asked Leandra as she plucked out a berry and eyed the boy from the corner of her eye.

"My home. It is called the Veiled Oasis," he replied anxiously.

"Is your home in Savenius?" Leandra then asked curiously, remembering she had left her own home with Wesdin. She then frowned when Dondree shook his head to say no. "Hmm," she murmured while contorting her face in mild frustration. "I suppose I should get more rest," she finally said. Taking the basket, she handed it back to Dondree, her appetite suddenly gone.

"As you desire," replied Dondree with a slight nod. "More logs are there. I shall be here," he said pointing to a small stack of wood as he sat on the ground where he had rolled out a blanket. "Do not fear to wake me should you require assistance," he said as he laid down with his back to Leandra.

Leandra sat staring at Dondree's back. After a time, she laid down and pulled the blanket up to her chin with her back pressed against the cold wall. *"Ami... Api... Wes... where are you?"* she thought to herself before squeezing her eyes closed which forced a torrent of tears from the corners of her eyes.

CHAPTER 24

The subtle vibration in the cavern unsettled Wesdin, and he abruptly turned before racing out. Uncertain of where he was going, he unknowingly became even more disoriented in the maze of tunnels. After a while, Wesdin felt his eyes becoming heavy with fatigue. Exhausted, he began searching for a place where he could rest and eventually discovered an area with torn covers and stale straw.

"This is fine," grumbled Wesdin as he heaped the shredded blankets and hay together before placing his cloak over the pile. He dropped his pack at one end before gradually lowering himself onto the makeshift bed, using his bag as a pillow. Turning on his side, he pulled the other half of his cloak around himself before falling into an agitated slumber.

"Why are the passages so great?" wondered Lana as she walked through a wide tunnel. As she continued to wander aimlessly, beads of sweat began forming along her hairline. After a while, salty streams flowed down the sides of her face. "Ugh," she grumbled aloud to herself. "It feels as if I am standing under the sun at its highest point," she groaned while wiping her face on her tunic irritably. As she rounded a corner, she saw a red glow. Cautiously, she pressed herself against the wall and crept forward. When she was close enough, she realized the increase in temperature was due to the stream of molten lava. "Oy!" she exclaimed, drawn to the destructive river. Without her realization, she left the passage and stood on a stone archway that provided access over the magma below.

Click, click, click, click.

Lana gradually became aware of a *clicking* noise on the opposite side of the bridge from where she had arrived, and she felt her body tense in response. She slowly rose to her feet, and then looked at the end of the overpass before hesitantly walking forward. "Who is there?" she demanded firmly but received no answer. Remaining where she stood, she raised her lamp and nervously glanced down the gloomy tunnel.

Abruptly, the *clicking* sound resumed, and Lana wasted no time in hurrying after it. "Wait!" she called out in the darkness. "Who are you?"

Amaruq heard the girl following behind him, and he knowingly navigated through the maze of passageways. Eventually, he led her to the corridor of abandoned *fire hound* nurseries where her companion was already sleeping.

Lana panted as she chased after the strange sound. Not paying attention, her foot became entangled, and she fell to the ground. "Oof!" she cried out in surprise. As she turned on her side, her gaze was drawn into a nearby cavity where a dim light was pulsing. Quietly standing, she then crept forward. "Oy!" she gasped quietly when her eyes landed on Wesdin, his locks illuminating the area around him faintly. "Hmm," she pondered to herself as she surveyed the area before deciding the lay down beside him. As she faded from consciousness, she unknowingly snuggled closer to the protective figure beside her.

* * *

"Khan. Khantessa," greeted Captain Quilaro as Avenor and Galhix arrived at the corral beside the stables where the *ephalants,* along with Drayd and Pylo, stood waiting patiently.

"Captain Quilaro," replied Avenor with a curt nod of his head. "The others?" he then asked as he surveyed the area.

"There," she replied simply as she jerked her chin upward and pursed her mouth, pointing with her lips.

Avenor turned in the direction Everita had indicated, and he instantly recognized the giants as they strode toward him menacingly. "The lot of you," he said with a shake of his head and a faint grin. "You appear of average height from a distance..." he purposefully paused before saying, "but tower over even the tallest of *ShadowRunners.*"

Novex led the *Apex* members and knocked his right forearm against Avenor's when he was within reach. "Not by much," replied Novex casually before appearing to look over Avenor's head. "Perhaps by a foot or so," he then added with a chuckle.

"Hah!" snorted Avenor as he placed a hand on Novex's chest and gave him a shove, completely aware that Novex had been standing on his toes. Turning to face the others, he then asked, "You all are certain?" Avenor dipped his head slightly after hearing their unanimous agreement. "Very well. Select a mount," he then said and pointed toward the corral.

"Oy!" exclaimed Novex in awe as he approached the enclosure and stared with his mouth agape. "What are those beasts called?" he asked aloud to no one in particular.

"They are called *ephalants,* Ambassador," answered Everita with a grin as she looked at Novex's dumbstruck face.

"They come from where?" inquired Novex as he walked through the gate that Everita held open for him and the other members of the *Apex.*

"An islet just South of the Eastern most fishing village of Itagrio. If my memory serves me well," Everita paused as she tapped her chin lightly in thought, "it is the village of Sedwin. It is believed that the desert island formed after the *Great Rift,* forced up from beneath the waters as VerTexItas was divided," she cheerfully expounded on the topic. "They are docile and incredibly obedient."

"Astonishing!" Novex gushed as he peered up at the creature. "Never have I seen such a robust beast that towered over any Weretigal!" he admitted with admiration.

"Your Grace," came a familiar voice which caught Avenor's attention at once.

Azelly pulled Avenor into a crushing hug, only releasing him after he grunted. "I am joining as well," she informed him, her tone welcoming no disagreements.

"It is a pleasure to see you as well," he grumbled before softening his response with a grin.

"Your Grace," Azelly then said as she greeted Galhix. "I intend no disrespect; however, I have requested two additional healers accompany us."

"Your actions are appreciated," Galhix replied sincerely as she stood beside Avenor.

Avenor quickly looked toward the animal pen and took note of those who were present and those who had yet to arrive. At that moment, two healers emerged from the stables and ambled toward the corral. He shifted his attention to Azelly with an arched brow before glancing away after she had nodded in confirmation that they were the two joining the expedition. "It is time," he said quietly to Galhix as he guided her to Pylo who stood beside Drayd. Effortlessly, the two mounted their steeds; Avenor then guided Drayd to the front of the group to explain the plan.

Everita stood at the gate of the enclosure, and she waited patiently until Avenor had completed his briefing. As Avenor guided Drayd forward, Everita then unbolted the lock and pulled the gate open to allow the patrol to exit. "May the speed of light be with you," she called out as the steeds were ushered into a gallop.

* * *

In the dark of night, Avenor and Galhix cautiously guided the expedition along the main trail used by the Grand Military scouts. Grateful that the specialized soldiers had cleared the route over the cycles, it allowed the group to travel swifter to the *Forbidden Pass* – the pathway that allowed access between Savenius and the *Forbidden Wilds.*

"Puq…" cursed Avenor aloud as he pulled on Drayd's reins. Standing at the summit of the steep mountain path, he frowned as he peered down the opposite side. "Major Teyio!" he abruptly called out as he turned to look for the man.

"Your Grace?" answered Jonetal as he guided his steed alongside of Avenor's jaguar.

"The most recent map… is it in your possession?" questioned Avenor curtly.

"Aye," replied Jonetal as he reached into a compartment on his saddle and withdrew a piece of rolled leather. He then passed it over to Avenor.

"My thanks," replied Avenor as he accepted the map and unfurled it. After orienting the map to his current position, Avenor examined the possible routes. *"Puq!"* he cursed again before motioning Azelly to come forward. "There appears to be five ways to reach our destination. I propose we take this one," he informed her as he leaned over and pointed to one of the passages. "What say you?" he then asked, turning to face her.

"It is a sensible choice," Azelly finally replied and nodded her head. "From the looks of it, we will exit the path here," she said as she pointed at an arrival place in the *Forbidden Wilds.* "It is centrally located. It would allow us to expand and scout this area while maintaining sight on one another," she finished explaining.

"Agreed," replied Avenor. He then shifted his attention to Galhix, "Agreed?" he asked her.

"Aye," replied Galhix with a nod.

Avenor then shifted in his saddle and faced Jonetal. "Agreed?" he asked as he rolled the map back up and extended it to the Major.

"Aye," replied Jonetal as he took ahold of the map, and he placed it back in the same compartment he had removed it from.

"Excellent," Avenor replied brusquely. "Move out," he then announced as he gently nudged Drayd in the side. He immediately leaned back in his saddle as the beast moved forward. "Oy!" cried out Avenor in surprise as he felt his steed slip. "Halt! Dismount!" he abruptly roared, and the progression of the entire group instantly stopped and hastily alighted to the ground. Wordlessly, he unfastened a rope that had been affixed to the side of his saddle, and without hesitation, he tied one end to the pommel of his riding seat before tossing it to Galhix. "Fasten it to your steed. Then pass it along to the next with the same message," he instructed her.

Silently, the expedition secured their mounts together. Aylox, securing the rear of the formation, finished tying the rope as instructed. He then raised a hand and hollered, "Ready!"

"Remove pickaxes," bellowed Avenor as he removed the one attached to his saddle. "The trail is steep. Move sideways. Use your axes to maintain your footing. Call out in warning if you must," he instructed loudly. With a heavy sigh, Avenor turned back to look at the steep path. *"Steady, boy,"* he said in Drayd's mind. *"Unhurried is flawless. Flawless is swift,"* he added, reminding the enormous jaguar that in such a perilous situation, advancing slowly resulted in fewer injuries or errors, thus allowing the expedition to continue without the need to stop and heal.

* * *

"Mmmm," groaned Wesdin as he flopped onto his back and extended his arms above his head, languorously stretching with his eyes still closed. "Gah!" he abruptly exclaimed when something sharp pricked at his hands. Bolting upright, he turned only to realize it was pieces of hay that had poked through the torn blanket; immediately, he sighed with relief and began rubbing the crusty buildup from his eyes. Preoccupied with self-grooming, he gradually became aware of someone snoring behind him; he instantly froze in fear. He then hesitantly rotated at his hips, and he looked over his shoulder before exhaling forcefully. A glower distorted his face as his gaze landed on Lana sleeping peacefully. "Where did you come from?" he hissed at the sleeping girl.

"What?" squealed Lana as she shot straight up to a sitting position and grabbed ahold of Wesdin, startled awake by his harsh question. "What happened?" she asked, her voice trembling with panic as her eyes tried to focus in the dark.

"Ugh," Wesdin groaned to himself in annoyance. "Release me," he said while shaking his arm and prying himself away from Lana with a grimace of disdain.

Lana instantly reached out for Wesdin again and clutched at the back of his tunic. "Where… where… is your torch?" she stuttered. "Please… please light… light it," she begged as she scooted even closer to him. "I cannot even see the tip of my own nose," she whispered bleakly.

Wesdin rolled his eyes and scoffed lightly. As he was about to ignore her request, a thought suddenly occurred to him. *"Oy! If I do not, she'll be a continuous leech!"* After spending time contemplating his options,

Wesdin finally grumbled under his breath, "Give me a moment to find it."

"Very well," sighed Lana, but she still did not relinquish her unyielding hold on Wesdin.

"Hmm, I suppose I would be scared if I could not see," he silently thought to himself as he was about to irritably bark at Lana. With a huff of resignation, he reached back and picked up his travel bag. A gasp escaped his lips as he lifted the flap and was greeted by the *Drachen Tome;* he removed items from his pack until it was empty, and he placed the tome on the bottom before replacing his belongings. *"Oy... I am grateful she cannot see in the dark! I did not think I would see her again!"* he mutely admitted as he recalled how he had taken time to read through the tome as he wandered on his own.

"Have you found it?" asked Lana anxiously, keenly aware that Wesdin still had not provided the requested light.

"The torch, aye. I am searching for my kindling and striker," he readily replied. Pretending to fumble through his belongings, he then said with forced enthusiasm, "I've found them!" Not caring to utter another word, he then struck the stones together. "Bah!" he grunted when the spark did not take. Repositioning the rocks in his hand, he then forcefully clashed them together and grinned when a flame sprung to life.

"Phew!" exhaled Lana and finally relaxed her grip on Wesdin's tunic. "It is much appreciated," she then said to Wesdin with a light pat to his back. "It is unnerving here," she finally whispered.

Wesdin canted his head to the side and arched a brow. "How do you mean?"

"I... we... umm... I think there is..." she stammered nervously, trying to find a way to tell Wesdin what was on her mind without appearing daft.

"Aye, I believe we are not alone as well," he agreed with her as he stood. He emitted a short laugh at the astonished look on Lana's face, and he held out his hand to her. "Come," he said as he pulled her to her feet.

"I heard some sort of sharp *tapping* sound. I followed it," she admitted to Wesdin as they stood shoulder-to-shoulder peeking out from the safety of the grotto they had slept in.

"As did I," he informed Lana as he stepped out into the deserted passageway. "Well... let us hope they are friendly," he added with a shrug of his shoulders.

"What?" asked Lana. Frozen in place, she stared at Wesdin as if he had two heads; her face was a mask of disbelief. "You desire to seek the stranger out?" she questioned in appall.

"Would you rather he or she come search for us?" he countered over his shoulder.

"Bah!" huffed Lana in exasperation before rushing after Wesdin.

The pair walked in peace down various tunnels, and they pointed out strange markings and engravings as they saw them.

"I have seen this before," Wesdin whispered in awe. Reaching out, he placed his hand against an image that had been etched into the wall. Lana stood beside him, and they inspected what appeared to be a drop of water divided in four sections.

"Are those the elements?" Lana inquired quietly. With her head tipped to the side, she studied the signs that reminded her of a mound of boulders, gusts of wind, a fire, and waves.

"It appears so," replied Wesdin slowly, recalling the precise images he had seen in the massive cavern prior.

"Where have you seen this before?" questioned Lana as she remembered Wesdin's comment.

"Hmm?" hummed Wesdin before replying. "Oy, uh-hmm… on a pendant belonging to my Ami. She said it belonged to my Grandapi. It is the only thing she possess from her Api or Ami."

Lana instantly stiffened at the mention of Wesdin's mother, and her eyes darkened as she recollected every word told to her regarding her father's siblings. "I see," she said tersely before spinning away from the image and crossed her arms over her chest. "Shall we continue?" she then ground out between clenched teeth.

"Aye," responded Wesdin slowly, taken aback by Lana's abrupt shift in her mood. *"Oy! I have nearly forgotten… her Ami was just slain,"* he reminded himself. Sighing, he assured himself the mention of his own mother brought back memories of her mother's recent passing, and that was the reason she had become disgruntled.

Becoming lost in their own thoughts, they continued calmly ambling with no set destination in mind. Suddenly, the unnerving *clicking* sound resumed ahead of them. Simultaneously, the two turned, and their gazes locked. Without a word, they hurried after the repetitive noise. Without realizing it, the tunnel ended, and they found themselves standing in what appeared to be an arena.

* * *

Snap!

Leandra opened her eyes at the unexpected noise, and she remained motionless until her vision adjusted to the dim light. After quickly surveying the small space, she realized the sound came from Dondree as he forcefully shook the dirt off his blanket.

Sensing someone was watching him, Dondree spun around to find Leandra scowling at him. "Uh... apologies," he said nervously and quickly finished the task at hand. "It is near time for morning feast," he said as he rubbed his neck uneasily. "There is a chamber pot there. Self-care items there. Clean attire there," he informed her without making eye contact. "I shall wait at the entrance to escort you out," he finished before leaving.

Sitting up gradually, Leandra contemplated if she should tidy herself up before following after Dondree. "Hmph!" exclaimed Leandra as her stomach suddenly grumbled, deciding for her. "I dare not starve," she finally decided. After glancing at the empty doorway, she scrambled off the bed; she hastily disrobed before donning the softened leather outfit. Immediately, she rinsed her face. As the water dripped from her chin, she felt an uncomfortable pressure in her bladder. Anxiously, she hurried to the chamber pot and sighed with relief as she voided. Once done, she rinsed her hands before picking up the fragrant twig set out for her; she chewed one end before using it to scrub her teeth. "Ah," she said as she savored the refreshing minty flavor.

Dondree stood in the shadows just inside Overlook Cave, avoiding the sweltering heat from the sun, as he waited for Leandra to appear.

"Uh-hum," coughed Leandra softly, clearing her throat to garner Dondree's attention.

Dondree spun around and instantly smiled when he saw Leandra walking toward him. "I am glad to see you," he said once she stood beside him. "Come," he then said and led the way toward the feasting area.

"It is a pleasure to see you up and about," said Reeyah as she caught sight of Dondree and Leandra. "My son says you are called Leandra."

"Aye," replied Leandra meekly as she tried to hide behind Dondree, feeling her face flush in response to the countless stares while equally trying not to gawk at their deformities and abnormal protrusions.

After raising her arm and dipping her head once to signal the start of morning feast, Reeyah then turned her attention back to the beautiful little girl sitting beside her son. "Tell me... where are you from?" Reeyah suddenly asked.

"Uh..." she began nervously before Dondree leaned over to whisper in her ear. "Apologies, Overlord Reeyah... my home is Capitalia," she answered before glancing at a girl, dragging a lame leg, setting down a platter in front of her.

"Capitalia… is that part of the Feral Unknown?" asked Reeyah with an arched brow and probed further when Leandra shook her head. "What of Feralia?"

"I have never heard of such places," responded Leandra with her brows knitted together.

"Is that so?" retorted Reeyah skeptically. "No matter…" she said and purposefully paused before adding coldly, "it is unlikely you will ever return to this Capitalia place you speak of."

Leandra tried to keep her emotions at bay in response to Reeyah's heartless comment, but her expression betrayed her concern. After a few deep breaths, Leandra decided to remain silent and refuse to acknowledge such harsh words.

"As such," continued Reeyah callously, "since Lord Dondree has taken a fancy to you, you will be promised to him."

"Say again?" gasped Leandra, certain she was hearing things. With her mind racing, she studied Reeyah's smirking face. She then turned to look at Dondree who sat beaming at her expectantly. Leandra abruptly shifted her gaze to Reeyah and watched the woman snickering. Just as Reeyah opened her mouth, Leandra interrupted with, "I am already promised."

Reeyah stared at the girl for a moment, her face void of emotion, before suddenly erupting into a fit of laughter. "Oy, child," she said before chortling again. "It is unlikely anyone will discover your whereabouts. Nevertheless… if within a fortnight your betrothed arrives… you shall be free to depart with him," she finished with an amused look.

"But mother!" cried out Dondree, ready to dispute her words.

Reeyah raised a hand, silencing her son's objection. "Otherwise… you **will** be promised that day and fully mated when you come of age," she then sneered to Dondree's delight. When Leandra sat in stunned silence and refused to answer, Reeyah chortled mercilessly before leaning back to enjoy the nourishments set before her.

CHAPTER 25

The caravan of slow-moving individuals with their steeds had just finished navigating the steep trail and reached a level area when the sun had emerged over the horizon.

"Oy," grumbled Galhix as she used a hand to fan herself. "The heat... it is unbearable," she said as she removed her cloak and unfastened the ties of her tunic at her neck.

"Indeed," agreed Avenor as he peered up in the direction of the rising sun. "General Arteno," he then called out as he shifted his attention to Azelly.

"Your Grace?" replied Azelly in a questioning voice as she strode toward Avenor.

"Details regarding the terrain," he responded curtly as he surveyed the foreign territory.

"Beasts are strange here. Do not trust what you see. This green area is relatively flat. There are hills but few in numbers. This place is surrounded by desert wastelands. There is a swamp section in that direction. A cluster of sparkling pools eventually spill out to form the stream with fresh water," she finished without providing specific details regarding the known dangers.

"The wastelands," began Avenor as he cast a sideways glance at Azelly and noticed her jaw muscles jump.

"Major Teyio," Azelly finally called out, knowing it was better for him to inform Avenor on his scout's missions.

"Aye, General?" he replied as he hurried toward her.

"The Khan desires to know what is past the edge of the wilds," she said uneasily.

Jonetal glanced from Azelly to Avenor and back again before swallowing hard. "Your Grace," he said slowly before continuing, "my scouts have been unsuccessful in exploring the desert. The heat is deadly. They have not discovered a water source. Scouts that have been unfortunate to remain out there during waking hours have perished," he informed Avenor quietly.

"How is it that you are certain they perish?" questioned Avenor with a brow raised.

"I received multiple reports when we first began exploration missions. My scouts failed to return. It was then that I decided to have future troops deploy with a tether before daybreak. The soldiers remaining at the edge of the desert became concerned when they noted the leads no longer moved **prior** to morning meal. As they hauled the line back... they learned they were dragging their deceased comrades," answered Jonetal with a scowl on his face.

"Oy!" exclaimed Galhix as she overheard Jonetal's report.

"Understood," replied Avenor as he wiped sweat from his brow. "If that is the case... we make camp and rest now. We will revise the plan at dusk. Inform the others," he instructed Jonetal. Grunts and mutters of understanding were made as word spread from one to another regarding their current situation; needing no further guidance, the lot began setting up their tents in the shade of the trees.

* * *

Enormous sections of the ceiling above the Ring of Blood had been carved out ages ago, creating a handful of roosts for the immortal *Drachen* that brought peace and prosperity to the land. Having already made himself comfortable as he waited for the children to arrive, Ignahzel lounged toward the rear of his perch where he remained hidden from view.

Boom!

Ignahzel smirked to himself as he heard the heavy doors of the arena close. Lifting his head, he peered over the edge and saw the two youths hesitantly walking to the center of the enclosure.

"Hello?" said Lana nervously as she clung to Wesdin's arm, her head swinging from side to side as she tried to peer into the darkness beyond the circle of light provided by the torch Wesdin carried. "We mean no harm," she said again, her voice cracking at the end.

"*So... it is true,*" he thought to himself as he felt a long-forgotten thrumming of energy gradually awaken within his being in the presence of the *Queen's* bloodline.

"Is anyone there?" asked Wesdin as he peered into the darkness before turning in a circle. As he turned, he noticed the high walls with strange seating arrangements beyond. Tilting his head back, he gazed up at the ceiling and observed the same symbols they had seen earlier. "Odd," he whispered to himself.

At that moment, Ignahzel decided to make his presence known. Without moving, he inhaled deeply before focusing on the marble pylons strategically built along the wall of the battleground. With a single, forceful exhalation, he released a flaming stream and set all fifteen pillars ablaze which brightened the entire cavern.

"Eep!" squealed Lana as she clutched Wesdin even tighter and buried her face against his arm.

"Oy!" exclaimed Wesdin with his eyes wide as he watched the river of fire encircle them. As it ceased, Wesdin turned and peered up in the direction it had come from.

"Who are you?" demanded a thunderous voice from above them, causing Lana to tremble uncontrollably.

"I am called Wesdin... Wesdin Crusendir," answered Wesdin as he squinted, continuing to find the source of the threatening voice.

"The other one?" snapped the malicious stranger when Lana did not answer.

Wesdin turned and shook his arm lightly before nudging Lana in the side with his elbow. "Answer," he seethed under his breath.

Lana fearfully raised her head, her eyes wide with terror, before answering. "Lana... I am... I am called Woblana Pey... Peygulroq," she managed to say as her voice quivered and cracked.

Ignahzel glowered at the two children skeptically as neither family name was the name he desired to hear. "There is no other surname?" he then demanded.

"Nay," replied Wesdin in a certain tone before gazing at Lana from the corner of his eye. He felt her stiffen at his side and heard her forcefully swallowing.

"Well?" roared the stranger, causing the entire cavern to shake in turn.

"*Blutdrache!*" screamed Lana in response as she buried her head in Wesdin's arm again. "I have been told my name is Woblana *Blutdrache!*" she cried out as terror possessed her.

"*Blutdrache,*" repeated the harsh voice. "We never anticipated the return of the *Blutdrache* lineage," he continued in a softer tone. A peculiar noise from above them attracted their gaze, and the two children gasped in surprise as they watched a massive, red serpent like creature emerging from one of the roosts.

"Wesdin," whispered Lana as her legs wobbled before completely giving way under her, and she fell unconscious to the ground.

"Wesdin Crusendir..." said the colossal beast as he climbed out of his perch before extending his wings. Gracefully, he took flight and circled the arena before landing with a *thud* directly before Wesdin and the comatose Lana. "I am called *Lord Ignahzel Feuerdrache.*"

Wesdin's eyes remained wide with disbelief as he eyed the incredible creature towering over him. He opened his mouth to greet the dragon, but he abruptly snapped his mouth closed as Lana stirred beside him. He then knelt beside Lana and helped her back to her feet once she woke completely.

"I am called *Lord Ignahzel Feuerdrache,*" repeated Ignahzel as he watched the two, one stoic while the other cowered.

"It... it... is a... a... pleasure to... to meet... you... *Lord Ignahzel Feuerdrache,*" stammered Lana as she used Wesdin to steady herself.

Wesdin remained unmoving as he studied *Ignahzel.* Instead of a simple greeting, he felt an unknown sensation from the deepest part of his being compelling him to formally acknowledge the beast.

Ignahzel's gaze briefly shifted to the amber-eyed girl before settling back on the black-eyed child curiously. *"His body betrays him, and yet..."* the dragon silently observed, hearing Wesdin's frantically beating heart and the sporadic nervous hitch in his breath. *"He has not shown the terror he feels."*

Allowing instinct to guide him, Wesdin knelt on his right knee; he then brought his hands up to the center of his chest. He kept his left elbow down, his left hand opened and his fingers together while pointing upward. He proceeded to fist his right hand, and he placed it against the palm of his opposite, opened hand, while simultaneously keeping his right arm parallel with the ground.

Ignahzel felt the corners of his mouth twitch ever so slightly as he studied Wesdin. When he saw the boy bowing his head, Ignahzel immediately followed suite and assumed the same position as the youth.

"Nahm-Aztey, Lord Ignahzel Feuerdrache," greeted Wesdin in his mother's native tongue.

"Ahz-sulam oo-laikim, Wesdin Crusendir," boomed Ignahzel in return as an overwhelming sense of calm flooded through his entire being before saying, "rise."

"What is he doing?" Lana muttered to herself as she gawped at Wesdin.

Wesdin frowned and shook his head briefly before standing. *"Oy... why did I do such a thing?"* he silently pondered to himself.

"One claims to be *Drachen.* Yet... the other speaks *Drachen,*" *Ignahzel* spoke with a bemused tone. "Remain still," he instructed firmly. Without another word, he extended both of his massive hand-like claws to each child. With a single razor-sharp nail, he pierced through the flesh of their foreheads.

"Ah!" shrieked Lana while Wesdin simultaneously hissed, "sssssss!" in response to the short-lived pinprick pain that erupted throughout their minds.

Ignahzel wordlessly rifled through the children's memories, those they were aware of and those forced back to their subconscious minds. A progressive feeling of derision began entering his heart as images of deceit and treachery were exposed. Once he finished scouring their memories, *Ignahzel* retracted his claws and blew a warm breath over them, healing the wounds. Like a statue, he remained glaring down at the youths, feeling his crystal-like golden-orbs begin to smolder with uninhibited fury.

* * *

"Discard perishables you do not plan to consume immediately," said Jonetal as the envoy began packing up their belongings. "It is only added weight and spoils quickly. Take the dried meats and unleavened bread instead."

"Feed them to the *ephalants,*" instructed Azelly as she removed two apples and held them up to her steed as she munched on one of her own.

"Aye," agreed Valcaly as she removed a pouch of nutrient packed berries and consumed a handful before offering the remaining ones to her eager beast.

Once the group had finished sorting through their belongings and packing what was required, they cautiously navigated their way to the cool stream to replenish their flagons and water their mounts.

"Hail!" a feminine voice suddenly rung out from the opposite side of the river.

"Who goes there?" demanded Novex as he abruptly sprung forward without hesitation and landed waist deep in the refreshing water.

"Oy!" exclaimed the stranger as she emerged from a nearby bush. Her attire closely matched the surroundings thus cloaking her presence from the expedition until she emerged. "Greetings," she then said with a slight dip of her head.

"Who are you, and how have you come to be here?" demanded Novex as he glared at the woman.

"We mean no harm. We are simple nomads," answered a deeper voice just before another figure appeared beside the first. "I am called Segos. This here," he paused as he placed a hand on the woman's shoulders, "is Lynn. She is my wife."

Novex stared at the two nomads intently before finally relaxing and making his way back to the others. Before emerging from the cool water, he dipped below the surface. "Ah," he sighed before hoisting himself out. "You should give it a try," he said to his brothers with a grin.

"Nomads?" repeated Avenor once he stood after filling his flagon. "What brings you here?" he questioned after he secured the sloshing containers to his saddle and turned to face the two newcomers.

"Same as you," replied Segos as he knelt beside the stream and began filling multiple containers with the life sustaining liquid. Lynn set a lid over the containers and tied a rope over them to keep the contents from spilling out.

"Why have my soldiers never seen you?" asked Jonetal as he watched the pair work silently.

"Soldiers?" returned Lynn with a questioning look. "We return only when our water has been depleted. Otherwise… we are out there," she finished while pointing in the direction of the desert.

"How do you manage to survive?" asked Galhix curiously, recalling Jonetal's words regarding the searing heat.

"We have been here many cycles. We have established resting places," answered Lynn hesitantly as she knelt beside the stream. She then removed the hood from her head before splashing water on herself and cleansing the grime from her face.

Avenor's eyes instantly narrowed on the maroon-colored strands of the stranger. He noted that she wore her hair short and disheveled on top while the sides and back of her head were shaved except for the slight stubble where it was growing back.

Segos was aware of the blue-skinned man's attention on his wife, and he protectively stood behind her with his arms crossed. "You shamelessly eye my wife," he then accused.

Avenor felt a scowl form on his face at the accusation before lifting his gaze to meet the steely glare of Segos. "Indeed," admitted Avenor unabashedly as he crossed his arms over his own chest. Remaining still for a moment, he then continued just as Segos was about to respond. "How could I not when it has been many cycles since I have gazed upon the beauty of…" Avenor purposefully stopped mid-sentence and turned to peer back down at Lynn as she twisted her hands together anxiously.

"Do not even dare…" fumed Segos, suddenly fearful the group of strangers were not friendly.

"High Cleric Wynox," finished Avenor quietly.

Segos felt his jaw drop as he fell to his knees beside his wife. Absentmindedly, he reached for her hand and clutched it tightly in his own.

"It has been too many cycles, High Knight Wynox," Avenor then said as he turned to stare at the baffled face of Segos.

"Who are you?" Segos then asked, his voice trembling with uncertainty.

"This is Khan Avenor Crusendir," answered Azelly suddenly as she placed a protective hand on Avenor's back and eyed the two vaguely familiar faces.

"Avenor?" gasped Lynn as he eyes widened in disbelief while pressing her hands to her quivering lips.

"What is this?" asked Mikela telepathically to the other tigals as she stood at a distance and watched the scene unfolding.

"Uh... so..." fumbled Novex as he thought about a way to tactfully inform his family and the Khantessa about the strangers. *"The Khan had been promised before. But his betrothed vanished. These are her parents,"* he said in a rush.

"Promised before?" said Galhix incredulously. *"He has never said such a thing,"* she said with a frown on her face.

"Aye... but I cannot say more, Your Grace," Novex added uneasily. *"It would be best for you to discuss this with His Grace."*

"Hmph!" grunted Galhix as she glared at Avenor's back and furiously crossed her arms over her chest. She remained mute and decided it was a conversation better left for a different time.

"Please," said Avenor after the surprise had dissipated, "join us." The group exchanged pleasantries, information, and learned of the dangers they would encounter. Josegos and Bebelyn provided relevant knowledge before Josegos removed a folded, piece of leather from a compartment in his tunic.

"We found this just the other day," confided Josegos as he held out the item for Avenor to take. "We were returning here when we spotted a scuffle."

"What sort of scuffle?" asked Aylex curiously as he inspected the unkempt couple.

"A scuffle between *fire hounds* and *desert scorpions*. It was strange because we thought we saw people," recalled Bebelyn. "We saw a single wolf escape that way with something dangling from its mouth while the *scorpions* headed that way," she said with a faraway look in her eyes as she pointed in the two directions.

"Odd," grunted Jonetal as he glanced at Valcaly with a brow raised. He then shrugged his broad shoulders and shook his head from side to side, indicating he knew nothing of the beasts.

Avenor carefully opened the scorched leather, revealing a detailed map. "Oy!" he exclaimed as he inspected the map carefully. "Do you know these places?" he suddenly asked to which the couple shook their heads.

"We have only been as far as here," admitted Bebelyn as she removed a rolled parchment from within her own wraps and extended it out to Avenor.

Avenor waved the others over as he placed the maps on the ground for everyone to see. As the entire consortium listened to Josegos and Bebelyn, they began sharing ideas and revising their plan accordingly.

* * *

"Where do you suppose he went?" asked Lana in an anxious whisper as she continued looking around. She had been unable to relax from the moment the creature had revealed himself.

"To find something suitable for his evening meal rather than us," retorted Wesdin smartly as he rolled his eyes while reaching for his pack.

"How can you be at such ease?" she asked hotly while pacing in front of Wesdin as he casually sat leaning his back against the arena wall.

"Mmm-uhhmmm," mumbled Wesdin in response with a nonchalant rise and fall of his shoulders. "Why are you so troubled?" he inquired, recalling how a sense of tranquility had engulfed him at *Ignahzel's* touch. When Lana did not respond, he shook his head and held out a container to her. "Here," he said before taking a swallow from another vessel he held to his lips.

"Ugh," gagged Lana as she sniffed the contents. "What is this?" she asked while eying Wesdin drink from the container in his hand, shuddering with disgust after each gulp.

"Meal mush," answered Wesdin after he forced down another mouthful before placing the cork back in the opening.

"What is meal mush?" Lana asked after a while, still uncertain if she should drink the contents.

"What?" gasped Wesdin as he tilted his head to look up at her. "You've never had meal mush?" he countered skeptically. "Oy," he then said when she slowly shook her head from side to side. "Well... it provides all the necessary nutrients one needs in a single dish," he informed her. "It is not the tastiest... but it is better than starving," he admitted as he skewed his face.

Lana looked at the container suspiciously before her attention was drawn back to Wesdin.

"Give it here if you do not plan to consume it," Wesdin snapped while holding his hand up expectantly.

Lana made a face in return before hastily raising the vessel to her mouth and forcefully gulping down some mouthfuls. "Gah!" she finally groaned as she replaced the stopper and tossed the container back to Wesdin. "Not my favorite," she groused with a shudder of revulsion.

"Nor mine," admitted Wesdin with a snicker of amusement.

Just as Lana was about to retort, a deafening roar was emitted above them. She instantly dove to the ground beside Wesdin and scooted as physically close to him as possible. As the first thunderous sound began to fade, three more erupted around the two children.

Wesdin watched in awe as *Ignahzel* flew in graceful circles. The unexpected appearance of three more dragons caused Wesdin to gasp in surprise, and he sprung to his feet to watch them elegantly dance through the air with one another.

Lana remained frozen on the ground, watching through terror-stricken eyes, as a brown, blue, and silver dragon appeared to float beside the ruddy one she knew was *Ignahzel*.

The four magnificent beasts gradually landed, each settling opposite of another, along the arena wall and examined the two children keenly.

"Remarkable!" said the silver dragon breathlessly as she leaned over the barrier, her grey eyes twinkling with excitement and her tail slashing from side to side behind her.

"Aye, *Lady Azkaiel Vvindrache,*" agreed the cerulean dragon with a swipe of his tail behind him.

"Your doubt is no longer, *Lord Ahkuahel Wasardrache?*" asked *Ignahzel* as he turned to observe the blue beast that had agreed with the first.

"Hmph," snorted *Ahkuahel* in response and dipped his head once before turning to look at the russet-colored female. "What say you, *Lady Terranel Eradrache?*"

Terranel canted her head from one side before tilting it to the other as she stared deeply at the two humans through her jade-green eyes. After a while, she shook her mighty frame starting with her head and allowed the force to send a ripple through her scales all the way down to the tip of her tail. "Aye," she finally answered with a single swish of her spiked tail.

"It is settled then," boomed *Ignahzel* as he looked from Wesdin to Lana and back again. "Let the *Battle of the Blutdrache* commence."

As *Ignahzel's* words reverberated throughout the cavern, Wesdin turned and looked at Lana over his shoulder before turning to stare at the red dragon.

"*Lord Ignahzel,*" called out Wesdin as he respectfully bowed before the creature. "We do not understand," he admitted uneasily.

"Indeed," replied *Ignahzel* with a curt dip of his head.

"That one," crooned *Azkaiel* with admiration, "is honorable. While the other," she snapped abruptly, her voice becoming ominous, "is full of malevolence."

Wesdin looked between the two and a perplexed expression distorted his face.

"*Tchah!*" gasped *Azkaiel* as she tried to calm her heart as it hammered against her chest. "He is not aware?" she suddenly asked, her fierce gaze locking with *Ignahzel's.*

"I am not aware of what?" interrupted Wesdin just as *Ignahzel* was about to respond.

Ignahzel turned his yellow-golden eyes, shimmering once more with fury, to Wesdin and he responded truthfully. "She has threatened your mother's life by forcefully removing 'the source' from her soul." *Ignahzel* observed the various emotions contort Wesdin's youthful face; he watched as Wesdin's expression became a mask of disbelief before he twirled around and hissed at the stunned girl.

"Is what he says true?" demanded Wesdin as he took a threatening step toward Lana.

"What if it is?" sneered Lana callously as she closed her eyes. She then began changing into the peculiar form she was still not accustomed to.

* * *

"Remember, follow the ground that is both cooled magma and hard-baked earth. Use the stone archway to cross over the lake of lava. Hug the base of the mountain, and you will eventually discover a monstrous staircase. What lies beyond... we know naught," reiterated Bebelyn as she pointed to each place on the sketch drawn into the sand.

"Understood," said Galhix quietly as she studied the map intently before turning to look at Azelly. "Are you ready General Arteno?"

Azelly shifted uneasily in Drayd's saddle as the jaguar threw his head back; the large cat released a vigorous yawn and finished off with a loud roar before shaking his head. "Throw me kitty, and it will be the last thing you ever do," warned Azelly as she tightened her grip in the feline's fur sensing the animal was taunting her. "Aye, Your Grace," she then answered Galhix.

237

"Play nice, Drayd," warned Galhix with a chuckle as the beast flicked his tail from side to side before twitching one of his ears. "She will skin you… and I will allow it!" she then added with a smirk as the animal flattened his ears against his head. A chorus of chuckles sounded nearby at Galhix's threat.

"You will not survive the trek across the desert," Avenor reminded his mount as he pressed his forehead against the jaguar's and felt the creature's reluctance. "She is my sister. I will personally make you an ornamental floor piece if you purposefully throw her," he then scolded. "That is what I thought," he finished sternly once Drayd accepted the situation.

"Feisty that one is," Mikela said to Avenor with a chuckle as he mounted the *ephalant* that Azelly had been riding.

"Aye," Avenor responded once he settled himself on the extremely tall creature. "Like Novex if I remember correctly," he then added as Novex guided his steed between Avenor and his mother.

"Ey!" protested Novex upon hearing Avenor's statement.

"Dare tell me I have misspoken," taunted Avenor with a smirk plastered on his face as he waited for Novex to respond.

Novex pursed his lips and scrunched his nose in annoyance before nudging his steed in the side, prodding her to move forward. His silence triggered Mikela and Avenor to erupt into laughter.

Avenor then guided his steed over to where Pylo stood patiently with Galhix astride his back. "Be it you or be it me… we will find Wesdin," he assured Galhix seriously.

"Swear no longer than a *sennight*," demanded Galhix in return as she clutched Pylo's reins and willed the unshed tears out of her eyes.

"I vow to return in no longer than a *sennight*," Avenor assured Galhix as he placed his right forearm against his chest in salute. "I look forward to when we meet again… My Khantessa."

Galhix felt her breath catch when she heard Avenor use his endearing name for her, but he had already turned and nudged his mount forward before she could respond. *"You promised no more than seven days and seven nights!"* she silently yelled as she took one more glance at Avenor's back. She then tugged on Pylo's reins lightly. *"Let's go, boy,"* she spoke telepathically to him. Suddenly, she cried out, "Chah!"

"Chah!" bellowed Azelly in turn as she pressed her knees into Drayd's side and leaned down over his neck as he sprang forward.

Aylox filed last behind the others as he was accustomed to; without instruction, he swiveled his head from side to side and kept a vigilant watch for possible threats.

Aylex glanced at his father's imposing frame and allowed his gaze to slide to a familiar, smaller rider; he then gradually pulled his gaze away and returned his attention back to the group that was preparing to depart.

"Don't look so sad," teased Daylin telepathically for everyone to hear. *"That toothpick wielding lady will return ta fare-you-well,"* he finished with a snicker of amusement.

"Ey... how about you shut it?" retorted Aylex as he shot his brother a murderous glare, to which those aware of the conversation then burst into uncontrollable chortles.

"Senior Sergeant Agoreena," began Avenor with a grin as the master Priestess neared him, "pay them no mind."

"As you command, Your Grace," replied Eventi as a smile played at the corner of her lips.

"Ready when you are, Your Grace," called out Josegos from the *sand rider* which he and Bebelyn were standing on.

"Lead the way!" replied Avenor as he made a signal with his hand, motioning Josegos to begin the journey. Every person watched with fascination as Bebelyn and Josegos began simultaneously cranking a device in the center of their flat-bottomed, barge-like *sand rider*. Gradually, the satin sail began billowing as the pair began to increase their momentum before it completely opened with a *snap!*

"Oy," gaped Avenor as he watched the bizarre ship lurch forward before abruptly grumbling, "bah!" as he realized he and the others had not followed suite. "Chah!" he then roared and charged after the swift moving vessel with the remaining troops following close behind.

CHAPTER 26

The sun had set, and soft voices wafted on the occasional breeze after evening feast had been shared. Dondree sat outside of his mother's tent with a pensive look on his face as he waited for her to finish discussing hunting matters with Demic and Dimor.

"Good eve, Lord Dondree," greeted Dimor as he stepped out from behind the leather flap and dipped his head respectfully to the youth.

"Good eve, Dimor," replied Dondree as he stood and nodded his head in return just as Demic appeared. "Good eve, Demic," he then greeted.

"Lord Dondree," said Demic as he tipped his head. "Overlord Reeyah is aware of your presence. You may enter," he finished saying as he held the entry barrier to the side for Dondree to pass.

"Overlord Reeyah," Dondree said quietly once he entered. As he waited, he watched his mother burning inscriptions into a piece of large rawhide.

"Lord Dondree," Reeyah finally said as she set her metal scribing nail down near the small flame burning on the table beside her. "What troubles you?"

"I uh… uh…" he stammered under his mother's fierce gaze and lost track of his own thoughts when she suddenly barked at him.

"Spit it out, Boy!" growled Reeyah irritably. She then forcefully slammed her hands down on the table as Dondree stuttered. Reeyah's eyes narrowed as she watched Dondree open and close his mouth repeatedly, but no words emerged.

"Leandra is already promised," he finally managed to squeak out under his mother's terrifying glare. "How can you force her to be promised to me?" he inquired tentatively with his eyes downcast. The tense silence that followed was suddenly disrupted by Reeyah's manic cackling, and Dondree snapped his head up to stare at his mother in bafflement.

"Oy, Dondree..." sneered Reeyah as she openly glowered at her own child. "Do you truly believe her beloved will come for her?"

Dondree frowned at his mother's remark before answering softly. "He would not survive the trek through the desert."

"Precisely!" she then yapped harshly.

"But... I could travel with her... escort her back to her home," he offered innocently.

"Hah!" she then scoffed. "How do you suppose her family will react when they see someone as hideous and deformed as you returning with their child? They will automatically suspect you were the one to take her. They will attack first and not care to ask questions until it is too late," she spat vehemently. When Dondree remained mute, she added, "that is how I can force her to be promised to you. Or would you rather another warrior stake claim to her instead?" she continued mercilessly as she crossed her arms over her chest. "I thought not. Now go assist Demic and Dimor with the new scorpions," she concluded and dismissed him coldly.

"Aye, Overlord," he responded dully, lost in his own thoughts. *Why has she become so heartless? How can she say such things? I was certain she would be glad to be able to return to her home.* With no answers to his questions, Dondree went to seek out Leandra before obeying his mother.

* * *

The four *Archaic* winged-beasts watched in fascination as Wesdin's silver highlights began pulsing with energy while untamed rage coursed through him; dark power surged within him, and the lavender flecks in his eyes began to glow faintly as he locked his deadly sight on Lana.

"Rrgh!" grunted Lana as she felt her body beginning to change. The *ripping* sound of cloth caught the attention of all four creature, and they shifted their gaze to Lana. "Agah!" she shrieked as her bones shattered before reforming themselves and mending back together. "Ugh!" she muttered as she fell to her hand and knees as wings, darker than night, sprouted from between her shoulder blades. As her spiked tail emerged from the last section of her spine, she felt her entire being growing and becoming stronger while her teeth elongated into fangs.

"Ah... so the prophecy has come to light," muttered *Lady Azkaiel,* recalling her vision eons ago as provided by her power of Foresight. "She has indeed entirely transformed even though she is not mated," she noted solemnly of the young dragon as it could only mean one thing. "The child possesses "the source" of both *Primus Devotion* and *Primus Valor.*"

241

"And the outcome? Or is it still vague?" inquired *Lady Terranel* telepathically. Thoughtlessly, she used her power of Brawn and unintentionally crushed the wall where her claws had settled. *"Apologies,"* she immediately said sheepishly before shifting her position and watching the broken pieces float like powder to the arena ground.

"As clear as swamp water," answered *Lady Azkaiel,* obviously disheartened.

"Phew," sighed Lana as she staggered from exhaustion. After a moment, a frown creased her brow as she progressively became aware that her physical form had altered even further than before.

Wesdin pulled his shoulders back, and he glared into Lana's blood-red eyes without an inkling of fear in his stance.

Lana chuckled maliciously as she took unsteady steps toward Wesdin before falling to her forearms, still unaccustomed to her cumbersome frame. "Come, Wesdin. I shall kill you like your mother slaughtered my father!" she roared.

The glimmering glow surrounding Wesdin suddenly burst into a blinding light, causing every dragon to avert their eyes, and time seemed to stand still as ethereal whispers caressed Wesdin's mind. *"Lineage of Elemperia Blutdrache. Untainted. Nobel Drachen. Pure. Innocent. Worthy. Venerable Rex der Drachen. Hark unto us, precious one. Beseech your Bloodline."* As Wesdin listened in a trance-like state, he felt a weightlessness engulf him.

"Honoritus Ancestriantus… ezcuhear meeyan petishiano…" Wesdin instinctively began imploring, guided by the archaic memories buried deep in his subconscious. As he cried out the last words, begging for assistance to restore balance and prosperity, he felt debilitating agony seize him, and his eyes fluttered closed just before he faded into oblivion.

* * *

Azelly prodded Drayd, and he lunged forward to take lead of the formation as they dashed across the solid ground. "There!" she bellowed and pointed at the looming stone bridge.

"Chah!" screamed out Galhix as anxiety gripped her fueled by the uncertainty of her son's safety. Pylo instantly obeyed and surged ahead along with his brother.

"Ugh… I feel like I am going to be…" groaned Aylox under his breath as he leaned over the side of his steed's neck. "Blaagh!" grunted Aylox as he unceremoniously retched from the unpleasant sensation of riding an *ephalant.*

The harsh huffing and puffing of the steeds echoed across the barren land as they charged over the rock archway; while simultaneously, deep in the wastelands, the band of *ephalants* pounded the sand under their hooves as they careened over the shifting particles effortlessly.

"Avoid the mounds!" yelled out Josegos as he veered the *sand rider* away and formed a large arc around the *fire hound* den.

"And the *boulder fiends!*" shouted Bebelyn as she pointed to various clay figures.

"What of them?" bellowed Avenor in return as he glanced in the distance at the motionless statues.

"If close enough, they waken!" she hollered back as she and Josegos skillfully navigated through the desolate terrain.

Avenor expertly guided the herd of *ephalants* as gradually brought them to a halt as the ship slowed to a standstill in front of a small den.

"This one is abandoned," Josegos answered the silent question in Avenor's eyes. "We rest here. The sun will rise soon. We do not want to find ourselves out there without shelter," he then added as he jumped off the boat.

"Very well," replied Avenor with an understanding nod. "Dismount," he then commanded the troops. Immediately, the men and women descended from the backs of their steeds. Cautiously, they then filed into the den while leading their assigned beasts by the bridle of their head harnesses.

"Clear!" called out Novex as he eyed the passage that appeared to continue deeper than where he had decided to stop.

"Make camp," instructed Avenor as he gently encouraged his *ephalant* to lower itself to the ground.

"Brother," said Novex quietly through their mind link as he peered toward the entrance where Avenor stood.

"Aye?" responded Avenor as he glanced up and caught sight of Novex's apprehensive expression.

"There appears to be a passage. I do not believe the den ends," he silently voiced his concerns.

"Fear naught," replied Avenor with a nod. *"There are no signs of recent habitation. Remain vigilant but do not overly concern yourself,"* he assured his *hamigo* before they finished settling down to recover from their ruthless trudge through the dunes.

"Your Grace," shouted Azelly as she reached over and grabbed ahold of Galhix's reins. "Whoa!" she then called out. "Whoa!" she repeated and slowly brought the two felines to a halt as they reached the gigantic steps leading into the smoldering mountain.

"How dare you!" shrieked Galhix as she turned a deadly glower to Azelly.

"Khantessa," groaned out Aylox as he guided his steed abreast to the two jaguars. "We must recover before blindly charging in," he then grumbled.

"You would betray me?" seethed Galhix as she turned her furious glare to Aylox as he dismounted and began striding toward her.

"Khantessa, you know what you speak is not true," retorted Azelly as she swung her legs over and slid down from Drayd's back. "But we must rest. We know naught what we will encounter," she reminded the reckless woman.

An unexpected sob escaped from Galhix's quivering lips as her strength abandoned her; weakly, she fell from Pylo's saddle, but before she hit the ground, Azelly's strong arms wrapped around her waist. "We **will** find him," Azelly said sternly as she pulled the distraught mother closer. With Galhix cradled against her chest, Azelly refused to accept the idea that any harm had befallen her nephew. "Make camp there," instructed Azelly as she pointed to a covered fissure between the crag base and a massive heap of boulders.

From his lookout post, Amaruq watched the foreigners approach *Burg der Drachen*. Remaining hidden from view, he crept along the concealed path until he was crouched above the strangers. As he sniffed the air, a familiar scent assaulted his senses. At once, his ears flattened against his head; without a second thought, he turned and dashed toward the Ring of Blood.

* * *

Dimness flooded Wesdin's mind as his physical form dissipated into infinite miniscule particles. In the farthest reaches of his memories, where shadows and vast darkness reigned, he watched as brightly illuminated flecks were strewn about like dazzling jewels on a black canvas.

His spirit soared through the *Celestial Realm,* and he watched with wonder as *Divine* revealed all to him. He observed how the world was formed with just a breath from *Divine*. Atop the highest peak, in an aerie woven from threads of gold, adorned with the rarest of gems and ore, *Divine* settled a clutch of five – four in a circle with the last egg in the center. The immortals would eventually serve and protect all of humanity.

As each whelp hatched, Wesdin instantly recognized the *Archaic* beasts. Wesdin sensed *Divine* was pleased that he recognized his children, and formally introduced them as they emerged.

Lord Ignahzel Feuerdrache, First Born, Ruler of Fire and Hellhounds, Harbinger of Inferno. Guardian of his Brethren.

Lady Azkaiel Vvindrache, Second Born, Ruler of Air and Wyverns, Beholder of Foresight.

244

Lord Ahkuahel Wasardrache, Third Born, Ruler of Water and Sirens, Bestower of Life.

Lady Terranel Eradrache, Fourth Born, Ruler of Earth and Golems, Provider of Brawn.

Regina Elemperia Blutdrache, Queen of Dragons, Last Born, Ruler of All, Power of All. Guardian of her Brethren.

Wesdin felt himself admiring the newborn dragons, and he watched in amazement as they summoned their respective creatures to serve as their defenders. All except *Regina Elemperia.* She summoned a *hamrammr drake* – a four-legged wingless dragon with the ability to shapeshift into whatever creature *Elemperia* commanded.

To guide, teach, and protect his children, *Divine* gave rise to humans. *Regina Elemperia* eventually became enamored with a human, and she forsake her immortality to share her blood. Upon the exchange, *Elemperia* gained the ability to transform to a human while her mate gained the ability to transform into a dragon, thus becoming the first *King of Dragons – Rex der Drachen.* However, humans were foolish and unwise; even after *Divine* provided them with all they could desire, the evil in their hearts festered with greed and arrogance.

They sought to destroy *Drachenia,* the land of Dragons. To protect his children, *Divine* allowed the humans to become enslaved. As time passed, *Prince Klause Blutdrache,* the holder of "the source" for *Primus Valor - Power of Courage in the face of Adversaries,* became smitten with a slave, and he took her as his mate. This was forbidden, and so he removed "the source" of *Primus Devotion – Power of Love -* from his sister so that the *Drachen Reign* would end. From there, Wesdin watched the history he knew unfold from the *Great Falling* to the *Great Rift* until the present.

Divine allowed Wesdin to see the truth behind creation; he showed the innocent and kind child the truth of Dragons and humanity. As a sense of tranquility washed over Wesdin, he heard *Divine* whisper, *"Wake pure one with a tender heart. Restore Drachenia. Bring balance and peace once more."*

As soon as *Divine* finished speaking, Wesdin felt as if he was pulled into a whirlwind. He felt his shapeless form beginning to swirl faster and faster! His vision became blurred! Until abruptly… it all came to a halt!

Wesdin blinked once. Twice. A third time. Gradually, the dimness cleared from his vision, and he saw the astounded faces of the *Archaic* immortals and the defiant one of Lana.

"Hah!" taunted Lana as she glared at Wesdin. "This changes nothing!" she then shrieked furiously. Her angry scream soon became a *deafening* roar just as she charged Wesdin.

* * *

Raaaaaaaaawwwwwwwrrrrrrrrrrr! The thunderous roar echoed throughout *Burg der Drachen* with such a force that it reverberated through every passageway until it finally escaped through the stairway where the small patrol had prepared their camp.

"Ah!" screamed Galhix in surprise while leaping off the ground.

Aylox tensed as his gaze locked with Azelly's as she scowled with uncertainty.

"What the *puq* was **that**?" asked the accompanying healer Senior Sergeant, Soother Baeson Samsedir. Though he tried to remain calm, his voice quivered and cracked with fear.

"We will learn soon enough," replied Galhix with her eyes wide in terror. With trembling hands, she began donning her armor and weapon. "Suit up," she commanded in a strained voice.

"You are serious?" squawked Baeson as he stared at Galhix incredulously. "Whatever **that** was... sounds as if it could **devour us!**" he yelled, stressing certain words as he spoke.

"Sit your arse down and keep an eye on the mounts if you are too frightened," snapped Azelly unkindly, her eyes narrowed and throwing daggers at the healer.

"But... it's... I... that... how... what if..." stammered Baeson, opening and closing his mouth like a fish before snapping his mouth closed with a look of determination flashing in his eyes.

"Then do as our Khantessa commands... and **suit up!**" growled out Azelly as she cinched down the clasp of her gauntlets.

In silence, the group anxiously prepared for the upcoming battle. Azelly knelt and waved Jonetal over as the others stood around them in a circle listening intently to the plan of attack.

"Vice Commandant, will you take point?" asked Azelly as she glanced up at the towering man.

"In tigal form, aye," he replied without hesitation, as he was the only melee warrior who had the ability to see in the dark.

"Excellent," she then replied. "Major Teyio will follow, then Khantessa Galhix with primary heals to you both. I will follow Khantessa and lead Overseer Truceran and Maestro Samsedir. Senior Sergeant, primary heals for Overseer Truceran and me," she informed everyone hastily. "Questions?"

"Nay," rang out a chorus of voices in unison.

Poof! Poof! Both Aylox and Galhix transformed to Weretigals.

"Very well. Fall in!" she then ordered. Wordlessly, the patrol formed a single-file in accordance with Azelly's plan. Aylox waited for Azelly's hand signal, and he immediately began cautiously advancing upon receiving it.

CHAPTER 27

In unison, the four magnificent beasts tossed their heads back, and they released a continuous breath of fire while simultaneously roaring as Lana charged toward Wesdin. The display was short-lived, a herald at the initiation of the *Battle of the Blutdrache*.

Wesdin unsteadily side-stepped Lana's attack, and he spun around in time to watch her momentum carry her forward before she careened into the arena wall.

"Ey!" hollered *Lord Ahkuahel* as he leaned back slightly in amusement. "What?" he asked with a frivolous shake of his head as *Lady Terranel* gave him a displeased look. "We have never seen fledglings battle. It is quite amusing," he admitted with a snicker.

"Indeed," agreed *Lady Azkaiel* with a short giggle before reverting her gaze to the arena once more, a slight smirk still on her face.

Just then, *Amaruq* appeared beside his master. *"Lord Ignahzel,"* he spoke only to the red dragon. *"More humans have arrived,"* he informed him curtly.

"Guide them here," Ignahzel replied without turning away from the battle below. *"They come for the children,"* he said knowingly.

"As you command, My Lord," Amaruq responded with a bow of his head. Upon rising, he turned and hurried back in the direction from which he came, setting ablaze the torches as he went.

"Ugh," grunted Lana as she swayed from side to side upon regaining her footing. Turning, she glowered at Wesdin. *"How did he do it?"* she silently pondered as she eyed his marvelous form. Across from her stood a brilliant white dragon. His eyes were blacker than night except for the colored ring. It was a vibrant lilac color and a stark contrast to the darkness that surrounded it. Each spine of his wings was the same purple hue with a spike at both ends. The barbs along his tail continued up his back all the way to the base of his neck. Her form was bulkier and cumbersome, and it made it difficult to maneuver. She noted how Wesdin's form was trim and muscular which allowed his to move swiftly and elegantly. Lana glared at Wesdin, and she became enraged when she noted she stood the same height as the younger dragon. She snorted furiously, and a puff of smoke emerged from her nostrils.

"The fight is now fair," said Wesdin quietly. Confidently, he stamped one of his front claws on the ground; then he proudly pushed out his chest where his snow-white scales shimmered in a rainbow of pastel colors. "Unlike what you did to my Ami!" he then spat with hostility.

"He is absolutely impeccable!" exclaimed *Lady Azkaiel* as her smokey orbs twinkled cheerfully.

The youths emitted a roar at one another while simultaneously rearing up on their hind legs. After landing with a heavy *thud*, the two wasted no time in racing toward one another.

* * *

Aylox led the patrol, hugging the wall as he went, while keeping a vigilant lookout for possible enemies; just as he rounded the corner, he abruptly stopped upon seeing a flickering glow ahead.

"Damn, Aylox!" hissed Jonetal, having collided into the massive feline's rear end. "Can you not warn a man," he continued with a scowl as he swatted Aylox's tail.

Aylox turned to glare over his shoulder and purposefully flicked his tail in Jonetal's face before facing forward again.

Just then, an unsettling *clang* sound rang out followed by other nerve-wracking noises.

"*Puq!*" grunted Azelly as atrocious growls, snarls, and roars boomed through the gigantic passages

Aylox instantly froze with his tail in Jonetal's face; Jonetal remained motionless, appearing to have forgotten the black satin appendage was dangling in front of his parted mouth.

"Advance," shouted Azelly in a forced whisper as she clenched and unclenched her fists, feeling perspiration forming within her armor-clad hands.

Jonetal was startled out of his shocked state at Azelly's command, and he instantly swatted at Aylox's tail. "*Puq,* man!" he ground out between clenched teeth. "Keep your tail to yourself!" He then glowered over his shoulder when he heard muffled chuckles and snickers.

Aylox felt his muscles bulge as he visibly tensed, and he purposefully flipped his tail in Jonetal's face once more; after taking a deep breath to calm his rattled nerves, he finally began to edge forward once more.

"Go along with them," instructed Galhix telepathically to Aylox as she noticed the first torch followed by many others in a single passage, completely illuminating the wide interior.

"Aye, Your Grace," Aylox replied. Needing no further instruction, he cautiously navigated through the corridor using the flames as a guide.

Click, click, click, click.

The entire patrol instantly halted upon hearing the unanticipated *clicking* coming from somewhere in front of them.

"Show yourself!" demanded Jonetal as he peered around Aylox. As they waited for a response, a wolf-like creature appeared in the center of the passage. "Oy!" gasped Jonetal as he eyed the beast that was nearly twice the size of Aylox.

Azelly instantly waved the other two behind her forward, and the three of them posted themselves on the opposite side of the hall from their comrades in a defensive position.

Amaruq remained motionless for a brief time; once he knew they had seen him, he then turned his head and slightly lifted his snout before slowly walking in the direction he had faced.

"Your Grace," said Azelly quietly as she looked across at Galhix. "It appears the beast desires we follow it." Azelly waited until she saw Galhix cast her a sideways glance. She then heard the Khantessa's quiet chuff while nodding her head.

Aylox stood sideways watching Azelly and listening to her speak with Galhix; after confirming what action to take, Azelly then nodded to Aylox and motioned to him to go after the *fire hound.*

* * *

Lana and Wesdin crashed violently into one another. Upon impact, they began clawing and snapping at each other.

Wesdin managed to settle on Lana's back, and he clamped down at the base of one of her wings.

"Argh!" shrieked Lana as Wesdin's fangs pierced through the thin hide of her wings and tore through it. Abruptly, she fiercely kicked her hind legs up and outward, bucking Wesdin off.

"Ugh!" grunted Wesdin as he landed in a heap to the side of his opponent in a surprised daze with his sensitive underbelly exposed.

Lana spun around; when she saw Wesdin still on the ground, she seized the opportunity and lunged toward him. Extending her wings, she lopsidedly closed the distance before forcefully landing on Wesdin. Without hesitation, she sunk her two-inch razor-blade like claws into his belly and began slashing at him ruthlessly.

"Argh!" roared Wesdin as Lana tore open his flesh. Forcing the pain from his mind, he then rolled completely to his back. He placed his hands and feet against Lana, and using all his might, he thrust upward and to the side to dislodge her. "Ugh," he grunted as he rolled to his side. Becoming weaker by the moment as blood gushed from under him, he made his way to Lana.

Lana struggled to regain her footing as she slipped and slid from the blood coating her claws. Watching Wesdin approach, she hastily tried to turn but only managed to slip once more. The momentum of her spin caused her to land on her back. "Gah!" she cried out as she thrashed her arms and legs wildly in the air.

Wesdin hobbled around Lana, keeping away from her claws, and he approached her from the side. Just as Lana flung her head from one side to the other, Wesdin lunged forward and clamped his fangs deeply into her neck. With his jaws firmly locked, he began aggressively swinging his head from side to side. A flood of warm fluid filled his mouth, and he grunted in satisfaction as he tasted Lana's blood.

Amaruq entered the arena stadium at that moment with the humans not far behind. He headed toward *Ignahzel* without pause, and he sat beside the red dragon.

"Oy!" exclaimed Jonetal as he walked into the massive cavern beside Aylox who had his mouth hanging open in disbelief.

"Come, humans," said *Ignahzel* as he briefly looked at their flabbergasted expressions. "I assure you... an attack will be to no avail," he informed them.

Poof! Poof!

Aylox and Galhix simultaneously reverted to their human forms. Mutely, the entire patrol then moved forward, their gazes locked on the red beast. As they stood at *Ignahzel's side,* the sudden screech from below startled them, and they all jumped in response.

"Oy," breathed out Azelly as she gaped at the two magnificent beasts wrestling about in a field of blood.

As Lana struggled, she curled herself upward and successfully hooked the claws of one of her hindlegs under Wesdin's chin.

Wesdin growled menacingly as Lana's claws pierced into his neck. Clamping his teeth down tighter, he then placed one of his front claws on Lana's head to hold her in place. As Lana kicked her foot, she ripped through his neck and face. Snarling his displeasure, he prepared to yank his head back and rip Lana's throat out.

At that moment, his attention was drawn by a glinting in the stand above him. Without opening his mouth, he shifted his eyes upward and recognized Azelly's iridescent armor. His forehead crinkled as he scowled, and he allowed his gaze to travel from end to the other of the group of individuals.

251

Galhix stood unmoving as she watched the bloody match; without knowing why, her heart hammered against her chest uncontrollably as she watched blood oozing from the white dragon.

Wesdin abruptly released his hold on Lana who remained motionless on the ground, and he took a stunned step back. With his eyes locked with Galhix's, he felt a single word escape him.

"Ami," breathed out Wesdin before he fell to the ground.

"Wesdin?" whispered Galhix in confusion as she stared disbelievingly at the unmoving beast.

"Aye, it is your child," announced *Ignahzel* as he peered down at the trembling woman.

"Wesdin!" she then shrieked in terror. With a *poof*, she assumed her feline form and buried her nails into the stone wall of the arena. She then proceeded to swiftly crawl down to a reasonable height before she jumped to the ground. She then dashed across the bloody ground to Wesdin. She pressed her head against his, trying to nudge him awake. She then raised one of her paws and pushed against his chest softly, but he still did not respond. At that moment, Galhix watched as he took one last ragged breath. *"Wesdin!"* she screamed silently as she watched her baby die before her eyes.

"No," breathed out Azelly in a whisper as she watched the scene unfold. "No, no, no," she continued to repeat.

As the deafening silence filled cavern, Galhix swiftly stood looking down at Wesdin with her own head over his. As she inhaled deeply, a faint white glow emanated around her before gradually brightening. Exhaling slowly, she concentrated on the light, and it became a concentrated orb of blinding luminescence as it hovered above Wesdin. Abruptly, the floating sphere burst into countless flecks before settling on Wesdin's still frame. As each speck landed, it gradually penetrated through his flesh.

Azelly held her breath as she watched intently; it was cycles ago when Galhix had performed the same miracle on her. As she anxiously waited, her eyes widened in astonishment as she witnessed every one of Wesdin's wounds mended and flesh regenerated. She finally sighed with relief as she observed Wesdin's side rise and fall with each breath.

"Ugh," groaned Wesdin as he slowly blinked his eyes. *"Surely it was a dream,"* he thought to himself as he thought about his mother. Just then, a rough tongue swiped over his face and he abruptly turned. "Ami!" he shouted in excitement, however, as a dragon, it escaped as a roar.

Poof!

"Wesdin! Oy, my boy!" cried out Galhix as she hugged the gigantic beast and allowed hysterical sobs to wrack her frame.

A soft and pleasant melodious metallic *tinkling* sound filled the cavern as reflective specks appeared where the white dragon had been, and in its place stood Wesdin in his human form.

"Ami," he whispered softly as he hugged his mother tightly while silent tears poured down his face.

"Ey!" cheered *Lord Ahkuahel.* "He lives!" he said with a grin.

"Aye, and **not** because of you," snapped *Lady Azkaiel* as she glowered at her brother.

"Had Khantessa Galhix not arrived, I would have revived him," he huffed in return and shrugged a shoulder nonchalantly.

"What… who…" stuttered Galhix as she finally managed to control her heart wrenching sobs as she pointed and glared at the lifeless black dragon.

"Oy," said Wesdin quietly with a sorrowful expression on his face. *"She was not so bad. She was deceived by those who only sought power,"* he mused to himself. He remained still as he struggled to make sense of his own internal debate. Finally, he turned to gaze up at his mother. "Ami…" he began nervously before turning to look back at the felled creature. "It is Lana. I beg… please revive her," he then pleaded.

"You are serious?" questioned Galhix with her mouth agape. "After all she has done?" she continued as a glower appeared on her face.

"Aye," replied Wesdin with a slow nod as he turned to face his mother again. "She deserves to be forgiven. She was deceived by those closest to her," he answered truthfully. "Deep in her heart, I know she is good."

Galhix gasped in surprise at her son's wise words; she then smiled as she extended her hands and caressed his cheek lovingly. "As you desire, my beloved," she finally answered before becoming a tigal once more. She then completed the ritual once more and sighed in relief when she heard the black beast emit a low grumbled.

"Oy," groaned Lana as she opened her eyes to see a white tigal towering over her. "Ah!" squealed Lana in surprise as she rolled to her side. Her gaze was immediately drawn to Wesdin. "You…" she said with a shake of her head. "We… how… I passed…" she muttered as her mind raced, recalling the darkness that had surrounded her as she entered the *Celestial Realm.*

"Aye," Wesdin replied quietly with a nod of his head. "My Ami revived you," he informed her.

"Why?" Lana blurted out as she turned her tear-filled eyes to Galhix after she had reverted once more to her human self.

"It was his request," replied Galhix as she placed a hand on Wesdin's shoulder.

"Why?" repeated Lana hoarsely, unable to comprehend the reason he would save her.

"I have seen your heart and soul," he said seriously. "You were misguided. I feel it is right to forgive you and grant you another chance to prove what I believe. That you truly are good," he said while closing the distance until he stood directly in front of Lana.

Lana shook her head vehemently. "Nay. I have..." she began to protest.

"Silence!" Wesdin said firmly. "It is forgiven," he repeated as he placed a hand over Lana's heart. "Make amends through future actions," he told her softly to which she could only nod in response.

"All hail Wesdin Crusendir, *Rex der Drachen!*" roared the four dragons in unison before unleashing a volley of fire blasts upward as they acknowledged Wesdin as their king.

CHAPTER 28

Novex dashed through the desert in tigal form alongside Avenor in his shadow form; the journey was longer than anticipated for Novex because of the loose particles easily giving way under his weight. However, the pair traveled faster than the entire patrol and had decided to scout ahead before the others.

"Well?" asked Josegos immediately upon Avenor and Novex's return.

"There is no other option than to arrive openly," answered Avenor with a huff as he took ragged breaths. "One path. Surrounded by mountains. Perfectly fortified," he continued between gasps as he pulled deep breaths into his hungry lungs.

"I see," replied Josegos as he dipped his head in acknowledgement. "How far do you suppose?" he then asked.

"Not far at the speed we have traveled," said Novex as he placed a hand on Avenor's back. "We suggest waiting to depart until half the night has passed. That way when we arrive, the sun will be close to emerging but still us time should we need to make a hasty retreat."

"Aye," agreed Avenor after his breathing had become even. "We do not desire to arrive in the dead of night to surprise those there. If it is not necessary, I wish to avoid any skirmishes," he finished.

"Agreed," voiced Mikela and Bebelyn in unison as they listened to the proposed plan.

"Very well," said Avenor with a sigh. "Refresh yourselves and your steeds. While we do not desire a fight, we must still be prepared."

Time seemed to pass in a blur when Avenor finally looked up at the night sky. "Finish packing up," he announced. "We move out soon."

"Aye, Your Grace," replied Mikela as she ushered the others to do as commanded. Silently, the patrol members filed out of the den that had offered reprieve from the scorching rays during the day and mounted their steeds.

"Move out," called out Avenor after he ensured everyone was mounted and waiting for his signal.

In the dead of night, the pounding of *ephalant* hooves and the *whooshing* sound of the *sand rider* as it sliced through the sand disturbed the silence as Avenor and Novex warily guided the expedition toward the hidden encampment.

"Whoa!" said Avenor quietly as they approached the trail. He raised a hand to halt the others while gently pulling on the reins of his steed. Without speaking, he made a signal and was instantly obeyed.

"We desire to join you," whispered Bebelyn as she approached Avenor. "We have traveled this desert for many cycles... but we have never been this far," she admitted sourly.

"Very well," replied Avenor with a curt nod, understanding her desire to enter the foreign camp.

"My thanks," she then gushed before turning to hurry back to Josegos.

"Secure your steeds to the *sand rider*," offered Josegos in a hushed tone as the group contemplated where to tie their mounts.

Avenor nodded his head in agreement, and all the *ephalants* were tethered to the barge. Avenor then motioned for the individuals to circle him. "We advance quietly. Remain calm and make no sudden movements." After instructions were given, Avenor looked from one to the next and assessed their expressions. "Questions?" he asked and released his anxious breath when every person shook their head from side to sided. "Very well. Move out," he then said briskly. The patrol automatically assembled in the position assigned by Avenor, and they wordlessly followed behind the Khan.

Dondree sat with his feet dangling over the ledge just past the entrance of Overlook Cave lost in his own thoughts. *"I cannot obey... I cannot see her become like mother. She will not even speak to me,"* he thought of Leandra and felt a tightness in his chest. *"If I leave now... mother will know. I must prepare... We will not make it far. They will come for us on the scorpions. One of the new scorpions! I can tame one!"* he contemplated excitedly as he developed a plan to escape with Leandra.

"Puq!" cursed Eventi under her breath as she accidently kicked a rock as the patrol hesitantly trekked down the stairs. As the stone rolled, it suddenly fell over the edge and tumbled down the stairs. With each *knock* and *bang* it made, she contorted her face and flinched as the sounds resonated like thunder.

"What was that?" Dondree mused to himself. He then turned in the direction of the path and was thankful for the illumination provided by the moon. Gradually, he watched as several figures appeared, and he immediately felt the hairs at the nape of his neck stand on end. Just as he opened his mouth to alert the compound, he frowned and thought of Leandra once more. *"Can it be? They are here for her?"* he considered hopefully. Having decided, he jumped to his feet and crept toward the trail and headed toward the strangers.

Avenor watched as a youth emerged at a distance in front of him; slowing his pace, he watched as the boy appeared to be sneaking along as he sidestepped piles of gravel and rubble. Avenor did the same and guided the others around the loose mounds that would betray their presence.

"Greetings," said Dondree in a hushed voice once he was within hearing range of the newcomers.

"Greetings," returned Avenor in similar fashion. "I am called Avenor Crusendir," he informed the youth.

"I welcome you, Avenor Crusendir," replied Dondree with a slight bow. "I am called Lord Dondree."

Avenor raised a brow skeptically as he eyed the child but did not question him. "We have come in search of a boy," he then said.

Dondree made a face as he canted his head to the side and arched a brow as he recalled the incident when he had saved Leandra. "Oy," he finally groaned as he shook his head. "There is no boy here."

Avenor scowled in return as he sensed Dondree was not being truthful. "Lord Dondree…" he said as he took a single step forward.

"But there is a girl…" Dondree said abruptly and effectively interrupted Avenor.

"A girl? What girl?" inquired Avenor. *"What girl? I am not aware of another child missing?"* he demanded in question telepathically to the family of tigals.

"We know naught, Brother," responded Novex after he exchanged befuddled glances with his mother and brothers.

"She was with a boy and another girl," continued Dondree uneasily, sensing the change in Avenor's mood.

"Three children?" seethed Avenor furiously in the telepathic link he shared with the tigals. *"How has **my** son and two more children gone missing with no one aware of it?"* he fumed. While he spoke, he visibly stiffened as he tried to maintain his composure.

"The boy and girl… they were taken by a *fire hound,*" admitted Dondree as he watched the emotions on Avenor's face change from disbelief and ultimately despair.

"And the girl here?" Avenor ground out between his clenched teeth.

"She currently sleeps. I can guide you to her," replied Dondree as he turned. "Come," he said before abruptly stopping. "You must be silent. Overlord Reeyah has not been well lately," he said of his mother.

"Very well," agreed Avenor as he and the others trailed behind Dondree wordlessly.

Demic sat outside of his tent sharpening his spear in preparation for the early morning hunt when a *clattering* noise drew his gaze. Curiously, he watched Dondree make his way to the single point of access for the oasis. His lips then turned down as he watched the boy leading a band toward *Overlook Cave*. Without hesitation, Demic stood and entered a nearby tent.

"She is there," said Dondree as he pointed down a passage.

Avenor looked sideways at the boy before peering down the short tunnel. He then took a breath before stepping forward.

Novex reached out and grabbed Avenor's shoulder at that moment. *"Should I accompany you?"* he inquired in Avenor's mind.

"Aye, it cannot do any harm," he replied after considering the question. The pair then noiselessly crept along until they reached a leather hide blocking an entryway. Nervously, Avenor grabbed one side and pulled it open. "Oy!" he exclaimed as his breath hitched, seeing the adorable face that he cherished as much as his own son.

Novex glanced past Avenor and inhaled sharply. "Leandra," he said in a barely audible whisper.

Avenor released the flap and crossed the distance and knelt beside the girl. Tenderly, he reached out his hand and caressed her cheek lovingly. "Lea," he said gently.

Leandra frowned in her sleep and mumbled incoherently as she pulled the blanket over her head causing Avenor to chuckle.

"Leandra... we must go home," Avenor informed her as he pulled the blanket and uncovered her face.

"Uncle..." she grumbled and tried to regain the blanket before saying, "not now." After tugging without success, Leandra flopped on her back with a huff. She opened her light-brown eyes and stared into a familiar pair of solid black ones; she blinked rapidly before bolting upright and throwing her arms around Avenor's neck. "Uncle Avenor!" she cried out as she buried her face in his neck.

"Shh, shh, shh," he hushed her softly. "You are safe. I am here now," he assured her as he embraced her protectively. "It is time to return home," he repeated as he stood with Leandra cradled against his chest. Avenor turned and smiled at Novex. "Time to go," he then said to Novex who nodded in agreement.

"I am indebted to you, Lord Dondree," said Avenor genuinely as he stood before the boy. "This child... she is my niece," he admitted with tears in his eyes as he gazed down at Leandra.

"I am glad you have found her," replied Dondree with a sad smile on his lips as he risked a glance at Leandra.

"My thanks," whispered Leandra as she peaked at Dondree briefly before burrowing her face back into the crook of Avenor's neck.

"Come. I will guide you back," said Dondree as he spun on his heels and began leading the others out. As they reached the end of the path from *Overlook Cave*, a malicious voice cut through the silence.

"What do we have here? A traitor in our mist," spat Reeyah as she eyed Dondree with contempt.

"Overlord Reeyah," said Dondree in surprise. "Her uncle has arrived!" he informed her quickly.

"Is that so?" barked Reeyah as she shifted her gaze to look at the man carrying the child. "It is unfortunate you have come this far only to leave empty handed," she then sneered.

"We do not desire to fight," Avenor replied monotonously as he eyed the woman. "We will take the child and leave," he said and took a single step forward.

"Tsk, tsk, tsk," chided Reeyah. "You cannot come here and just take what does not belong to you. Had it not been for me, that child would be dead," she fumed while pointing at Leandra.

"You have my thanks for saving her," Avenor responded. "Here," he then said and removed a sack of gems and coins and tossed them to Reeyah. "Payment for your efforts."

"Hah!" scoffed Reeyah as she dropped the sack. "Your payment is of no value here. But the child... she can be mated," she added unkindly.

"Overlord Reeyah!" cried out Dondree as he rushed to his mother's side and grabbed ahold of her arm. "I beg of you! Let Avenor take his niece home!"

"Release me!" hissed Reeyah as she forcefully withdrew her arm. As she glared at her son, his words finally registered. "Avenor?" she repeated as she turned her eyes back to the man.

"Aye," replied Avenor curtly as he eyed the insane woman.

Without warning, Reeyah was possessed by a fit of hysterical cackling and crowing. "Oy," she finally managed to say. "How I yearned for this day!" she said as all mirth vanished from her eyes. "And now it is here," she spat vehemently.

"Explain yourself," returned Avenor flatly as he glowered at the woman.

"You truly do not recognize me?" she sneered as she removed the hood from her head. "One would believe you would never forget your betrothed," she then hissed furiously.

Confusion gradually gave way and Avenor sucked in a breath sharply as recognition appeared in his eyes. "Sedria…" he finally whispered incredulously.

"Sedria is no more!" she suddenly roared. "That weak, pathetic girl is gone. She passed when you never came. I am Overlord Reeyah!"

"Sedria?" came a soft voice from behind Avenor. Bebelyn and Josegos rushed forward but were held back by Novex and Mikela. "Sedria!" Bebelyn suddenly cried out as she gazed upon her daughter after so many cycles.

"Who dares say that name?" snarled out Reeyah as she turned her hostile gaze upon Bebelyn.

"Sedria… it is us… Ami and Api," answered Bebelyn as she held her hands out to Reeyah.

"Hah!" retorted Reeyah as she rolled her eyes. "I have no Ami and Api. If I did, they would have come searching for me cycles ago."

"My beloved child! Your mother speaks the truth!" interjected Josegos as he struggled against Novex's vice-like grip. "We have searched this entire time!" he wailed.

Reeyah ignored the two claiming to be her parents, and she turned her steely gaze back to Avenor. "The child stays," growled out Reeyah once more.

Reeyah's brutal voice pierced through Avenor's dumfounded silence, and he shook his head to clear the fog. A myriad of emotions flowed through him, but her cruel words warded off any feelings of remorse.

Dondree felt helpless as he eyed his mother, and he could not believe the words she had spoken. With a heavy heart, he walked to stand beside Avenor.

"What are you doing?" demanded Reeyah furiously. "You would betray me for them?" she shrieked.

Dondree looked up at Avenor and lifted the corner of his mouth ever so slightly. Under his breath, he then said, "Challenge her for the right of Overlord."

Avenor peered down at Dondree's sorrowful eyes and nodded once. "My thanks," whispered Avenor in return. *"Take Leandra,"* he then wordlessly told Novex. He then carefully placed Leandra in Novex's arms before facing Reeyah once more. "I challenge you for the position of Overlord," he announced sternly as he eyed the woman he was once betrothed to.

* * *

Lana stood staring at the closed-door contemplating on knocking or not. Finally deciding she would not, she jumped when the door abruptly opened.

"I can sense your presence," said Wesdin with a sheepish grin as he looked at his cousin.

"Uh... I see," mumbled Lana nervously. "Would you walk with me?"

"Ami... I am going with Lana," Wesdin informed his mother before closing the door behind himself. "What is it?" he finally asked after they had walked for a while.

"I... uh... I... I am sorry," she said in a rush before looking away from Wesdin as a splash of redness stained her cheeks.

"I accept your apology," Wesdin returned as he reached out and took Lana's hand. "We are family," he added before beaming up at her happily.

Lana returned his smile with one of her own. "You will return home," she stated as she withdrew her hand.

"Aye," agreed Wesdin. "I have spoken with the others. I have requested you be Regent Regina in my place."

Lana's eyes widened and she turned to stare at Wesdin in disbelief. "What? Why?"

"You are not comfortable to be with my Ami or me. *Drachenia* must be restored. Balance and prosperity must return. It is only possible if all five *Drachen* work together to accomplish such a task," he said with a smile.

"You would trust me? After all I have done?" she countered apprehensively.

"Aye. Remember though... I am but a brief flight away," he replied while waggling his brows at her playfully. "I am certain one of the others will demand my return if needed."

"Aye," said Lana with a giggle as she interlocked her arm through one of Wesdin's. "It is good to know my cousin is my ally," she said as a tear slipped from the corner of her eye, overjoyed with the notion she had a true family.

"Indeed," agreed Wesdin. The two walked in silence as he escorted Lana back to her own chamber. "Rest well," he said before turning and making his way back to the quarters he decided to share with his mother to rest and recover before embarking on the journey home.

CHAPTER 29

Avenor stood unphased as Reeyah cursed and shouted obscenities at him while discarding unnecessary attire. With purposefully unhurried movements, he reached up and loosened the ties of his tunic at his neck; he then slowly rolled his sleeves up to his elbows. He considered removing his weapon, but at the last moment decided to keep his *battle-staff* strapped to his back. With mastered concentration, he then assumed his shadow form.

Reeyah smirked at Avenor as he stood still, and she began mumbling quietly. With a wicked grin on her warped face, a crimson silhouette steadily began forming until her entire body was radiating with the translucent illumination. Pulling her lips back, she revealed her knife-like fangs as she continued muttering unintelligibly to herself as she assumed a solid stance. A continuous *clinking* sound instantly came from Reeyah as she felt her armor-like scales emerge in a ripple from her head down to her toes.

Avenor crossed his arms over his chest in an unimpressed gesture and arched a brow inquisitively as his only outward response. "Shall we begin?" he asked casually once he sensed she was finally ready.

Reeyah stood with her feet shoulder width apart, one slightly farther back than the other; she then bent her knees and held her arms out to her sides before *hissing* furiously at Avenor's disinterested reaction.

With his black eyes fixed on her familiar face, Avenor and Reeyah began walking in circles while facing one another; they gauged each other's stances and assessed one another for any possible weakness. Avenor covertly observed as Reeyah's feet appeared to slither in the sand, and he noticed a brief pause before she moved the other. With that in mind, he decided to make the first attack.

"Afraid oh mighty Khan?" jeered Reeyah as she watched Avenor's eyes flicker from her feet back to her face. "You try to conceal..." she began but her voice soon trailed off.

Avenor commanded the shadows, and they obeyed at once. As Reeyah was distracted with taunting him, he instructed the shadows to seize her feet. Reeyah's smirk vanished from her face as she risked a look down at her feet. At that moment, Avenor skillfully reached for his *battle-staff*; in a single, fluid motion, he brought his staff forward and grasped it in both hands before forcefully jabbing the end into Reeyah's chest.

"Oof!" grunted Reeyah as she staggered backward and clutched her chest. Her eyes narrowed on Avenor as she *hissed* once more. Without hesitation, she then lunged at Avenor's shadowy form.

Avenor remained in place, only rotating his shoulders, and lightly whacked Reeyah on her back as she stumbled past him. "We can end this now," Avenor said coldly as Reeyah spun around and glowered at him.

"Hmph!" she grunted and rotated her shoulders. "We are only just beginning," she spat in return. With a hand extended out toward Avenor, she began chanting loudly. "Tuyom lifexia et soulexia sar **meyah**!" she finished in a scream. Instantly, her scarlet specter appeared; with a blood-curdling shriek, it darted directly to Avenor.

Avenor's eyes widened at the appearance of the crimson phantom. "Ugh," he groaned and dropped to one knee. He frantically reached up, and he clutched at his chest as he was overcome with a sense of impending doom.

Reeyah snorted in disgust as she watched Avenor's circle of swirling shadows become smaller as her specter began siphoning his lifeforce and redirecting it to Reeyah. "You appear frightened," she blatantly ridiculed him as she felt a newfound surge of power and energy blooming within her.

Avenor felt his strength fading and darkness threatening the edges of his vision. As he fell to both knees, Leandra's frantic screams penetrated the haze. Gripping his staff, he abandoned his shadow form to preserve his energy; he then began hastily reciting an incantation and erecting an invisible shield around himself. The phantom released an ear-piercing screech as it was abruptly interrupted and could not continue draining its prey. Avenor took ragged breaths before silently reciting various incantations. Immediately, he felt his health restored and his strength return. Using his staff for support, he managed to stand. After focusing on the ghastly specter, Avenor extended a hand.

Reeyah sprang forward, sensing Avenor was focused on her demon. She immediately began clawing and slashing at the invisible shield, knowing it could only sustain a finite amount of damage. Pausing briefly, she then hastily recited another incantation, and a glowing cylinder emerged between her hands. With a snarl, she forcefully threw her hands outward and flung a *luminosity flare* at Avenor.

The amount of damage caused by the *flare* broke through Avenor's shield, and he winced in pain as he felt the flare strike him squarely in his chest; even with the immense discomfort, he did not lose his focus. Sweat began profusely pouring down his face, evidence of his extreme exertion, and he clenched his teeth together as he finally gained control of the frenzied phantom.

Furiously, Reeyah grunted before yelling out another incantation, and a dazzling golden orb appeared in her hands. She then viciously hurled a *searing star* at Avenor.

Avenor staggered back as he felt every inch of his body consumed be an unseen inferno.

Reeyah threw her head back and unleashed a crazed chortle as she watched Avenor lose his footing. As he crashed to the ground, Reeyah appeared at his side within an instant. As she leaned down toward him, Avenor suddenly reached up and grabbed the front of her tunic. He then brought one foot up and kicked her forcefully in the stomach. Using the momentum of his own kick, he then threw Reeyah behind him and over his head.

"Ah!" screeched Reeyah as she flew from one end of the circle of onlookers to the other. "Oof!" she then grunted as she landed on the hard, sunbaked ground.

Standing and picking up his staff, he then drew a symbol in the air and muttered under his breath before pointing his staff at Reeyah, instructing the apparition to attack her.

Reeyah immediately frowned as she watched her abominable creation race toward her; suddenly, she began shrieking and thrashing about wildly as an unconceivable anguish ripped through her.

As Avenor watched in horror, he felt his own health and strength rejuvenating as the phantom drained Reeyah's life essence and transferred it to him.

Just as she thought her life would end, the specter vanished because its time was expended, and her tormented screams ceased. On her hands and knees, Reeyah whispered another chant. Her health was partially restored as she lacked the energy to completely heal herself. With a ragged breath, she began chuckling sporadically and stumbled to her feet.

"Do you yield?" thundered Avenor as he glowered at Reeyah.

"The challenge is **always** to the death," sneered Reeyah in return just before she slithered toward Avenor; when she was close enough to him, she launched herself upward.

Stunned by her movements, Avenor was caught by surprise as Reeyah came down with her fist drawn back; her blow was delivered with precision, and she landed in a kneeling position directly in front of Avenor.

"Ssss," seethed Avenor as he felt Reeyah's armored scales slice through the flesh of his face. Before she could recover, Avenor grabbed the back of her head while simultaneously jerking his leg up and smashed her face against his knee.

"Argh!" cried Reeyah as she was sent sprawling backward before abruptly standing again with a snicker. "I am invincible," she then said with a smirk. "My armor is impenetrable."

"Invincibility is but an illusion," retorted Avenor as he tossed his *battle-staff* to Mikela. He then stood at a slight angle, with a strong base and his fisted hands raised for hand-to-hand battle. Before Reeyah could plan her next attack, Avenor bolted forward and grinned to himself as he watched her charge forward as well.

Just as Reeyah thrust one foot into the ground with all her might, propelling herself upward, Avenor viciously curved his arm back and swung his fist down. Avenor delivered the blow with such a force that it halted Reeyah's forward progression and snapped her head backward.

"Ugh," moaned Reeyah as she writhed on the ground, trying to regain her bearings, before rolling onto her stomach. Shen then shoved herself up onto her knees as she prepared to stand.

At that moment, Avenor lunged at Reeyah and pinned her down from behind with his legs astride her hips.

"Ah!" shrieked Reeyah as she to push herself off the ground before screaming and yelling incomprehensibly when she felt Avenor lock his legs around her waist.

Without hesitation, Avenor then slipped one arm around Reeyah's neck while holding it in place with his other. As she flailed and kicked disgracefully, Avenor began tightening his hold until he could hear Reeyah's breathing becoming ragged and labored. He then snarled, "Do you yield?"

"Never!" Reeyah grunted, sending spittle flying out of her mouth and dribbling down her chin as she slowly suffocated. Feeling the burning in her lungs intensify, she began clawing at the arm around her neck.

Avenor shook his head ever so slightly in disappointment; he then pressed a brief kiss to Reeyah's temple before whispering against her ear so only she could hear him. "You have my sincerest apologies. I failed you as your betrothed. I only desire you will find peace." As soon as he finished speaking, Avenor readjusted his grip and violently twisted Reeyah's head.

Crack!

A silent tear escaped from the corner of Avenor's eye as he gently untangled himself from Reeyah's motionless body. He then carefully laid her on the ground and smoothed back her disheveled locks from her face.

"Oy," breathed out Novex as he approached Avenor and held out his hand. Once he hefted Avenor to his feet, he pulled him into a firm half-embrace as Leandra hugged him fiercely as well. After separating, Novex passed Avenor a flask. "Have some *restoradria*," he said with a sheepish grin as he attempted to ease the uncomfortable silence.

Avenor shook his head and erupted with laughter as he removed the stopper. "You have my thanks," he finally said and took a long drink. After wiping his mouth on the back of his hand, he gazed down at the lifeless frame of his former betrothed and felt his eyes swell with unshed tears.

"Avenor..." said Dondree quietly as he stood beside the taller man.

"Hmm?" murmured Avenor as he turned and looked down to see Dondree's despondent expression. "Oy," he whispered as he placed his hands on the boy's shoulders. After a moment of brief hesitation, Avenor pulled the youth into his embrace. "I offer my sincerest apologies about your mother," he said quietly.

Dondree shook his head against Avenor's chest and stepped out of his embrace. "You have my thanks. But... she was not my mother," he replied in a low voice as tears streamed down his face.

Josegos cradled Bebelyn as she clung to his chest while her body shook with silent sobs. A curious look appeared in his eyes as he overheard Avenor speaking with the boy, unable to recall what he had said previously. "Avenor," said Josegos as he guided Bebelyn along.

"Aye?" answered Avenor as he shifted his attention to the other man.

"Sedria... Reeyah... he... he... called her mother," Josegos stammered anxiously as he looked at the boy with maroon colored hair.

"She was my mother," interjected Dondree with his eyes downcast.

"Oy! Flesh of my flesh!" exclaimed Bebelyn abruptly before fiercely grabbing Dondree and dragging him into her embrace.

"They are the parents of your mother," Avenor said with a smile as he saw the shock and confusion on the boy's face. "Will you return with us?" he then asked Bebelyn and Josegos.

Josegos exchanged a look with his wife before turning to answer. "Your Grace... we have been nomads for far too long. We cannot fathom returning," he spoke truthfully. "We would also prefer to remain here, with Sedria's child. Our grandchild."

"Understood," replied Avenor with a curt nod. "Lord Dondree," he then said as he placed a hand on the boy's shoulder once more. "I must return to my home. I appoint you as Overseer," he then announced with a half-smile.

"You are certain?" questioned Dondree with his eyes wide.

"Aye," reaffirmed Avenor. "These two are excellent advisors. Heed their words," he added as he dipped his head at both Josegos and Bebelyn. "Should you ever require assistance… consider me your ally," he finished warmly.

"You have my thanks, Avenor," returned Dondree with a broad smile. At that moment, Bebelyn leaned over and whispered something to her grandson. Dondree's eyes instantly widened, and he placed his right forearm over his chest. "You have my thanks, Khan Avenor Crusendir. I am honored to have you as an ally."

Avenor looked at Bebelyn and noticed her fair skin becoming a shade of pink. Giving her a knowing smile, he then returned the boy's salute. "As I am honored to have you as an ally… Overlord Dondree."

Bebelyn looked toward the sky at that moment and placed a hand on Avenor's forearm. "The sun will soon rise. Remain here until nightfall," she stated in a pleading manner.

"Very well," said Avenor as he turned to Dondree. "We must fetch our mounts."

"Bring them. There is plenty of shade near the water," replied Dondree without delay. As he watched Avenor and the others make their way to the trail, Dondree noticed someone kneeling beside the frail shell of his mother. After taking a deep breath, he walked over to the lone individual. "Demic," he said and waited for the man to reply.

"Overlord Dondree," he responded with a sniffle but did not lift his gaze to meet the boy's.

"I… she… you… can…" stumbled Dondree with uncertainty as he tried to express his sorrow and gratefulness for the times Demic had supported and protected his mother.

"Say no more, Overlord," said Demic gruffly as he stood to finally face Dondree. "You were correct. She was no longer our Reeyah," he admitted as he placed a hand behind Dondree's neck. He then pressed his forehead to the youth's. "I harbor no ill feelings. You have my support, Overlord," he said before leaning back and placing a firm kiss on Dondree's temple before solemnly stalking away.

CHAPTER 30

Wesdin peacefully strolled through the illuminated passages and nodded his head to the *fire hounds,* recalling how they were truly known as *hellhounds,* as they guarded the corridors. As he passed a certain *hellhound,* the wolf snorted and blew Wesdin's hair. Wesdin instantly stopped and turned to face the arrogant beast; suddenly a grin appeared on his face.

"It is good to finally meet you, *Alpha Amaruq,*" he informed the canine as he reached up and lightly scratched the animal's chin.

"It is a pleasure to have you here, Rex Wesdin Crusendir," returned *Amaruq* telepathically, having an immediate mind link with the boy as he ruled all dragons and those they dominated over. *"We are all jubilant for the return of our beloved Blutdrache and revival of this desolate land."*

"Aye, I am certain of it," replied Wesdin with a slow nod of his head. "*Alpha Amaruq...*" began Wesdin with a brief paused before continuing, "I have a request."

Amaruq knelt before Wesdin, and he immediately tilted his head to the side which exposed his neck as a sign of submission. *"I am here to serve, Rex Wesdin."*

"I will return to my home. My cousin... Lana *Blutdrache* will rule here as Regent *Regina.* She will be the one to restore *Drachenia.* My request is that you respect her as you respect me."

"As you desire, my Rex," *Amaruq* answered without hesitation before rising once more. *"With the guidance of the Archaic Drachen, the Regent Queen will also be guided and learned well."*

"You have my thanks, *Alpha Amaruq,*" Wesdin replied with a dip of his head. "I will take my leave. I must rest before the journey back to my home," he then said as he began to turn but abruptly halted as another thought entered his mind. *"Alpha Amaruq,"* he said with a concerning tone.

"Aye, my Rex?" returned *Amaruq* with a slight crinkle between his brows as he canted his head to one side curiously.

"The day you brought me here… there was another girl," said Wesdin uneasily, reaching up and rubbing the back of his neck before asking, "do you know what has become of her?"

Amaruq instantly stiffened as he recalled abandoning the other child, uninterested in her as *Blutdrache* blood did not course through her veins. Hesitantly, he shook his head to indicate he did not. *"Nay, my Rex. I vow unto you that I will discover her whereabouts before your departure,"* he promised.

"You have my thanks, *Alpha Amaruq,*" replied Wesdin as he nodded his head before turning.

Amaruq instantly threw his head back and released a long howl that reverberated throughout every cavern and corridor of *Burg der Drachen,* summoning an elite pack of *hellhound* trackers. As they arrived, *Amaruq* instructed them on the mission of finding the missing girl their *King* was adamant about locating. With a ferocious growl, *Amaruq* dismissed the pack of wolves; they instantly turned and dashed through the various tunnels that led to the distant dens throughout the lands.

* * *

Leandra clung to Avenor's leg, and she followed him wherever he went. Avenor placed a hand on her head and lightly caressed her head.

"Fear naught, Lea," he said calmly as he peered down at the girl and smiled when she turned to look up at him. "We will return home at nightfall," he assured her.

"Aye, Uncle Avenor," she returned as she tightened her hold on his leg, causing him to chuckle.

"Come," he then said as he leaned down and picked the child up as if she weighed nothing at all. "Let us explore this *Veiled Oasis* as we wait."

"Very well," replied Leandra as she placed one arm over Avenor's shoulder with the other around the front of his neck so she could lock her fingers together on the side of his neck.

"Overlord Dondree," greeted Avenor as he walked through the center of the camp. "Is there anything of particular interest here?"

"Your Grace," replied Dondree with a salute he had been taught by Josegos and smiled when Avenor returned the salute respectfully. "Unfortunately, there is not much. The only thing would be at the far side of the pool, one can occasionally see an *armored culebra.*"

"An armored serpent?" retorted Avenor in question.

"Aye," answered Dondree with a slow nod. "Reeyah obtained one of their rare scales. She used her twisted, dark magic to create an elixir that allowed her to partially gain their skills and traits."

"How do you know this?" asked Avenor with a frown.

269

"One of our warriors, Demic… he informed me," he answered apprehensively. "She also created a similar elixir for me," he then added.

"An elixir for you to become an *armored culebra?*" questioned Avenor with his brows arched in surprise.

"Nay. A *fire hound,*" responded Dondree as he took a nervous step back, unsure how Avenor would respond.

"Fascinating!" exclaimed Avenor. "Would you demonstrate?"

"Uh," said Dondree, having not expected such a reaction from Avenor. "Aye," he finally agreed before taking a deep breath. Standing before Avenor and Leandra, Dondree heard the audible cracking of his bones as they broke. His face became distorted as it became more animalistic than human. Maroon fur, the color of his hair, sprouted over his entire body while he grew in stature. His hands and feet resembled paws while his nails elongated into dagger-like claws. Once his transformation was complete, he opened his eyes and sat back on his haunches.

"Oy!" exclaimed Avenor as he peered at the hideous beast.

Leandra suddenly grinned and wiggled against Avenor. "Uncle… set me down," she pleaded as she pat his chest repeatedly.

"Hmm?" hummed Avenor before he nodded and bent to set Leandra on the ground.

"Dondree," she said softly with a smirk.

"Aye?" said Dondree as he lifted his eyes and peered curiously at the girl.

Poof!

"Oy!" gaped Dondree as he looked at the unfamiliar creature standing where Leandra had once stood. "Wha… what is she?" he inquired with his eyes wide as he turned to peer at Avenor.

Avenor grinned as he reached down and gently caressed Leandra's head before scratching behind her ear. "She is what we call a *Weretigal.*"

"Indeed," replied Novex with an impish grin.

Poof!

"Ah!" yelped Dondree as he saw Novex's larger feline form. Timidly, he took an unconscious step back as his eyed widened even more. "There are more than just Leandra?" he questioned with his mouth hanging open.

"Heh," chuckled Avenor as he cast a sideways glance at Novex. "Aye," he nodded as he pointed to Novex's mother and brothers. "They, too, are tigals."

Dondree turned his wide-eyed gaze toward the other giants and stared at them uncomfortably before exhaling forcefully with his cheeks puffed, letting out a low whistle. "Do they speak?" he suddenly asked when he realized the two cats had not said a word.

"Not aloud as you do. There is a way to communicate silently with one another," answered Avenor.

"Hmm," mused Dondree before nodding his head. "I understand. Are you like them?" he abruptly asked Avenor.

Avenor instantly erupted with laughter at the accusing look on Dondree's face; he then shook his head from side to side with a smirk. "Nay. I only assume a shadow form."

"Only," muttered Dondree. As he rolled his eyes, Avenor roared with merriment, and he doubled over to grab his aching side; Dondree then shook his head as he recalled how Avenor had completely merged with the shadows, almost undetectable except his figure was darker than the shadows he blended with.

Avenor spoke with Leandra, and she confirmed she was comfortable being left with Dondree. He then went in search of the others with Novex at his side; he wanted to discuss the return route they would take later that evening and plan for the journey.

* * *

The day passed peacefully without any issues; Wesdin slept in his mother's protective embrace as the others rested in separate quarters. As evening neared, the group of individuals began to stir and soon emerged refreshened from their slumber. A selection of meats had been roasted for the humans by their *Drachen* allies, and they consumed the nourishments with gratitude. Wesdin sat in silence as he anxiously waited for word from *Amaruq*.

"My Rex," *Amaruq* said from behind Wesdin and startled the boy by his unexpected appearance.

Wesdin turned around in his seat; instead of speaking aloud, he decided to attempt to communicate telepathically with *Amaruq*. *"Alpha Amaruq,"* responded Wesdin and popped up and down in his seat excitedly when *Amaruq* responded.

"The pack of trackers has returned. They have located the girl," he informed Wesdin briskly.

"Is she safe? Where is she? Is she harmed?" Wesdin immediately began asking questions in a hurry without giving *Amaruq* time to answer.

"Aye, Rex Wesdin. Aye," *Amaruq* interjected sternly which halted Wesdin's rapid inquiring. *"She is with one that looks as you do. Blue-fleshed. There are others... like Sir Aylox,"* he then added calmly to which Wesdin crinkled his nose.

"Api? Onio Novex?" Wesdin silently ruminated to himself. *"Where are they?"* he then asked *Amaruq*.

271

"In the hidden haven of the Barbarians," replied *Amaruq* with a slightly wrinkle between his brows. *"The trackers could not gather more than that,"* he added with an apologetic tone. *"The Barbarians... they consume our kind."*

"Oy!" exclaimed Wesdin with a look of horror on his face. *"I am glad to know the tracker did not risk his life to inspect further,"* Wesdin finally responded.

"It does appear they will depart this eve as you, my Rex," Amaruq added slowly. *"Should they travel swiftly as your patrol... you will intersect with them at the place where I discovered you and Regent Regina Lana."*

"Oy!" gasped Wesdin in surprise at how soon he would be able to see his father and closest friend. *"You have my thanks, Alpha Amaruq,"* he then thanked the highest-ranking canine.

Once the sun dropped below the horizon, Azelly led her subordinates to prepare the small herd of *ephalants*.

"I do not plan to be riding back," said Aylox as he eyed the beast and placed a hand on his stomach as it began to turn at even the thought of riding the animal. "Nay," he said while shaking his head back and forth numerous times. "Not again."

"You are serious?" asked Azelly with a chuckle as she eyed the intimidating tigal. "A touch of stomach sickness has got you?" she taunted him in jest.

"Hmph!" snorted Aylox as he glared at Azelly and crossed his arms over his chest.

"Indeed," answered Valcaly for the silent feline as she gave him a playful jab to his shoulder. "You did not hear him retching on our trek here?" she then asked as she turned to face Azelly.

"Oy," said Azelly as she arched a brow, "is that so?" she then asked with a grin.

"Aye," returned Valcaly with a bark of laughter as redness crept up Aylox's neck, over his face and to his ears.

"Oy, leave the man be," interrupted Jonetal as he appeared at Aylox's side. "We all cannot have stomachs of steel. Although," he paused and gave Aylox a sideways look, "I have never known of a warrior to lose his meal from a little ride," he finished while impishly waggling his brows.

"Ey!" snapped Aylox as he shrugged away from Jonetal and gave him a forceful shove in his chest. A chorus of laughs and chortles rang out as the group teased Aylox before finally settling down as Galhix and Wesdin emerged.

"Vice Commandant has offered his steed to Khanzito Wesdin," said Azelly as she tried to stifle her chuckle as the others muffled their snickers.

"You have my thanks, Vice Commandant," replied Wesdin as he saluted the disgruntled tigal and began climbing up with Azelly's assistance after the man returned his salute. "Your Grace," she then spoke to Galhix, "we are prepared when you are."

Galhix nodded in acknowledgement before approaching Pylo; the jaguar lowered himself to the ground and waited for Galhix to settle herself before rising once more. She then peered over at Azelly; once Azelly sat astride Drayd, she gave the General a signal and Azelly issued the command for the group to begin the trek back toward Capitalia.

* * *

Avenor took one more look around at the smiling faces of the *Deflings* as they continued to press multiple gifts forward as a way of showing their sincere appreciation for his healing their long-standing affliction. Avenor had detected a contamination in their water source; while the former *Barbarians* had believed the *Filth* surrounded them and was in everything, the searing heat had purged it from the land, except for the underground caverns of water. Avenor had sensed it and was able to detract the remnants and purify their water.

"The offer will always remain, High Knight," said Avenor after he had assisted Leandra up onto his steed.

"You are most generous, Your Grace," replied Josegos as he grabbed Avenor's right forearm with his own before giving him a firm hug. "Perhaps one day."

"I bid you well," Avenor responded before turning away and mounting the *ephalant* behind Leandra. "Are you ready to go home?" he then asked as he leaned to the side and peered down at the girl sitting in front of him.

"Aye!" Leandra instantly squealed happily as she clutched the reins in her hands.

"Give the command," Avenor said in a whisper just loud enough for her to hear him.

"Oy!" gasped Leandra before bellowing out in her high-pitchy child voice, "move out!"

At once, the *ephalants* jolted forward and were gently prodded into a steady gallop. The patrol gradually moved into position with Avenor and Leandra safely in the center while Novex took point. With a comfortable pace set, the small troop expected to make it to the *Forbidden Wilds* well before sunrise.

* * *

"Look there!" hollered Jonetal as they approached their destination and pointed out toward his left where a trail of sand was

Kimberly Evette Ortuno

settling. Following it forward, he saw the gaggle of *ephalants* trotting along at a casual pace.

"Avenor," breathed out Galhix with a sigh as she caught sight of him.

"Your Grace," shouted Novex as he held out his arm in the direction of the two jaguars leading the remaining *ephalants*.

"Oy," he breathed out nervously. Squinting, he peered at her intently and instantly felt his heart drop when he did not see Wesdin sitting with her. "No," he whispered as he clenched his hands around the reins until his knuckles turned white. *"Tell me it is not true,"* he wordlessly thought, not bothering to examine the remaining *ephalants* and their riders.

Azelly and Galhix guided their steeds and forced them to veer to the side; Pylo and Drayd instantly released thunderous roars in unison upon spotting the others.

Novex tugged the reins of his *ephalant* and headed toward the giant white jaguars that were racing toward him. Just before the two separate formations collided, Novex and Azelly turned in time, and the two units seamlessly converged together for the remainder of the brief ride to the safety of the green territory.

* * *

"Whoa!" hollered Azelly as the entire patrol arrived at their destination, and progressively slowed their mounts to a stop. With an inquisitive look on her face, she approached Avenor; she placed a hand on his knee and gave it a brief squeeze.

"Why the drawn face, Brother?" Azelly asked as she stared up at Avenor.

"Hmm?" mumbled Avenor as he peered down at Azelly, the look in his eyes distant as he appeared to look through her. "Wesdin..." he croaked out as his eyes instantly welled with tears.

"Aye?" replied Azelly with a brow arched.

At that exact moment, Avenor heard an excited squeal that made him abruptly snap his head in the direction of the sound.

"Api!" shouted Wesdin as he rushed toward his father.

"Oy!" gasped Avenor as he swung his leg over the side of the *ephalant*. "Azelly," he then said, as he clutched a bundle in his arms. "You will be startled and pleased to have this returned to you safely," murmured as he passed the bundle down to her.

"And what is this?" she responded as she accepted the wrapped parcel. Cautiously, she pulled back a section of the blanket, and she instantly released an audible gasp as her eyes flew to Avenor's. "How?" she asked as she clutched Leandra against her chest without caring for a response. She returned her focus to her daughter and lightly shook her awake. "Lea!" she cried softly as tears streamed down her cheeks.

"Ami!" exclaimed Leandra as she awoke to find a familiar pair of eyes peering down at her. After struggling to free herself from the confines of the blanket, she then threw her arms around her mother's neck and squeezed tightly.

Just as Avenor's leapt down to the ground, Wesdin charged toward him and hopped into his waiting arms. "Api!" he shrieked out again happily as he wrapped his arms around his father's neck, and he hugged him with all his might.

"My boy," exhaled Avenor as he held Wesdin tightly while twisting from side to side at his waist. "Now tell me..." said Avenor sternly with a frown, "how is it that you and Leandra are here?"

"I... uh... well, Api..." he stammered as he shifted his eyes to the ground. "I was saddened," he finally admitted.

"By what, my beloved?" asked Galhix as she joined her son and husband, and she placed a comforting hand on Wesdin's back.

"The *paahkias* and other cubs that have *transformed*... they spoke unkind words. They... they... told me I was not worthy to be future Khan," he admitted as a single tear slipped from the corner of his eye.

"Oy," whispered Galhix, feelings of empathy suddenly flooding her, feeling sorrow for her son.

"And what of you?" demanded Azelly as she leaned back and glared at Leandra.

Leandra's eyes instantly dropped, and she sucked her bottom lip between her teeth nervously. "Umm... the night we left... there was a bunch of noise... the master healers were being summoned... I looked out the window... I saw Wesdin... I thought he was out playing late... I followed him... then I learned he was running away... I could not let him leave alone... so I went with him," she mumbled under her breath.

"Oy," groused Azelly as she pulled her daughter tightly against her once more. "You are truly fortunate that you were not harmed," she whispered as she stroked Leandra's hair gently.

"Indeed," agreed Avenor as he disheveled Wesdin's hair lightly.

"You will be the death of me," scolded Valcaly as she reached out and lightly jabbed Wesdin in his shoulder before taking the boy from his father's embrace, having been terrified to speak to him at the castle.

"You have my apologies, *Onia*," he replied as he hugged Valcaly and gave her a kiss on the cheek.

"You must also apologize to the *Apex*," she instructed him seriously. "The fear we have all experienced from your disappearance has been intense." Valcaly watched as Wesdin audibly gulped and nodded his head slowly with shame. Reaching up, she placed a hand under his chin and lifted his head. "Keep your head held high," she told him quietly. "As future Khan, you accept your mistakes and offer your apologies with humility and grace," she finished, and she set him down.

"Aye, *Onia* Valcaly," replied Wesdin as he took a shaky breath before walking toward Aylex and Daylin. "Aylex. Daylin," he said while meeting their stares with his own. "I offer my sincerest apologies for the fear and concerns I have caused you."

"We accept your apologies, Khanzito," replied Daylin with a smile as he reached out and ruffled Wesdin's hair.

"Aye," agreed Aylex as he saluted the child. "I have but one request… let's not do that again, eh?" he finished with a grin.

Wesdin grinned sheepishly as he returned Aylex's salute and nodded his head. "Agreed," he then replied before giving the man a cheerful hug.

"Your Grace," said Jonetal as he approached Avenor. "Do you wish to rest here, or should we press onward to Capitalia?"

Avenor glanced in the direction the sun would soon rise, and he quickly decided. "We should move closer to the *Forbidden Pass* since we must make plans to traverse the steep trail. We'll rest there," he said with a frown as his mind began racing with possibilities.

"Understood," replied Jonetal with a nod. He then turned and gave instructions to the others to mount up in preparation to move out. Swiftly, the patrol obeyed Jonetal's command, and they completed the brief journey before the sun crested over the horizon. They then made camp, watered their steeds, and replenished their flasks with fresh water.

CHAPTER 31

"General Crusendir," greeted the dockmaster with a salute as Manijor slowly crossed the gangway and disembarked the ship.

Manijor half-heartedly returned the salute and grumbled incoherently but did not stop to converse with the man. Instead, he snapped at a nearby guard and demanded a wagon be prepared.

"Aye, General," replied the soldier without hesitation. At once, he departed to complete the assigned task.

A plain, wooden box was brought off the ship, carried by troops with sorrowful expressions plastered on their faces. Without instruction, they carried it and gently placed it in the back of the wagon.

Manijor instantly clambered into the back of the cart with the container, and wordlessly sat as Leander climbed into the driver's seat. Leander glanced over his shoulder at the absentminded man, and said softly, "Steady yourself, General." After Manijor nodded his head, Leander faced forward and gave the reigns a quick snap. "Chah!" he called out, and the zebrils lurched forward. Mutely, Leander guided the zebrils from the dockyard to the palace.

* * *

"Our claws slice through the stone with ease," said Novex as he stood at the base of the steep trail, examining the abrupt incline with his head canted to the side. "We could hastily create stairs," he then said as he glanced over his shoulder at his father and mother. "What say you?"

"Aye," replied Mikela and Aylox in unison as they faced one another and nodded their heads in agreement.

"Boys!" Mikela abruptly bellowed. Her commanding voice rang out intensely, and the two tigals instantly ran to their mother's side.

"We will dig out stairs for the mounts. Otherwise… the trek will be too dangerous for them," said Novex as he clapped his younger brothers on the shoulder as he stood between the two of them.

"Ver' well," replied Aylex with a slow nod of his head.

"Shall we?" then asked Novex as he dropped his arms and walked toward the path. *Poof!* Immediately after assuming his tigal form, he began cutting out sections of the stone with ease. He then shoved the block, and he watched as it tumbled downward to land at the base of the mountain.

"Hmm," grumbled Avenor as he watched the rocks beginning to build up, creating a barrier. "Clear them out," he then instructed the others standing about.

"As you command, Your Grace," responded Azelly. She locked eyes with her subordinates, and they instantly moved forward to begin clearing the debris.

"You two remain there," said Avenor sternly as he pointed to Leandra and Wesdin.

"Aye, Api," replied Wesdin as Leandra nodded her head obediently.

"It will take a long time," said Leandra after a while as she watched the adults working.

"Indeed," replied Wesdin with a slight frown. After contemplating his actions for a short time, he finally said, "I will assist."

"Oy!" exclaimed Leandra as she reached out and grabbed Wesdin's arm. "Your Api instructed us to remain here," she reminded him lightly.

"Aye, I remember," he said with a small smile. "But I believe he will be glad I have assisted," he added slowly. Without another word, he then stood and approached the base of the mountain. "Api!" he shouted before approaching his father.

"Aye?" grunted Avenor after he hefted a large block from the ground and turned to face his son.

"Would you please call the others down?" he asked as he clasped his hands together and fiddled with his fingers nervously.

"For what reason?" asked Avenor after he dropped the stone.

"I have a suggestion," answered Wesdin with apprehension.

Avenor arched a brow as he peered down at his son. "Very well," he finally replied, deciding it would be good to rest for a while. "Bring it in!" shouted Avenor as he raised his arm and waved everyone toward him. "Water break!"

Wesdin waited patiently for the *Apex* members, the last to rejoin the group, as they grab their flasks and random food items before flopping down on the ground in the shade.

Avenor turned to Wesdin and dipped his head slightly. "Alright, Wes," he said before taking a long swallow of water. "What is this suggestion?"

Wesdin grinned impishly at his father; he then took a deep breath. With his brows furrowed together, he focused on his physical self. Progressively, Wesdin summoned forth his power; the lavender flecks in his eyes began to glow while his silver highlights hummed with energy. As the radiance became stronger, it surrounded Wesdin until it suddenly exploded into a blinding light, forcing every pair of eyes to turn away. As the group shifted their gazes back to Wesdin, multiple gasps escaped passed stunned lips as they gazed upon Wesdin's magnificent white dragon form.

"Oy!" exclaimed Avenor as he bolted to his feet and approached his son in awe. "What is this?" he asked incredulously as he reached out and felt his son's armored scales.

Galhix smiled broadly as she stood and placed a hand around Avenor's waist. "We will discuss it in detail once we are home," she informed him with a grin.

"Oy," repeated Avenor as he gazed at Wesdin with awe. "Very well," he replied slowly before stepping back.

"I will complete the task," Wesdin finally said as he turned and flew up the mountain where Aylox had been. With ease, he hastily clawed out chunks of stone from the mountainside and sent them tumbling down the steep trail. With his barbed tail, he smoothed out the crude steps. With his wings extended, he sliced through the walls to create a place for individuals to grab a hold of. At the peak of the mountain, he turned and flew back to the bottom. At the base, he used his tail and swept the debris to the side, making two large piles. After he was done, he shook off the dirt before *transforming* back to his human form.

"Impressive, Khanzito," said Novex with a long whistle while nodding his head approvingly.

"Indeed," added Avenor as he reached out and tousled Wesdin's hair. "Now, you should be confident in your ability to *transform*," he finished with a proud smile.

"Aye," replied Wesdin with a bashful grin.

"Well then…" said Avenor as he looked up at the completed set of steps, "who desires to ride back or stay and recover longer?" he asked as he turned to face the wide-eyed members of the patrol. "Mount up!" he then cried out enthusiastically after the unanimous bellows of agreement to return.

* * *

The newly formed steps made the once treacherous trek not as deadly, and the expert riders easily guided their steeds up the path. At the peak of the pass, Azelly wrapped her arms tightly around Leandra; she then leaned back to remain in the saddle as she encouraged her *ephalant* into a light canter, allowing the downward momentum to propel the animal along the steady decline. Every rider followed suite without incident. As the last soldier reached the bottom, the sun had just set below the horizon.

"Almost home," breathed out Wesdin quietly to himself. He inhaled a deep, peaceful breath as he watched long shadows stretch across the familiar terrain in the last bit of lingering light.

"Aye," agreed Galhix as she brought Pylo to halt next to Wesdin. "Shall we?" she then asked with a tip of her head forward, noticing the others had gained a significant distance ahead of them.

"Oy... aye!" exclaimed Wesdin with a sheepish smile. "Chah," he said while pressing his heels into his steed's flanks.

"Let's go, boy," called out Galhix as she gave Pylo a light prodding in his side. "Chah!" she then shouted and raced alongside of Wesdin.

The steady clopping of *ephalant* hooves forewarned the sentinels posted in the watchtower over the city's back gate.

"Riders approaching!" shouted a sentinel as she pointed out toward the dense forest; a cloud of dust rising from above the shorter trees and the rhythmic pounding the only signs of the gaining riders. "Open the gates!" she then immediately hollered as her eyes landed on a familiar jaguar and rider wearing a specific tabard. "Khan Crusendir has returned!"

Below her, soldiers sprang to action; the heavy wooden gates, having remained closed since Avenor's departure, were forced open.

A smile tugged at the corner of Avenor's lips as he watched the guards proudly salute, and he instantly brought his right forearm to his chest as he returned their sign of respect as he passed through the open gates. Avenor slowed the pace as he led the way to the palace stables, and he gradually brought Drayd to a halt. He then swung his legs over the side before jumping to the ground. "Good boy," he said as he pressed his forehead against the massive animal's. Drayd chuffed once in return before continuing to pant frantically.

"Your Grace!" greeted Everita with a hasty salute as she rushed out from the stables.

"Captain Quilaro," replied Avenor as he saluted the Stable Master in return, and he smiled with appreciation as she took the reins from him.

"Khanzito?" inquired Everita with apprehension in her voice.

"I am here," said Wesdin as he guided his *ephalant* to stand beside Drayd. Carefully, he dismounted from the beast and beamed up at Everita.

"Oy!" exclaimed Everita as she reached out and grabbed Wesdin. She then squeezed him fiercely before drawing back just enough to peer down at him. "You best not be doing that again!" she scolded.

"Understood," said Wesdin before standing on his toes to kiss the Stable Master's cheek.

"Oy... no you don't!" she said as she stepped back from the boy and pointed a finger at him. "You won't be getting off that easy. No amount of sugar is going to keep you from cleaning the stalls!"

"Oy," grumbled Wesdin. "I shall be here after Erudition."

"After?" scoffed Avenor as he crossed his arms over his chest. "Both you and Leandra will be here before Erudition and after," he said firmly.

"But... but... but..." stammered Leandra as she heard her name and rushed to stand beside Wesdin.

"Do not sass your uncle," barked Azelly as she crossed her arms and stood beside Avenor. "We will decide on a suitable punishment in the morning," she finished sternly.

"Indeed," agreed Galhix after she passed Pylo's reins to another soldier and placed an arm around Avenor's waist.

Just as Leandra and Wesdin began whining in protest, a palace sentry interrupted them brusquely.

"Khan Crusendir," said Kalven, drawing everyone's attention. The grave expression he wore instantly silenced the exhausted gaggle as they milled about.

"Speak, Captain Weelton," commanded Avenor as he physically tensed, detecting the man's uneasy aura.

"General Akeenil," began Kalven woefully and swallowed hard past the lump in his throat. After taking a deep breath, he said, "your Ami..." and allowed his voice to trail off.

Without waiting for further explanation, Avenor shot Galhix a desperate glance before sprinting for the palace. *"Ami..."* he silently said to himself, feeling a sense of dread spiraling out of control within him.

"What of General Akeenil?" demanded Azelly as she grabbed Kalven by his shirt.

"She has passed," responded Kalven in a barely audible whisper with his eyes downcast.

"No!" screamed Wesdin as he overheard Kalven's reply. Turning, he raced toward the castle with his mother and the others hot on his heels.

Crash!

Avenor barbarously barged threw the door of his parent's personal chambers, sending the wooden barrier open wide with such a force it smashed against the wall and fell in splinters.

Manijor jumped at the sudden intrusion, and he glared daggers at the individual. However, he immediately slumped back in his chair when his eyes landed on the distraught face of his son.

"Api... tell me it is not true," begged Avenor as he stared at his mother's motionless figure. Slowly, he walked to the edge of the bed and fell to his knees; with a shaky hand, he reached out grabbed a hold of one of his mother's. "When? How?" he asked in hoarse whisper as he gazed upon his mother's frozen flesh, absentmindedly recalling how master Wizard's would freeze the fallen to preserve their flesh before a proper *ceremonial burning*. In his grief, Avenor never heard his father's lack of response as his questions fell on deaf ears.

Manijor remained silent aside from the occasional sniffle, lost in his own thoughts. "No!" he gasped as hysterical crying invaded his ears. He jumped to his feet and rushed to the doorway just as Wesdin came charging through. Manijor instantly scooped the boy up and crushed him to his chest.

"Grandami!" wailed Wesdin as he fought against Manijor's hold. "Grandami!" he continued screaming at the top of his lungs. As he pounded against his grandfather's chest, silent sobs choked off his breathing, gradually suffocating him.

"Shhh," crooned Manijor as he held the boy tightly. "Shhh," he hushed repeatedly while swaying from side to side.

"No! She... ca... n't be!" shrieked Wesdin hysterically before passing out from shock.

Without releasing the boy, Manijor sat back down and cradled Wesdin tenderly. He lightly caressed the boy's childish features and admired his brows that resembled Everly's. Aside from quiet sobs and sniffles, the chamber was silent.

"It is prepared," said Betaro as he appeared beside Manijor and placed a comforting hand on the younger man's shoulder.

"Very well," replied Manijor, his voice husky from the frequent crying. "Her *burning* will be this eve," he said solemnly, addressing the questioning gazes from those standing around him.

"Eve," whimpered Valcaly as she pressed a hand to her lips, suppressing the shrieks that threatened to spill forth from her mouth.

"No... Grandami... I love... You can't go," muttered Wesdin as he tossed his head from side to side in his sleep. Without warning, he sat upright in Manijor's arms. "Grandami!" he shouted and startled those present.

"Shh… you are home," said Manijor quietly as he tucked Wesdin's wild locks of hair behind his ears. "We will send your Grandami to the next world this eve," he said somberly.

"Set me down!" growled out Wesdin as he struggled against Manijor's hold; immediately, he rushed to Everly's side and placed his hands on either side of her face. "Grandami! It is not your time!" he said quietly.

"Wesdin," snapped Avenor as he stood up and glowered at his son. "Do not…" he began sternly but abruptly stopped as he watched Wesdin transforming.

"Oy…" gapped Manijor as he watched the bright luminescence radiating out from his grandson before being forced to look away by the blinding light. "Surely I am dreaming," he whispered as he turned to find a brilliant snow-colored dragon in place of Wesdin.

Wesdin crouched beside the bed where his grandmother lay; without saying a word, he closed his eyes and inhaled deeply. Calling upon the *archaic blood* coursing through his veins, he summoned forth his powers as were revealed to him by *Divine*. A translucent sky-blue mist poured from his pursed lips carrying with it radiating, neon, cerulean speckles, and crystal-clear flecks. The mist wafted over Everly's still form, and it remained hoovering above her. Wesdin hesitantly opened his eyes; as he gazed lovingly at his grandmother, he began reciting the ancient words that whispered through his mind.

"Leave her be," ground out Avenor between clenched teeth when nothing happened.

Wesdin ignored his father's words and exhaled lightly over his grandmother once more; with his second breath, the ethereal mist settled onto his grandmother's lifeless body. Wesdin remained still, watching his grandmother expectantly.

"Wesdin!" barked Avenor as he rounded the edge of the bed, preparing to berate the boy for his nonsense.

"Oy…" escaped passed Everly's lips as she felt the chill fade from her body, bringing Avenor to an abrupt halt.

"Grandami!" roared Wesdin in his excitement.

"Oy!" exclaimed Everly as her eyes flew open to find a spectacular pair of solid black eyes with a ring of lavender peering down at her.

"Oy…" whispered Avenor as he turned to Wesdin. "You have my sincerest apologies, my son," he apologized profusely.

Wesdin nodded slightly to his father, wordlessly accepting his father's apology, knowing his outburst had stemmed from grief.

"Everly!" cried out Manijor as he lurched forward and wrapped his arms around his wife's cool body. He planted numerous kisses over her face as she laughed.

"Mani!" she exclaimed and pushed against his lightly. "Calm yourself!" she said with a chuckle.

"Ami," breathed out Avenor as he cautiously approached his mother. "You... you... live," he finished with a mask of disbelief on his face.

"Indeed," she said with a soft smile as she turned to face Wesdin. "A miraculous thing, really. Your *friend* informed me that it was not my time to remain in the *Celestial Realm*. He assured me that you would bring me home," she said while lightly caressing Wesdin's scaled cheek.

"Divine?" he inquired with a sparkle in his eyes.

"Aye," answered Everly with a knowing grin as she nodded her head.

"Oy!" exclaimed Wesdin excitedly before he transformed back to his human self and climbed onto the bed with his grandmother.

"What else did he say?" asked Wesdin as he waggled his brows playfully, causing Everly to erupt with laughter.

"Mmm," she murmured as she tousled his hair, "he revealed much. But none that I can share with you now," she said before reaching out and tapping Wesdin on the tip of his nose.

"Bah!" grunted Wesdin as he crossed his arms over his chest.

"Well...," said Everly with a purposeful pause before continuing, "all except you have exceeded his expectations and will surpass your father's reign."

As the cycles passed, Everly's proclamation held true; with the guidance of his family, closest confidants, and *Divine,* Wesdin was raised to be a kind, honest, and virtuous leader with friends at every border. Upon Wesdin's coronation as Khan, he was received with love and adoration from his citizens and those of his allies.

END